The Forgiving Hour

ROBIN LEE HATCHER

WATERBROOK
PRESS

THE FORGIVING HOUR
PUBLISHED BY WATERBROOK PRESS
5446 North Academy Boulevard, Suite 200
Colorado Springs, Colorado 80918
A division of Random House, Inc.

Scriptures taken from the *New American Standard Bible®* (NASB).
© Copyright The Lockman Foundation 1960, 1962, 1963,
1968, 1971, 1972, 1973, 1975, 1977. Used by permission.
Scripture quotations marked (NIV) are taken from the *Holy Bible,
New International Version®*. NIV®. Copyright © 1973, 1978, 1984 by
International Bible Society. Used by permission of Zondervan
Publishing House. All rights reserved. Scripture quotations marked
(TLB) are taken from *The Living Bible* copyright © 1971.
Used by permission of Tyndale House Publishers, Inc.,
Wheaton, Illinois 60189. All rights reserved.

The characters and events in this book are fictional, and any resemblance
to actual persons or events is coincidental.

ISBN 1-57856-150-7

Printed in the United States of America
1999—First Edition

10 9 8 7 6 5 4 3 2 1

*To Francine Rivers, who first inspired
me to write for the Lord.
To the women writers of the LoveKnot,
who fanned the flames of that desire.
To the pastors and teachers who gave me
a hunger for the Word,
especially Hank Aguilera.*

Thank you.

Prologue

BOISE, IDAHO

The sky that Saturday in May was a brilliant, cloudless blue, sunshine kissing the earth with a promise of the summer to come. There was the scent of green on the afternoon breeze, and windows throughout the subdivision had been thrown open to let it in. Flowering trees were in full bloom; tulips and daffodils bobbed colorful heads at passersby, as if in welcome. Sprinklers kept time on neighborhood lawns with a steady *chick-chick-chick-swoosh...chick-chick-chick-swoosh...*while the laughter of playing children filled the air.

It was the perfect sort of day to meet one's future daughter-in-law.

Claire Conway checked the grandfather clock in the entry. Dakota and Sara should be arriving at any moment.

I love her, Mom, and you're gonna love her just as much as I do.

She smiled as the two-month-old memory filled her thoughts. She'd been living and working in Seattle on a short-term assignment for her employer, and Dakota had arrived for a visit. They'd just finished supper, her six-foot-four-inch son having polished off two helpings of his favorite casserole and, for dessert, a large slice of cherry cheesecake. And then he'd told her he'd met someone special and was engaged to be married.

1

It was difficult for her to accept that her son was old enough to be engaged, let alone planning a wedding for July. It shouldn't be this hard to accept, but it was.

At twenty-four, Dakota was six years older than Claire had been when she wed his father.

And he's twice as mature as his father ever was, she thought with a twinge of the old bitterness.

But mature or not, Dakota remained her little boy, all six feet plus of him. In her mind, she knew he was a grown man. In her heart, he was the towheaded kid with skinned knees, mussed hair, and a smile that made her melt on the inside.

I love her, Mom, and you're gonna love her just as much as I do.

Claire didn't doubt for a second that she would love Sara Jennings. She trusted Dakota's judgment. Besides being mature beyond his age, he was intelligent, kind, and generous, a man of integrity and deep moral convictions. If he thought Sara was the woman with whom he wanted to spend the rest of his life, then Claire believed it too. Sight unseen.

Sara's a little older than I am. Seven years to be exact. She thought it should matter—to me and to others—but I convinced her it didn't. She's made me the happiest guy in the world by accepting my proposal.

The rumble of the Jeep engine pulled her thoughts to the present. She drew in a deep breath and let it out slowly before walking to the door and opening it. Stepping into the afternoon sunshine, she watched as Dakota hopped out of the Jeep, then strode around to the passenger side of the vehicle. Once there, he offered his hand to help the young woman disembark.

Claire put on a welcoming smile. She knew Sara had to be even more nervous than she was, and she wanted to do all in her power to make this first meeting a pleasant one. It could set the tone for the rest of their lives. She wanted to prove that mother- and daughter-in-law relationships didn't have to be strained or antagonistic.

A glance at her son's face confirmed the depth of his feelings for the woman on his arm. A warm glow spread out from Claire's heart. To see him like this made all the difficult times of the past fade into obscurity.

Dakota shifted his gaze from Sara to his mother. He grinned. "Hi, Mom."

"Hi, yourself."

"Mom, this is Sara. Sara, my mother, Claire Conway."

Claire offered her hand to the young woman, for the first time taking a good look at her. She was tall—at least five ten—and striking. She had cat-green eyes, long and curly burgundy-colored hair, a flawless complexion, and a perfect figure.

For just a moment, Claire wondered if they'd met before. There was something familiar about her.

"It's a pleasure to meet you, Mrs. Conway."

Claire gave her head a slight shake. "Please, call me Claire." That was much easier than trying to explain it was *Ms.* rather than *Mrs.*

The younger woman revealed a hesitant smile. "I'd like that... Claire. Thank you."

"Come inside. I've got decaf ready, and I made a coffeecake for the occasion."

"You *baked?*" Dakota's voice was filled with mock surprise.

Claire shot him a censuring glance but couldn't maintain it for long. When he laughed, so did she.

"Like I told you, Sara, Mom nearly forgot how to find the kitchen after I moved out. Now she only cooks at Thanksgiving, at Christmas, and on rare special occasions...like this one. Right, Mom?"

"Right."

Claire led the way into the house, then left Dakota and Sara in the living room while she proceeded into the kitchen. She heard the young lovers conversing softly as she poured coffee into three china cups and placed them beside the creamer and sugar bowl on a polished silver tray. Even from the other room, she could discern the happiness in her son's voice. Again, she was warmed by it. What mother wouldn't be?

Dakota's early teen years had been hard ones. He'd gotten into more than his fair share of scrapes, taking out his anger and bitterness with rebellious and sometimes reckless behavior. Of course, his anger and bitterness had been no worse than her own, betrayed as they'd been by his father.

Remembering her ex-husband brought a frown to Claire's brow. Foreboding followed on memory's heels, a sense that something was about to go wrong.

But that was ridiculous. Nothing was going wrong. There was no room for anything but joy in this house today. The past was the past. Today they were celebrating the future.

Coffee tray in hand, Claire stepped through the kitchen doorway, then paused, unnoticed, to observe the two young people. Sara was looking at a display of photos on the mantel. Dakota stood with his arm around her shoulders, smiling contentedly.

"Who is this?" Sara asked him, pointing to a framed snapshot.

Dakota glanced at it. "That's me and my mom when I was...oh, about five, I think."

"Where was it taken?" Sara sounded odd.

"That's our old house on Garden Street. It's where I grew up. Mom sold it after she got a divorce, right after I finished grade school."

"Dakota...what was your father's name?"

Lowering his voice, he answered, "I've told you why I never talk about him. I promised Mom I wouldn't."

Still, after all these years, he was keeping his promise to Claire, a promise she never should have asked him to make. It had been wrong of her to ask it, no matter what the reason. At the very least, she should have released him from it this spring.

She almost spoke up, almost told him so, but something kept her silent...

Something about Sara.

The younger woman looked up into Dakota's eyes with an unwavering gaze. "What was his name?" she repeated in a hoarse whisper. "I need to know. I *have* to know."

"Does it matter that much to you?"

"Yes. Yes, it does."

Claire was struck again by that sense of impending doom. Something was pressing on her lungs, an enormous, unyielding weight. Each breath came hard.

At long last, Dakota answered Sara's question, "Porter. His name was David Porter." There was no bitterness in his reply. He'd forgiven the man long ago. "Why?"

As if sensing Claire's presence, Sara turned. Her eyes were wide and filled with horror. "Claire...*Porter? Dave* was your husband? He's Dakota's father?"

Claire remembered now. She remembered where she'd seen Sara

before. The coffee tray slipped from her hands and crashed to the floor.

It had been twelve years, and the young college student had become a woman. Sara had changed. Her hair was long, full, and curly instead of cropped short. Her figure had blossomed, no longer the stick-thin girl she'd been. She'd grown only more beautiful with the passage of time.

But it *was* her.

"What's going on?" Dakota asked, glancing back and forth between his mother and his fiancée in confusion.

Sara looked at him. Her voice quavered as she asked, "Did your dad call you Mikey?"

"Where did you hear that?"

Sara took a faltering step backward, out of his reach. "It can't be. It can't. God wouldn't do this. He wouldn't do this to us." She shook her head, almost keening the words. "He wouldn't do this."

"Would someone *please* tell me what's going on?" Dakota looked from his fiancée to Claire. "Mom?"

Sara turned toward her too. "Say it isn't true. Please say it isn't true."

But Claire couldn't comply.

Because it *was* true.

Her thoughts hurtled back twelve years to the first—and only other—time she'd seen Sara.

Sara Jennings…

The other woman…

The girl who'd destroyed Claire's marriage, her home, her life.

Hell was real. Claire knew it…because she was in it now.

Part One: *Betrayed*

Bread obtained by falsehood is sweet
to a man, but afterward his mouth
will be filled with gravel.

— PROVERBS 20:17

Chapter One

APRIL—TWELVE YEARS EARLIER

"Patti?" Sara called as the door to their apartment swung open. "Are you home?"

Her roommate didn't answer.

Sara dropped her books and backpack on the rickety table near the door and headed for the refrigerator. As usual, she was hungry at the end of a school day.

Just before she reached the kitchen, a man appeared in the doorway. Sara let out a squeal of alarm as she jumped away from him—and found herself pressing against the back of the love seat, unable to go farther.

She glanced toward her backpack. A spray can of Mace was in the side pocket. Her brothers insisted she carry one now that she was out on her own. If she could reach it before he—

The stranger raised his right hand, like a traffic cop warning her not to move. He was holding a hammer. "I'm here to install the new kitchen cabinets," he explained quickly, before she could make a dive for her bag. "Mrs. Hilton let me in. I thought I'd be done before anyone got home, but I ran into a few problems."

Her pulse began to regulate. She remembered now that her landlady had said the carpenter was coming today.

"Sorry I startled you." He grinned. "I don't generally frighten women. Honest, I don't."

His smile made Sara's heartbeat jump into overdrive a second time. For a different reason.

"The name's Dave Porter." He switched the hammer to his left hand, then offered his right to her.

After a moment's hesitation, she took hold of it. It was large, warm, callused. She liked the feel as it enveloped hers in a firm grasp. "I'm Sara Jennings."

"I'll get out of your way as fast as possible. Shouldn't take me all that long to finish up."

She peeked around him into the kitchen. The new cabinets were a huge improvement over the old. "No hurry."

He gave a quick nod, then returned to his work.

With his back toward her, Sara was able to watch him, unabashedly enjoying the view. The sleeves of his blue-and-white plaid shirt were rolled up to his biceps, biceps that flexed and bulged as he used the hammer with precision. His shoulders were broad, his hips narrow. His worn Levi's fit him like a glove. And when his physique was taken into consideration along with his handsome face and devastating smile, he made one definite knockout package.

Her gaze shifted to his left hand. No wedding band. She breathed an unexpected sigh of relief. "You don't care if I get myself something to eat, do you? I mean, I won't be in your way, will I?" She wasn't hungry any longer; she just didn't want to leave the kitchen.

Dave glanced over his shoulder. His dark blue eyes seemed to say he knew the truth. "No, you won't be in my way. I like company while I'm working."

Sara opened the refrigerator and grabbed the first thing in sight— some leftover fried chicken.

"You a student at Boise State?" he asked her.

"Yes."

"Like it?"

"Mostly."

"I attended the U of I. A long time ago now. I had plans to be an architect, but money ran out after that first year. Circumstances changed, so I had to quit school." He pounded another nail. When he set the hammer on the counter, he continued speaking. "But I've built myself a pretty good carpentry business over the years, so it hasn't turned out all bad. I like working with my hands."

His hands. She wondered what it would feel like to have him caress her cheek with those work-roughened fingertips. A shiver ran up her spine.

"What's your major?"

His question jerked her unruly thoughts back to the present. "Theater arts. But I don't know what I'll do with it after I graduate." She gave a shaky little laugh. "It's not like I expect to be a movie star or anything."

He turned, leaned his behind against the edge of the counter, crossed his arms over his chest, and gave her a long, thorough look.

Her stomach tumbled, and again she shivered. She'd never had anyone look at her in quite that way before.

"You're sure pretty enough to be a movie star, Miss Sara Jennings."

She felt the heat of a blush flood her cheeks. He thought she was pretty. In a reflexive but purely feminine gesture, she ran a hand over her hair.

"You a senior?"

"No," she replied. "A freshman."

"Eighteen, huh? Man, I can hardly remember what it was like to be that age. Ancient history for me."

"I'm nineteen, and you don't look like you're all that much older than me."

He studied her again. She shifted, unsettled by the way his perusal made her feel. This was no college boy. This was a man. All male. Masculinity emanated from him in a way she'd never experienced before.

"I'm thirty-two." There seemed to be an unspoken question included in that simple statement.

She shrugged, hoping he wouldn't guess that her heart was pumping a million miles an hour. "That's not so old."

"You know…" He glanced at the cabinets, then back at her. "It doesn't look like I'll get these finished today. It's going to take a bit longer than I thought at first. I'll need to come back tomorrow. Take my time and do it right. Don't want all your dishes getting busted."

"No, that wouldn't be good." She forced herself to take a breath; she didn't want to pass out from lack of oxygen. "I don't have any classes on Thursday afternoons. You won't need Mrs. Hilton to let you in."

She didn't have a clue why she'd said that to him.

His smile was slow, his gaze mesmerizing. "Fine. I'll come straight to your door. About two o'clock?"

Maybe she *did* know why she'd said it.

She nodded, saying, "I'll be here."

Claire Porter had just finished setting the dining room table when the back door opened and her husband entered the kitchen. Her heart skipped, as it always did, at the sight of him.

"Hi, honey," she said, walking over to give him a welcome-home kiss.

"Hi." Dave dropped his tool belt on the floor beside the washing machine. Then he brushed his lips across hers before stepping around her and moving toward the stove. "What's for supper?"

"Pot roast with potatoes and carrots."

He lifted the lid, as if to see if she'd told the truth, then nodded. "I'll wash up."

He strode out of the kitchen, and a few moments later, Claire heard water running in the bathroom sink.

The back door opened again. This time her towheaded, twelve-year-old son burst into the room. The knees of Mike's jeans were covered with dirt, his tennis shoes were caked with mud, and the underside of his fingernails looked like they hadn't been cleaned in a year.

"Hey, Mom. Sorry I'm late." He removed his shoes. "I was helping Mrs. Applegate put in her garden and lost track of the time."

Claire smiled. It was just like Mike to help their elderly neighbor.

She gave him a hug, thinking how lucky she was. She had a husband she adored and a son she wouldn't trade for all the gold in Fort Knox. What more could any woman want?

He stepped out of her embrace, looking up at her with excited blue eyes, a paler version of his father's. "Mrs. Applegate says she'll pay me three dollars a week if I'll help her weed her garden this summer. I told her she didn't have to give me nothin', that I'd be glad to help her. But she insisted. So is it okay if I let her pay me? I only need another thirty dollars in my savings account to get that new bike I've been wanting."

"You bet it's okay," Dave answered as he reappeared from the hallway.

"Hey, Dad. You heard?"

"Our son's a real entrepreneur." Dave grinned at Claire. "Next thing you know, I'll be going to the boy for my business loans instead of the bank. Isn't that right, Mikey?"

"Ah, Dad. I wish you wouldn't call me that. I'm not a baby anymore."

Contentment flowed over Claire. Dave worked long hours, and sometimes he could be short-tempered with both his wife and his son. But not this evening.

Again she thought how lucky she was. She and Dave had weathered more than their share of rough times—both financially and emotionally—in the almost thirteen years of their marriage. They were so young at the start, just kids really, with a baby already on the way. There was the disappointment that had come when they'd learned Claire couldn't have any more children after Mike was born. There was the year when they'd nearly lost the house after construction work in the Boise area dried up. And there was a period, a few years back, when Claire had wondered if Dave still loved her, had even wondered if he'd been unfaithful to her, although she'd never had anything but her gut feelings upon which to base her suspicions.

But those times were behind them now. They had come through with flying colors. They were happy. They were a whole family.

No other woman alive was as lucky as Claire.

Chapter Two

Sara didn't hear a single word her professor was saying. Her thoughts were too full of Dave Porter and the way he'd looked, standing in the efficiency kitchen of her apartment. She kept trying to figure out why he'd affected her the way he had. It wasn't as if she'd never met a handsome member of the opposite sex. She'd met plenty of them. She'd dated her share of them. Of course, they'd all been boys, not men.

Thirty-two years old. Her brothers would have a cow if they knew she was interested in a man that age. They still considered her the baby of the family—the little princess—and probably always would.

She smiled to herself. The three Jennings brothers had picked on and protected Sara throughout her life. They'd scared more than a couple of would-be suitors off their parents' farm when they hadn't thought the guy worthy of their sister's affections. Oh, how she'd hated their meddling. All three of them—Tim, Josh, and Eli—had been royal pains in the neck throughout her high school years. But if she was honest, she'd have to admit she missed being around them since she'd started attending the university.

But I don't miss them right now.

The last thing she would have wanted or needed was to suffer her brothers' interference in regard to Dave Porter.

She glanced at her watch.

The butterflies started fluttering in her stomach again. Three hours. Just three more hours and he would return to her apartment. Was it only to finish the cabinets? Or was he coming to see her?

She answered her own question: *He's coming to see me. He could have finished yesterday, but he wanted to see me again.*

Sara knew she was right. There'd been some sort of connection between them. Something special, something unique. Could this be what was called "love at first sight"?

She scrawled his name across a sheet of lined notebook paper. *Dave Porter.* It had a nice sound. *Dave Porter.* Simple. Strong. Straightforward.

She looked at her watch again. If it weren't for the sweep of the second hand, she'd have thought it wasn't working. Time seemed to stand still. She wanted it to be two o'clock.

When class was over, she bolted from the room like a kid on the last day of school before summer vacation. She didn't hang around to visit with any of her friends. She didn't look for her roommate or walk to the student union building for lunch as she often did. Instead, she slipped her backpack over her arms and started jogging toward her apartment building, about six blocks away from the university.

She hoped against hope that Patti wouldn't decide to cut her Thursday afternoon class. It wouldn't be unprecedented if she did. Patti Cooper hated her math class—and the professor who taught it.

Once home, Sara bustled around the apartment, picking up dirty clothes and straightening magazines and books. She applied the broom to the scruffy hardwood floor, sweeping up the collection of dust bunnies from beneath chairs and tables. There wasn't a lot of furniture in the tiny living room, and what there was looked old and ratty. The typical college-kids-on-a-shoestring style of decorating. Parents' castoffs and Salvation Army purchases. She hadn't given much thought to how the apartment looked before now. It was just a place to crash between classes and parties and college ball games. Most of her friends' off-campus apartments looked much the same—or worse.

But Dave wasn't a college student, and she didn't want him to think of her as one.

By one-forty-five, Sara had taken a shower, reapplied her eye shadow and mascara—the only makeup she wore—and was dressed in her favorite, wine-colored jeans and a mauve blouse. As she stared at herself in the full-length bathroom mirror, she wondered if she ought to change again. The outfit made her look too young, too unsophisticated. Which she probably was.

A dress might be a better choice. She had a nice green number with a super-short skirt that showed off her long legs and—

There was no time to finish the thought, let alone follow through, before the doorbell rang. Sara's pulse quickened in direct proportion with her now rapid breathing. She tried to hide how nervous and uncertain she felt.

"Too early?" Dave asked the moment the door opened before him.

"No," she answered, "you're right on time."

He grinned, as if he understood she'd been watching the clock in anticipation of his arrival.

Sara held the door open a little wider. "Come on in."

"That's why I'm here." He grabbed his toolbox and stepped inside.

He was dressed much as he'd been the day before, only this time his plaid shirt was red and white. The sleeves were rolled to above his elbows again. The hair on his arms, she noticed, was gold instead of light brown like the hair on his head.

She followed him as far as the kitchen doorway, wondering what excuse she could use to stay right there.

He fastened his leather tool belt around his waist, placed a level, a hammer, and some nails on the countertop, then glanced behind him, meeting her gaze. He smiled at her in that special way of his. "So tell me about yourself, Miss Jennings. Like I said yesterday, I enjoy company while I work."

"There's nothing very interesting to tell," she answered, pleased that he'd asked, that he'd given her a reason to stay.

"I bet that's not true. Start with your family. Are they from around here?"

Sara had never been the type to say much about herself to new acquaintances, but with Dave, for some reason, she didn't feel her usual reticence. Maybe it was the way his blue eyes met hers without wavering. Or maybe it was his slightly crooked smile that made warm feelings curl in her stomach. Whatever the reason, she wanted him to know all about her, just as she wanted to know all about him.

"My folks have a farm outside of Caldwell. Dad grows corn and sugar beets."

"Brothers and sisters?"

"Brothers. Three of them. All older."

Dave whistled through his teeth. "Bet you were one spoiled little baby doll."

If someone else had said that to her, she'd have been insulted. "I suppose so," she admitted. "But I was pestered plenty too. Their favorite game when I was five or six was 'let's ditch Sara.' I was left behind in the strangest places."

He laughed.

"It wasn't funny at the time."

"Bet not." As he spoke, he started to work on the cabinets. "What got you interested in the theater?"

"I don't know." Sara settled onto one of the two barstools at the counter that separated kitchen from living area. "I just always loved to act."

Dave had a way of drawing out more and more information. Over the course of the next hour, she told him the names of her three brothers as well as the names of her parents, disclosed her passion for horses and barrel racing, announced she had the lead role in Boise State's production of *Cat on a Hot Tin Roof,* and confessed her fondness for Chinese food and chocolate cake with dark fudge frosting.

It was only when he started packing up his tools that she realized she hadn't asked him a single question about himself, and now he was getting ready to leave. A wave of panic struck her in the midsection.

"Well, that should do it. Now you can put your dishes away." He picked up his toolbox.

"Dave…" She let his name drift into silence, afraid to continue. What if she'd misread him? What if he wasn't interested in her?

"Yeah?"

"I, ah, I have a couple of tickets for the play. For *Cat on a Hot Tin Roof.* It starts next Friday. A week from tomorrow. If you'd like to use them…" Again she failed to finish her sentence.

He smiled. "I'd love to come."

She couldn't remember when she'd felt this nervous or excited. If he would just—

His voice lowered a notch as he continued, "But I'll only need one of those tickets. I'll be coming alone." He set his toolbox on the floor, then took a step toward her. "Although I hope I won't end the evening alone. Will you be my dinner date after the play?"

She swallowed hard. "Your date?"

"They do still call it that, don't they?" His eyes twinkled with amusement. "A date. You know? When a guy asks a pretty girl out."

She nodded.

"So will you? Go out with me?"

"Yes." She sounded as breathless as she felt.

"Great. Friday night it is. Give me your phone number, and I'll call you. Okay?"

"Okay." She thought he might try to kiss her.

Instead, he pulled a small spiral notebook and a pencil from his shirt pocket. "Sara Jennings," he said as he wrote on one of the pages. Then he looked at her expectantly. "Your number?"

Just as she finished answering him, the apartment door opened, and Patti entered. She stopped and stared at Dave. Her expression changed quickly from surprise to frank appreciation. Sara felt a rush of relief that her roommate hadn't returned sooner.

Dave grinned at the newcomer. "You must be Patti."

"Yes." She glanced at Sara, one eyebrow cocked in question.

"I'm Dave," he answered before Sara could. "Your friendly neighborhood carpenter." He picked up his toolbox again. "And I'd better go. I'm already behind schedule on my next job."

Patti stepped aside so he could walk past her. Sara followed him out to the open-air landing, purposefully closing the door behind her.

He paused at the top of the stairs. Glancing over his shoulder, he said, "I'll call you on Monday."

"I'll be waiting." She immediately regretted the words. She sounded too anxious, too much like a teenager.

His smile made her forget everything else. "Talk to you then."

Chapter Three

Claire dipped the tops of the éclairs in the chocolate ganache glaze, then put the dozen rich desserts into the refrigerator to chill.

Not for the first time, she glanced at the clock on the kitchen wall. Dave should have been home by now.

"Please don't forget we've got company coming for dinner," she muttered.

If he did forget, it wouldn't be the first time. Dave was notorious for losing track of the time or forgetting an obligation. And he hated it when Claire reminded him. He detested being nagged, and that's exactly what he accused her of doing, no matter how carefully she selected her words. They used to fight about it all the time until she'd made the decision it wasn't worth the grief. Her husband was a hard worker and a good provider. He labored six days a week and occasionally on Sundays too.

So Dave had a slight character flaw. Wasn't love about accepting a man as he was?

"I'm done setting the table, Mom."

She turned. Mike stood in the archway between kitchen and dining room.

"Can I go over to John's now?" he asked, referring to his best friend.

"You're sure Mrs. Kreizenbeck won't mind you coming so early?"

He laughed. "You know what it's like over there. John's mom probably doesn't even know when there's an extra kid around."

Claire couldn't disagree. There were ten children in the Kreizenbeck household, and she'd never been inside their home when it wasn't in total chaos. Maybe there was peace in the middle of the night, when everyone was asleep, but certainly never in the light of day.

She lifted a paper plate covered with aluminum foil from the counter and held it out to her son. "I made some frosted sugar cookies to take with you. They are *not* just for you and John. Understood? You be sure to share them with his folks and brothers and sisters. There's plenty for all."

"I will."

"And you give Mrs. Kreizenbeck a hand with whatever she asks."

"I will. I always do." He shifted his weight from one foot to the other, trying to hide his impatience.

"Have you got your dress clothes packed so you can go with them to church in the morning?"

"Ah, Mom, you know I do."

Claire grasped his shoulders and dropped a kiss on his forehead. "Okay, get going. Have a good time and behave yourself. Be home by one o'clock. And be sure you're careful crossing Orchard Avenue on your bike. You know how busy—"

He was off and running before she could finish her words of caution.

She smiled. Some of her friends had to worry about their children all the time, but Mike rarely gave her any concern. He did his homework, usually without being told, and brought home good grades with every report card. He was active in the Boy Scouts. He was considerate to old people, like their neighbor Mrs. Applegate. He always helped around the house, washing dishes, running the vacuum, making his bed. She'd never once suspected him of smoking or drinking, although she knew some children his age were already into such things. And he never sassed her.

Suddenly she chuckled. If someone could read her mind, they'd think her son was a candidate for sainthood, which wasn't the case either. Despite all his good points, Michael Dakota Porter was still just a normal boy who could get into more than a little mischief when he was so inclined.

With a shake of her head, Claire returned her attention to the dinner preparations.

The Italian stuffed veal breast, along with carrots and new potatoes, was roasting in the oven, filling the air with the delicious scents of onion, garlic, and sage. A salad of mixed greens was prepared, as were two homemade dressings. The last thing she had to do was put the rolls into a serving basket and warm them, but that could wait until after her guests arrived.

She glanced at the clock again. "Oh, Dave, *please* don't be late tonight. Please don't forget about dinner. Not with all these guests coming."

Maybe she should have reminded him, even if he would have gotten angry and called her a nag. He'd been so preoccupied the last couple of days. Like his thoughts were in a far-off place. Sometimes when he looked at her, she didn't think he saw her. Instead, he seemed to look right through her.

She frowned. Last night, she'd worn the nightgown he'd given her for their last anniversary, and he hadn't even noticed. He'd just given her a perfunctory kiss good-night, rolled over, and gone to sleep. If that black satin negligee couldn't get his attention, he was sure to forget a dinner party, especially one given in honor of her best friend, Alana Moncur, and her husband, Jack.

"Couple of stuffed shirts," Dave had said when she'd told him she wanted to give this party for the Moncurs' tenth wedding anniversary. "Haven't you ever noticed how he lords it over the rest of us common folk? He's always bragging about how much money he makes and what a success he is."

"He does no such thing," she'd protested, despite knowing it wouldn't change Dave's mind. Her husband rarely changed his mind about anything.

Claire yanked off her apron and left the kitchen. Unless she wanted to greet her guests in her faded Levi's and oversized cotton blouse, she'd better get changed. Worrying about whether Dave would arrive before everyone else wasn't going to get him there any faster.

❦

Waiting for Monday—and that anticipated phone call from Dave—was going to drive Sara crazy.

It was only Saturday, and she'd already spent far too much time staring at the telephone, waiting for it to ring. She'd tried watching television, but she couldn't find a single program that interested her. She'd tried reading a new novel by her favorite author, but even a great love story couldn't hold her attention. Patti was off playing tennis with a group of friends, so she couldn't while away the day exchanging mindless gossip with her roommate. She found no enjoyment, as she usually did, in rehearsing her lines for the upcoming production. If she didn't do something to take her mind off Dave, she would be a basket case by Monday.

So Sara did what came naturally. She went home to see her family.

Her parents owned three hundred and twenty acres in western Canyon County. The farm had been in the family since the late twenties, purchased with money Sara's great-grandfather, Horace Jennings, had made as a bootlegger during the Prohibition years—a story her dad liked to retell at every Jennings family reunion.

For decades, the rich soil had produced crops of sweet corn and sugar beets to be sold at market. It also nurtured an immense garden of vegetables to help feed the family. A few calves, raised for the beef that would go into the Jenningses' deep freeze, grazed on pastureland alongside several saddle horses. Huge poplars, oaks, and maples filled the yard, providing shade, and one tree offered a gnarled limb from which hung an old rope-and-board swing. The two-story white house that had sheltered several generations of Jennings kids was large and drafty, like most seventy-year-old farmhouses.

Sara had never minded any of the imperfections in her childhood home. Not the creaky stairs or the groans from the attic on dark windy nights. Not the icy floor on an early winter morning. Not the faded flowered wallpaper in her bedroom. Not even the hairline cracks in the claw-footed bathtub or the leaky faucet in the sink. Nothing would ever make her think there was a better place for children to grow up than in this old house.

She arrived at the farm at suppertime. She hadn't planned it that way, but she wasn't sorry either. Although her mom wasn't a fancy cook, nobody knew better than Kristina Jennings how to fill up a husband and three strapping sons with plain, hearty, just-tastes-good food. Tonight she was serving poor boy stew, made with hamburger, onions, carrots, potatoes, and tomato sauce. Before Sara scarcely knew what was happening, she'd been seated in her old spot at the table between her dad and her eldest brother, Tim.

"You're too thin," Kristina fussed as she set before Sara a large bowl of stew and a chunk of fresh-baked bread with ample butter spread on it. "You're wasting away to nothing."

It was what her mother said every time she saw Sara. A woman of short stature, Kristina was round and soft, reminding Sara of the Pillsbury Doughboy in a curly red wig.

"I'm *not* too thin." Sara glanced to her left. "Tell her I'm okay, Dad."

Her father, Jared Jennings, had a face like an old weathered glove, browned by the sun and creased by the heat, cold, wind, and constant worries that came with farming. He also had eyes that twinkled with the mischief of a small boy.

"She's okay, Kris. Leave her be." He winked at Sara. "Besides, them college boys like 'em skinny as beanpoles. Ain't that right?"

Heat rose in her cheeks as she remembered Dave telling her she was pretty enough to be a movie star. He wasn't a college boy but—

"Well, I'll be!" Tim exclaimed. "Look at her blush. I don't think I've ever seen her blush before."

"The princess has gone and got herself a boyfriend," Josh said with a laugh. Her middle brother was a ruthless tease, and now that he thought he had something to razz her about, this was sure to be a long evening.

Sara groaned inwardly. She didn't need this. She'd come home to take her mind *off* Dave.

"Who is he?" Eli asked. "Do we know him?"

"I *don't* have a boyfriend. And if I did, I sure wouldn't tell any of you buffoons." She picked up her spoon and stared into her stew. "I'm not *that* naive."

"Come on, Sara," Eli wheedled. The closest to her in age, he'd been the one she confided in most often during her girlhood. "Tell us about him."

Glancing up, she met her mother's watchful gaze. Kristina would know if she tried to bluff her way through. Her mother had always known when any of the Jennings kids told a lie. It was a sixth sense with her.

Sara released a sigh, feeling like a punctured tire with the air rushing out. Then she looked around the table. "Okay, I've met someone. I think he's nice and I think he's cute, but I don't know much about him yet." *Nothing at all, actually.* "We've never been out on a date. I hope we will soon." *Friday night. I'll see him Friday night.* "Now, that's all I'm going to say about him. Nothing may come of this, you know, so don't get yourselves all in a lather."

"Don't you think you oughta let one of us have a look-see?" Josh leaned forward in anticipation. "I'd be happy to check him out. What's his name?"

Sara laughed. "Not a chance, Bro. You couldn't drag his name out of me. Not even if you torture me with bamboo shoots and hot irons. My lips are sealed."

The three brothers started talking at once, the decibel level rising steadily as they listed all of their sister's former boyfriends, then detailed the reasons those boys hadn't been good enough for Sara, along with a few reasons why she couldn't find the right fellow. The teasing seemed to go on interminably.

But it only took a few softly spoken words from their mother to bring it to an end. "That's enough, all of you." Kristina waited for silence, then said, "Your supper's getting cold. Sara, I want to see you eat all that stew. I don't care if those boys over in Boise do like their girls thin. You eat."

"Yes, Mom."

With their mother's gaze moving from Sara to each son in turn, she added, "Go ahead, all of you."

Chapter Four

The Porter home on Garden Street was a small, older house, not much different from the neighboring houses that lined the street. It wasn't large or fancy, but Claire loved it. She'd spent years decorating it from pennies pinched from her grocery budget, trying always to make it special, a place where everyone felt comfortable and welcome.

This night, with four couples around the dining room table and laughter punctuating the air, Claire felt aglow with success.

Alana leaned toward her. "That was an incredible meal. I can't thank you enough."

"You know I love entertaining. And I wanted to do something special for you and Jack."

"I've never known anyone who thrived on being 'the little woman' the way you do."

Claire knew her friend didn't mean for her words to be insulting, nor did she take them as such. She *did* thrive on it. She'd never had any aspirations to have a career. She'd always been content to be a wife and a mom and a homemaker. Nothing more and nothing less. No apologies to the liberated superwomen of her generation.

She looked toward the opposite end of the table, her gaze settling on her husband.

She remembered the first time she'd seen Dave as if it had been yesterday. September. The month of warm days and cool nights. The first day of school, her sophomore year at Borah High, between second- and third-period classes. He was a senior, the star pitcher of the varsity baseball team. He'd come striding down the crowded hallway, a head taller than most of the other boys. Tall and gorgeous with a killer, self-confident smile. She couldn't help but notice him. All the girls would have died for a chance to go out with him. But he'd picked Claire.

She still sometimes wondered why.

They'd dated all that year, two kids desperately in love. Then, the following September, Dave had left for the University of Idaho in Moscow, and Claire had despaired of losing him to someone else, to someone prettier and older, to someone who wasn't "stuck in the morals of the past," as he put it.

When he'd come home the summer between his freshman and sophomore years, Claire had given in to her fear of losing him and to his constant pressure to "let me love you completely." Shortly afterward, she'd started taking the pill, but it was already too late. Before he left for school in September, she'd had to tell him she was pregnant.

It hadn't been the ideal way to start a marriage, she thought now. Dave had been forced to leave college in order to support his bride and the baby who arrived seven months after the hastily arranged wedding. But they'd made it work, and in another five months they would celebrate their thirteenth wedding anniversary.

"You know"—Alana's voice intruded on Claire's private thoughts—"you still look at him the way you did when you were fifteen."

Claire smiled as she watched Dave lean toward Jack's cousin, Ty Boston, the two men deep in conversation, probably about one sport or another. "I love him just as much as I ever did. More, really." She turned toward her friend. "I'm terribly happy, you know."

Alana nodded. "I know."

"But you didn't always think I would be, did you?" It was a rhetorical question. Claire's best friend had made it clear, back in high school, how she felt about Dave.

He's going to break your heart one of these days, Claire Conway. You just wait and see. He's too full of himself. He wants to be the star. Especially when it comes to girls.

"I'm glad I was wrong," Alana whispered.

"Me too."

"I hope you're always this happy."

"We will be."

The clinking of a dinner knife against a wine goblet drew everyone's attention toward Jack Moncur. He stood, glass in hand.

"I'd like to thank all of you for coming tonight to help us celebrate our tenth wedding anniversary." He patted his trim abdomen. "Especially Claire for preparing that fantastic meal. And, of course, Dave for opening his home to us." He turned his eyes on his wife. "Most of all, I want to thank Alana for loving me and putting up with me while I learned how to be a husband. You all know it couldn't have been easy for her. Honey, you're the best." He lifted his glass. "To you, my darling. I love you."

They all took sips from their glasses.

Claire glanced down the length of the table. Her gaze met Dave's.

She expected him to smile that special secret smile, a smile that would say *I love you too. I think you're the best. Thanks for loving me and putting up with me.* But he didn't smile. Instead, his gaze shifted abruptly back to Jack.

He couldn't have meant to make her feel rejected. Dave had simply wanted to see what gift Jack was presenting to Alana at that very moment. That's all. Claire knew he loved her. He would never hurt her intentionally.

Nonetheless, the evening had lost some of its luster.

⸎

Sara loved the smell of spring on the farm. The pungent scent of freshly turned soil warmed by the sun. Flowering trees in bloom. Even the smell of cow manure wasn't bad when mingled with that of alfalfa hay.

As dusk settled over the earth, Sara stood in the corral with her quarter horse gelding, Rusty. She and Rusty had taken a few barrel-racing championships during her high school years. Last year, they'd come in second at the Snake River Stampede.

"You miss it, fella?" She stroked the white blaze on the sorrel's face.

As if understanding the question, Rusty snorted and bobbed his head.

Sara chuckled. "I'll bet. You're getting fat and lazy, standing around, waiting for me. If you weren't so ornery, maybe one of the guys would saddle you up."

"He could use a good run."

She turned, brought out of her reverie by her mother's unexpected presence.

Kristina leaned her arms on the fence. "He does miss you, you know."

"I wish I had time to come out for a ride now and then. I didn't know being in a play and keeping up with the rest of my studies would be so time consuming." Sara gave Rusty's neck a final pat, then strode across the corral to where her mother stood. She stepped up on the bottom rail of the whitewashed board fence, twisted, and sat on the top rail, her gaze returning to her favorite gelding.

For a while there was silence, a comfortable silence between a mother and daughter who'd survived the turbulent teen years and hysterical hormones and were now becoming friends.

"You nervous about the play?" Kristina asked at long last.

"Not really. I've got my lines down pat. I think I could say them in my sleep. In fact, I *do* say them in my sleep. I think I'll do okay on opening night."

"You'll do more than okay." She patted Sara's hand. "Dad and I are coming to the Saturday performance. Uncle Peter and Aunt Betsy are joining us. The boys all have other plans, but they said they'd be there on closing night."

Sara hoped her brothers would behave themselves. She could only imagine what shenanigans they might cook up.

"Would you like us to come early? We could all go out to eat, the five of us."

"I couldn't possibly eat before the play, Mom. I'd throw up."

"Which means you *are* nervous."

She laughed. "Yeah, I guess it does."

"What about this young man you mentioned at supper? Will *he* be at the play?"

Sara glanced down at her mother, not even trying to disguise the truth. "I hope so, Mom. I *really* hope so."

Kristina stared back, her gaze thoughtful. "Don't forget what's important, Sara Teresa."

The words were few, the reminder gentle, but Sara understood what her mother was saying. There were certain values the Jennings children had been raised with, certain standards of conduct that were expected of them, whether they were teenagers living at home or adults out on their own.

She thought of Dave again, of the strange way he affected her by his mere presence.

"I won't forget," she answered softly, hoping her promise was true.

Dave shoved the drawer closed, cursing angrily. "Jack Moncur's a jerk."

"Dave. Really."

"He didn't have to give her that diamond necklace at the party. He did it to show off, to make the rest of us guys look bad."

Claire pulled the brush through her hair. "That wasn't why. It was their anniversary party. Of course he would give it to her here. We're her friends."

"You know what's wrong with you, Claire? You don't have a clue about anything." He stormed out of the bedroom, slamming the door behind him.

Her hand stilled in midstroke. She was stunned by his rage. What had she said that was so terrible?

This isn't about Jack, a small voice warned.

She dropped the brush onto her dressing table and hurried after him. She found him sitting on the front stoop.

"Dave?" She placed a hand on his shoulder. "What's wrong?"

"Nothing," he grumbled. Silence. Then, "Everything."

"Is it work?" She sat beside him.

Instead of looking at her, he turned his eyes toward the sky. Claire followed the direction of his gaze.

Overhead, stars sparkled against an inky black backdrop. Night sounds drifted to her on a breeze, whispering through the green leaves on the trees that surrounded the Porter home. A cricket chirped its evening song. Someone's radio played near an open window, the music vying with static.

"Claire?"

"Hmm?"

"Do you ever wonder what would have happened to us if you hadn't gotten pregnant?"

Her heart nearly stopped beating. *I didn't do it on purpose, and I didn't do it alone.* After a few painful moments, she answered him, "No. No, I've never wondered that."

"Sometimes I do. I wonder what our lives would have been like if I'd had the chance to finish college. Maybe I'd have more money than Jack by now."

"Oh, Dave," she whispered, "we're rich in all the ways that count."

He looked at her. "I guess you got everything you wanted, didn't you, Claire? A husband, a son, a house." The anger was back, making his words harsh. "Just the way you always wanted it to be."

"I don't know what you mean." Her throat hurt. Her chest hurt. "It's what you wanted too."

"I think you know better than that."

She took hold of his upper arm, hanging on like a woman about to drown. "No, Dave, I don't. Tell me. Explain it to me. I'm your wife. You can tell me anything. I love you. If you're not happy, then let's do something about it."

He turned his eyes skyward again, not saying anything more.

His silence was worse than his anger.

Chapter Five

"How 'bout a sharing a burger over at the Burger 'n' Brew?" Luke Chambers, one of the cast, suggested to Sara on Monday afternoon at the end of rehearsal.

"Can't," she answered as she gathered her books. "I've got an appointment."

It was only a little white lie. She didn't have an appointment exactly, but she was expecting an important phone call. She had to get home. She didn't want to chance missing it.

"Maybe tomorrow?" Luke persisted.

She shrugged. "Maybe."

He gave a self-deprecating laugh. "I know a brush-off when I hear one." He grinned, obviously not heartbroken by her refusal. "Well, I hope the guy's worth it."

"So do I." She smiled back at him and took off for her apartment.

The sky had turned cloudy while she was in the rehearsal hall, and there was a sharp bite in the blustery wind that buffeted her back, pushing her along the cracked sidewalk. The weather felt more like February than April. She hugged her arms in front of her chest and quickened her steps. She was certain that rain would fall in the valley before evening, and if it stayed this cold, there could be a fresh dusting of snow on the mountain peaks by morning.

Sara was so intent on reaching the warmth of her second-floor apartment that she didn't see the tall man leaning against the stair railing until she was almost upon him.

"Oh!" She stopped, looked up, then felt her heart somersault.

"Hi." His smile hadn't changed. It was as devastating as she remembered.

"Dave."

"So you haven't forgotten my name."

"Of course I haven't forgotten. But I…I thought you were going to call. I wasn't expecting to see you until Friday night."

His smile faded. "Did I come at a bad time?" He moved as if to leave.

"No!" she answered hurriedly. "No, it isn't a bad time. Come inside. It's too cold to stand out here."

She stepped by him. In her haste to unlock the door, she dropped the key. Dave bent to pick it up. When he straightened, Sara found her nose suddenly mere inches from his.

"You're very pretty, Miss Jennings," he said, his voice low and husky. "Have I told you that before?"

She swallowed. *Yes*, she mouthed, although no sound came out.

He kissed her, right there on the landing. It was a chaste kiss, a mere brushing of lips, almost too brief to notice, and yet she was exploding inside.

This had to be love.

What else could it be?

It was after nine o'clock before Claire cleared the table. Dinner had gone mostly uneaten.

"Want me to do the dishes, Mom?" Mike asked as he followed her into the kitchen.

"No, sweetheart. It's time you were in bed. School tomorrow."

He touched her arm. "Dad's okay."

"I know." She forced a shaky smile. "He always forgets to look at his watch, doesn't he?"

Mike's smile was as artificial as hers. "Sure does. All the time."

Claire kissed his cheek and gave him a gentle push out of the kitchen. "Go on now. I'll load the dishwasher, and then I'll be in to tell you good night."

Without a word of protest, he obeyed.

As soon as Mike left the room, Claire went to the window and stared out at the dark street.

What if something *had* happened to Dave? What if he'd fallen on a job somewhere and no one knew it? Claire wouldn't even know whom to call. He hadn't told her where he was working. What if it was a new construction instead of a remodel? What if he was lying in some unfinished house in an empty subdivision and nobody found him until a crew arrived in the morning? Or what if there'd been an accident while he was driving home? What if his truck had been hit by another vehicle? What if they couldn't find his wallet before they took him to the hospital? What if—

Calm down. Stop it.

It wasn't as if he'd never failed to come straight home from work before. There had been other nights when he'd stopped for a drink

41

with friends and lost track of the time. She knew the likelihood was small that he was injured and helpless.

She hated giving in to her fears, hated the feeling of helplessness, of weakness in her own personality. Dave hated it too.

"Come home. Don't do this to me."

Claire wiped away the tears that had spilled onto her cheeks.

"He's fine," she berated herself, "and I'm not going to say a thing to him about this when he gets home. Not one word. So help me, I won't."

Sniffing, determined not to cry anymore, she returned to the kitchen. Quickly, she tossed the wasted food into the trash, rinsed the plates, and put them one by one into the dishwasher. Within minutes, all traces of dinner had vanished, the countertops were wiped clean, the dishwasher was whirring away, and Claire had brought her tears under control.

By the time she reached Mike's room, he was already in bed, his light off. But he wasn't asleep.

"What if something *has* happened to Dad?" His question was an echo of her own.

She sat on the edge of his bed. "Your dad is okay. I'm sure of it. Don't worry about him."

"Well, if he's not hurt, how come he does this stuff to you? How come he has to make you cry?"

"He doesn't mean to. Grownups aren't perfect. We make mistakes, just like kids."

"He oughta be nicer to you."

Her heart ached, and she didn't know if it was more for herself or her son. "He loves us," she answered softly. Then she ended the conversation by leaning forward to kiss his forehead. "Good night, honey."

"'Night."

❧

The greasy spoon, located east of the city, was noisy with conversations and loud music from the jukebox. Several couples played pool at tables set near the back, the women clad in tight jeans and short-cropped tops, the men looking like cowboys right out of an old black-and-white movie, complete with boots and Stetson hats. The air was filled with cigarette smoke and the scent of hot cooking oil. Old barn wood paneled the walls. The floor, stained and sticky with spilled beverages, was nothing but a concrete slab.

In the dim light of the restaurant, Sara watched Dave pour beer from a frosty pitcher into two glass mugs. It had been three hours since they'd eaten their dinners of deep-fried prawns and thick french fries, three hours of talking, laughing, and holding hands beneath the table, and still neither one them seemed ready to leave.

"I really shouldn't have any more to drink," she protested as he slid the mug across the marred surface of the table. "I'm feeling a little tipsy." She didn't mention that she was underage or that her parents would skin her alive if they knew she was drinking. There was no point in reminding him of their age difference.

"You're not driving, Sara. Go ahead. It won't hurt you."

Not wanting to disappoint him, she lifted the mug and took a sip. She didn't care for the taste of beer, but she wasn't about to tell him that either. She wanted only to please.

He grinned, as if he understood her thoughts. Then he reached out and touched her lower lip with his index finger, wiping away a trace of moisture. The caress sent a shock wave through her body. His smile disappeared.

He leaned toward her. "I like what you do to me."

She was held, mesmerized, by his gaze.

"I wasn't expecting to ever feel like this, Sara."

"Me neither."

He kissed her, a different sort of kiss than the one they'd shared earlier. This one was unhurried, slow, and deep, as if he were savoring every moment, every taste, every sensation. This was the way a man falling in love kissed a woman. She was certain of it.

When their lips parted, Dave cleared his throat. "I'd better take you home. It's getting late."

She wished they didn't have to leave, but she knew he was right. She had classes tomorrow. He had work.

He stood and held out his hand to help her out of the booth. He didn't let go until they reached his pickup truck. Before he opened the door, he pulled her back into his arms and kissed her again, with more passion this time. The intensity half frightened her.

"I wish you didn't have a roommate," he whispered huskily in her ear.

Sara knew what he meant. She was a virgin—not an easy thing to be in this sexually permissive age—but she wasn't a fool. She'd felt tempted before. She'd heard all the persuasive arguments of her teenage boyfriends. But her parents had drummed into her head from an early age the importance of waiting for love and marriage, and it hadn't been terribly difficult to adhere to that teaching.

Until now.

Was it *really* so important? she wondered as she looked into Dave's eyes.

"I've never felt like this before," he told her. "I don't know what you're doing to me."

The words caused her heart to soar.

"Come on. Let's get you back to your apartment."

Once in the cab of the pickup, Dave drew Sara over close to his side. As soon as they were on the highway headed toward town, the truck in fourth gear, he put his right arm over her shoulders. It seemed a safe and wonderful place to be; she wished she never had to leave it.

Neither one of them said a word until the truck came to a stop in front of Sara's apartment building. With a twist of the key, the engine died. The silence of night surrounded them. The light of a waning moon turned the hood of the gray truck silver. Sara could hear the rapid beat of her heart. Or was it his heart she heard?

Dave's arm tightened as he turned and kissed her temple. "What time do I need to pick you up on Friday?"

"We're supposed to be there by six-thirty."

"Then I'll be here at six. Until then, I'll be thinking about you all the time."

Sara undressed in the dark, doing her best to be quiet.

"Forget it," her roommate said from the corner of their shared bedroom. "I'm not asleep."

"Sorry."

Patti turned on the lamp beside her bed. She covered her mouth to hide a yawn, then blinked sleepily. "You're really falling hard for this guy, aren't you?"

She shrugged, not sure she was ready to talk about it yet.

"Hey, remember me? It's Patti. No romance escapes my notice, and you know it."

Sara laughed softly. "Yes, I know it."

"So?" She sat up on the bed, leaning her back against the wall. "Tell me all about him."

"He's...special."

"Well, aren't they all when you're falling for them? That doesn't tell me a thing. Come on. Give me particulars, Sara."

"You mean besides the fact that he's the most gorgeous man I've ever seen in my life?" She assumed the duplicate position of Patti, hugged her legs to her chest with her arms, and rested her chin on her knees. She closed her eyes. His image came immediately to mind. "When Dave looks at me, I go all warm inside. Like I'm melting or something. He likes all kinds of sports. He used to play baseball back in high school. He was the pitcher. He has his own ski boat, and he said he'd teach me to water-ski this summer if I want him to. He doesn't like cats, but he has a dog, a black lab, and he used to go hunting on horseback with a good friend of his. Which means he knows horses, at least a little. He's smart. He went to U of I for a year but had to give it up for lack of money. He's had his own carpentry business for the past ten years." She paused, then added, "I like his laugh."

Patti seemed to consider everything she'd been told before she asked, "Ever been married? He *is* over thirty, after all."

"Yes. He's got a little boy named Mikey whom he doesn't get to see much because of his ex-wife. She must be an awful person, keeping a son and father apart. He doesn't like to talk about it—I could tell by the look in his eyes when I asked him if he'd been married before."

Her roommate frowned. "How long has he been on his own? You don't want to get mixed up with some guy on the rebound."

"I'm not sure." What exactly had Dave said about that? His reply eluded her. "I got the feeling it's been a long time. Years."

"Sara...be careful."

She remembered the way he'd kissed her. "Don't worry, Patti. I know what I'm doing."

Lying on the bed in the darkened bedroom, Claire heard the truck pull up next to the house.

Dave was home.

She opened her eyes and looked at the clock radio. The red glow of digital numbers stared back at her: eleven o'clock. Should she get up and go to meet him? Would it be better if she simply pretended to be asleep? But if he was hurt, if something was wrong...

She tossed aside the sheet and comforter, sat up, and reached for her robe at the same time she slid her feet into her slippers. She cinched the belt of the robe tight as she left the bedroom. She was nearly to the kitchen before she heard the back door click shut.

He was trying so hard not to make a sound.

She flipped the light switch.

In that first burst of light, Dave turned toward her, eyes wide with surprise. Then the surprise was gone, replaced by irritation.

"I didn't expect you to still be up," he said.

"I was worried when you didn't call."

"I'm not going to report in like some kid to his mommy." He cursed. "I don't need you mothering me. Mikey needs mothering. Not me."

Beer and smoke. He reeked of both. She wanted to ask him where he'd been. She wanted to ask him whom he'd been with. She wanted to demand an explanation. She wanted him to hold her and tell her he loved her. What she didn't want was to burst into tears, the very thing she felt close to doing.

He pointed at her. "Don't start in on me, Claire. I mean it. A working man deserves a few hours of pleasure without being nagged."

She couldn't think of any reason for him to be acting this way. Hadn't she been thinking, just last week, how perfect her life was? What had gone wrong? She felt as if a train had broadsided her.

"And don't tell me we need to talk either," he added, his voice dripping with disdain. "Talking's the last thing I want to do."

If he'd struck her, it couldn't have hurt worse.

"I'm tired. I'm going to bed." With that, he strode past her, leaving her standing alone in the middle of the kitchen.

It was just like a few years ago when she'd wondered if he—

No, she wouldn't think about that. All marriages went through difficult periods. Whatever was bothering him would pass if she was patient. She merely had to let him know she loved him. She mustn't nag or cry. She just had to wait it out.

They would be fine.

She turned off the kitchen light and made her way down the darkened hallway. A pale sliver of moonlight spilled across the bed, and she could see that Dave was already beneath the covers. He was lying with his back toward Claire. After dropping her robe onto a nearby chair, she slipped between the sheets, trying not to cause so much as a ripple in the mattress.

Hold me, Dave.

She turned her head on her pillow, gazing over at him. She wanted to speak her request aloud, but she couldn't. He wanted her to leave him alone. She had to honor that request. She didn't want to give him any more reason to be angry with her.

We're going to be fine.

She rolled to her right side, feeling as if an ocean separated them instead of the intervening space on the queen-size mattress.

Sleep didn't come for hours.

Chapter Six

Friday was Claire's day to volunteer at Mike's school, her favorite part of every week. She'd first volunteered when her son started kindergarten and had continued through each grade of elementary school. Next year he would be in junior high, and she would no longer be needed.

But she tried not to think about that. She wasn't ready for her son not to need her, not to want her around when he was with his friends. Thankfully, it hadn't happened yet.

This afternoon, Mrs. Blackwell's sixth-grade class was visiting the Boise Public Library, and Claire was trying to help keep track of thirty eleven- and twelve-year-old students. It was no simple task.

"Mrs. Porter?"

She glanced down at the freckled face of Teresa Dawson. "Yes, Teresa. What is it?"

"Would you show me again where to look for stuff in the card files?"

"Of course." She placed her hand on the girl's shoulder, and the two of them walked to the bank of small file drawers filled with index cards. "What is it you need to find?"

"My report's on how the pilgrims came to America."

"Well, then, let's start with the letter S for ships."

Ten minutes later, Teresa had a list of books and their numbers written on a slip of scrap paper. Happily, she trundled off to find them.

"You have a way with children," Mrs. Blackwell said as she stepped up beside Claire. "Have you ever considered becoming a teacher?"

"Me?" Claire laughed at the idea. "Heavens, no."

"Maybe you should."

She shook her head. "There's no time for me to go to college. I work three mornings a week, and the rest of the time I'm busy taking care of my husband and son. Besides, I'm happy with things as they are."

Happy with things as they are…

She frowned. Was that true?

Dave had been moody all week. One moment he seemed himself, but the next he was surly and out of sorts. He'd made it clear they weren't going to discuss why he came home late on Monday, so Claire had let it drop. She didn't want to add tension to the situation. She'd told herself it wasn't important. And she must have been right—Dave had wanted to make love to her last night. If something were truly wrong between them, he wouldn't have wanted to make love.

Would he?

"Mrs. Porter?" Teresa's voice intruded on her unsettling thoughts. "I can't find this one." She handed the slip of paper to Claire. "Can you help me?"

She smiled at the child, glad for a reason to think of something else. "Let's look together, shall we?" She took hold of the child's hand.

*

"So what d'ya think, Mike?" John whispered. "D'ya think you could go?"

"I don't know. My dad's always sayin' we don't have the money to do stuff like this."

"Yeah, but two weeks in Montana!"

Mike opened the glossy brochure again. Pine trees and lakes and horses made the camp look like paradise.

"Maybe you could get some jobs mowing lawns this summer to help pay for it. We wouldn't go till August." John punched him in the arm. "At least ask."

If he went, that would leave his mom all alone. He hated to do that to her right now. She tried not to show it, but she was sad a lot of the time. She would miss him real bad if he was gone for a whole two weeks.

My dad wouldn't miss me. That's for sure. He didn't like the way that thought made him feel.

"You gotta at least ask," John persisted.

"Okay. When the time's right, I'll ask my mom. Just don't count on me gettin' to go, that's all."

*

Two hours later, with Mrs. Blackwell's class safely returned to the school, Claire walked the half-mile to her home. The brief cold snap that had blown in from the northwest earlier in the week had disappeared, and the weather was once again delightful.

Claire loved springtime, loved the budding of new life, the lawns turning from brown to green, the tulips pushing up to reveal the first bright colors of the year, the birds nesting in leafy trees, the calves and colts frolicking in pastures.

It had been a day much like this when Mike was born. Two weeks ago, the Porter family had celebrated Mike's twelfth birthday, but the memory of the first time she'd held her son in her arms, all eight pounds four ounces of him, was as fresh as if it had happened only yesterday.

In her mind's eye, she saw her husband standing in the hospital room near her bed. Mike was no more than six hours old at the time. Dave looked surprised and a little dazed, like many new fathers. Her parents, George and Lisa Conway, were there, too, along with her younger brother, Harold. Her dad declared the baby the spitting image of Claire when she was born. Her mother merely smiled and tried to blink away tears of joy and relief. Fifteen-year-old Harold, bored and impatient with all the fuss and falderal about a baby, just wanted to get out of there.

How happy Claire had been on that day. How perfect her life had seemed. Just like one of those television families from her childhood in the fifties and sixties. Like the Cleavers or the Stones. It hadn't seemed possible that anything could go wrong. Not ever.

But, of course, things hadn't been perfect. Six weeks after her son's birth, she'd learned she would never have another child, and before Mike's third birthday, her parents had been killed in an automobile accident, the driver of the other car drunk behind the wheel. As for her brother, Harold had gone to college back East the same year as their parents' deaths and never returned to Idaho. She hadn't seen him in over eight years, although she wrote to him semiregularly and he called her a few times a year.

She was suddenly overwhelmed by a sense of aloneness. She felt abandoned, cut adrift by those she'd depended upon most. She longed to be able to hug her mother and ask for advice. Lisa Conway would have known how to fix what was wrong with Claire's marriage. Her parents had been married over twenty-five years, and her dad had never been unhappy or discontent in all those years. She was positive he hadn't.

She thought of Dave again, of his dark moods, of his frowns and his tempers. She'd tried to convince herself that nothing was amiss, that it was all related to stress from long hours at work and that it had nothing to do with their home life. But in her more honest moments, she knew better. Not even their lovemaking last night could have made everything all right.

With those heavy thoughts on her mind, Claire made her way up the sidewalk and let herself in the back door.

She paused on the threshold, staring at the signs of this morning's hasty departure. Breakfast dishes stained with dried egg yolks were stacked in the sink. A skillet with bacon grease turned white and solid in its center sat on the old electric stove. Bread crumbs surrounded the toaster. Chunks of dry dog food were strewn in front of the washer and dryer. Dave had kicked the dog's dish this morning as he was leaving, spilling the contents, but he hadn't bothered to clean up the mess he'd made.

He never did pick up after himself, Claire thought with a spark of irritation. He always left everything to her. Sometimes she felt more like his maid than like his wife.

She was immediately ashamed. This was what she wanted, what she'd always wanted, to be a wife and mother and homemaker. She wouldn't even work those three mornings a week in Jack Moncur's office if she and Dave didn't need the money to see them through the leaner times that came with the construction business.

The phone on the kitchen wall rang. Claire closed the door behind her and crossed the room to answer it. "Hello."

"Good. I caught you at home."

"Dave?" She couldn't hide her surprise. He rarely called her in the middle of the day.

"Listen, I've got a lead on a big remodel job up above Idaho City. I mean big. It could see us all the way through summer, maybe even to next Christmas if we're lucky. But if I want to get the job, I've got to go up there today. Right now. I don't know who all I'm going to have to see or how long it'll take me to drive up and back. I hear there's still some snow on the roads. It'll probably be well after midnight before I get home. I just didn't want you to worry if I was late."

"I appreciate that, Dave, but couldn't you—"

"I've gotta run. I don't want to miss out on this. I'll tell you all about it in the morning."

The line went dead.

Sara didn't know if she was more nervous about opening night or seeing Dave again. Combined, they seemed overwhelming.

While she waited for his arrival, she stared at her reflection in the full-length mirror, picking out all of her flaws. She didn't have much of a figure. Small breasts. Narrow hips. Long but too-thin legs. She didn't like her dark red hair; it was much more fashionable to be blond. Her eyes were probably her best feature, but if a guy—if Dave—was close enough to see them, he was close enough to see the smattering of pale freckles that spilled across her cheeks and the bridge of her too-long nose.

"How many times are you going to change outfits?" Patti asked as she entered the bedroom.

Sara met her roommate's gaze in the mirror. "Until I get it right." She turned around. "What do you think of this?" She held out her arms, then pirouetted, awaiting judgment.

She wore a short-sleeve knit top, the same light green color as her eyes. Her skirt, hitting her at midthigh, was a darker forest green. Black pantyhose encased her long legs. She'd always thought the outfit flattering, but tonight…

"I think I'd kill to look like you."

Sara turned back to the mirror. "I don't know. Maybe I should try—"

"Don't even think about it." Her friend stepped in front of the closet and threw herself against the door in an I'm-willing-to-die-for-it gesture.

Before Sara could react, the doorbell announced Dave's arrival.

Patti grinned in triumph. "Besides, you don't have time. *He's* here."

The butterflies in Sara's stomach went into full flight. She glanced once more at her reflection, then went to open the door for him.

"Hi." Dave smiled that heart-stopping smile of his the moment their eyes met.

"Hi."

His gaze moved down the length of her, unhurried, filled with appreciation for what he saw before him. It returned at the same leisurely pace. His perusal seemed more intimate than a physical caress would have been.

"You look beautiful," he said at long last.

She was glad she hadn't changed again. "So do you."

He chuckled as he stepped toward her, drawing her to him. "I'm beautiful, huh?" He kissed her until she was weak in the knees.

It was the sound of applause—reminding them that they weren't alone—that ended the kiss. Sara knew she was flushed as she stepped out of his embrace and turned toward her roommate.

Patti lifted an eyebrow, then looked at Dave. "You treat her good, Mr. Porter."

"Patti!"

"I mean it," her friend continued, unfazed by Sara's embarrassed protest. "You be careful with her, or you'll answer to me."

"I promise I'll be careful, Miss Cooper." He sounded just as serious as Patti did.

Mortified, Sara hurried into her bedroom where she grabbed her purse, jacket, and bag of personal items that she would need at the theater. She returned quickly, not wanting to leave Dave alone with her roommate any longer than necessary. "I'm ready," she announced as she stepped to his side.

"Break a leg, Sara." There was a note of apology in Patti's voice.

"Thanks," she mumbled, not yet ready to forgive. She took hold of Dave's arm and urged him out of the apartment.

"Patti's a good friend to you," he said as they descended the steps.

Reluctantly, "Yes, she is."

He squeezed her arm against his side. "She just doesn't want you to get hurt."

"I know you wouldn't hurt me." She spoke the words in a whisper.

Dave stopped on the sidewalk, pulling her to a halt with him. Taking hold of her upper arms, he turned her to face him.

She met his gaze. "You wouldn't *ever* hurt me." Louder this time.

"How can you be so sure?"

"Because I just know you wouldn't."

There was a trace of sadness in his smile. "You are very young, Miss Jennings."

"I'm not too young to know what I want or what I believe."

"Sara—"

She placed an index finger over his lips. "Shh. There's no point in arguing with me. Now get me over to the theater. I don't want to be late for my first lead performance."

Chapter Seven

Mike didn't get a chance to ask his mom about camp. The "right time" he'd told John he was waiting for never came.

That night Mike and his mom went out for burgers, then to a movie. It was something they often did together, just the two of them. He liked the movie *Back to the Future* a lot, but he didn't think his mom did. She didn't laugh. Not even once during the whole show.

That night, the light seemed to go out of her. Despite her best efforts not to let him see what she was feeling, Mike wasn't fooled. He knew his dad had done something to hurt her.

That was the night he started to hate him.

Lying in his bed after they got home, Mike stared up at the ceiling in his dark room and wished his dad wouldn't ever come home. Not if he was going to make Mom look so sad. Not if he wasn't gonna treat her right. He didn't mind so much for himself; he was used to doing things without a dad around. His dad didn't ever spend much time with him. Not the way John's dad did. Mr. Kreizenbeck coached softball in the spring, led their scout troop, and taught sixth-grade Sunday school. He was involved in everything his kids did. And he was always doing nice things for Mrs. Kreizenbeck too.

It wasn't fair, Mike's mom not getting treated like that. Somehow, he knew, he had to make that up to her.

⟨◦⟩

The play was a blazing triumph; Sara received a standing ovation. But it was Dave's praise that made her feel truly a success. All through the late supper they shared, he told her how amazing she was, how beautiful she was, how sexy she was. By the time they returned to her darkened apartment, she'd started to believe him.

"I suppose I shouldn't come in," Dave whispered as they stood on the threshold. "Don't want to wake up Patti."

"She's not here. She went to Pocatello this weekend. That's where her folks live."

"You mean we have the place to ourselves?"

Her pulse quickened. "Yes."

"Then, Miss Jennings, I think I should kiss you. Thoroughly."

His mouth covered hers, and her mind went blank. She was vaguely aware of the sound of the closing door, but she didn't know how they ended up across the room and on the sofa. Just suddenly she was lying across his lap as he continued to smother her with earthshaking kisses.

Somewhere in the back of her mind, a small voice, sounding far too much like her mother's, warned her that she was venturing out of her depth, that she was treading in dangerous waters. But she didn't want to listen to her conscience or to her mother. She wanted to make Dave Porter love her. She'd already fallen hard for him.

It had to be fate, their meeting. They were meant for each other. So why wait?

"I've never known anyone like you," he whispered in her ear. "No woman's ever made me feel this way before."

He thought she was a woman. Wouldn't he see her as a mere girl if she denied him what he so obviously wanted? They belonged together. Waiting wouldn't change that.

"Sara?"

"Yes."

It was more than a response to her name. It was a decision. It was inevitable that they become lovers, and now was surely the time.

Claire leaned her forehead against the cool glass of her bedroom window. *Please, God. No.*

She knew. Deep in her heart, she knew he was with someone else tonight. And she wanted to die. Dave was her life. She'd loved him since she was fifteen. If he stopped loving her…

Should she confront him? Or was it better to ignore it? Last time…

It was like a knife piercing her heart. Yes, there had been a last time. She might as well admit it. It wasn't just suspicion. It was fact. Dave had carried on an affair before.

But he hadn't left Claire. She had to remember that. Whatever the cause of his dalliance, he hadn't wanted to end his marriage. He loved his wife and son. Deep down, he had to love them. He would always love them.

*O God…*She looked up at the heavens. *If You exist, don't let it be true.*

She turned her back to the window and sank to the floor. Tears streamed down her cheeks. She felt so alone. So utterly and completely alone.

Why was this happening to her? Hadn't she been a good wife to Dave? Hadn't her concern always been for his needs, for his happiness? What had she done to deserve his betrayal?

She struck the floor with her fists as a moan issued from her throat. "What do I do now?"

If there was a God, He didn't answer her. There was only the silence of the bedroom, the emptiness of her heart, the despair of a life crumbling around her.

∽∾

Sara felt Dave sliding away from her and stirred in her sleep. "Mmm," she mumbled. "Where are you going?"

"It's time I left for home."

Opening her eyes, she made out his form. He was sitting up on the side of the bed. She reached out and touched his back with her fingertips.

"You should have told me this was your first time, Sara." There was a hint of accusation in his voice.

"I didn't think it would matter. Did it?"

Without answering, he rose from the bed and started to dress.

Even though she couldn't see him clearly in the dark bedroom, Sara blushed and glanced away, embarrassed. Now that the sweeping passion was over, now that she was fully awake, she experienced her first wave of guilt and shame. She pulled the sheet up to cover her nakedness.

But what should she feel guilty about? They were two consenting, single adults. They weren't harming anyone. She refused to accept the guilt. She refused to be ashamed. These were the eighties, after all. The days of puritan morals were long since past, killed in the sexual revolution of her parents' youth.

"I love you," she whispered, unable to keep the words to herself any longer. Then she waited to hear him repeat the words to her.

He didn't.

She fought tears. "Dave…"

Dressed now, he put one knee on the bed and leaned over her. "It's okay, Sara. I'm not angry. I just don't want us to get carried away or do anything rash."

Sara should have realized what a ludicrous thing that was for him to say, given they'd gone to bed on their first date. But recognizing it would be to accept her culpability. She wasn't prepared for that.

"I understand," she managed to say around the lump in her throat.

He kissed her forehead, kissed the tip of her nose, kissed her on the lips. "You said Patti's out of town for the rest of the weekend. Why don't I come by tomorrow evening?"

"I can't. Not tomorrow." Her fingers tightened on the sheet she was holding over her breasts. "My parents are coming to Boise to see the play."

"Oh, yeah. That."

He sounded as if he'd forgotten the play completely, as if he'd never seen her in it.

He kissed her again, then stood. "Don't get up. I'll let myself out."

"You'll call me?" She couldn't disguise the desperation she felt.

"I'll call you." He walked across the room, pausing in the doorway. "Sara?"

"Yes?"

"You'd better get on the pill. We don't want any unpleasant surprises."

It was only common sense. So why did she feel another surge of shame? At least it meant he was coming back, that he wanted to continue to see her.

"You'll take care of that on Monday?" he asked. "You'll get a prescription?"

"Yes, I will."

"Good." He disappeared into the hall.

A moment later, she heard a faint squeak as the front door opened.

"Good night, Sara," he called softly.

The door closed before she could reply.

Chapter Eight

Old habits die hard.

Claire didn't confront Dave about her suspicions. Not on that first night when he didn't come home until two in the morning and not on any of the similar occasions in the weeks that followed. It was easier to slip back into pretending her life and marriage were everything they were supposed to be.

Dave told her he didn't get the job north of Idaho City, but he had plenty of other reasons for staying out late or being away on weekends. And she let his explanations fall between them, unchallenged.

April became May.

May rushed toward June.

Although it seemed impossible, Mike was set to graduate from elementary school in two more weeks. There were times Claire couldn't even recall the cute toddler he'd been. Judging by the high-water position of his trouser cuffs, he'd sprouted another two inches since Christmas. His voice had started to crack in midsentence, announcing his headlong plunge into adolescence and then manhood.

How did a mother prepare herself for that?

But what truly disturbed her was the constant tension and bickering between Mike and his dad. It didn't seem to matter what one of them said, it irritated the other, and before she knew it, they were yelling at the top of their lungs. The fights usually ended with Mike being sent to his room and Dave storming out of the house.

On this Sunday morning, it was about to happen again.

As usual, Mike was getting ready to go to church with the Kreizenbecks. Dave made a crack about holier-than-thou people and all the garbage they were putting into his son's head. Mike told him that wasn't true. The Kreizenbecks were nice, real nice, and he liked going to church with them and learning about God.

"And it's *not* garbage," he ended emphatically.

"It's for sissies, boy. A crutch for idiots."

"It is not."

"Sissy."

"I'm *not* a sissy!"

"Dave, please—" Claire began.

"Is that so?" he continued, ignoring her. "You are if I say you are. I shouldn't let you go with that Kreizenbeck jerk. I don't like the guy. I don't trust him, and I don't want you turning out like him."

"At least Mr. Kreizenbeck knows how to be nice to Mrs. Kreizenbeck and his kids. It wouldn't hurt you to be nice to Mom once in a while."

Claire leaned over to pour Dave another cup of coffee, cutting off his view of their son and hoping it would stop the snowballing argument. It didn't work.

Dave stood and stepped around her, his body rigid, his voice level rising. "Don't you talk back to me, Mikey Porter. You hear me?"

"Don't *you* call me Mikey," the boy shouted in reply. "I hate it."

"I'll call you whatever I want." He grabbed his son by the shoulders and gave him a rough shake. "Now, you apologize to me for mouthing off like that."

Instead of obeying, Mike thrust out his chin and leaned forward, fists clenched at his sides. "I *won't*. I'm *not* sorry. You're always making Mom cry. Why do you have to do that? How come you can't be nice to her? She's the best mom in the world."

Dave shoved Mike away from him, then spun toward Claire. "You've made a mama's boy out of him."

"That's not fair," she protested. "I haven't—"

He muttered a curse, then stormed past her. The back door opened …and slammed closed. Less than a minute later, the truck roared to life and pulled out of the driveway.

An oppressive silence filled the kitchen.

"I'm sorry, Mom. I didn't mean to make him mad at you. I just—"

"It isn't your fault, honey." She sank onto a chair with a sigh, fighting the threat of tears. She was tired of crying.

"He *is* mean to you, and I hate him for it."

"Oh, Mike…"

"It's true. He's grouchy all the time, and he makes you cry, and he never does anything with us. And I don't care that he doesn't. Who wants to be with him? Not me."

She wondered what she could say to change his mind about his father. Maybe Dave was right. Maybe this *was* her fault. She'd let their son see her unhappiness, let him feel her tension. She'd let him see her tears. She should have sheltered him from it. He was only twelve years old. He couldn't begin to understand the complexities of a marriage, the ups and downs, the ebb and flow of life that affected every couple.

"Your dad's just going through a difficult time." The excuse tasted like sawdust on her tongue.

"But he shouldn't take it out on you."

How simple life was for the young. Things were either black or white, right or wrong.

Mike stepped forward and put his arms around her, as if he were the adult and she the child. "Don't feel bad. I'm here."

It took all her internal fortitude not to crumble at his brave words.

A horn honked, announcing the arrival of the Kreizenbeck family.

"There's your ride."

"Why don't you come with us, Mom? You'd like church."

"Not today. Another time maybe."

"I should stay with you."

"No." She put on a smile. "You go on. I have a lot to get done this morning." She gave him a hug. "And don't you worry about your dad and me. When he gets home, we'll talk it all out and things will be fine. Just like it used to be. I promise. You'll see."

His blue eyes—so like his dad's and yet so different—called her a liar.

Another beep of the horn broke the silence between them.

Claire gave him a gentle shove. "Hurry up now, or you'll make everyone late."

Sara was both surprised and delighted to see Dave when she opened the door. She hadn't expected him until Monday night.

He leaned his shoulder against the doorjamb, looking moody and charming at the same time. "Hi."

As usual, her pulse quickened at the sound of his voice. "Hi."

"I'm going for a drive in the mountains. Up to Lowman. Maybe as far as Stanley. Care to come along?"

"I'd love to."

"Good. Let's go."

It became quickly apparent, as Dave drove his truck up Highway 21, that he hadn't invited Sara along for the scintillating conversation. She tried more than once to introduce a topic of interest to him, failing miserably each time. Mostly, he grunted and frowned in response, his expression growing darker with each passing mile.

It frightened her, seeing him this way.

Many things frightened her. She was afraid her parents would learn that she'd become physically intimate with a man outside of marriage. She was afraid Dave didn't love her, despite all the times she'd told herself he must or he wouldn't keep coming to see her. She was afraid he would tire of her because she was young and made so many mistakes. She was afraid because he refused to talk about himself beyond the very basics. She was afraid when he didn't come to see her, and she was afraid, when he did, that he only came for sex. She longed for him to call her sometimes, just to talk, just to say he missed her. He never did. He hadn't even given her his phone number; when she looked for it in the telephone directory, she'd discovered it was unlisted.

Just yesterday, Patti had said, "Say what you want, Sara. I don't trust him. There's just something—"

Sara hadn't let her friend finish. She didn't want to hear anything negative about Dave. She had to believe in his love for her, in their future together. If she didn't, if she let doubts creep in, if…

"How'd you like to go to Portland with me for a couple of days?" he asked, breaking into her agitated thoughts.

"Portland?"

"Yeah, there's some business opportunities over there I want to look into."

"Are you thinking of moving?" Alarm tightened her gut.

"Maybe." For a fleeting moment he met her gaze, then looked back at the winding road. "Think about it. We could have a couple nights in a nice hotel, just the two of us." He grinned, and it was clear what he was imagining. "No roommates. No phone calls. No interruptions."

Is that the only reason you want me along, Dave?

She couldn't speak the question aloud. To do so would be to admit her secret doubts.

"How about it?"

"I've got a job lined up for the summer," she answered at last, "but it doesn't start until the fifth of June. I suppose I could go before that. Just for a couple of days."

"That's my girl." He placed his arm around her shoulders and drew her close. "It'll be good for us both. I don't know about you, but I could sure use a little vacation. I'll bet you could too."

His girl. He'd called her his girl. Surely that meant her doubts were baseless, that he cared, that he loved her as much as she loved him— even if he didn't say so.

She smiled, her heart lifting. Of course that was what it meant. She had nothing to fear. Nothing at all.

Claire wandered through the house, feeling listless, aimless, and empty. She wanted to do something to take her mind off Dave and her suspicions, but nothing she tried worked. A woman's instinct told her he'd gone to see his lover after his fight with their son.

She paused at the living room window and stared through the glass at the front yard. Sunlight filtered through lacy branches of the curly willow tree, causing a crisscross pattern of shadows to flutter over the lawn. At each of the front corners of the yard were huge lilac bushes. A warm spell in March had caused them to bloom early in the season. Now the purple blossoms were gone, and all that was left was green. She wished she could still cut a fresh bouquet and fill the house with their scent.

She remembered the spring she'd planted the lilacs. They'd been hardly more than twigs. Mike, a toddler at the time, had sat nearby, wiggling his toes in the grass and laughing as the green blades tickled the bottoms of his feet.

That was the same day Dave had brought home the new truck. New to them anyway. Claire had baked a cake to celebrate that milestone in their lives. Success and prosperity had seemed just around the corner. How perfect her little world had been. How inviolable.

Like a jag of lightning piercing the sky, an ache shot through her heart. She was filled with an overwhelming desire to fall to her knees and wail in lamentation, as for the dead. Because if something wasn't already dead, it was surely dying. If not her marriage, then her dreams of what a marriage should be.

No. Please, no. Don't let it be true. Oh, please, don't let this happen to me. To us. I'd rather die.

71

Chapter Nine

"How about stopping for pizza?" Dave asked as they neared Boise's city limits. "I'm starved."

"Sure. I'd like that."

Sara was glad he wasn't taking her straight home. She was happier when with him, her fears silenced, at least momentarily. But she knew that once she was back in her apartment and was alone with too much time to think her doubts would resurface. She wasn't ready to end what had turned out to be a perfectly delightful afternoon.

"I know a little hole-in-the-wall pizza parlor that makes the best deep-dish pizzas you've ever tasted. Great brew too." He downshifted as he approached a stop sign, then flipped on his turn signal. "That okay with you?"

"Whatever you want to do is fine."

"That's what I like about you, Sara. You know how to make a man feel good about himself. No pressure. No worries. No strings attached."

She wished those words sounded more like a compliment than they did.

At the parlor, Dave ordered a large, thick-crust pepperoni and sausage pizza, no olives, and a pitcher of whatever was on tap, as long as it wasn't light. Then he ushered Sara to a booth in the back corner of the parlor. He filled a frosted mug with beer and slid it across the table.

A spark of rebellion left a metallic taste in her mouth. *I'd rather have orange soda with pizza. And I hate pepperoni.*

Why didn't she tell him so? She'd never been afraid to speak her mind to guys before. She'd always been frank with her brothers and boyfriends. So why was she afraid to speak up to Dave?

Because, she answered herself with brutal honesty, she was unsure how he felt about her. And if he didn't love her, then…

"Why so serious, babe?" He took hold of her hand across the table and gave it a squeeze.

She couldn't tell him, so she made up something. "I was thinking about Portland."

"We'll have a good time."

Warmth wrapped around each of his words, tugging at her heart, giving her hope.

Softly, she asked, "Do you really think you want to move there?" *Will you want me with you then too? Will you ask me to marry you?*

"I'll just have to wait and see." He shrugged. "Depends on the work I find."

"It's so gray and rainy near the coast."

"Yeah, but not as cold in the winter as it is here. Hardly ever snows."

"No, I guess not."

He leaned toward her. His eyes were more ebony than blue in the dim light of the parlor. The corners of his mouth curved infinitesimally. "Would you miss me if I moved away?"

"You know I would." Her reply was almost inaudible.

But he heard it. And seemed pleased by it.

She swallowed, trying to calm the flutter of nerves in her stomach.

He appeared on the verge of saying something. Perhaps he was ready to tell her he loved her. Maybe he was ready to ask that all-important question.

The address system crackled and sputtered, then a loud voice blared, "Number forty-eight, your pizza's ready. Number forty-eight."

"I think that's us." Dave glanced at the ticket stub on the table. "Yeah, it is. Sit tight and I'll get it."

Just inside the entrance of their favorite pizza parlor was a room filled with video arcade games.

"Can I have some quarters, Mom?" Mike asked as they stepped from daylight into the shadowy restaurant.

"Sure." Claire plucked the coins from a zippered pouch on the side of her purse. "You want the usual?" She placed the quarters in the palm of his outstretched hand.

"Uh-huh."

"I'll come get you when our order's out."

"Okay."

She watched as her son made a beeline for the Donkey Kong machine. He dropped his quarter into the slot and quickly positioned his hands on the controls as the familiar theme song began to play.

Claire felt her spirits lift. After all, how bad could things be as long as there was Mike, pizza, and Donkey Kong?

She walked to the counter and stood beneath a sign that proclaimed *Place Orders Here.*

A teenage girl, wearing a narrow-brimmed baseball cap, a bright red shirt, and navy slacks, flashed a silver-metal grin at her. "Welcome to Pizza Den," she chirped—for that was the only word that could describe the perky, almost annoying cheerfulness of her voice. "Can I take your order?"

"Yes. I'd like a medium pepperoni and sausage with black olives. Thin crust, please. One salad with Thousand Island dressing. And two mugs of root beer."

The girl scribbled the order on a standard green-and-white form, then tore away the number at the bottom along the perforated line. "Here you go." She handed the ticket stub to Claire, still grinning and showing the braces on her teeth. "We'll call your number when it's ready. You want your salad and drinks now or with your pizza?"

"With the pizza is fine, thanks."

"Sure thing."

Claire was just turning back toward the arcade room when familiar male laughter reached her ears. Her breath caught in her throat. Her pulse went into overdrive. She turned slowly, searching the room.

His back was toward her, but she knew it was Dave.

And he was with *her.*

The light was too dim, the corner too distant, for Claire to see clearly. It was more an impression than anything else, yet one that seared into her soul.

The woman was young. Painfully so. Just a girl. Pretty. Dark hair cut in a cap of short curls. Reed-thin. She was leaning toward Dave in the manner of one totally engrossed in another person, of a woman yearning for a man.

As if feeling Claire's gaze upon her, the girl abruptly glanced in her direction. Claire stumbled backward, out of sight, ragged breaths tearing at her throat and lungs. She leaned against the wall, wondering if she was going to do something horrible like faint.

What should she do? Should she confront Dave and that…and that…

A torrent of vile names filled her head, and she wanted to screech them all. She wanted to rip that girl's hair out by the roots. She wanted to drag her out of that booth and kick and scratch her.

Nauseated, Claire closed her eyes. She'd guessed Dave was having an affair, but seeing the proof of it before her eyes was worse than she could have imagined. She wanted to die. She wondered if she might die. Right here. Right now.

A momentary numbness washed over her. She felt disembodied, separated from herself, unable to move. Then the Donkey Kong music filtered into her brain, reminding her that Mike was just a few yards away, that Mike might see his father with that girl if Claire didn't do something quick.

She pushed away from the wall and hurried toward the arcade. Her son was feverishly working the controls on the video game. "Mike, come on."

"Boy, that was fast." He glanced over his shoulder, then back at the screen. "I'll be there in a minute."

"Now, Mike. We're leaving."

"Leaving?" He turned toward her, puzzled.

"Yes." She held out her hand toward him. "Come on."

"But what about the—"

"*Now*, Michael Dakota."

Mike understood what she was saying, just like every other kid understood. When a mother addressed her child with both first and middle names, it meant *Don't argue with me; I mean business.* He followed her out to the car without another word.

Claire didn't look at her son again, even though she knew he was casting furtive glances in her direction. It took all her concentration to maintain a facade of composure for his benefit. She didn't want him to see her shatter into a thousand pieces. That would have to wait until she was alone. It couldn't happen in front of him.

But in her heart, devastation reigned unchecked.

✥

The minutes dragged by, late afternoon fading into evening, darkening into night.

Claire waited in the living room, all lights turned off, her hands folded in her lap, clenched so tight her fingernails bit into her flesh. She knew Mike had been alarmed by her behavior but she couldn't help it. She'd sent him to bed an hour ago and only hoped he would be asleep before his father returned.

If his father returned…

Honey-coated laughter echoed in her memory. It was a sound she knew well—or *used* to know well. Did Dave ever laugh like that around her anymore?

He'd loved her once. She could make him love her again. She was only thirty. That wasn't old. She hadn't let herself get fat. She was still attractive. It wasn't hopeless. It couldn't be hopeless. She wouldn't let it be.

Headlights flashed against the window. Claire caught her breath and held it, listening as the truck rumbled into the driveway. The pickup stopped; the engine died. Silence. The truck door slammed. Silence again. Then the back door opened and closed.

Claire rose from the sofa, staring at the kitchen doorway, waiting.

Dave didn't see her standing there until he flicked on the hall light. He stopped abruptly, looked at her, frowned. "What are you doing up?"

"Do you love her?"

"What?"

Louder, "Do you love her?"

"Love who? What're you talking about?"

"Mike and I went for pizza."

A vile curse assaulted her ears a split second before Dave threw a punch at the wall. The plasterboard crumbled, leaving a fist-sized hole.

Shocked by the unexpected violence, Claire stumbled backward. Her legs hit the sofa, and she sat down.

"Can't you leave anything alone?" he shouted as he moved toward her, his posture threatening.

She shrank against the back of the sofa. Her gaze darted toward the hall. "Please, Dave. Mike's asleep."

He swore again, turning away while raking his fingers through his hair. His shoulders rose and fell with the drawing in of a deep breath. After a long while, he strode to the overstuffed chair opposite the matching sofa, turned, and sat down.

"So what now?" he asked.

"Do you love her?"

He frowned, shrugged, and then shook his head. "No, I don't guess I do."

"Then why? *Why?*"

"I don't know. She's young and pretty. She makes me feel good."

She made him *feel* good? What sort of answer was that? What sort of reason for adultery?

"It just happened, Claire. I wasn't planning it."

She'd loved him from the time she was fifteen. She'd been his wife for nearly thirteen years. She'd tended him when he was sick. She'd borne his son. She'd cooked his meals and cleaned his house and shared his bed. She'd rejoiced with him when things went right and shouldered his burdens when things went wrong.

And she was forgotten because that pretty young thing made him *feel* good.

She wanted to hit him. She wanted to pound him with her fists the same way that he'd struck the wall. She wanted to hurt him. Hurt him like he was hurting her.

"I guess it's too bad you wanted pizza." One corner of his mouth turned upward, that teasing, you-never-could-hold-anything-against-me-for-long grin of his.

There was a cold, hard lump in the pit of her stomach. "This isn't anything to joke about."

"Look, it happened. I'm sorry." His scowl returned. "Now let's forget it and go to bed."

"Not till we get this settled between us." Her voice rose to match his. She'd forgotten Mike and the need for quiet. *Just forget it?* The desire to shriek at the top of her lungs was almost overwhelming.

"And how do we *settle* it?" he asked.

"I want us to see a marriage counselor."

He laughed, a sound devoid of humor. "Not a chance. I'm not getting all touchy-feely with some crackpot shrink. You can go talk to whoever you want, but leave me out of it." He stood and strode down the hall.

She quickly followed him into the bedroom, closing the door behind her. "We're not finished talking."

"Yeah, we are." He started to undress.

She wondered how often he'd disrobed in front of that girl. How often had the two of them shared a bed? The thought was sickening; it drained the strength right out of her. She leaned back against the door.

"I love you, Dave. Doesn't that matter? Isn't our marriage worth saving?"

His silence was worse than a shout…and more eloquent too.

"Dave?"

"Aw, Claire, you're making too big a deal out of this. Sometimes men stray. It happens all the time." He yanked back the covers and got into bed. "Now let it go." He rolled onto his side and closed his eyes.

"Are you going to see her again?"

"Good night."

"Are you, Dave?"

He sighed. "I'll tell her it's over. Okay? Now turn out the light and let me get some sleep. Tomorrow's a workday, and I'm beat."

She flipped the switch, plunging the bedroom into darkness, but she didn't move away from the door, didn't attempt to undress and go to bed. She couldn't. Her body was as paralyzed as her mind and heart.

Oblivion, she discovered, was better than pain, better than the heartache she knew she would feel tomorrow. So she allowed the lethargic cocoon of numbness to embrace her.

Chapter Ten

When Sara hadn't seen or heard from Dave for a week, panic set in. Had she said something when they were last together that had upset him? Had he been in some sort of accident on the job or in his truck? No one would know to notify her. She'd never met any of his friends. What if he was hurt, maybe dying?

But that didn't bear thinking about.

Another week passed, and the day she and Dave were scheduled to leave for Portland was approaching. Still she hadn't heard from him. She was beside herself with worry. She tried to weasel his unlisted phone number out of the operator, telling her it was a family emergency, but it didn't work. She tried the same story at the post office with the same result.

Then it occurred to her to check the city directories at the public library. Success at last. She found listings for two David Porters in the current year's directory, one who lived on Five Mile Road, the other on Garden Street.

Garden was closer; she drove there first.

Sara was still a block away when she saw Dave. He was headed toward his truck, parked on the side of the road. She didn't have to get closer to recognize him. Her heart knew him immediately.

He's all right.

Her hand flew to the horn. Then he turned back toward the house, and something caused her to hesitate before honking. Her gaze followed his…to a woman standing just inside the doorway of the tree-shaded house.

Sara didn't remember pulling over to the curb, didn't remember cutting the engine, but there she was, the car parked and silent. She leaned forward, gripping the steering wheel with both hands.

Dave returned to the front door. He gestured emphatically as he spoke to the woman on the other side of the storm door. Sara wished she could see her clearly, then was glad she couldn't. Although she tried to tell herself there were a dozen—no, a hundred!—different reasons for what she saw, in her heart, she knew there was only one reason for that woman to be standing inside the doorway of Dave's house. She was his wife.

Dave Porter wasn't divorced, as he'd told her. He was a married man.

But maybe they were separated. Maybe they were getting a divorce. They were arguing. Maybe…

No, if that were true, he would have told her. He wouldn't have lied about it. And it *was* a lie. Whether by omission or commission, it was still a lie.

But maybe…

Dave opened the storm door, leaned through the doorway, took the woman by the shoulders, and kissed her on the mouth, dashing the last glimmer of Sara's hope.

Claire knew Dave believed his kisses could make her forget what he'd done, but it wasn't going to work this time. She'd begun to realize how often he used his body in the place of meaningful communication. Her husband thought sex could solve anything, but it wasn't going to solve this.

"Think about it," he said as he stepped back from her. "It would do us good to get away. It's only for two or three nights. The Kreizenbecks could keep Mikey while we're gone. He practically lives over there anyway."

How would you know? You're almost never at home.

"I'll think about it," she answered without enthusiasm. A month ago she would have jumped at the chance to go to Portland with her husband. Why not now?

"How long are you going to punish me?" A frown darkened his face. "So I made a mistake. It isn't that big a deal. What do you want from me? Blood?"

Yes! The force of her anger shocked her. *I want blood. I want you to suffer as much as I'm suffering. I want vengeance.*

He must have read the answer in her eyes. With an angry curse falling from his lips, he spun on his heel and strode toward his truck for the second time.

She stood there, rooted to the spot, until he drove away. Then she closed the door, surprised to find she wasn't crying. She didn't know quite what to think about that. Was it a good thing or a bad thing to run out of tears?

She walked to the kitchen and began to clean up. For the past two weeks, Dave had come home for lunch every workday. He'd also pulled into the driveway no later than five-thirty every evening. She might have seen it as his renewed commitment to her. She might have—if it weren't for the martyred expression he frequently wore and his continued refusal for them to seek professional help for their marriage.

"This wasn't the first time it's happened," she'd said to him last night. "Is it, Dave?"

His stubborn silence had been answer enough.

A wave of nausea rushed through her as she recalled the conversation. Bracing the heels of her hands against the counter, she leaned over the kitchen sink, swallowing the bile that rose in her throat.

"Mom?"

She glanced toward the back door.

"Mom, are you okay?"

She nodded, unable to speak.

"You don't look so good." Mike hurried across the kitchen. "Need me to call the doctor?"

"No." The reply was more groan than word. She shook her head, then repeated, "No."

"Is it Dad? What'd he do to you this time? What'd he say to you?"

Pain sliced into the deepest part of her soul. She closed her eyes. How much did he know? What had he overheard and how much had he guessed? She'd tried hard to shield him; she hadn't wanted him to know what was happening between his parents.

But she'd failed. The same way she'd failed at so many things.

Sara's eyes were swollen and red from crying when she answered the knock at the door that afternoon. The last person she'd expected to find standing there was Dave.

84

"Hi." He smiled, looking sexy and confident.

Fury erupted in her chest. "What are you doing here?"

His smile faded. His eyebrows rose in question.

"I don't ever want to see you again." She swung the door toward him.

He stopped it with the toe of his boot. "Whoa!" He pushed it open. "What's going on?"

"It's over." She clenched and unclenched her fists at her sides.

"Over?" He tried another smile, this one pleading and boyish. "And to think I came over just to see if you're ready for our trip to Portland. Are you mad 'cause I haven't called or been by? I've been real busy with work or I would have. I thought you understood about that." His voice was husky, masculine, and suggestive. "I wanted to clear everything off the calendar so I can give all my attention to you."

"Can it, Dave. I saw you with your wife. I went by your house and I saw you with her."

A part of her longed for him to deny it; a part of her ached to hear him ask what on earth she was talking about. She hoped to see confusion flash in his beautiful blue eyes and honest puzzlement color his handsome face.

It didn't happen. Instead, he muttered something unintelligible under his breath.

She tried to close the door again, but he pushed his way inside. She probably should have been alarmed, but she was too furious to consider that she might be in danger from this man who had lied to her, used her. "Get out!"

"Sara…" He reached for her shoulders.

She knocked his hands away.

"Look, I'm sorry. I should've told you about Claire. But it doesn't have anything to do with us."

"Nothing to do with us!" She stared at him in amazement. "Do you think I'm that naive or just plain stupid?"

"My marriage is on the rocks. I've only stayed because of my boy, Mikey. But what you and I have—"

"You and I have nothing. Nothing except a pack of lies. We've got lots of those, don't we?"

"You love me, babe." He grinned. "You know you do."

She slapped his cheek. Hard.

He cursed then. Cursed her and his wife and all women.

"Get out." Her anger was gone, icy resolve in its place. "Go away and never come back."

"What were you doing sneaking around my place anyway? How'd you find out where I lived?"

It was such an inane thing for him to say that she almost laughed aloud. He was implying this was *her* fault?

"If you send me out that door"—he pointed toward it—"don't expect me to ever come back again."

"I don't *want* you to come back. I thought I loved you, but I was just in love with falling in love. I'll get over it." She took a step backward. "And I'll get over you too. I suppose I should even be thankful for the lesson you've taught me. I *was* naive. But I won't ever be that gullible again. I'm just glad I never introduced you to my parents."

His expression darkened as he leaned toward her. "You're gonna miss me, Sara Jennings."

She remained mute, hoping he couldn't read the truth in her eyes. She *would* miss him. She *had* loved him, however misguided it had been. His lies and betrayal hurt more than anything had ever hurt before.

She was ashamed too. Ashamed because she was forced to admit her part in this affair. She'd behaved recklessly. She'd intentionally ignored all the values her parents had taught her, telling herself they didn't apply in today's world. Now she was paying for it with her heart.

Dave turned away, strode to the door, then looked over his shoulder. In a low, dismissing tone, he said, "If you find yourself in trouble, don't come looking to me to bail you out. You're on your own. Get my meaning?"

Before she could think of a reply, he slammed the door closed.

And just like that, Dave Porter was gone from her life.

❦

The disintegration of a marriage, Claire discovered, was something that happened in tiny increments. A word here. A gesture there. It happened over months, even years, with the parties involved often unaware it was happening.

Then one day, a person woke up and discovered it was too late to salvage what had once seemed indestructible.

Those were Claire's thoughts as she watched Dave loading the back of his gray pickup on a Saturday in June. He was going to Portland, but he no longer wanted her to go with him. He was taking Jazz, his black lab, and the speedboat he'd bought a couple of years before. But he wasn't taking his family; he didn't want them along, wife or son. He'd made it clear he had no intention of coming back. He was leaving them for good.

She should have been afraid. She should have been terrified of being on her own. She knew almost nothing about their financial condition. She had only a part-time job and no education beyond high school. How were she and Mike going to get along?

At one point she'd wondered if he was taking that girl with him. *That girl.* His mistress. Claire didn't even know her name.

She should have felt *something.* If not fear, then rage or sorrow or self-pity. Something. *Anything!*

Dave jerked a tarp over his belongings in the truck bed and tied it down with bungee cords. When he was satisfied that all was secure, he strode up the walk toward Claire. "Where's Mikey?"

"He went over to John's."

"If he thinks I'm chasing after him to tell him good-bye, he's mistaken."

She crossed her arms over her chest. "I don't think he wanted to say good-bye."

"He's probably run off to cry on his friend's shoulder. The boy's weak, Claire. You've got him tied to your apron strings." He pointed at her. "It's a good thing we didn't have any more kids for you to ruin."

She couldn't feel anger or hurt over that comment. She'd stopped feeling anything in recent weeks. Intuition told her that pain would return, along with a host of other unwelcome emotions, but for now she felt nothing.

She watched Dave leave as if this were happening to someone else.
And perhaps that was true.
For Claire Porter would never be the same again.

Part Two: *Bitterness*

For I see that you are full of bitterness

and captive to sin.

— A C T S 8 : 2 3 , N I V

Chapter Eleven

OCTOBER—THREE YEARS LATER

Claire parked her car in a visitor's space in front of the school. She made no move to get out of the car, needing a moment of stillness first.

Dakota was in trouble again. It was only October, and this was the third time some sort of infraction had caused the school's secretary to call her. This time the principal, Martin Hathaway, had asked to see her in person.

Following a resigned sigh, she opened the door of the faded blue Mazda and got out, then stood staring at the main entrance of the high school. It hadn't changed much since she had been a student. Temporary classrooms dotted the lawn behind the science and math building, and a new roof had been added to the gymnasium. But overall, it looked the same as it had in the seventies.

It seemed only yesterday that she'd walked those hallways, clutching textbooks to her chest, giggling with her girlfriends, waiting for another breathless moment alone with Dave, feeling all the anxiety of a fifteen-year-old girl in love.

A familiar spark of anger ignited at the memory. This was her ex-husband's fault. Silently cursing his name, she slammed the car door closed and headed for the school's administrative offices.

A few minutes later, when she entered the reception area off the main lobby, she saw her son sitting on a corner chair. His head was tipped toward his chest, his eyes downcast, staring at some spot on the floor. His long legs, holes in the knees of his Levi's, were stretched out before him and crossed at the ankles. Studied nonchalance. Practiced indifference. That was the impression he was trying to give, and Claire knew it. She also knew he didn't feel as blasé as he looked.

"May I help you?" the woman on the opposite side of a long counter asked.

"I'm Claire Conway. I'm here to see Mr. Hathaway."

Dakota straightened, his gaze meeting hers. Regret flashed across his face, replaced quickly by a look of defiance. He got up but didn't say anything.

Her only child was six feet tall and still growing. His eyes were a piercing shade of light blue, his blond hair the pale white-yellow color of straw. Claire was glad he didn't physically resemble his father—she didn't need a constant reminder of the man who'd broken her heart—but Dakota did have the same sort of magnetism for members of the opposite sex. Too handsome for his own good, Claire often thought, judging by the number of girls who called him in the evenings and on weekends.

The secretary buzzed the principal. "Mr. Hathaway? Ms. Conway is here to see you."

A few moments later, the nearby door opened, and a smallish, middle-aged man appeared. His salt-and-pepper hair was thinning on top, and his scalp glowed in the sunlight that streamed through a window to his left.

"I'm Mr. Hathaway." He motioned toward his office. "Won't you come in?"

She glanced at Dakota. Her son's expression remained wary and unrepentant.

Hathaway answered her unspoken question. "We'll have your son join us in a bit. I'd like to talk to you privately, if I may."

"Of course."

He stepped aside and allowed her room to enter. "Please have a seat," he said after closing the door. Then he strode to his chair on the opposite side of the desk. "Did Miss Prescott explain the nature of the problem when she called you?"

"Not really."

The principal flipped open a file folder in front of him and studied the paper on top. "Dakota is apparently quite bright, but our concern isn't about his grades. It's his attitude. An attitude that seems to extend toward any person with authority. He has a boulder-size chip on his shoulder and is daring one and all to knock it off."

Claire nodded. The principal's assessment wasn't news to her. She'd watched Dakota's attitude evolving over the past three years, her sweet-natured son turning into this belligerent teen. What she didn't know was how much of it was because of his age, how much had to do with his father's desertion, and how much was her fault.

"Ms. Conway, have you considered getting counseling for Dakota?"

She hated discussing her private affairs with this man or anyone else. But if it would help her son...

"We both saw a counselor three years ago." She lowered her gaze. "That was right after his father and I got divorced. But I couldn't afford to continue the sessions. We hadn't any insurance coverage, and I couldn't pay without it."

"I see."

Yes, he probably *did* see. He probably saw plenty of such situations nowadays. This high school had to be filled with kids from single-parent homes. But did most dads just disappear, cut off all contact, and seem to forget they'd ever fathered a child? That's what Dave had done.

Claire thought back to the summer of her divorce. She'd taken back her maiden name as a small act of defiance and hadn't been particularly surprised when her son said he wanted to change his name too. He didn't want to be Mike Porter, he'd said. It reminded him of his dad calling him "Mikey."

So, with his mother's help, Michael Dakota Porter had petitioned the courts to legally become Dakota Conway. Claire had expected Dave to object. She'd secretly hoped it might bring him to his senses. But he hadn't cared. He'd signed the necessary forms without missing a beat, allowing all traces of familial ties to be erased by the stroke of a judge's pen.

There'd been no contact from him since. She didn't even know where he was living. The last time she'd tried to write to him at his Portland address, her mail had been returned as undeliverable.

"Ms. Conway?" The principal's voice intruded on her thoughts.

She looked up, straight into Mr. Hathaway's compassionate gaze. "He's not a bad boy."

"No, I don't think he is," he replied softly. "But he's heading for real trouble if something doesn't change. I'd like to find a way to turn things around before it's too late."

"Please, tell me exactly what happened this morning."

⁂

Dakota stared at the closed door, wondering what Hathaway was saying to his mom. He'd felt ashamed when she walked into the office, ashamed because he was the cause of her having to leave work, ashamed because when he faced her again, he knew she would look at him with those sad, confused eyes of hers. She would blame herself; she always did. But he knew she wasn't to blame. He was. Of course, he didn't mean to disappoint her like this, any more than he'd meant to mouth off to his U.S. history teacher.

Still, he wouldn't have done things any differently this morning. Mrs. Foster had been riding Sally Thompson extra hard, harder than usual, picking on the girl when it was obvious Sally couldn't answer the questions. The teacher had intentionally embarrassed his classmate, and everybody knew what the old hag was doing. Sally was nearly blind without her bottle-thick eyeglasses, the ones she'd lost last week.

About the fourth time Mrs. Foster called on Sally, Dakota had just plain had enough. So he'd told Mrs. Foster what she could do with the Bill of Rights, in graphic terms.

That was when he'd been sent to the principal's office.

Dakota shifted on the hard wooden seat of the chair. What was taking them so long in there?

"Hey, man. What's going on?"

He turned toward the main door. "Hey, John." He shrugged. "I'm waitin' to see Hathaway."

John Kreizenbeck entered the room and came over to sit beside him. "Kids are sayin' you really told old Mrs. Foster off."

"Yeah."

"Your mom in there?" John jerked his head toward the principal's office.

He nodded.

His friend let out a low whistle. "Foster probably had it coming, but I think you'd better get control of that temper of yours before you land in *real* trouble."

"You think?" The two words were laced with sarcasm. The last thing Dakota needed was a lecture from his best friend, even if John was right.

John obviously wasn't offended by the remark. He grinned, slouching in the chair, at ease as usual. "Yeah, I think." He glanced out the window, watching students as they headed for their next class. "The youth group at church is going bowling tonight. Care to join us?"

"I got a feeling I won't be going anywhere for quite a while. By the time Mom's finished in there with Mr. Hathaway, I'll be lucky if I get to leave the house again before I'm thirty."

"Bet you're right." His friend chuckled. "Well, just thought you should know we all miss you and wish you'd start coming again. We've got us a great new youth pastor. Things're really happening."

Dakota grunted his response.

It was a long time since he'd done anything with the Kreizenbeck family. After his mom had been forced to sell the house, they'd moved away from the old neighborhood, and with Dakota's whole world turned upside down, he'd become an expert at avoiding people—especially a family that was as happy and whole as the Kreizenbecks. He couldn't bear to see others who were content. Not when he had to watch his mom struggling to hold things together, scraping to pay the rent and put food on the table. Things were tough, thanks to Porter's skipping town and saddling his mom with all the unpaid debts.

Porter. He muttered a curse beneath his breath, and his mouth thinned into a hard line.

He never thought of Dave Porter as a dad. As far as Dakota was concerned, he didn't have one. *He* was the man of the family now. It was up to him to take care of things for the two of them, up to him to make sure his mom was okay.

And you're doing a great job of that, aren't you?

His face grew hot with shame. His mom shouldn't have to be in there with Hathaway. Why'd he have to mess up all the time, giving her all this grief?

John leaned toward him. "There's somebody that can help you, man."

"Who?"

"You know who."

Dakota gave his friend a hard look. Bitter words rose in his throat but wouldn't come out. Through the haze of time, he remembered the peace he used to feel, sitting in church with the Kreizenbecks. He'd liked listening to the pastor, liked hearing the choir sing. Back then, he'd believed everything was going to be okay. Really okay.

John seemed to understand. "Nobody said life was gonna be easy. God never said things would always go our way. He just said you wouldn't have to go through it alone." He punched Dakota in the arm. "You think about it." He lifted a hand in farewell. "Catch you later."

The glass door to the main hallway swung closed behind John mere seconds before the principal's door opened and Mr. Hathaway appeared.

"You can come in now, Dakota."

Only the twenty-fifth of October, and it was snowing outside Sara's fifteenth-story office window. The flurry of white was so thick she could barely make out the building across the street. That meant the drive home would be treacherous. Denver freeways at five o'clock were a wild and wooly experience under the best of circumstances. But throw slick roads and low visibility into the mix...

A knock at the opening of her small cubicle drew her attention from the window.

"Sara?" Melanie Slade leaned in. "Are you sure you don't want to change your mind about tonight? My brother's keen on meeting you."

"No, but thanks." She reached for her purse. "I want to get home before it really dumps on us."

"You need to get a life, girlfriend."

Melanie's parting comment echoed in Sara's mind as she drove out of the city, heading north. She knew her coworker was right. She didn't have much of a life.

At the end of her freshman year of college, Sara had come to Colorado, hoping to escape the memories that were around every corner in Boise. She'd found a place to rent, taken an entry-level clerical job at Richards and Clemmons, and burrowed in to nurse her wounded heart. More than three years later, she was still nursing it.

She tried not to think of that dark spring, but the unwelcome memories lingered, worsening whenever a man indicated interest in her. She would look at him and wonder, *Are you lying to me too? Are you another Dave? Do you have a wife and child at home?* She never stayed around long enough to find out. It wasn't worth the risk.

"You ought to find a church to attend, dear," Kristina Jennings had said over the telephone last night. "It would do you good, and you might meet some nice young men there. And what about your acting? There must be a community theater in your area. They would be thrilled to have someone with your talent, and you're sure to make some new friends if you get involved."

But that suggestion only caused Sara to remember opening night of *Cat on a Hot Tin Roof,* to remember the applause she'd received, to remember Dave and the night she'd given herself away so easily, so cheaply.

How sordid the affair seemed to her now. How foolish and naive she'd been. But at least she would never play the fool again. She'd rather live and die all alone than trust another man with her heart.

By the time Sara turned into the parking lot of her apartment complex, she was thoroughly depressed. This wasn't what she'd expected out of life, to live like this. She'd always been the darling of the family, the spoiled one—and she'd known it too. Everything had come easily to her. Now she was far from her parents and brothers, just getting by on her lousy salary, living in a one-bedroom apartment with only her cat to keep her company.

Maybe she should have gone with Melanie and the others tonight. Dinner, a drink, maybe some dancing. It might be nice to do something different for a change.

But what if she liked Melanie's brother? No, it wasn't worth the risk.

She nearly slipped and fell on the slick sidewalk as she made her way from the carport to the stairs. It wouldn't have surprised her if she had. It would be just her kind of luck to break her tailbone or ankle or something.

Sara's calico cat meowed a greeting as the door swung open. The feline twisted, serpentine, around the legs of the wooden rocker in the living room, her tail sticking straight up in the air.

"Hello, Gretchen."

Sara lifted the cat into her arms and rubbed her cheek against warm, soft fur. Her reward was a loud purr of contentment.

"It's not so bad, just the two of us, huh? It's just the way we like it. Right?"

Chapter Twelve

The tip of Dakota's cigarette glowed red as he took a deep drag. He wished he had one of those beers he'd stashed in the garage, but he didn't dare leave his room. He was taking a chance just sitting here on the windowsill.

He ought to throw some things in a duffel bag and take off. He could hitchhike over to Portland or down to San Francisco or L.A. He could pass for eighteen if he had to; he was plenty tall enough. And lots of guys his age were on their own, not having to put up with being grounded by parents or listening to a mental school principal or jerk teachers.

Yeah, it would be easy to just take off.

Like you-know-who did.

That was an unpleasant thought. He didn't want to be anything like Dave Porter. Not in any way. But leaving his mom would make him the same, and he knew it.

Dakota muttered a few choice swearwords. He hated school and his teachers and Mr. Hathaway, hated never having any money to call his own, hated just about everything and everyone. He definitely hated the man who'd been his father. He even hated himself.

The one person he could never hate was his mom. She'd done everything for him. She'd sacrificed everything for him. He couldn't remember the last time she'd bought herself something that wasn't a dire necessity. When there was any extra money, which there rarely was, she spent it on him.

There's somebody that can help you, man.

Sure, he knew what John had meant. He'd been talking about Jesus Christ. But Dakota didn't belong in church, not with all this ugliness inside him, and he knew it even if John didn't.

Nobody said life was gonna be easy...He just said you wouldn't have to go through it alone.

"Well, that'd sure be nice if it was true."

I AM TRUE.

Guiltily, he flicked his cigarette out the window and jumped up from the sill. He turned toward the door. No one was there. The Voice had seemed so real, but his mind must have been playing tricks on him. Still, his heart continued to pound at a rapid rate.

"Too weird."

There's somebody that can help you, man.

What if John was right?

⚉

Claire looked up from the pile of papers on the kitchen table. The clock on the wall read eleven-fifteen. Weariness blurred her vision, but there was no stopping now. She needed to get these bills paid. Some were already a week late.

Suddenly overwhelmed by her circumstances, she pressed her forehead against the heels of her hands. Hot tears burned her throat and the backs of her eyes. Every month it was the same thing, robbing Peter to pay Paul, choosing whom to pay now and whom to pay late—or not to pay at all.

More than once she'd considered filing for bankruptcy. It would be a way out from under all this. But she'd always resisted the temptation. Maybe pride kept her from it. More than likely her belief that doing so would give Dave another victory kept her from it.

Bitterness, all of it centered on the memory of her ex-husband, twisted her heart. If Dave would make even an occasional child-support payment, it would help. But he never did. Paying even a little would have tipped off the authorities that were charged with finding deadbeat dads. But the real reason he didn't pay was because he simply didn't care what happened to his ex or his son.

Claire often wanted to give up, to just curl into a fetal position and die. If it weren't for Dakota…

She straightened and looked toward his bedroom door. What was she going to do about her son? There was so much rage walled up inside of him. She recognized the feelings because they were a reflection of her own. Even the changing of their names was an extension of their shared bitterness.

Looking down at the stack of bills, she reminded herself that there were plenty of good reasons for Dakota to hate the name of Porter and the man who'd given it to him at birth. Claire also knew it was wrong for her to encourage those feelings, but she couldn't help it. The same hate festered in her soul.

A soft moan slipped from her lips. Oh yes, she hated Dave. She hated him much more than Dakota did. She hated him for betraying her. She hated him for stealing the dreams and expectations she'd once had. She hated him for not being the man she'd thought him to be.

It wasn't only his affair with that girl she'd seen him with. Claire probably could have gotten over that, given time. She'd believed in him and the sanctity of their marriage. She'd meant the promises she made on their wedding day, even if he hadn't. Being his wife had defined her existence. Being Mrs. Dave Porter—and mother to his son—was all she'd wanted to be.

Without him, it seemed she'd vanished too.

She sighed, remembering it all. She'd loved him so very much, enough to forgive him anything, even infidelity. Now she could forgive him nothing. Not after he'd deserted their only child. She could never forgive that. The pain in her son's eyes wounded her beyond the healing hand of time.

How could Dave have done it? How could he have tossed aside Dakota as if he didn't exist?

Claire abruptly shoved away her checkbook and the bills, rose from her chair, and walked into the living room of the small house she rented in an older section of town. The insulation was poor, and cold air seeped in around windows and exterior door frames. Even with the curtains drawn, she could feel the draft.

Just one more symbol of her miserable existence, of her string of failures.

"I certainly know how to feel sorry for myself," she whispered in disgust.

She crossed to the living room window and drew aside the faded drapes to look outside. A streetlight illuminated her lawn and the misshapen oak tree in her next-door neighbor's yard. Across the street, the Thorndike home was decorated for Halloween with carved pumpkins and a straw-stuffed scarecrow. A family lived in that house. A *whole* family—dad, mom, and kids. Just like the Porters used to—

"Mom?"

She gasped and spun around, pressing her right hand against her speeding heart. "Dakota, what are you doing up?"

"I couldn't sleep." One corner of his mouth curved in a crooked, halfhearted grin. "Sorry I scared you."

Her laugh was shaky, still affected by the surprise he'd given her. "You should be."

"Mom...I...ah..." He dropped his gaze to the dull hardwood floor. "I just wanted to say I'm sorry for the trouble I caused you today. You shouldn't have to leave work on account of me. I really am sorry."

"I know you are."

He met her gaze once more. "I don't mean to do things like that. It's just sometimes—"

Again, more softly, "I know."

"Well, I just wanted to tell you."

"Thanks, honey."

He turned toward his room, then looked over his shoulder. "John invited me to start going to his church's youth stuff again. They still meet on Wednesday nights. You think I could go? I mean, I know I'm grounded but..." He let the words fade into silence.

Claire's chest was tight with emotion as she met her son's hopeful gaze. Part tough guy. Part little boy. Full of promise of the man he would one day be. She'd failed him countless times. She'd been a less-than-perfect parent.

What was the best thing to do in this instance? Let him go or be strict and stick to the punishment?

How am I supposed to know what to do?

There had to be an answer to her silent question; only Claire didn't know where to look for it.

"I'll think about it," she answered at last.

He nodded, then went off to bed, leaving Claire once again with her troubled thoughts.

Chapter Thirteen

Best Homes Real Estate had a large office on one of the busiest streets in town. Claire usually went into the office, which she now managed for Jack Moncur, at seven in the morning, just to beat the worst of Boise's rush-hour traffic. She tried to leave by four in the afternoon for the same reason. It didn't always work out that way.

On this particular Friday, there had been one of those last-minute closing crises that were not uncommon in the real-estate business. Claire had spent the better part of the afternoon chasing down signatures and delivering them to the title company so a young, extremely anxious, highly agitated couple would be able to start moving into their new home over the weekend. Now she was trying to get her most pressing duties done so she could call it a day and go home.

The building was almost deserted as five o'clock drew near, but the receptionist, Nancy Bartlett, was still at her desk, and George Mitchell, one of Best Homes' top agents, was in the copy room, using up reams of legal-size paper.

Claire stared at the blinking green cursor on her computer screen. Her eyes hurt. Her head ached. But she was determined to get these entries made today. Otherwise, she would start off next week already behind. And the end of the month was always a zoo with more things to do than seemed possible to handle.

The intercom buzzed, and Nancy's voice came through the speaker. "Claire, there's a Mr. Kreizenbeck here to see you."

Surprised, she pressed the button. "Send him in, Nancy. Thanks." She stood, but before she could step around her desk, Maury Kreizenbeck appeared in her office doorway.

John's father was a shorter, heftier version of his son. He had one of those pleasant, unremarkable faces, the kind that if a police officer asked for a description, the answers would include words like *average, ordinary, usual.* One thing that wasn't ordinary was his smile. A look of genuine pleasure that went way beneath the surface. Even though she hadn't seen him in at least two years, Claire remembered that smile and was warmed by it now.

"It's good to see you, Mr. Kreizenbeck," she said, stepping around the desk to offer him her hand.

"And you, Mrs. Porter. Sorry. It's Ms. Conway, isn't it?" His fingers closed around hers, warm and firm. "But let's make it simple for both of us. Call me Maury."

"And I'm Claire." She motioned toward the chair beside her desk. "Won't you sit down?"

"Thanks." He released her hand. "I won't keep you long. I wasn't even sure I'd catch you in. But I was in the area and thought I'd take a chance."

She could only assume that Dakota had told John where she worked and that John had told his father.

When they were both seated, Maury Kreizenbeck said, "I'm here about Mike. I mean, Dakota. Can't quite get used to the name change for him either."

Claire folded her hands on top of her desk and waited for him to continue.

"John told me Dakota's having a bit of trouble at school. I thought maybe I could be of some help."

A part of her bristled at the implication that she couldn't handle her own son. Another part felt a rush of relief.

Maury leaned forward. "It isn't my intention to interfere, Claire, but I've always been fond of your boy. He was like one of our own. We've missed having him over to the house." He drew a deep breath. "I know things have been difficult for you both these past few years. They always are in a divorce."

There was a wealth of kindness in the tone of his voice as well as in the expression on his face, and a lump formed in Claire's throat in response to it.

"God knows what you're feeling, Claire. He'd like to help you."

She watched him through a veil of unshed tears.

"Do you believe that?"

Abruptly, she swiveled her chair, turning her back to him. She opened a drawer in the credenza and yanked a tissue from the box.

Did she believe God knew what she was feeling? She supposed so. She couldn't quite deny the existence of a Supreme Being, although sometimes she would like to. But of what importance was she to Him or Him to her? If He wanted to help her, why didn't He?

No, God might be in His heaven, but Claire Conway was stuck here on earth with a son who was angry at the world, a stack of unpaid bills, a fifteen-year-old car that was threatening to give up the ghost, and a bed as empty as her heart.

"Claire…"

She dabbed at her eyes, blew her nose, took a deep breath, and faced Maury again.

"May I pray for you?" he asked.

"*Now?*" She shook her head, then glanced toward the outer office to see if Nancy was anywhere nearby. "I don't think that would be appropriate. Not here."

His expression told her he disagreed, but he let it drop. "John tells me Dakota is grounded and the reason why. But my wife and I were hoping you would allow him to come to church with us this Sunday. John can pick him up and bring him home again. You have my word that they won't go anywhere else."

She remembered how Dave had hated his son going to church. And maybe religion *was* just a crutch for people with no backbone, as he'd said. But recalling his objection was enough to help make up her mind.

"I suppose it might be good for him," she replied at last. "Dakota always enjoyed going to church when he was younger."

Maury's gaze was unwavering, seeming to say, *It would be good for you too. Why not join him?*

"I really must get back to work." She stood. "I appreciate your concern for Dakota. Really, I do. Have John tell Dakota what time he'll need to be ready on Sunday morning. He knows where we live."

There was no possible way Maury Kreizenbeck could misinterpret his dismissal, but he appeared to take no offense. In fact, his smile as he rose from his chair seemed warmer than ever.

He offered his hand to her again. "If you need someone to talk to, give Gloria or me a call. Anytime at all."

"Thank you. I will," she answered, knowing full well that she wouldn't.

❦

The Rough Riders Bar and Grill was as noisy and raucous as its name implied.

Seated at a high, round table, Sara twisted on her barstool and looked toward the dance floor through the blue veil of cigarette smoke. An attractive singer, with straight black hair that reached to her thighs, crooned "Sweet Dreams." Couples were slow dancing, most of them holding each other close, each woman's head resting on her partner's shoulders.

It had been a long time since Sara had danced like that. She missed it more than she wanted to admit. Listening to the lyrics of one of her mother's favorite country "sad songs" didn't help matters any.

Melanie Slade jabbed her in the arm with an index finger. "Find your smile, Sara. You're scaring off every good-looking guy in the joint. You'll never meet anybody with that morose expression on your face."

"I'm not sure I want to meet any of them. Bars never seemed like a good place to find a guy."

"Then why'd you agree to come?"

Because I couldn't stand another evening alone in my apartment. Sara released a sigh, shaking her head in reply.

"I should have called my brother. He'd have—" Melanie's words were cut short when she was bumped from behind, causing her to spill her drink across the table.

"'Scuse me, miss," the tall cowboy said as he tugged his black Stetson's brim and offered a grin.

Melanie's eyes widened as she looked over her shoulder. Whatever sharp retort had been on the tip of her tongue was forgotten. "That's okay. No harm done." She returned his smile, obviously captivated.

"I'd be obliged if you'd let me buy you another drink." His gaze swung to Sara. "You too miss."

She nodded without comment.

He moved to stand between Melanie's and Sara's barstools. "Haven't seen the two of you here before, and believe me, I'd remember two attractive girls like you."

"It's our first time," Melanie answered. "Quite the crowd. Is it always like this?"

"Usually. Sometimes it gets *real* noisy and rowdy, but you get used to it."

"Noisier than this?" Melanie gave a throaty laugh, flirting with her eyes, then pointed at Sara. "That's Sara and I'm Melanie."

"Glad to meet you, Melanie and Sara. My name's Bernard Willis. But the last fella who called me Bernard got punched in the nose, so my friends call me Jet." He turned his hundred-watt smile on Sara. "Care to dance?"

"I'd better not. My country swing's a bit rusty. Maybe you should ask—"

"No problem. Just follow my lead." Jet gently but firmly took hold of her arm and drew her to her feet. Glancing at Melanie, he said, "I'll bring her back." Then he led the way to the dance floor, holding Sara's hand in his.

With expertise, Jet guided her around the dance floor in time to the music. It was surprising how quickly the steps came back to her, and before long, she was enjoying herself as she hadn't in ages.

Maybe it hadn't been such a bad idea to come tonight.

For the next hour, Jet danced with both Sara and Melanie, although his obvious preference was for Sara. She had to admit she was flattered by his attentions. It felt good to be noticed and complimented.

Between dances, she learned that Jet was a professional rodeo cowboy. She'd suspected as much; she'd known enough of them in her barrel-racing years that she could usually spot one at fifty paces. Jet told her he was from a small town in Wyoming. "A wide patch in the road," was how he described it. He had two younger sisters, and he would be twenty-seven on his next birthday, a month from now. She enjoyed his easy smile and his infectious laughter.

Sara thought she could learn to like him a lot.

Closing time loomed, and the two of them were on the dance floor again. The band was playing another slow song. Jet held Sara close as they moved in time to the music.

Midway through the song, he whispered in her ear, "How about I give you a lift home? It'd be a shame to let the evening end this soon. I want to be with you."

She leaned away from him, tipping back her head so she could look him in the eyes. The lust in his gaze confirmed the meaning of his suggestion. She hadn't misunderstood him.

And why was she surprised? He was a man, after all.

She stopped dancing and pulled away from him. Not bothering to give him a reply, she turned and walked to the table where Melanie was visiting with the waitress.

"I'm leaving," she said as she grabbed her purse.

"Leaving? But—"

"I'll see you Monday."

"But—"

"Hey!" Jet had followed her off the dance floor. "What's wrong?"

Sara ignored him.

"Look at me." He grabbed hold of her arm.

Despite herself, she did as he demanded.

He must have seen her loathing—of herself or of him, she wasn't sure which. His eyes narrowed as he said, "So, are you frigid or something?"

For a heartbeat, she couldn't speak. She felt as if he'd slapped her. She longed to do the same to him.

"Good night, *Bernard.*" She yanked free of his grasp.

She didn't look behind her as she hurried out of the Rough Riders Bar and Grill, hoping with every step that he wasn't following her. Once inside her car, she locked the door and leaned her forehead against the steering wheel. She didn't know if she wanted to scream or cry. Maybe both.

Was it just her luck? Or were all men creeps?

Chapter Fourteen

Dakota was unusually nervous as he walked into the teens' class at John's church the next Sunday. A lot had happened to him in the three years since he'd last been here. His parents had divorced. His dad had skipped town. They'd had to sell their house, and the car had been repossessed. Everything in his life was different—and so was he. He wasn't sure what the others would think of him. He still believed he wasn't good enough to be here.

He tried to look cool and unaffected as he sauntered into the upstairs room. If he didn't pull it off, no one let on that they noticed. Several of the kids recognized him and made a point of welcoming him back, asking how he'd been.

After a few minutes, John tapped him on the shoulder. "Hey, Dakota. I want you to meet Henry Forester. He's the youth pastor here at Sunrise Fellowship."

Dakota turned, but he didn't find the man he expected.

Henry Forester looked nothing like a pastor to him. Pastors, he recalled from when he used to attend church, were gray-haired and bearded. They looked like kindly old grandparents.

Pastor Henry, on the other hand, wasn't much older than most of the kids in the room. Maybe twenty-three, twenty-four, tops. He had hair the color of ink, worn in a short, spiky fashion, and he was clean-shaven. He was about the same height as Dakota, Jimmy Stewart–thin, and moved in a loose, disjointed manner.

"It's a pleasure to meet you, Dakota."

Church is for sissies, boy. His father's condemnation made Dakota mentally cringe.

But the pastor's handshake was firm, and the look in his eyes declared there was nothing sissified about him. Dakota sensed that Pastor Henry was rock solid and strong in every way that counted.

"We hope you'll join us often."

"Thanks," Dakota answered. "I just might."

Pastor Henry released his hand, then swept his gaze over the other teenagers in the room and said, "Let's get started, shall we?"

Folding chairs were pulled into a circle, and everyone took a seat.

"Anybody have a prayer request?" The pastor once again looked at each kid, slowly this time, silently encouraging each one of them to open up.

"Yeah, I do."

"Go ahead, Rick."

Dakota listened as the boy, a stranger to him, shared about his aunt who'd been diagnosed with terminal cancer. "She knows the Lord, so she's pretty much at peace about dying. But Uncle Lou's havin' a rough time with it. He's started drinking again. Mom says he's feeling helpless and angry and is just striking out. She says he needs lots of prayer to see him through this."

Dakota understood that sort of anger. He'd struck out plenty.

Next, a girl asked for prayer about her biology class, saying she feared she was going to flunk because she wouldn't accept the theory of evolution as fact. Her teacher frequently belittled her in front of the other students. She said she didn't mind that so much, but she was planning to go into veterinary medicine, so she needed good science grades.

Did God really care about grades in a biology class?

More petitions, both big and small, followed.

Finally, when no one volunteered another request, Pastor Henry leaned forward, resting his forearms on his thighs. With hands folded and head bowed, he began to pray in that soft, soothing voice of his. "Father God, we're so glad to be here with You this morning, to know You're here in our midst because You promised to be..."

Dakota didn't so much hear the words as feel them. *Father God...*

God, the Father. A Father who loved him. A Father who would never leave him. Was God really like that? Years ago, Dakota had believed it, but he'd been a little kid back then.

He opened his eyes and glanced across the circle at the pastor. It was clear this man believed with all his heart that God was his heavenly Father, that he experienced no doubt about having the ear of God as he prayed.

But if God cared, how come there was pain and suffering on earth? How come He didn't do something about it? And how come Dakota's mom had to struggle the way she did, when she'd never hurt anybody in her entire life? How come she had to be alone and unhappy? How come he wasn't a better son to her, and how come...

At that moment, the strangest thing happened. The questions that raced through his mind were silenced. A peace stole over him. A peace like the hush before a storm when even the earth holds its breath.

He couldn't explain it, but Dakota knew something extraordinary was happening to him.

And nothing was ever going to be the same again.

Claire lay on the sofa, trying to read the paperback novel in her hand. It was her favorite kind, a murder mystery, but she couldn't seem to concentrate. Time after time, she had to go back and reread a page.

The house seemed too quiet. On a Sunday morning, Dakota was usually in his room with his stereo blaring out some sort of rock music. This morning, he'd gone to church.

Had it been a mistake to let him go? She'd done it as much out of defiance toward Dave as for any help she'd thought it might be to Dakota. What were they teaching there? About a God of love?

Ha!

Why would anyone believe that? Wasn't it just setting a person up for more disappointment, more disillusionment? God didn't care what happened to the people on earth. If He was watching from heaven, it was only for entertainment purposes. All a big joke.

As much as she was loath to admit it, she thought her ex was probably right about organized religion. But on the other hand, if he was wrong and if God and heaven existed, then there was also a hell. And if there was a hell, then Dave Porter would burn for all eternity in it.

Just as he deserved.

Blurry-eyed, with Gretchen leading the way and noisily demanding a saucer of milk, Sara shuffled into the kitchen of her small apartment. Like Gretchen and her milk, Sara was desperately in need of that first cup of coffee.

Sleep had eluded her again last night. She hadn't slept well since her encounter with that jerk, Jet Willis, last Friday. She couldn't seem to shake the sound of his voice as he'd suggested they spend the night together, the look in his eyes that said he thought she would be willing to go to bed with a man she'd just met.

Did she *really* look the type? Did she have a big red *A* tattooed on her forehead or something?

She reached for the coffee carafe and filled it with tap water.

You ought to find a church to attend, dear. You might meet some nice young men there.

She tried to shut out her mother's voice as she scooped coffee grounds into the filter. The last thing she needed was to go to church and be made to feel guilty. She didn't need people judging her for the mistakes she'd made. She could judge herself without any help, thank you very much. She knew what she'd done.

But it wasn't like her affair with a married man had been her fault, she argued silently. She hadn't *known* Dave was married. And once she knew, she'd told him to get lost.

With a moan, she set the carafe on the counter, leaned forward and, with her eyes squeezed shut, repeatedly bounced her forehead against the cupboard door. When was she going to get over it? Over *him?* When did she get to put the past behind her, once and for all?

She would be twenty-three in a couple of months. These were the eighties, for crying out loud. Men and women lived together all the time, even had children together, without being married, and no one seemed to notice or care.

Sure, there were a few, like her parents, who still taught their children that sex was wrong outside of marriage. But weren't they just being puritanical?

Of course they were.

Sara dearly loved them, but her folks were as old-fashioned as they came. They didn't understand how society worked these days. Sara lived in a different world from the one Kristina and Jared Jennings had grown up in. Young people were more sophisticated, more in tune with their needs and desires.

That was a good thing. Right?

With a deep sigh, she refocused her attention on the coffeemaker. "Why does it have to be so hard?" she muttered. "Life isn't fair."

She pressed the button to start the coffee brewing, then headed for the bathroom and one of her famous three-minute showers. According to Patti Cooper, her old college roommate, no other female alive could shower as quickly as Sara.

Thoughts of Patti caused a sadness to tighten her heart. She'd been dreadful about answering letters. A year ago her friend had apparently given up on her; she'd stopped writing altogether. Now Sara didn't even know where Patti lived.

Why did I let that happen? Why did everything have to fall apart for me?

No, life just wasn't fair.

Chapter Fifteen

The small narthex of Sunrise Fellowship had been decorated for Christmas with a real pine tree, large wreaths, red ribbons, holly, and silver balls. In the sanctuary, someone was playing the organ, and the melody of a familiar carol drifted through the closed doors.

Dakota paused for a moment to take it in. In the five weeks since he'd encountered Jesus in that upstairs Sunday school room, this church had come to feel like a second home. A place of warmth, comfort, and security.

Now, looking at all the special decorations, he felt as never before the wonder of this season. For the first time in his life, he truly understood what it was about. It wasn't about giving or getting presents. It wasn't about a ten-day vacation from school. It was about love, the kind of love only God could give.

He wished the whole world understood that. He wished his mom understood it.

With a sigh, he headed down the hall to the youth pastor's office.

When Pastor Henry saw him, he rose from the chair behind his desk. "Come on in, Dakota. You're right on time." He waved him in. "How are you?"

"Confused."

The pastor grinned. "Most of us are when we're fifteen."

Dakota released a humorless laugh of agreement.

"Doesn't help, huh?" Pastor Henry pointed to a chair opposite him. "Well, sit down and we'll talk. See if we can't find a solution to whatever's troubling you."

It wasn't easy for Dakota to open up and share his innermost feelings. He'd become an expert at keeping his thoughts private. He looked down at the book he'd brought with him. The study Bible, a version specifically created for teens, had been a gift to him from the Kreizenbecks.

"I've been reading the Bible every day," he began. "John told me to stick with the New Testament at first, so that's what I've been doing. I understand a lot of it. It's helped me figure out some things. Only...only I still don't know what to do about..." He stopped, unsure how to put his thoughts into words.

He lifted his eyes, looking across the desk. Even though Pastor Henry was gazing directly at him, Dakota suspected he was praying at the same time he was listening. For some reason, that made him feel better.

"It's about my mom." He paused, then added, "And my...dad." The word felt odd on his tongue. As if he'd spoken it in a foreign language instead of English. And he felt guilty for saying it.

"Go on, Dakota."

He drew a deep breath and let it out slowly. "My folks are divorced. My father...walked out on us over three years ago. He was cheating on Mom. He hurt her real bad." He felt a spark of anger and unconsciously tightened his hands into fists. "He took off and Mom was left with all the problems. We had to sell our house and the car was taken back by the bank. Mom's always worryin' about how to pay the bills. And we've never heard from him since the divorce. No letters. No child support. Nothing. It's like we never even existed. She hates him because of it."

Dakota gripped his Bible, staring down at it as he continued.

"I've hated him too. Hated him more than anything. But I...I know I'm supposed to forgive him." He met the pastor's understanding gaze. "Aren't I?"

"Yes."

"I think I'm gonna need help with that."

Pastor Henry leaned forward, resting his forearms on the desk. "God will give you whatever help you need to obey Him. We have His promise."

Dakota nodded.

"There's more, isn't there?"

"Yeah. It's...well..." He felt frustrated by his inability to articulate his feelings and thoughts.

Use the Word. Sure. That was the best way to explain.

He flipped open the Bible, then looked up. "It says here in Ephesians 6 that I'm supposed to obey my parents 'cause it's the right thing to do. And it says I'm supposed to honor them so things'll go well for me. Right?"

"Right."

"Well, I figure I can forgive my father, since that's what Jesus says to do. And I think I can stop being so mad at him. I guess that'd help with the honoring part." He pointed to the scripture. "Trouble is, I made a promise to Mom that I'd never talk about him or tell anybody what he did. My dad, I mean. She made me promise I wouldn't even say his name aloud, not even when she isn't around." Dakota shook his head slowly. "That was the day we went to court to change my last name to be the same as hers. We were both pretty angry back then." As an afterthought he added, "My dad's last name is Porter, not Conway."

Pastor Henry nodded but made no comment.

"I promised Mom I'd do just what she wanted. But shouldn't she know I'm gonna forgive him? And if I tell her, she's going to be hurt. I know she will."

Dakota imagined the look that would be in her eyes when he told her he was forgiving his dad. She would feel betrayed again, this time by her son. He hated the idea of causing her more pain. If only there was another way.

In a soft voice, the pastor said, "Maybe she'll understand better than you think."

"No, she won't." Dakota's shoulders slumped as he stared at the frayed laces of his shoes.

"The Bible tells us to speak the truth in love."

He nodded as he raised his eyes to meet the pastor's gaze. "What if I tell her and she still doesn't want me to talk about him? What should I do if she wants to hold me to my old promise?"

"As long as what your mother asks isn't contrary to the will of God, then you should honor her by obeying."

"You mean, forgive him but still not mention him?"

Pastor Henry nodded.

"I could do that." He released a sigh. "I just don't know how I'll tell her."

"You'll have to trust the Lord to guide you, Dakota. Let's pray about it. Shall we?"

After nodding, he bowed his head, closed his eyes, and hoped God would speak really loud so he couldn't miss hearing Him.

❦

"But it won't cost you anything, Sara. Dad and I will send you the airplane ticket. It will be one of our Christmas gifts to you. Won't you at least consider coming home? We haven't seen you in such a long time."

"I don't know, Mom," Sara answered. "Things are busy at work this time of year, and it's tough to get extra time off around the holidays."

Kristina Jennings wasn't giving up that easily. "You won't need time off. Christmas is on a Monday this year, and there are direct flights between Denver and Boise, so it won't take you long to get here and back. You can fly to Boise on Friday after work and we can get you back to Denver on Christmas night. We've checked with our travel agent. There are still openings if we book right away, but they're going fast. Please say yes, Sara. We miss you so much."

"Oh, Mom…"

"Please."

There was no denying she wanted to see her parents and brothers. She missed them all, and three years was a long time.

"Sara, it's important to us."

With an internal sigh, she relented. "All right, Mom. I'll come home for Christmas."

"Oh, honey, that's wonderful. Wait until I tell your father. He'll be so delighted. And the boys too. In fact, Josh has a surprise for you. He's been wanting to tell you in person."

"A surprise? What is it?"

Kristina laughed. "I can't tell you. Josh wants to do it himself."

A short while later, Sara said good-bye to her mother and hung up the phone. But the conversation lingered in her mind.

She couldn't help wondering if she was doing the right thing, going home for the holidays. Boise held so many painful memories for her. Would this visit put them to rest or make them worse?

She wished she knew.

Claire basted the fabric according to the pattern's directions, the hum of the sewing machine drowning out the drone of the television news coming from the other room. She had never been a great seamstress, but she was determined to get this shirt made before Christmas. It would probably be the only gift Dakota got this year. The bank account was empty, and the heating bill was bound to be high because of the extended cold snap.

"Hey, Mom?"

At the sound of Dakota's voice, she jumped up from her chair and tried to hide what she was working on. "I thought you were in bed."

"I couldn't sleep." His mouth was pressed into a straight, thin line while a thoughtful frown drew his brows together above the bridge of his nose. "I need to talk to you."

"All right."

She quickly shepherded him toward the living room, flicking off the kitchen light as she passed through the doorway. While Dakota sat on the chair next to the sofa, Claire turned down the sound on the TV. When she faced him again, she felt a twinge of alarm. His expression was so troubled.

What now?

Things had been going well in the past few weeks. Dakota had seemed…different somehow. Happier maybe. More content perhaps. There'd been less swagger in his walk, less anger in his voice. She sincerely hoped that wasn't all about to evaporate like a wisp of smoke.

She wanted to demand immediately that he tell her what was wrong, but she managed to hold her tongue, knowing it was better for him to do it in his own way. She could see that he was struggling to find the right words.

At long last, he leaned forward, forearms resting on his thighs, his hands clasped together between his knees, his gaze downcast. She saw him nod, as if agreeing with someone. Then he straightened and looked at her.

"Mom, I've got something to tell you, and I need you to hear me out without interrupting. Okay?"

"All right." She went to sit on the sofa.

"Remember a few Sundays back, when I started going to church again with the Kreizenbecks?"

"Of course I do."

"Well, something happened to me that day. I sorta tried to tell you what it was."

129

She hid a smile, remembering how he'd come home that day, babbling something about God loving him and making him new. His enthusiasm had reminded her of the little boy he'd once been, all smiles and goodness.

Dakota drew in a deep breath as he looked her straight in the eyes. He wasn't smiling now. His look was intense. "Mom, I asked Jesus into my heart that day. He's changed me. I've been born again."

"Oh." What else did one say to a statement like that?

"Jesus loves you too."

She stiffened. "You're not going to start preaching at people on street corners, are you?"

For just an instant, he grinned. "I might."

"Dakota—"

"No." He raised a hand to silence her. "Let me finish. Please."

She acquiesced but didn't relax. If she wanted to hear a sermon—which she didn't—she could flip on the television on Sunday morning.

"Mom...do you remember the day we went to court to legally change my name?"

Claire drew back, surprised by the sudden turn he'd taken. "I remember."

"Remember how you asked me never to talk about...about my father again? Not even when you weren't around? Not ever, to anyone."

"Yes." The reply was short and clipped, and even she could hear how much bitterness was contained in that one, simple word.

"Well, I need to talk about him to you now. Pastor Henry says I need to be honest with you, to let you know what's happening."

She longed to forbid him to mention Dave, no matter what some preacher said, but she knew it would be wrong of her to do so. She bit her lip to keep herself silent.

"Jesus says I need to forgive anybody who's wronged me, just like He forgave me for my sins."

"*Your* sins?" Her sarcasm was as obvious as her bitterness. "You're just a boy. You're not old enough to be worried about sinning."

"I've hated my father, Mom, and it's a sin to hate a parent, no matter what he or she might have done wrong. I don't want to hate my dad anymore. A little while ago, in my room, I prayed and I told God that I was forgiving my dad for leaving us, for never coming back to see me, for forgetting me and you and everything else. I'm not going to hate him any longer."

He might as well have shoved a knife right into her heart, the way it hurt. "How can you say that, after everything he did to you?" she whispered hoarsely. "After everything he did to me?"

"Because…it's what I'm supposed to do. As a Christian. Jesus expects it of me."

"And you think it's that easy? Well, I've got news for you, little boy. It doesn't work that way. Life's hard, and you have to take your knocks, and some of them are going to leave you hating something or someone. I guarantee it." She stood, her entire body shaking with anger as she pointed a finger at him. "You don't talk about that man. You hear me, Dakota? You don't ever talk about him again. Not to me. Not to that pastor whatever-his-name-is. Not to anybody. You promised me you wouldn't. He hurt us. He deserted us. I hate him, and I'll hate him until the day I die. You should too."

On the verge of tears, she fled to the solitude of her bedroom, slamming the door behind her.

Alone in the living room, Dakota bowed his head. It hadn't gone the way he'd hoped it would, but he couldn't say he was surprised.

I don't think I handled that too good, Lord.

He knew what he'd wanted to happen. He'd hoped his mom would say she needed to know Jesus. He'd hoped she would immediately forgive his dad and find out how much better it was to let go of all those ugly feelings inside. Dakota didn't fully understand how it worked. He just knew God had changed him, that God loved him, and that he'd been happier since accepting Christ than in all the rest of his life put together. That moment five weeks before, when Pastor Henry and John prayed with him after Sunday school, had changed everything.

Maybe if he...

Let it go for now, he told himself.

But he couldn't seem to do that. He wanted to make everything okay. He wanted to fix it. If he could just find the right words to make his mom understand what he was telling her. He knew how much she loved him, how much she'd sacrificed for him, how hurt she'd been by his dad. He didn't want to add to her hurt. That wasn't his intention.

OBEY HER, DAKOTA.

But if I could just make her see—

HONOR YOUR FATHER AND MOTHER.

I know the verse, Father. But if I could just—

TRUST IN MY PROMISES, MY SON.

"Okay, Lord," he whispered, "that's what I'll do. I'll honor my mom by keeping my promise. If she doesn't want me talking about my dad, then I won't. Not for as long as it takes."

He wondered how long that would be.

Chapter Sixteen

Feeling the plane's landing gear descend, Sara leaned closer to the window so she could see the lights of Boise as they came into view.

"Your family's going to be mighty glad to see you," the elderly woman in the center seat said.

Sara glanced toward her and smiled. "Yes. And I feel the same."

"Next time, don't wait so long between visits." The woman patted the back of Sara's hand with her fingertips. "Time rushes away from us before we know it."

She nodded, then turned her gaze out the window again.

The elderly woman was wrong about time passing quickly. At least, it sure seemed to crawl in Denver, Colorado. Sara wondered if it would have been different if she'd had the courage to stay in Boise. Probably not.

She pressed her forehead against the cool glass. If she'd stayed, would she have seen Dave again? Had he left his wife and son, she wondered, or had he and Claire Porter put their marriage back together? If Sara hadn't sent him away that day, would there have been a chance the two of them could have…

She closed her eyes, at the same time mentally closing off the direction of her thoughts. Three and a half years should have been long enough to rid her of the memories. They'd had an affair. Nothing more. She'd thought she was in love with him. She'd been wrong. Why did it still haunt her?

"You all right, dear?"

Sara looked at her seatmate. "Yes, I'm fine. I was just remembering the last time I was home."

"Well, I hope you have a lovely Christmas with your parents and brothers."

The plane touched down. Tires screeched. Jet engines roared.

The elderly woman's eyes rounded as she gripped the armrests. "Oh my," she said breathlessly. "I do hate this part."

To distract her, Sara asked, "Did you say your son would be here to meet you?" She already knew the answer. It was one of the many things the two of them had talked about during the two-hour flight.

"Yes, he'll be here."

By this time, the plane was taxiing toward the terminal, and Sara looked out the window again. Anticipation quickened her pulse.

Despite the bad memories, it was good to be home.

⟨✤⟩

The mall was packed with shoppers on this Friday evening, three days before Christmas. Dakota's friends were all headed to the music store, but Dakota had something else in mind.

"Listen," he told them, "I'll meet you guys up in the food court in an hour."

"Sounds like a plan," Rick Smith agreed.

"Want me to come with you?" John Kreizenbeck asked.

"Nah." He waved, then allowed himself to be swept along by the crowd.

A short while later, he stood in front of the jewelry counter in the Bon Marché, staring at the bracelet. He'd seen his mom admiring it a couple of months ago, but there was no way she could spare the money to buy something so frivolous for herself. He could almost hear her saying those exact words.

"May I help you?"

Dakota glanced up at the salesclerk and nodded. "Yeah, I'd like to buy that bracelet." He pointed. "That one there. The Black Hills gold one."

The clerk raised an eyebrow as he looked at the worn condition of Dakota's coat. His gaze seemed to say, *You can't afford that. Go away and don't waste my time.*

"I'm buying it for my mother for Christmas." *Jerk.* "Could you get it out so I can see it close up?"

With obvious reluctance, the clerk unlocked the showcase and withdrew the bracelet, placing it on the glass counter between them. "The price is one hundred and fifty dollars." His tone could only be described as condescending. He was obviously waiting for Dakota to admit he didn't have enough money and leave.

"I know." *Major jerk.* "I've looked at it before."

"Would you care to see something else? Something...more affordable?"

"No." He felt his temper rising.

BE ANGRY, AND YET DO NOT SIN.

Okay, Lord, but this guy is asking for it. He needs somebody to tell him—

Dakota could almost see God shaking His head.

Okay. Okay already.

Pressing his lips together, Dakota withdrew his wallet from his pocket and started counting out the cash. "How much with sales tax?"

Clearly surprised, the salesman answered, "A hundred and fifty-seven dollars and fifty cents. One moment, and I'll ring it up."

"I'm gonna want it gift-wrapped." He paused, then added, "Please."

While the clerk hurried to complete the sale, Dakota thought about how surprised his mom would be when she opened her present on Christmas morning. Dakota had mowed a lot of lawns the last two summers. He had been saving up for a radical new CD player and speakers. But this morning, he'd realized that buying a gift for himself wasn't nearly as important as doing something special for his mother. She deserved it.

The past couple of weeks hadn't exactly been easy for her. She was having a hard time with his decision to forgive his father. He understood why. He'd been there. He knew all about hanging on to bitterness. He also knew how much better it was to let it go. But how did he show her? She wasn't about to let her fifteen-year-old son tell her what to feel or do.

And she'd made it clear she didn't want to talk about his conversion any more than she wanted to talk about his dad.

He sighed, shaking his head slowly. *How come she can't see the truth?*

Pastor Henry said Dakota's job was to be obedient and to leave the rest up to God. That wasn't as easy as he made it sound.

⚜

Sara's eyes brimmed with tears as she looked around the dining room table. "It's so good to be home," she said for what must have been the twentieth time since emerging from the Jetway and into her mom's outstretched arms.

Eli punched her shoulder in a playful manner. "Hate to admit it, Sis, but we've missed you too."

Tim echoed the sentiment.

Headlights flashed against the dining room window.

"There's Josh." Kristina rose from the table and hurried into the kitchen.

Sara was aware of a heightened sense of anticipation among the others in the room. She saw the secretive look that passed between Eli and Tim. What was going on? Just what was Josh's big surprise?

She twisted in her chair and stared at the kitchen doorway, waiting for her mother and Josh. The back door opened, and Sara could hear a hushed exchange of voices.

A few moments later, her middle brother appeared. And with him was a lovely young woman about Sara's own age; she was smiling shyly as Josh drew her toward his sister.

Sara knew now what was going on. She didn't have to wait for introductions. Josh was in love, and she would bet a month's salary a wedding was in the offing. Getting up, Sara embraced him, then turned toward the young woman whose arm was still around Josh's waist.

"Sara," he said, his voice full of pride, "I'd like you to meet Fiona O'Hara, my fiancée."

"I knew it!" She grabbed a surprised Fiona and gave her a tight hug. "This is so wonderful. Another female in the family. Mom and I've needed that for a long time." She hugged her brother a second time. "When? When are you getting married? I need to know so I can arrange time off to be here to see it."

"In the spring," Josh answered. "March 31. And you'd better be here. We want you to be in the wedding party."

Sara glanced toward Fiona.

The girl nodded, a smile in her ink-black eyes. "It would mean a lot to us if you'd be my bridesmaid."

"I'd love to." She took hold of both of their hands. "Come over here. Sit down and tell me how you met. I want to know every detail." She looked up at her brother. "And then I'm going to spill all the dirt about you, Bro, and you'd better hope she doesn't come to her senses after I do."

What followed was one of the most enjoyable evenings Sara had partaken of in years. The house was warmed by the laughter of a family who not only loved one another but genuinely liked one another as well. Brothers and sister teased and taunted, poked and jabbed. Fiona, the soon-to-be-newest member of the family, was regaled with stories of derring-do, some true and some pure fabrication.

It was late by the time Josh left to take Fiona home. Not long afterward, Tim and Eli departed for the apartment they shared in Boise. The house seemed far too quiet with all of them gone.

"Don't worry, Sara," her dad said. "They'll be back tomorrow."

She put her arm around his waist and laid her head on his shoulder. "Thanks for bringing me home, Dad." A lump formed in her throat, making it hard to say anything else.

"If it was up to me, I'd have you back here for good. Your mom and I rattle around in this big old house by ourselves, now that all you kids have moved out."

"Maybe someday I'll come back," she whispered.

"I don't see what's keeping you in Denver. You ought to be here with us. It's not like you've got yourself some high-and-mighty career there."

"Leave her be, Jared." Kristina gave him a pointed look. "Sara's a grown woman. She wouldn't live at home with her parents even if she did come back to Idaho." She suppressed a yawn, then added, "It's way past my bedtime. I'm going to turn in." She went over to where Sara was standing with her dad and kissed her on the cheek. "We love you, honey. It's sure good to have you home for Christmas."

"Thanks, Mom. I love both of you too."

"Guess I'll join your mother." Jared kissed his daughter's other cheek. "Unless you want my company."

"No, it's okay, Dad. I'm going to bed. It's been a long day."

Half an hour later, her teeth brushed and her face washed, Sara crawled beneath the down comforter on her twin-size bed, her back propped against two plump pillows. Before turning out the light, she let her gaze roam over the room. It seemed both familiar and foreign at the same time.

Her parents hadn't changed anything since she'd moved out. Her favorite posters still hung on the walls. Her many horse trophies still cluttered the top of the ancient dresser, one of them covering the spot where she'd carved her initials when she was eight. Her collection of stuffed teddy bears filled the wooden rocking chair that had belonged to her grandmother and spilled onto the floor around it.

It had been four and a half years since Sara had graduated from high school. The girl she'd once been seemed a stranger to her now. How simple she'd expected life to be. If only she'd known…

With a sigh, she turned the switch on the bedside lamp and plunged the room into darkness. Then she snuggled under the warm comforter, tired and wanting to sleep. Unfortunately, her mind was too full.

She thought of Josh, the first of the Jennings siblings to become engaged. More than once she'd heard her mother lament about not having grandchildren, wondering aloud when any of her children were going to get married and get on with the business of giving her some babies to spoil rotten. Apparently, Fiona and Josh hoped to oblige.

Sara remembered the blush that had colored Fiona's cheeks when Josh said, "Children are like arrows. A man is blessed whose quiver is full of them." He'd kissed Fiona's forehead. "We want a full quiver."

She'd been more than a little astonished to hear her brother quoting the Bible. Josh had always been the most reluctant to go to church when they were kids.

"Josh met Fiona when he visited Sunrise Fellowship," Kristina had explained. "Now we all go there."

That had surprised her too. Her parents had been lifelong members of the same large denominational church in Caldwell. Sara and her brothers had attended Sunday school, gone through confirmation classes, and sung in the choirs. What on earth had convinced her family to suddenly start going somewhere else? Was it just because of Fiona?

Come to think of it, there'd been lots of talk all evening about the activities and people at their new church. Even from her brothers. Something was different, but she couldn't quite put her finger on what. It was like…Oh, she didn't know. Like they were *excited* about going to church. All of them. But it wasn't just that. It was much more than a new place to attend Sunday morning services. Their lives were full of new friends and new interests. Sara had found it disconcerting.

She'd been left out, left behind. It took her a moment to pinpoint the exact nature of what she was feeling. She was jealous! Jealous that Josh was getting married. Jealous that Fiona was already looked upon as a member of the family. Jealous that her parents and brothers had moved forward with their lives while Sara was trapped in the past.

I'm being ridiculous.

She rolled to her left side and closed her eyes. She *wasn't* jealous. She liked Fiona. She was glad for her brother. She'd had a wonderful time tonight, being home with everyone. It couldn't have been more perfect.

Unless there'd been someone here with me. Unless Dave…

Dave. That's what—or rather, who was bothering her. Dave. She hadn't let go of him, of the memories, of her broken heart. Despite three years of trying, she'd still never let go.

And now it was time.

Chapter Seventeen

When Claire awakened on Sunday morning, she discovered that a thick blanket of snow had fallen during the night. Large, wet flakes continued to drift downward from a pewter sky. She longed to use the weather as an excuse to get out of her promise to Dakota.

"It's Christmas Eve," he'd said last week. "Please come to church with me, just this once."

She didn't know why she'd agreed to his request.

No, that wasn't true. She did know. It was out of guilt. Her reaction to Dakota's decision to forgive his dad was not what it should have been, and she felt guilty about it even though she couldn't change it. She shouldn't have responded to him in anger. Nor should she have demanded he hold to his promise to never speak of Dave.

Resentment flared. Even now, her ex-husband had a way of spoiling things. Silently, she cursed him as she headed toward the bathroom.

A few minutes later, she stood beneath the hot spray of the shower, the water hiding her tears. She used to love Christmas. The shopping, the lights, the get-togethers with friends, the sledding parties, and snowball fights. She'd especially liked Christmas morning, watching Dakota open his gifts.

But that was back in the days when she'd called her son Mike and there'd been money for presents. Lots of them, both toys and clothes. She didn't want to think about the homemade shirt wrapped in tissue paper beneath the puny tree in the living room. The only package there.

How could Dakota forgive his dad for doing this to them?

She leaned her forehead against the shower wall. "I'll hate you till the day I die, Dave. God or no God, I'll hate you till the day I die."

Sara's dad drove slowly along the interstate. Black ice was hidden beneath the snow, and they'd already passed three cars that had slid off the road.

Sitting in the backseat of the automobile, Sara stared out the window at the passing countryside. Farmland was quickly disappearing, replaced by new subdivisions and shopping centers and storage units. So much change, everywhere she looked.

But I'm the same. I'm still the same as I was in college. I shouldn't be, but I am.

The car fishtailed.

"Jared!"

"Be still, Kris, so I can concentrate."

Sara looked toward her parents in the seat in front of her. Remembering how often she'd heard similar exchanges, she couldn't help smiling. According to Kristina, her husband drove too fast, followed too close, and ignored all the rules of defensive driving. According to Jared, his wife was an accomplished backseat driver.

"Dear Jesus," her mother said, "please get us there in one piece."

Over the past two days, Sara had heard several little prayers like this one. Actually, they were more snippets of conversation than what she'd always thought of as prayer. Kristina hadn't used to talk to God aloud, but now it seemed to be a normal occurrence.

Everybody's changed except me.

That thought replayed itself in her mind throughout the remainder of the drive to Boise. But it wasn't until her dad had parked the car in front of Sunrise Fellowship and they were all standing on the sidewalk beside it that Sara realized what she wanted to do. What she *needed* to do.

"Mom. Dad. Can I borrow the car?"

"Of course, dear," Kristina answered.

"I mean now."

Her mother looked at her. "But what about church? And the roads are so slick. You shouldn't—"

"It's important, Mom."

Her dad took hold of her hand, turning it palm up. Then he placed the car keys in it and closed her fingers over them. "Drive careful. And don't forget to pick us up at noon."

"Couldn't this wait?" Kristina persisted. "Whatever *this* is."

"No."

Her mother shook her head, saying, "Your brothers will be disappointed."

"I'll come visit your church another time. I promise. And we're all going out to eat afterward. Right?"

"Yes."

"So I'll see them then."

"Sara, don't you—"

Jared laid a hand on his wife's arm. "She said it was important. Let her go."

Thanks, Dad, she told him with her eyes.

With a nod of understanding, he drew Kristina away. Sara watched until they disappeared inside before moving toward the driver's-side door.

Claire reacted as she always did when she saw a woman with short, dark red hair. Her heart seemed to skip several beats, her stomach wrapped itself in knots, and a kind of fear coursed through her veins.

As Dakota turned the car into the church parking lot, Claire craned her neck to get a better look at the woman, but it was already too late. She'd disappeared into her car.

"See someone you know?" Dakota asked.

She turned toward him. "No."

When would she get over feeling this way? For all she knew, that girl—Dave's mistress—had changed her hair color, grown fat, whatever.

Maybe she died. That would serve her right.

"Is something bothering you, Mom?"

"No." *At least, nothing out of the ordinary.*

Less than fifteen minutes after leaving her parents at their church, Sara parked the car across from the small house on Garden Street.

Her heart raced as she stared at it, memories spinning through her mind. She remembered green trees and lilac bushes and colorful flowers in bloom. She remembered a gray pickup truck and a woman in the doorway.

And she remembered Dave and the death of her dreams.

Her gaze flicked to the mailbox, decorated to look like a Christmas package. In addition to the street numbers, there was a name: *D. Moss.*

She let out the breath she hadn't known she was holding. He didn't live here anymore.

And then she consciously and deliberately let it all go.

She let go of her romantic notions. Let go of the pain. Let go of her shattered expectations. Let go of everything that had held her captive, that had kept her a naive nineteen-year-old for the last three and a half years.

Most of all, she let go of Dave. In that moment, she made up her mind to go forward and not look back.

"It's over," she whispered, still staring at the house. "It's finally over."

She knew there would be moments of regret, times when she remembered that spring and wondered *what if.* But no longer would she be held captive by it. She'd made a mistake. Now it was time to move on.

Thank God.

Relief filled her as she turned the key in the ignition. She didn't know what tomorrow would bring, but at least it no longer seemed to be just one of many unhappy tomorrows.

Sunrise Fellowship was packed that Sunday morning with members, guests from out of town, and visitors who only attended services at Christmas and Easter. They filled the pews and the extra rows of folding chairs that had been set up in the back of the sanctuary.

For Dakota, the morning was filled with mixed emotions. On the one hand, there was his overwhelming joy in the Lord. He was filled with wonder at the truth that God Himself had chosen to leave heaven and come to earth to provide salvation for someone like him. On the other hand, there was his awareness of his mother's discomfort.

Claire sat stiffly beside him, her gaze locked on the pulpit. But Dakota suspected she wasn't listening to what Walter Drake, the head pastor, was saying. He wished she could hear, *really* hear. Maybe he'd made a mistake, talking her into coming with him this morning. Maybe she wasn't ready.

Did I blow it, Father?

"Why don't we all take a moment to get acquainted with those around us?" Pastor Walt said. "Introduce yourself to at least one person you don't know."

His mom shot him a look of pure horror as people stood and began shaking hands, hugging and greeting one another. He gave her a helpless shrug just before the woman in the pew ahead of them turned and held out her hand toward Claire.

"Welcome to Sunrise Fellowship. My name is Kristina Jennings. Is this your first time with us?"

"Yes," Claire answered.

The woman proceeded to introduce Claire and Dakota to her husband, her three sons, and one son's fiancée. "We hope we'll see you both here again," she added with a smile.

Dakota didn't bother to tell the woman that he was here every Sunday, usually sitting in the balcony. If he did, then he'd feel like he was pointing out that his mom *wasn't* here every Sunday. And from the look on her face, he thought it was better to say nothing.

Claire was, indeed, angry. Rebellion raged inside her. She hated the sanctimonious smile on that woman's face, a look of I'm-better-than-you. Why? Because this Mrs. Jennings needed a religious crutch? Well, Claire didn't need one. She was just fine, thank you very much.

For the rest of the service, Claire continued to simmer, her gaze returning again and again to the large family seated in front of her. To the woman and her husband and her three sons and the soon-to-be daughter-in-law. To a whole family, a family unscarred by a husband's unfaithfulness, by a father's desertion.

And bitterness multiplied in her heart.

Part Three: *Loneliness*

God makes a home for the lonely;

He leads out the prisoners

into prosperity,

only the rebellious dwell

in a parched land

— PSALM 68:6

Chapter Eighteen

June—Four and a Half Years Later

"So? What d'ya think, Mom?"

Claire raised an eyebrow. "You don't want to know."

"Ah, come on." Dakota grinned, looking more like a youth than like a man. "It's the perfect bachelor pad. Great place to bring all those girls." He gave her an exaggerated wink.

"No self-respecting female would set foot through that door."

Her son laughed.

She pivoted slowly, memorizing every dreadful detail of the studio apartment, a converted room on the third floor of a one-hundred-and-ten-year-old house in the north end of the city. The linoleum in the kitchenette was curling up in the corners. The tile grout around the sink was green with mold. The ugly carpet reeked of stale cigarette smoke—or something worse.

She longed to ask him why he was so determined to move out when he had a perfectly good home in a nice neighborhood where he wasn't charged rent and had someone to cook for him. But she already knew the answer. They'd been over it numerous times.

Dakota was twenty years old, and he wanted a place of his own. He was ready for it. Deep down, she knew he *should* be. It was normal. But it didn't make letting go any easier. She counted herself lucky that she'd kept him at home as long as she had. For his first two years at the university, she'd been able to hold their precarious finances over his head. But with her new position at Best Homes Real Estate—and the new salary that came with it—plus Dakota's recently awarded full scholarship, she'd lost that advantage.

"This isn't Siberia, you know," he teased, still grinning. "It's only across town."

Reluctantly, she returned his smile.

"And I'm not exactly the type to be having wild parties, so you don't have to worry about that."

No, he certainly wasn't the type for that. In her wild and woolly youth, she would have labeled Dakota a square. A Jesus freak. She supposed there were worse things for him to be.

He put his arm around her shoulders, leaning down from his lofty height, making her all the more aware that he wasn't her little boy anymore. "I'm glad you're going to miss me."

"Who said I'm going to miss you?" she blustered. "I have every intention of changing your bedroom into a den or something. Maybe I'll take up sewing again."

"Sure you will."

She jabbed him in the ribs with her elbow. It was either that or burst into tears. She had no desire to be one of those clinging, cloying mothers, and she had all the symptoms of becoming precisely that.

"Hey," he said softly, his expression somber now. "I'm not going to disappear. I've got a phone, so I'll call you. I've got a car. I'll come see you. Often. I promise."

She nodded. She knew his intentions were good, but she also knew how seldom that "often" more than likely would happen. He would be busy with classes and his job and his church. And girls! They would probably call him twenty-four hours a day, now that he wouldn't have a mother answering the phone for him.

After another squeeze, Dakota released her and started opening the boxes he'd carried in earlier. Claire watched him for a moment, then went to the kitchenette and unpacked the pots and pans he'd purchased at the thrift store that morning. Next she checked the shallow cupboards. The one next to the sink held three stoneware plates, all of them chipped, six plastic glasses, and two discolored coffee mugs that looked like they'd been around since the discovery of coffee beans. The cupboard above the stove held a box of macaroni and cheese, two boxes of Rice-A-Roni, three cans of tomato soup, and a loaf of wheat bread. The tiny, under-the-counter refrigerator contained a half gallon of skim milk, a six-pack of store-brand colas, a tub of margarine, a bottle of ketchup, a small jar of Miracle Whip, and a package of thick-sliced bacon.

If this is all he has to eat, he probably will *come home often.*

As Claire closed the refrigerator door, her gaze alighted on the slender gold chain on her right wrist. A poignant smile curved her mouth. Dakota had used his hard-earned savings to buy the bracelet for her for Christmas a few years ago. Like it was yesterday, she could see the way his blue eyes lit up with excitement and anticipation as she'd opened the unexpected gift. She'd had him put it on her wrist right then, watching as he fumbled with the clasp, and she'd rarely taken it off since. The bracelet was lovely, of course, but the reason she wore it always was because it came from Dakota, because she knew what he'd sacrificed to give it to her.

Now, over four years later, he still didn't have that fancy stereo system he'd once wanted. He continued to do things for others instead of for himself.

She glanced across the room. Her son was kneeling on the floor, transferring folded clothes from a box into drawers built into the wall. She wondered what she'd done to deserve a child like him. She'd certainly made countless mistakes in her role as mother. But despite them, Dakota had grown into an incredible young man. Loving and honest and selfless. A man of integrity and honor.

Completely unlike his father.

The thought caused her eyes to narrow as she pressed her lips into an unhappy line. Only last week, Alana Moncur had told Claire she needed to get over her ex-husband.

"There are more good men in the world like Jack and Dakota than bad apples like Dave," she'd said. "You've made a fine art out of male-bashing, Claire Conway, and you know it. Some marriages don't work out. So get over it and get on with your life. It's been eight years, for crying out loud."

She knew her friend was right, but knowing and doing were two different things. Her feelings toward Dave were like an old pair of jeans—frayed around the edges but familiar and hard to throw out.

What am I going to do with myself now that Dakota's gone from home?

An empty life lay before her like a deserted stretch of highway across the plains of Wyoming.

⁂

Sara doubled over at the waist, allowing her long mane of hair to almost touch the ground. Then she captured it into a ponytail high on her head. As she straightened, she told her tennis partner, "Let's cream 'em."

Vince Lewis grinned wickedly. "You got it."

Every Saturday morning, Sara and Vince met Joyce and Chuck Carruthers at the tennis club for a friendly, if heated, match. The four of them enjoyed the good-natured competition as well as the exercise; their games were filled with plenty of laughter and teasing.

But they all liked to win, and no one more than Sara. Last week, she and Vince had lost to the married couple. She didn't want a repeat this week.

She got her wish. She and Vince were in fine form, playing flawlessly throughout the match. It was one of their easiest wins since they'd paired up four months before.

After the game, Sara showered in the locker room, then met Vince in the lounge area of the club.

He kissed her lightly on the lips before asking, "Where for lunch today?"

She named her favorite bistro in a little, out-of-the-way place north of Denver.

"Sounds good to me." He took hold of her arm. "I'm starving."

"Me too."

She smiled, thinking how happy she was. She liked Vince a lot, and she wondered if their relationship would deepen and grow. She thought it might. They seemed perfect for each other. The two of them had met when he had come to install a new computer system in Sara's department at work, and he'd asked her out before the installation was complete.

The best part of their relationship was discovering how many things they had in common. His folks had a ranch near Cheyenne, and he'd grown up riding horses. They both liked the outdoors, playing tennis, and going for long walks. Each enjoyed reading, although Sara's taste ran to romances and Vince's to thrillers. Their favorite date was a movie and a late dinner, then talking into the wee hours of the night while drinking cup after cup of decaffeinated coffee. And while Vince would obviously like their relationship to move in a more physically intimate direction, he hadn't pressed when Sara made it clear she wasn't ready for the same.

With the wind from the open window causing her damp ponytail to flap against her shoulders, Sara turned toward Vince. "My folks want me to come home for a visit next month. Eli's baby is going to be christened on the tenth. They said you're welcome to come too. Interested?"

"If I could swing the time off work, I would be." He glanced quickly in her direction, then back at the road. "You think I'm up to meeting your folks, your brothers and their wives, and all those nieces and nephews?"

"I think you could handle it."

"I guess I could."

They continued the drive in silence, Sara's thoughts drifting to her family.

All her brothers were married now, and each had given their parents at least one grandchild. Josh and Fiona had celebrated their fourth wedding anniversary in March. Their son, Ron, had turned three the same month. Their daughter, Theresa, would be a year old in July. And the couple thought Fiona might be pregnant again, although it was still a bit early to know for certain. Tim and Darlene had been married over three years now. Their daughter, Becca, was a year old, and Darlene was expecting twins in October. Eli had married Myrna two years ago come August. Their first child, Randy, had arrived last month.

Surreptitiously, Sara glanced once again toward Vince. She wondered if he wanted children. They'd never talked about that, she supposed, because they'd never talked about marriage either. For some reason, they'd both avoided broaching those subjects. Now she wondered why.

Would she want this man to be the father of her children? She thought she might. She would if she fell in love with him. *Was* she falling in love?

She wished she knew for sure. She wished she trusted herself to know.

Funny how life worked. She'd gotten over Dave Porter years ago. That Christmas Eve day when she'd parked in front of his old house, she'd let go of the heartache. But there was one residual of that disastrous affair that remained unchanged. It wasn't that she couldn't trust men—it was that she couldn't trust her own emotional response to them. She'd had several boyfriends in the past four years. She'd even received a proposal of marriage from one of them. But she hadn't been able to accept. She hadn't known for certain if she loved him or not.

"God has the right man in mind for you, honey," her mother had told her a few weeks ago.

Well, if *He* knew who the right man was, it would be nice if He'd let *her* know. It wasn't as if she hadn't asked. It wasn't as if she weren't trying to hear God's voice. In fact, in recent months she'd felt an ever-increasing desire to understand more about spiritual things, a yearning to know what God wanted for her and from her.

Her mother had assured her that those who sought the truth would find it. "It isn't about religion, Sara, or what church you go to. It's about a personal relationship with God."

She wasn't sure she understood what her mother had meant, but she was trying.

Vince pulled into the parking lot next to the Rocky Mountain Bistro, bringing Sara's attention back to the present. He steered his restored 1968 baby blue Mustang into the last space at the back, far from any opening doors that might scratch the paint job or put a dent in the side of his beloved automobile.

"I think I'm in the mood for some of their world-famous meatloaf and hand-mashed potatoes with gravy," he told Sara. "How about you?"

She laughed, her more serious thoughts evaporating for the moment. "The health nuts at the club would faint dead away if they heard you." She reached for the door. "And meatloaf and mashed potatoes sound good to me. Down with vegetarians!"

Chapter Nineteen

John leaned over on his right hip and stared at the sofa cushion. "Hey, Dakota. You've either got a spring about to pop through or there's a gremlin living in this thing."

"Very funny." Dakota handed his friend a mug of strong, black coffee. "What do you expect for fifteen bucks? Besides, didn't you notice that it's the same olive green as the shag carpet and the drapes? That means my apartment is color coordinated. That's real uptown, man."

"Hurray for you."

Dakota grinned as he sat on the floor, stretching his legs out before him, his back against the wall. Michael W. Smith's "I Will Be Here for You" played on the boom box, the volume turned low.

"So, how's your mom doing with this move of yours?" John asked, all joking aside.

"It hasn't been easy." He shook his head. "I've always come first with her, especially after it was just the two of us. I think she's feeling at loose ends. Not knowing what to do with herself."

"Too bad she won't start coming to church with you. From what I hear, Sunrise has got a great singles group for people her age. She'd probably enjoy the fellowship if she'd give it a try."

"Yeah, but she won't go. I've told her about it. Not for her, she says."

"Keep praying for her. It'll happen one day."

He nodded. He believed God never failed to answer prayers. It was simply hard to wait sometimes.

Unlike a lot of other kids, Dakota and his mom had remained close, even during the toughest of his teen years, even when he'd been so angry with the world at large and his dad in particular. He loved his mother. One of his greatest desires was to be able to share this most important part of his life with her. They'd always been able to talk about anything. But she didn't let him talk to her about God. She cut him off whenever he tried.

The jangle of the telephone interrupted his contemplation. He went to answer it, figuring it must be his mom calling. She knew he was always up early on a Sunday morning. And she was the only other person who knew his phone number besides John.

"Hello?"

"Hello. Is this Dakota Conway?" The female voice on the other end of the line was faint and unfamiliar.

"Yeah."

"You don't know me, but I...I'm calling about your father."

"My father?" He frowned. "Who is this?"

"My name is Wanda. Wanda Porter."

"*Porter?*"

"Yes. I...I'm Dave Porter's wife." She paused a moment, then said, "I'm his widow. He passed away Thursday evening."

Michael W. Smith crooned something about love carrying him away.

John got up from the lumpy sofa, a look of concern on his face.

The beige walls of the small apartment seemed to close in around Dakota. The air was too still, too stuffy.

Images of his dad flashed through his mind, distant and fuzzy. His dad teaching him how to fish. His dad dropping his leather tool belt beside the washer and dryer. His dad driving off to work in his pickup. His dad fighting with his mom.

"I do have the right person, don't I?" the woman asked. "You were born Michael Dakota Porter. Correct? And your dad called you Mikey?"

Not for a long time. Not for eight years.

"Hello? Are you there?"

"How?" he asked, his voice gruff. "How did he die?"

"Cancer. But it took him very suddenly." There was a lengthy pause. When she continued, her voice was soft and full of sorrow. "Just a few weeks was all he had after they discovered it."

"I'm sorry." His words seemed inadequate, but he couldn't think what else to say.

"The funeral is tomorrow afternoon."

"Where?"

"We live in Salt Lake."

Salt Lake City. Seven hours away. His dad had been as close as that.

"I…I just thought you should know," she continued, her voice cracking.

"Yeah. Yeah, I appreciate it." Was that a lie or not? He couldn't be sure.

"Dakota? Your father talked about you a lot toward the end. He was…sorry. Sorry for many things. He would have told you if he could. I…I thought…I hoped you might come to the funeral."

Old feelings of resentment welled in his chest, burned his throat, and stung his eyes. Instinctively, he wanted to strike out at something, hurt something. He wanted to shout at the faceless woman on the other end of the line. Shout and tell her he couldn't care less what she hoped.

John's hand on his shoulder stopped him from doing it.

Yeah, Lord, I know. We've been over that be-angry-and-don't-sin lesson before. But it's not easy.

"Listen," he managed to say at last, "can I take your number and call you back this afternoon? I need to think about this a bit."

"Of course." She gave him her phone number, adding, "Please do call me back."

"Yeah. I will." He hung up.

John's fingers tightened on Dakota's shoulder. "Your father died?"

He nodded.

"I'm sorry."

"Yeah."

"So what're you feeling?"

"I don't know. Anger mostly, but I'm not sure what I'm the most angry about." That his dad hadn't bothered to contact him in eight years. That he hadn't known where his dad was living. That his dad had married again, maybe even had other kids, kids he'd actually loved.

"You going to tell your mother?"

Dakota closed his eyes. "I don't know. That woman. His widow. She wants me to come to the funeral in Salt Lake. It's tomorrow."

"Are you going?"

"I don't know that either."

God, what am I supposed to do?

❦

When Claire had purchased the quaint, older house a year ago, there wasn't a single flower in sight. It had taken many hours of work, last summer and fall and this spring, but now the backyard was a blaze of glorious color—irises and azaleas, potentilla and dianthus. A stone bench was set in the shade of a large oak tree, near the fountain that Dakota had helped her create from granite hauled out of the Boise mountains. And in the center of this flowering oasis was the sundial that had belonged to Claire's grandmother.

Ada Conway had taught Claire the joy to be found in gardening. And it was here, working on her hands and knees, digging beneath the sun-warmed surface to the cool, dark soil below, that Claire found her greatest source of peace. She probably never would have discovered it without her grandmother's help.

Pausing in her weeding, Claire sat back on her heels and looked toward the sundial. She wished Grandmother Ada had lived long enough for Dakota to have known her. Her grandmother hadn't been a beautiful woman. She hadn't been educated or wealthy. But she'd had a great deal of wisdom and common sense, and she'd dispensed advice to her grandchildren in life lessons that were easily understood.

It had been her grandmother whom Claire had told first about being pregnant with Dave's baby. An August afternoon, the sun harsh, the air still. Grandmother Ada had taken her into the garden where

165

bees buzzed around flower blossoms; a fountain, much like the one Claire had now, had gurgled and splashed, bringing an illusion of coolness with its sound, and the sundial that had come with the Conways from Ireland had registered the passing of time. The old woman hadn't scolded Claire or condemned her. She had merely listened as Claire spilled out her heart, all the while holding her granddaughter's hand and offering silent comfort.

After a very long while, Ada had said, "Every foot is slow on an unknown path, my dear. Just face the sun and turn your back on the storm. It will all turn out right in the end."

"I wish you were here now," Claire whispered as she rose from the ground.

She placed her fingers against the small of her back and arched backward, stretching out the kinks. Then she walked toward the sundial. Judging by the shadow, it was shortly after noon.

"You could have told me how to accept things the way they are." She touched the face of the clock. "I'm so lonely, Grandma. I know some of it's my own fault, but I just can't seem to change it."

The screen door squeaked, then Dakota's voice called, "Mom?"

Surprised, she turned toward the porch. She hadn't thought he would come to see her so soon. Certainly, she'd expected it to be longer than twenty-four hours. Then again, it didn't surprise her. Dakota was always considerate of others. He'd probably been worrying about her. The realization caused her to smile.

One look at his face as he came down the steps disabused her of such sentimental thoughts. Something was wrong, and he couldn't hide it from her.

She yanked off her soil-covered gloves. "Dakota?"

"I need to talk to you."

"What is it?" She reached out, touched his arm.

"Can we sit down first?"

"Of course." She turned and led the way to a stone bench. After they were both seated, she said, "Tell me what's wrong."

"I got a call this morning, and I'm not quite sure how to tell you about it."

"A call?" Her heart was racing, her mind assailed by multiple possibilities. "From whom?"

Dakota stared her directly in the eyes. "From my father's wife."

That was the last thing she'd expected him to say.

"He died on Thursday."

Dave's dead?

For a moment, she felt nothing. No reaction whatsoever. Then a flood of old memories washed over her, reminding her of what she should feel.

Good! I'm glad you're dead. I'd dance on your grave if I could. I hope there's a hell so you can be in it.

Her son must have seen what she was thinking and feeling. She sighed as he glanced away. "I'm going to the funeral in Salt Lake."

"You're *what?*" She was on her feet in an instant, looking down at him in horror.

Dakota stood too. "I'm driving down to Salt Lake for the funeral."

"You can't be serious."

"I'm not sure I can explain why, Mom. I just know I have to go. I prayed about it, and I know God wants me to go."

"Spare me your religious drivel."

He reached to touch her again. "Mom—"

"Don't!" She stepped quickly out of reach. She was so angry she couldn't think straight.

Dakota lowered his hands to his sides. "Mom, I've done my best to keep my promise to you. I avoid talking about my father. And I'll go on keeping my word as long as you want me to. But this is the *right* thing to do, and I've got to do it. No matter what he did in the past, he *was* my father and I'm going to his funeral. But I couldn't go to Salt Lake without telling you first."

Sarcastically, "Thanks a lot."

"John's going with me. We'll be using his dad's car. It won't use as much gas as mine would."

Claire remained silent. She wanted to tell him she would never forgive him if he did this, but something kept her silent. Perhaps, even in this moment of hurt and rage, she knew she would be sorry if she hurled such words at him.

"We're leaving in another hour. I've got to get back to my place so I'll be ready when John gets there."

She still said nothing.

His eyes were filled with sadness as he said, "I love you."

Don't do this. How can you do this to me?

He answered as if he'd heard her, repeating what he'd said a moment before. "No matter what else he did, he was still my father." He turned away. "I hope someday you'll understand."

"I'll never understand," she whispered. "Never."

Claire sat in the dark in her favorite wing-back chair. It was three in the morning. For hours—for an eternity—she'd been reliving those horrible moments, days, weeks of that odious spring and summer when her world collapsed. She stared into the darkness of the room, unable to move, unable to escape. The memories and the emotions were strong, as if no time at all had passed.

She could still hear Dave's distinctive laughter rising above the din of conversations and video games. She could still see the young girl with short, dark red hair leaning toward him across the table. She could still smell the pizzas baking in the huge ovens.

So he had married her, his mistress, and they had lived in Salt Lake City. Did they have children? Had he become a loving father to another woman's babies when he'd been incapable of the same with Claire's son, with his firstborn?

Cold fingers of dread wrapped themselves around her heart and squeezed. What if Dakota liked her, this woman who had stolen Claire's husband, her hopes, her dreams? She knew he would forgive that harlot for what she'd done, just as he'd forgiven Dave. All for the sake of his precious Christianity.

"No," she whispered. "You can't. You can't do it."

She didn't cry. She was too dead inside to cry, her tears held captive within an unforgiving heart.

Chapter Twenty

Oriana Simpson, an attractive woman in her mid-forties, leaned back in her desk chair, her elbows on the armrests, her hands steepled in front of her chest. "Have you considered returning to college?"

Sara shrugged, then shook her head. "Can't afford it."

"I'll be honest with you, Sara. You're never going to move beyond your current position with this firm without at least an associate's degree."

What could she say to that? It was true. She'd been passed over for promotions plenty of times.

Twenty-seven and already trapped in a dead-end job.

"You're being wasted where you are. You know it and I know it." Her boss leaned forward, a small frown knitting her brows. "You're too bright for the work you're doing. Underutilized. I'm well aware of the real work you're capable of. You're a whiz with computers, and I've seen the way you brainstorm your way through a problem. You could go far at Richards and Clemmons, but our policy is strict. You *must* have a degree."

"I'd love to, but going back to college just isn't possible for me right now."

Sara looked out the huge glass windows that lined Oriana's spacious office. Amazing, she thought, how long the effects of a person's mistakes last. If not for her affair with Dave, she would have stayed in Boise, graduated from BSU, had a real career by this time.

"It just isn't possible," she repeated with a shake of her head. "I haven't the money."

"Actually, Sara, if money is the only reason, there is a way. The firm has a rather generous continuing education program that will pay the majority of fees if an employee maintains good grades. If you are willing to take classes at night, in your free time..." She let the sentence drift into silence, unfinished.

"Really?"

"Really." Oriana jerked open a drawer in the credenza behind her desk and withdrew a large envelope. Swiveling back around, she held it toward Sara. "Take this home and read through it. Then come meet with me tomorrow and let's see what we can do."

"I will." Sara smiled as she rose, feeling both bewildered and excited. This wasn't what she'd expected to happen at her annual performance review. She'd thought she would get a pat on the head and a moderate salary increase, as usual.

College? Could she really go back? All she'd wanted to do eight years ago was perform. But since then she'd discovered there were other things to challenge and interest her besides acting. A degree would open up a realm of new possibilities.

It would take sacrifice. Going to school and maintaining a full-time job wouldn't be easy. And what about Vince? When would she see him if she was working in the daytime, going to school at night, and studying on the weekend? How did one maintain and nurture a relationship if one didn't spend time on it?

But an education, a college degree, a chance to move ahead. How could Vince not want her to have those things if he cared about her?

These questions were still roiling in her head as she drove home after work.

It wasn't until she pulled into her apartment complex parking lot that she remembered something she'd heard on television the previous morning. She'd been surfing channels, looking for a show to watch, when she'd stumbled across a TV evangelist. She'd paused no more than a few moments before changing the channel again, and yet she remembered the man's words distinctly.

"The fear of the Lord is the beginning of knowledge; fools despise wisdom and instruction."

She trembled inwardly.

Is this what You have in mind for me? Is it going back to school instead of marrying and having a family? How do I know for sure? How do I know You're even up there and listening? And if You are, how do I know when You're speaking to me or when it's just me doing the talking?

The fear of the Lord…The beginning of knowledge…

A surge of excitement caused her to smile. She wanted this. And for some inexplicable reason, she believed God wanted it for her too.

❦

Dakota wasn't sure what he felt as he stared at his father's casket above the open grave. A little removed from the situation, he supposed. As if it weren't quite real. He didn't know the man who was being eulogized by his friends. The father Dakota remembered had been someone different.

A breeze rustled through the trees behind him. Before him lay the majestic Wasatch Range.

Odd, the things that came to mind when one looked upon a parent's grave. Things never considered before. When Dave Porter was the same age that Dakota was now, he'd had a wife and a four-year-old son to support. He'd had a mortgage and a truck payment and a host of other bills. He'd been forced to give up college, to get married, and to go to work. What must that have been like for him?

Dakota's mom had always tried to gloss over that she'd been a pregnant bride, but Dakota had figured it out long ago. Had Dave blamed Claire for getting pregnant? Had he resented his son for being born?

He wondered how different their lives might have been if his dad had stuck around. Might there have been a chance that father and son could have learned to really love each other? It was only in retrospect that he realized how very much he'd wanted his dad's love, both before and after he'd gone away.

"Dave Porter was a devoted husband to Wanda," a man said.

But he lied and cheated on my mom.

"Though he hadn't lived here many years, he quickly became a trusted and upstanding member of the community."

But he left my mom in debt and never paid child support.

A wave of sadness washed over him. A sadness for all the might-have-beens that would never be. He'd spent a lot of years being angry and bitter, and it was only thanks to God that he'd moved beyond those emotions. He'd forgiven his dad, but he wished he could have loved him as well.

Now it was too late.

"Good-bye," he whispered, pausing for a moment before adding, "Dad."

He looked up at the cloudless blue sky. Soaring on an updraft was a hawk, its wings spread wide. And like that bird soaring overhead, he felt himself set free from an old hurt he hadn't even realized was binding him. Maybe that was part of the reason for being there today. Maybe it was simply to call Dave Porter *Dad* one last time.

When the graveside service was over, Dakota lingered until the crowd of mourners had thinned, then he made his way toward his father's widow. Wanda Porter, a plain, plump woman with mousy brown hair, took hold of his hand, looking up at him with grief-filled eyes.

"Thank you for coming, Dakota."

He nodded.

"It would have meant so much to your father to have you here."

Again, he nodded, not knowing what to say.

"Are you certain you can't come back to the house? You and your friend are welcome to stay with me instead of at the motel. I have a guest bedroom as well as a Hide-A-Bed sofa in the den."

"Sorry. John and I both have to get back to our jobs." He squeezed her hand. "Will you be all right?"

"Yes." She gave him a sad smile. "I'll have my memories of your father to sustain me."

Dakota wished he could say the same. There were few memories, and most of those were tinged with unhappiness.

"Dakota?" Wanda said softly, drawing him back to the present. "I hope you'll come to see me again. I'd like to tell you about my husband. We were only married three years, but I think he must have been quite different from the man you remember." Her words echoed his earlier thoughts.

"Yeah, I think he must've been." Impulsively, he leaned down and kissed her on the cheek.

"If he'd had a little more time, I think he would have called you himself." Her eyes welled with tears. "He had many regrets."

Dakota discovered he couldn't form a cohesive reply, so he simply nodded. Then he turned and strode toward John, who was waiting beside the car.

"Claire?"

She looked up and suddenly realized Jack Moncur had been talking to her for several moments without her hearing him. "Sorry, Jack. What did you say?"

"I was asking about the Rinker closing. Have the papers arrived?"

"No. I'll call the title company right now."

He frowned. "Are you okay?"

"Yes." She reached for the phone. "Just a little distracted. Everything's fine."

Obviously, her longtime friend and boss wasn't fooled, but he let it go. "Let me know when those papers arrive," he said, then disappeared down the office hallway.

Claire finished the call, ascertaining that the courier service would be delivering the needed documents soon. She buzzed Jack in his office and relayed the information. But the moment she pushed the intercom button again, turning it off, her thoughts returned to her son. Dakota had called an hour before to say he and John were headed back to Boise.

"I'll call you as soon as I get to my place," he'd told her, "no matter how late it is." He knew her well, knew she would want him to call even if it was after midnight.

She hadn't asked him about the funeral, about his father or his father's widow. She hadn't asked if he'd found himself with a sibling or two. She hadn't asked any of the things she'd obsessed about for the past twenty-four hours. She was fairly certain she didn't want to know the answers.

Once again someone speaking her name interrupted her musings. This time it was Alana who stepped into her office. As usual, Claire's best friend, dressed in a chic Donna Karan outfit and wearing tiny diamond earrings glittering on her lobes, looked like a fashion plate.

"I was hoping I'd catch you here," Alana said as she settled onto the chair opposite Claire. "I need a favor."

"Sure." Her answer came quickly and easily. After all, Jack and Alana had done her many favors over the years. "What is it?"

"I'm giving a dinner party for some business associates of Jack's tomorrow night. They're coming in from Seattle. I'm short one person. Will you fill out my table?"

"I take it the odd person"—her pun was intended—"is a single man."

"Of course."

"Promise me you're not matchmaking."

"I promise." Alana crossed her heart, but there was a teasing twinkle in her eyes all the same. "Strictly business."

She suspected it wasn't *strictly* business. Her friend was a die-hard romantic who couldn't bear to see Claire still single after all these years. She'd made numerous attempts to pair her up with one man or another.

As if reading Claire's mind, Alana said, "It isn't as if Dakota isn't grown. He's gone from home. You don't have to worry about an evil stepfather."

"Alana."

"Well, isn't that the excuse you used to use?"

"It wasn't an excuse."

Her friend dismissed her comment with a wave of her hand. "One bad apple doesn't mean the whole barrel is rotten. You might find a real hero if you'd just open your eyes."

"You've been reading historical romance novels again. I can tell."

Alana stood. "And you're changing the subject." She smiled. "Dinner is at six-thirty, so please arrive by six o'clock. And wear that pretty black dress of yours, will you? It's smashing with your blond hair."

She was right. Matchmaking. "Whoever he is, I won't be interested. Just remember I told you so."

"We'll see," her friend answered breezily before leaving.

As fate would have it, Sara didn't have to worry about how going back to school would affect her relationship with Vince Lewis. That very same evening, when he came over for a barbecue in the apartment complex common area, he announced that he was being transferred to Atlanta within the month.

She halfway expected him to suggest she go with him.

He didn't.

Then she waited to feel disappointment.

She didn't.

"I'll miss our tennis games," he told her.

"Me too." She motioned for him to have a seat on the couch. "I've got news of my own. I'm going back to school. Just nights, but I've decided I want to get a business degree." She sat beside him.

"Good for you. I think that's a great idea."

"I was going over the information when you got here. I've got one year of college behind me already." She felt her earlier excitement bubbling up inside again. "I think if I applied myself and took classes in the summer, too, I could get my degree in four years."

Vince took hold of both of Sara's hands and squeezed them. "I know you can do it. Will you send me an invitation to your graduation?"

"You bet." But deep inside, she suspected they would have lost track of each other by then.

Who knew where either of them would be four or five years from now?

❧

Claire answered after the first ring, and Dakota knew she'd been sitting next to the phone, waiting for his call.

"Hi, Mom. It's me. We're back, safe and sound."

"Thank goodness."

"We made good time."

"I'm glad John could go with you. Be sure to thank Maury for letting you boys use his car. I'd have worried myself sick if you'd driven that clunker of yours."

"I'll thank him."

"Do you have to work tomorrow?"

"Yeah. Eight o'clock."

"Then I'd better let you get some sleep."

Ask me what happened, Mom. Let's talk, get it out in the open, then release it once and for all.

"I'm glad you're home, honey."

"Mom—"

"I love you."

He sighed. "I love you too."

"Good night."

"'Night, Mom."

A moment of silence, then the other end of the line went dead.

Dakota gently placed the phone in its cradle. He'd been praying for his mom for nearly five years. At first, he'd expected God to work an immediate miracle in her heart. After all, once he'd found Jesus, he couldn't understand why she couldn't see the truth too. But she couldn't see. The miracle hadn't happened. Not yet. If anything, she'd grown even more resistant with the passage of time.

I DESIRE ALL TO BE SAVED AND TO COME TO THE KNOWLEDGE OF THE TRUTH.

"I know, Father," he said, his gaze still locked on the telephone. "So when's it going to happen?"

MY SON, THERE'S AN APPOINTED TIME FOR EVERYTHING. WAIT UPON ME.

Patience, Dakota silently confessed, had never been one of his strong suits.

~~~

The golden days of summer marched onward. Long days that teased Boise residents with a breath of coolness in the mornings, then turned blistering hot beneath a relentless afternoon sun. The foothills to the north of the city turned brown. Newscasters warned of the fire danger; people made it a habit to check the sky for telltale signs of smoke drifting above the pine-covered mountain peaks. The reservoirs slowly emptied their contents, leaving boaters anxious about the demise of their favorite summer pastime. The Boise River ran low; more than one person taking a lazy float in an inner tube suffered a broken tailbone when they hit submerged boulders. Drought became an all-too-common topic of conversation. Not only between farmers but also between servers and customers in restaurants and between total strangers waiting at bus stops.

Feeling separated from her son emotionally as well as physically—a separation for which she was to blame but seemed unable to alter—Claire tried to fill the void in her life with busyness. She worked long hours at the office. She accepted more invitations to Alana's dinner parties and met a surprising array of single men. She joined a health club and worked out, losing five pounds and improving muscle tone and endurance. She gardened, and her skin took on a bronzed hue. She went to art-house movies, and she read big blockbuster novels and tell-all celebrity books.

She stayed busy, busy, busy.

Dakota called her, dropped by to see her, and tried to breach the invisible wall she'd constructed between them. She *wanted* him to breach it, and yet she caused him to fail. Her intractable nature kept the wall in place. She resented the peace and maturity she saw in her son even while she admired those same traits in him. As time for the new school year approached, he contacted her less frequently, his days eaten up by work and selecting classes, church activities, and, she suspected, a new girlfriend.

Claire felt displaced, perhaps even invisible. She was thirty-eight. Not old, yet there were times she felt ancient. Her role as someone's wife had ended eight years before. Her role as someone's mother was no longer preeminent. When she looked at herself in the mirror, she couldn't help wondering, *Who are you?*

She received no answer.

Part Four: *Faith, Hope, and Love*

Now abide faith, hope, love,

these three:

but the greatest of these

is love.

— 1 CORINTHIANS 13:13

Chapter Twenty-One

The airport terminal was crowded. Travelers pulled rolling suitcases behind them as they rushed to their appointed gates. Others, just arriving, hurried to the three carousels in the baggage claim area in the lower level. Small children played tag around rows of connected seats. A baby cried, either hungry or tired. The roar of jet engines rattled the glass windows as a plane lifted off the runway.

It was all a bit overwhelming for Claire, who was admittedly a nervous flier.

"This way." Dakota pointed toward Concourse B after grabbing her carry-on from the security checkpoint conveyor belt.

She nodded.

"It's not much over an hour-long flight. That's no time at all."

"I know."

"Read your book. You'll be there before you know it." He put his arm around her shoulders and gave her a reassuring squeeze. "Remember to have some fun while you're there. Don't just work twenty-four hours a day."

His reminder wasn't as necessary today as it would have been a few years back. Claire had come through a rough patch emotionally, but thanks to numerous self-help books, she'd overcome the worst of it. The breakthrough came when she stopped thinking about her deceased ex-husband. She never thought about him anymore. Well, rarely ever. And her relationship with her son was once again healthy and strong.

Now she was off to Seattle, Washington, to open a satellite office for Jack Moncur. Her stay there was temporary. Just a few months. But she'd discovered she was actually looking forward to the new challenge. The realization had taken her somewhat by surprise. She wasn't exactly the adventuresome sort, and she could count on one hand the number of times she'd been outside of Idaho.

She glanced up. "You've arranged for time off in March? You're still planning to come see me?"

"Don't worry, Mom. I'll be there for your birthday. I've already got plans for us to take the ferry up to Victoria for a couple of days." He frowned. "Hmm. I forget. Will you be twenty-nine this year?"

"Very funny, coming from my almost twenty-four-year-old son."

They found Claire's gate and sat in a pair of vacant seats near the Jet-way. Dakota placed his mom's carry-on bag on the floor between them.

"Any chance Cynthia will be coming with you?" Claire asked, refer-ring to the young woman he'd been dating this winter.

"No." He shook his head. "I told you. She's seeing someone else."

"I'm sorry. I liked her."

"So did I. But we weren't in love. If she'd been the right one, God would have worked things out between us."

Claire barely kept from rolling her eyes. She and her son would never agree about religion. She'd reached a point in her life where she realized that whatever she was, whatever she was going to be, was up to her. That good old-fashioned truism of pulling oneself up by one's own bootstraps was the motto she lived by nowadays. Life was what a person decided to make of it.

"You surprise me, Mom."

"What about?"

He leaned closer and, in a low voice, said, "Because you won't even consider getting married again, but you can't wait for me to find somebody and tie the knot."

"That's different."

"Is it?" He raised an eyebrow and gave her one of his most charming lopsided grins. "Why?"

"I don't need a man in my life. I'm older and settled in my ways. I've already had my family. I'm quite happy the way things are."

The look in his eyes said, *Are you?*

She ignored the unspoken question, turning to watch as disembarking passengers spilled from the Jetway of her arriving plane.

I am happy, she argued in silence. *I have a rewarding job, and I'm financially secure at last. I've raised a son and managed to put him through college. I have a lovely little home that I've decorated just the way I want, and my time is my own to do with as I please. Why wouldn't I be happy?*

"You'll call me when you get to your condo?" Dakota asked, wisely changing the subject to something more prosaic.

"Of course."

"Did I mention that I'll miss you while you're gone?"

As she turned her head to meet his gaze, she smiled and her irritation with him vanished. "Yes, but it's nice to hear it again."

A boarding announcement blared from the speakers in the ceiling, interrupting whatever he might have said next. She immediately got to her feet, then picked up her small carry-on bag. Dakota stood too.

"You'll go by the house once a week and make sure everything is okay there?"

"I will."

"Be sure the thermostat stays set at sixty. I don't want any pipes to freeze if Boise gets a cold snap."

He grinned. "It'll stay at sixty. No pipes will freeze."

"Check the mailbox, just in case something doesn't get forwarded."

"Okay."

"If there's a problem of any kind—"

"Then I'll take care of it." Chuckling, he leaned down and kissed her forehead. "Don't worry. Everything will be fine here. Just make sure you have a great time in Seattle."

Her row was announced.

Dakota walked with her as far as he was allowed. The flight attendant took Claire's ticket and welcomed her aboard. Feeling a sudden panic, Claire turned toward her son. He grinned, kissed her on the cheek, then gave her a gentle push toward the Jetway.

"Have a great time, Mom."

Oh, why did I ever tell Jack I would do this?

⁂

Dakota watched her go. When she reached the bend in the Jetway, she looked over her shoulder, as if hoping he would call her back. He smiled and waved, and at last she moved on, disappearing from view.

This experience was going to be good for her, he thought as he followed the corridor toward the security area and the escalators beyond. He was nearly there when he heard someone call his name.

He stopped and looked around.

"Over here." Eli Jennings raised an arm, catching Dakota's attention.

And right behind Eli, coming out of Concourse A, was the rest of the Jennings bunch, one of his favorite families from Sunrise Fellowship. They were all there—Kristina and Jared, their three sons and three daughters-in-law, and more grandkids than Dakota could keep track of.

Before he could ask what had brought them to the airport, his gaze alighted on the one unfamiliar face in the crowd. For one breathless moment, the world stood still.

"This is our daughter, Sara," Kristina said, but her voice seemed to come from far away. "Sara, this is Dakota Conway. He goes to our church."

She smiled. "Hello."

"Nice to meet you." He smiled back.

"Sara's been living and going to school in Colorado," Kristina continued, "but she's finally coming home to stay."

"Welcome back." Dakota held out his hand.

"Thank you." She took it.

He didn't want to let go. Ever.

"She's been hired to head up the personnel department at Master Resource Industries."

Dakota thought it was Jared Jennings who dispensed that bit of information, but he wasn't sure. He still couldn't drag his gaze away from the burgundy-haired vision before him.

If perfection existed, he was looking at it.

A blush colored Sara's cheeks. She dropped her gaze to his chest and gently withdrew her hand.

Realizing what he'd been doing—staring like an idiot, holding her hand as if his life depended upon it—he felt the heat of his own embarrassment inching its way up his neck. He cleared his throat as he took a step backward. "Hope to see you again soon, Miss Jennings."

She glanced up. Her smile returned. "I'll be at church tomorrow. Perhaps I'll see you there."

"Definitely." He felt like a kid who'd just won a trip to Walt Disney World.

Later he would wonder if he'd bothered to say good-bye to the rest of the Jennings clan. It was nothing short of a miracle that he found where he'd parked his car and managed to drive home without running a red light or ending up in the barrow pit.

⤛⤜

"Go on. Admit it," Darlene said to Sara a few hours later. "You *liked* Dakota Conway."

Sara placed some sweaters in the open bureau drawer. "I don't *know* him. How can I tell if I like him or not?"

Her sister-in-law chuckled. "I knew I liked your brother the second I laid eyes on him."

"All that does is prove you're certifiable," she replied, trying hard not to laugh as she met Darlene's gaze.

"A little bit of insanity can be a good thing. I'm still crazy about Tim."

Sara smiled, awash in warm, tender feelings. "I know." She sank onto the bed next to Darlene. "You know the best part about coming home? I'll finally feel like I'm really your sister. Yours and Fiona's and Myrna's. I'm glad my brothers were smart enough to marry you all."

"Likewise. You know—"

"Mama!" The bedroom door burst open and a pair of auburn-haired munchkins barreled into the room. "Mama!"

Sara couldn't understand anything else the three-year-old twins said as they climbed onto the bed and started pouring out complaints to their mother.

"J.J., that's enough," Darlene ordered firmly. "Lizzie, be quiet." When they obeyed, she continued, "You first, J.J. Tell me what's happened."

Sara left the room while the twins' mother was still sorting things out.

As she went down the stairs, she heard her father and brothers shouting at the television and knew they were watching either football or basketball. She veered toward the kitchen where the women had congregated. Except for the twins, her nieces and nephews were outside, enjoying the wintry sunshine.

She'd barely had time to pull a diet soda out of the refrigerator before Myrna said, "You sure bowled over Dakota at the airport."

Oh, honestly.

"I think Sara was a bit bowled over herself," Fiona chimed in.

"I was not."

Myrna and Fiona exchanged amused glances, then burst into laughter.

Sara popped the tab on the soda as she sank onto a chair at the table across from her sisters-in-law. "Where's Mom?"

"Outside watching her grandkids have a snowball fight," Fiona answered. "She's a glutton for punishment. Never gets enough of them."

Myrna nudged Fiona. "Have you noticed how good Dakota is around the little ones at church? The patience of Job. Why, he's almost a saint." She winked at Sara. "And imagine how cute his own kids will be…once he gets married and starts a family, that is. I bet he—"

"I am *not* interested." Sara felt her cheeks growing hot. "I came back for a job, not a man. And I don't want to hear another word about him."

Fortunately, the other two women backed off. Unfortunately, the image of Dakota Conway lingered in Sara's head even after the teasing stopped.

She had to admit, that guy would be called a hunk in any woman's book. Well over six feet tall. Sky blue eyes. Thick blond hair, pleasantly mussed, sort of begging for a woman to smooth it with her fingertips. A slightly crooked smile that revealed a dimple in his right cheek. Sort of a combination George Strait–Brad Pitt.

I wonder how old he is.

She gave her head a tiny shake and forced herself to concentrate on what Fiona was saying about her son, Ron.

"He loved kindergarten, but he's hated first grade almost from day one. It isn't his teacher. She's super. But I can't make him tell me what else it might be."

The topic of children filled the better portion of the next hour. Sara even managed to hear some of it, despite how frequently the image of blue eyes and a crooked smile popped into her head.

John poked Dakota in the arm. "What's with you this morning?"

"What?" He dragged his gaze from the main entrance and looked at his friend.

"Who are you expecting? The pope?"

He shook his head. "Nobody."

"To paraphrase the Good Book, you won't tell a lie to your friends. Remember?"

"Okay already. I'm waiting for the Jenningses."

Bemused, "The Jenningses?"

"You'll know why when they get here." He pressed his index finger against John's chest. "And just remember that you *are* my friend."

"Huh?"

The doors opened again, letting in a draft of cold air. Dakota turned toward them. A sense of relief swept over him when he saw Kristina and Jared Jennings step through the doorway. There was a breathless moment of anticipation, and then he saw Sara.

She looked even more beautiful today than he'd remembered. She'd used one of those hair claw things to draw her dark wine-red hair away from her face. Brown shadow dusted her eyelids, a pleasant contrast to the cat green of her eyes. The smile on her bow-shaped lips was tentative, almost poignant, and altogether lovely.

Beside him, John let out a low whistle.

"Back off, Kreizenbeck," Dakota said, his voice low and his meaning earnest. "I saw her first." Then he moved toward the Jennings family, his gaze locked on Sara even while he spoke to her parents. "Good morning, Mr. and Mrs. Jennings. Good morning, Sara. Welcome to Sunrise Fellowship."

"Thanks."

"This is your first time at Sunrise, isn't it?" There wasn't any way in the world he would have forgotten if she'd been here before. He was sure of that.

"Yes."

"I guess you haven't made it back to Boise very often since moving to Denver."

"Not often." Her gaze flicked to a place just over Dakota's shoulder.

He knew without looking that John was approaching and would want an introduction. Glancing to his right, he said, "Sara, this is John Kreizenbeck. John, Sara Jennings."

"Nice to meet you, Sara. Now I know why Dakota was waiting out here instead of getting a seat like he usually does. He's been waiting for you."

I can't kill him, Dakota reminded himself. But he was definitely going to make John pay for this.

"Why don't we all go in and sit down?" Kristina suggested as she took hold of her daughter's arm. Smiling, she added, "You boys are welcome to join us if you'd like."

John leaned close to Dakota as the three family members headed for the door of the sanctuary. "How old do you think she is? Thirty?"

"Who cares?"

"She might," John answered, then echoed Sara's mother. "You *boys.*"

"Once you're past twenty-one, a difference in age doesn't matter."

"Dream on."

Maybe he *was* dreaming. He'd never felt such a profound attraction before. Sure, she was beautiful, but it was something more than that. A connection. A rightness. Whatever it was, he wanted to explore it. He wanted to *know* Sara. He wanted to know the woman beneath the pretty exterior.

"Come on," he said to John. "Let's get inside."

He made a beeline for the sanctuary, but he was already too late. Sara was seated between her mother and one of her brothers in a pew full of Jenningses. He had to be satisfied with sitting a row behind her.

Not a bad place to be, as it turned out. During the next hour and a half, he was able to watch the way her thick, curly hair swished across her back whenever she moved her head. He was able to hear the crystal clear tone of her voice as the congregation sang songs of praise and worship. He was able to see the way she leafed through her Bible during Pastor Walt's sermon.

Could this be the woman You planned for me, Lord?

Only yesterday he'd told his mother that God would work things out when he finally met the right girl. And now he wanted to hear the Lord saying, "Yes, this is the one."

He knew he should probably add, *Your will be done and not my own,* but he just couldn't do it. Not when everything inside him wanted his own way this time around.

Chapter Twenty-Two

Claire got lost on her way to the office that first Monday in Seattle. She wasn't used to the network of streets and freeways, the strange numbering system, the blending of one town into another. She was feeling very provincial and unsophisticated and might have thrown up her hands and gone back to her temporary home—only she didn't know how to find it.

After stopping three different times to ask directions, she finally succeeded in locating the new offices of Moncur, Quade, and Associates—the Seattle satellite of Best Homes Real Estate. Jack's partner in this venture, Kevin Quade, was waiting for her. She'd met Kevin once before, when he'd come to Boise in the early stages of forming his partnership with Jack, and she recognized him immediately.

"I'm sorry I'm late," she apologized after they'd reintroduced themselves. "I took a wrong turn—several, actually—and got lost."

"Easy to do in a strange city."

Claire nodded, then glanced around the lobby. Except for an L-shaped desk, a secretarial chair, and a coatrack, the area was empty.

"As you can see," Kevin said, "you're starting from scratch." He held out his arm. "Here. Let me hang up your coat. Then I'll show you around."

She obliged him.

The tour didn't take long, but it was daunting all the same. Every room was stark and empty, awaiting Claire's numerous decisions. Some structural changes were needed, as was new carpeting, not to mention fresh paint throughout. Furniture had to be ordered. Prints for the walls chosen. Shelves built in the storage and copy rooms. Phone system selected, computers purchased, software installed, support staff hired and trained. The list seemed endless.

"There's an espresso place just across the way," Kevin said when they returned to the lobby. "Why don't we go there? We can start making plans over coffee."

"All right." It certainly sounded better to Claire than staying in this empty office where their voices echoed and she could see how much there was to be done.

A short time later, the two of them were settled in the back of the coffee shop. Frothy mugs of cappuccino sat on the table between them.

After stirring in three packets of sugar, Kevin took a sip. "Mmm." It was a sound of pure pleasure. Meeting her gaze, he said, "You'll find we appreciate our coffee here in Seattle. It's almost a religion." He wiped his upper lip with his napkin.

"So I've heard."

He rested his forearms on the table, his expression suddenly serious. "You know, I didn't properly thank you for agreeing to come to Seattle. It's a sacrifice and a big disruption in your life, and I realize that. But Jack said he wouldn't trust anyone but you to get it done right. He holds you in high regard."

Warmed by the praise, she smiled. "It's mutual."

"You've known Jack a long time?"

"Ever since his first date with Alana. She and I have been friends since grade school." She lifted her cup of cappuccino. "Don't ask me how long ago that was. Please."

Kevin laughed, a strong, pleasant sound.

"How about you? How long have you known him?"

"About eight years, I guess. We connected during the relocation of For Him Ministries. I handled the sale of homes of the employees here, and Jack sold them new ones in Boise."

"Oh yes. I remember. A rather strange group, as I recall."

"What makes you say that?"

"Are you kidding?" It was her turn to laugh, but it wasn't a pleasant sound as his had been. "They prayed before they sneezed, let alone before they made an offer on a house."

"And prayer's a bad thing?"

She didn't care for the way he was watching her, his gaze kind but penetrating. "Maybe not bad. Just…unnecessary." She looked down at the mug in her hands. "What good does it do?"

"A great deal of good, I assure you."

Oh no. Not him too.

As if reading her mind, he said, "I'm an elder in the same church many of those strange people attended when they lived here." He sounded amused. "I've done my share of praying with them."

She couldn't help looking up again. Shouldn't he feel angry or insulted by what she'd said? And how had she gotten into a discussion about prayer and religion with him anyway? She knew better than that.

"We Christians *are* strange, Claire. Even the Bible calls us peculiar."

"What?"

"It says we're a peculiar people, chosen to show forth the praises of God."

"You sound like Dakota."

Kevin raised an eyebrow.

"My son."

"He's a Christian?"

"Since he was fifteen."

"How old is he now?"

"Almost twenty-four."

"And you think he's strange?"

She scowled at him. "No, I do *not* think he's strange."

Again with the lifted eyebrow.

"All right. Maybe sometimes I do. But mostly it's in a good way. He's a wonderful young man. He would go out of his way to help anybody in need, whether he knew the person or not. He's never been into drugs or alcohol. He worked hard to help put himself through school. I'm proud of the man he is."

"And didn't his faith help make him who he is?"

The question gave her pause. She supposed her son's religious convictions had to have played a part in shaping him. And if she was so proud of him, why did she object to a faith that had helped make him who he was? She'd never looked at it quite that way before.

"Yes," she answered at long last. "I guess it did."

⟡

Kevin could see confusion swirling in Claire's eyes, along with some other emotions he couldn't so easily discern. Deciding it might be wise to give her a moment alone with her thoughts, he asked, "Would you like another?" He pointed to her mug.

She shook her head without looking at him.

Wordlessly, Kevin rose from his chair and went to the counter where he ordered one regular coffee. While he waited, he glanced over his shoulder. He was sorry that he'd been the cause of that frown furrowing Claire's forehead. She was much prettier when she smiled. Still, he didn't know what he could have said differently.

By the time he returned to the table, he'd made up his mind that a change of subject was in order. As he sat down, he said, "What do you plan to do while you're here? Besides work, that is."

"I don't know. I haven't given it any thought." She hooked a lock of dark blond hair behind one ear. "I don't know much about Seattle."

"Well, what do you do for fun in Boise? Got any hobbies?"

"I like to garden in the summer."

"And?" he encouraged.

"Just the usual. Going to movies. Reading books."

"How about the theater? I hear there's a great performing arts center in Boise."

At last, her smile returned. Her dark blue eyes twinkled, and a dimple appeared in her right cheek. "Broadway musicals. I love them. I remember going to see *Oklahoma* and *Carousel* and *South Pacific* and *Camelot* with my grandmother when I was still in junior high and high school."

"How about newer ones like *Cats?*"

"Yes, and *Les Miz*. I loved that one, even though it makes me cry. Oh, and I adored *Joseph and the Amazing Technicolor Dreamcoat*. The songs are wonderful."

"Have you seen *The Phantom of the Opera*?"

She shook her head. "It hasn't come to Boise, but I own the original cast CD."

"Tell you what. I'll check to see what's playing in the area over the next few months. Maybe we can get tickets to a musical or two."

Claire's eyes revealed her surprise.

Kevin was a bit surprised himself, and he wondered if he'd overstepped his bounds. Maybe she was seeing someone in Boise. "If you'd rather not go with me, just—"

"No, I'd like to go..." She hesitated a moment before adding, "with you."

Chapter Twenty-Three

Every night that week, Dakota looked up the phone number for Jared and Kristina Jennings in the church directory. And every night that week, he went to bed without dialing it. It took him until Saturday morning, a full seven days after meeting Sara at the airport, to work up the necessary courage to place the call.

Someone—a female someone—answered on the fifth ring. "Hello?"

Dakota didn't think it sounded like her, but he hoped it was.

"Hello," he said. "May I speak to Sara, please?"

He hadn't felt this nervous since he'd asked Pamela Marker to the junior-senior prom when he was sixteen. He was surprised his voice didn't crack.

"I'm sorry. Sara isn't here at the moment. May I take a message?"

"No." His disappointment was keen. "I'll call back another time."

"Wait. Is this Dakota?"

"Yeah, it is."

"Hi. It's Myrna."

"Oh. Hi, Myrna."

"Listen, Sara's moving into an apartment in Boise. Her brothers are loading boxes and furniture into their pickup trucks as we speak. I'll bet they'd be glad for another strong back. If you're not doing any-thing else, that is."

"No, I'm not doing anything else. I'd be glad to help." *Real glad.* He grinned.

"Just a second. Let me find the address. You can meet them there." She returned to the phone a few moments later. "Here it is." She gave him the address, followed by directions to the apartment complex near the river.

Dakota wrote it down, then asked, "What time should I meet them there?"

"Hmm…" She hesitated. "You know, I bet it'll take the guys another hour before they're all loaded up. But Sara's at the apartment now, unpacking things she took over herself, so I guess you could go whenever it's convenient for you."

"Thanks, Myrna."

There was a hint of laughter in her voice as she said, "No, thank *you*, Dakota."

He suspected she just might be playing matchmaker, but since she was aiding his cause, he didn't object in the least.

He made it across town in record time.

⟨⟨⟨⟩⟩⟩

Taking a break from her unpacking, Sara stood at the large picture window overlooking the tree-lined Boise River. It was a beautiful view—tall cottonwoods, their winter-bare limbs revealing nests; clear water rippling over smooth river rocks; stately homes on the opposite bank; and beyond them, mountains rising toward the sky.

The view was the main reason she'd chosen to rent this particular apartment.

It had been nice to be with her parents this past week, sleeping in her girlhood bed, joking and teasing with her family around the supper table, getting to know her sisters-in-law, nieces, and nephews better. But she had to admit it would be good to have her own place again. After so many years with only herself for company, she'd missed her privacy.

That thought made her smile. Who'd have believed she would ever crave solitude?

It hadn't been easy to reach this point. Those early years in Denver had been filled with pain, regrets, and loneliness.

But I'm never alone, am I, Lord? Thank You for that.

Her spiritual awakening hadn't been a sudden thing as it was for some. For Sara, it had been a slow and sometimes arduous journey, a path traveled by fits and starts and plenty of questioning. Then one day, about three years ago, the confusion had lifted, like a gigantic cloud blown back by a strong wind, and she'd seen everything clearly. She'd understood then that she wasn't alone. Not in Colorado. Not in Idaho. Not ever. God was always with her. He'd always been with her, even when she hadn't known it.

Smiling in contentment, she turned around, knowing she'd better get busy. There were boxes of glasses, dishes, and keepsakes still to be emptied before her brothers arrived with the furniture. She didn't want any breakables in the way of their clumsy feet.

She was headed for the kitchen when a knock sounded at her door.

"Oh no," she muttered. "Not yet. I'm not ready for you guys."

But when she opened the door, she didn't find her brothers waiting on the other side.

Dakota Conway smiled, just a bit sheepishly. "I came to help with the move."

"How did you know I was…" She let the question fade away, unfinished. She had a good idea what his answer would be. One of her sisters-in-law was behind this. She would bet money on it.

"I was supposed to meet your brothers here to help unload the trucks. They aren't here?"

"Not yet." Sara opened the door wider. "Come on in."

"Thanks." He stepped into the living room.

"I'd offer you a place to sit, but nothing's arrived yet." She swept back the straggling strands of hair that had escaped her ponytail and suddenly wished she'd bothered to put on at least some mascara this morning.

His smile broadened. "I didn't come to sit. I came to work." He motioned toward the boxes lining one wall of the dining area. "I can help you unpack while we wait for your brothers."

"Are you safe around fragile items?"

"I think so. Why?"

"Because my brothers most definitely aren't. That's why I brought this load over myself."

Dakota laughed.

Sara was certain she felt the laughter in her own chest.

"I promise to use extreme care," he vowed solemnly, the twinkle remaining in his eyes. "Just tell me where to put things, and I'll get them there in one piece."

Sara hesitated, mesmerized by the way he looked at her, forgetting momentarily where they were and what they were supposed to be doing.

"Shall we get started?" A corner of his mouth lifted in obvious amusement.

Hoping she'd turned before he could notice her flushed cheeks, she walked to the boxes, snapped open the lid of the one on top, and said, "These things go on those built-in shelves on either side of the fireplace." Without looking at him again, she grabbed another box of glassware and carried it into the kitchen.

❦

Dakota was encouraged by Sara's flustered state. With luck, it meant she felt the same attraction he did. Time would tell.

He set the box on the floor, crouched in front of it, and began removing the contents, each item carefully surrounded with bubble wrap. His grin returned as he looked at the collection of teddy bear figurines he'd uncovered. There was a bear dressed as Robin Hood. Next came Romeo and Juliet complete with balcony, followed by an Easter bunny bear, a Christmas angel bear, a little girl bear saying her prayers, a leprechaun bear with his own Irish blessing and pot of gold, and a pair of Thanksgiving pilgrim bears. By the time the box was emptied, he'd unwrapped over twenty-five of the figurines.

As he started carefully placing them on the recessed shelves that bordered the fireplace, he asked in a loud voice, "How long have you been collecting these?"

"What?"

"These little teddy bears." He glanced over his shoulder just as Sara stepped into view. "How long have you been collecting them?

"About three years now. I bought one on a whim, and the collection just grew from there."

"I like them." He liked the collector too.

Sara came across the living room. Picking up the leprechaun, she said, "This is my latest purchase. I love the blessing." She read it aloud. "May the road rise to meet you. May the wind be always at your back. May the sun shine warm upon your face. May God hold you in the palm of His hand."

"He always does, doesn't He? Hold us in the palm of His hand, I mean."

She met his gaze. "Yes. He always does." The look of peace in her eyes was suddenly replaced by one of regret, making her look as vulnerable and fragile as one of her figurines. "I wish I'd always known that. Maybe I wouldn't have made so many mistakes in my life."

"What sort of mistakes?" He asked the question without considering the wisdom of it. It wasn't what she'd done that he cared about, but why it made her look so sad.

"The stupid mistakes of the very young."

Dakota sensed that a wall had gone up. He wanted to knock it down. He hoped a bit of humor would do it. "And you're so terribly *old* now, you don't make mistakes anymore?"

At first there was no reaction. And then, slowly, she smiled. "Old?"

"Ancient wisdom," he continued. "I'll bet you're full of it."

"I'm not sure I care for the ancient part. Mind if we change it to mature wisdom?"

"No, I don't mind at all." *I don't think I'd mind anything to do with you, Sara.*

Her eyes widened, as if she'd read his thoughts. He was sorely tempted to kiss her. He wondered what she would think if he did.

Loud male voices from the landing announced the arrival of the

Jennings brothers a moment before one of them pounded on the door.

"Sara, open up!"

"Coming!" She stepped around Dakota and hurried toward the door, looking relieved.

It was probably for the best, he thought. It was too soon to kiss her. But kiss Sara he would, when the time was right.

❦

"I'm not a golfer," Claire muttered as she swung...and missed. Again.

Kevin swallowed a chuckle. Laughing at her wouldn't help.

She turned accusing eyes in his direction. "How did I let you talk me into this?"

"Because you knew a game of miniature golf would be fun."

"Fun?"

He ignored her sarcastic tone. "You've worked hard all week long. Relax, Claire." He set aside his putter and walked over to her. "Let me show you something." He took hold of her right hand and adjusted the way she held the club. Then he stepped behind her. "May I?" He held out his arms on either side of her.

She glanced over her shoulder. When she seemed to understand what he meant, she nodded.

He moved nearer, his chest against her back, and closed his hands over the tops of hers. "Bend your knees just a little bit. That's the way." He hadn't brought Claire here for this reason, but he had to admit she fit rather nicely in his arms.

"Now what?" she asked, turning her head slightly.

She smelled good too.

"Kevin?"

He cleared his throat as he released her and stepped back. "Now take a nice, easy swing, keeping your eye on the ball the whole time. Just follow it through. That's the way."

She made a beautiful putt, coming within a foot of the hole. When she turned around and smiled, Kevin felt as if he'd won an award.

This could get interesting.

       ⤨

At nine-thirty that night, the boxes unpacked and the furniture moved into Sara's apartment, the four Jennings siblings and Dakota sat around a table in a nearby pizza parlor, sharing two large combinations and one medium Canadian bacon and pineapple. Between bites, the brothers cheerfully dispensed one story after another about their "baby" sister.

Fighting her own laughter, pretending an offense she didn't feel, Sara looked across the table at Dakota and said, "Didn't you say you were an only child? Well, lucky you."

"I guess it does have its advantages. I *do* know a whole lot more about you than you do about me."

She swept a suspicious gaze over her brothers, wondering what they'd told Dakota when she'd been out of the room. Too curious not to, she asked, "Like what?"

"Hmm. Well, for one, you turned thirty-one on January ninth. A belated happy birthday, by the way."

"Thanks." She shot her brothers another look, this one of real disapproval.

Dakota continued with his list of garnered information. "When you were in high school, you won some awards in barrel racing and you competed at the Snake River Stampede. After graduating from Nampa High, you attended one year at BSU where you studied theater arts, but you finished your schooling in Denver, mostly by going to school nights while working a full-time job. Let's see. A business degree, right?"

"Right."

"You don't start your job with Master Resource until February, which means you've got lots of time on your hands for a few more weeks. Oh yes. I have it on good authority that you outranked your competition for that job by a mile."

Maybe it wasn't so horrible, having her brothers bragging about her.

"And one more thing," Dakota said, revealing that crooked grin of his, the one that made her pulse quicken.

"What's that?" She was breathless.

He leaned toward her, answering in a stage whisper, "Beyond the slightest doubt, Miss Jennings, you are the best looking of your parents' offspring."

Her brothers immediately erupted in protests.

"I beg to differ!"

"Wait just a minute!"

"What d'ya mean, Conway?"

Eli held the half-empty pitcher of root beer over Dakota's head and pretended he was going to pour out the contents. Then all their voices dissolved into laughter.

Sara felt warm inside. It was wonderful to be here with her brothers.

It felt good to joke and laugh. And it felt good to be with Dakota too.

As if reading her thoughts, he leaned forward again. "I mean it. You *are* pretty, Sara."

It wasn't fancy, as compliments went. She'd heard more flowery declarations. But it was probably the nicest one she'd ever received—because of who gave it to her.

⚉

Sara hadn't lain awake thinking about a guy in years. She tried to tell herself her wakefulness was due to her new surroundings. The apartment was strange to her. A sharp winter wind was whistling around the corner of the building. The light from an outdoor lamp tossed an odd shadow through the miniblinds and onto the wall.

It had to be something other than thoughts about Dakota Conway that were keeping her awake tonight.

That's a lie, and I know it.

Dakota was handsome and charming. He was friendly and helpful. He was a fellow believer. And her family liked him.

But none of that was enough to keep her awake at night. Was it? She'd known plenty of handsome men. She'd met Christian men who might have been interested in her, had she given them an opportunity. At least she thought she had. At the moment, she couldn't recall a single name or face.

I'm older than Dakota, she thought, not for the first time, *but by how much? And should it matter?*

She rolled to her right side and punched her pillow.

Maybe meeting Dakota is the reason I was brought back to Boise.

She groaned, closed her eyes, rolled over onto her left side.

That's ridiculous. I didn't come back here for a man. I came back here for a job. I worked hard for my degree, and now I'm being rewarded for that hard work. Dakota's a nice guy, but if I was in the market for a husband, I'd look for somebody older, somebody more mature. I don't want somebody who still has the same mistakes to make that I did.

Her arguments made perfect sense, all of them. Except Dakota's image remained. She could still see the sparkle in the startling blue of his eyes and the way the left side of his mouth lifted first in that charming grin of his. She could still hear the warm rumble of his laughter, the unique timbre of his voice. She could still smell the musk aftershave he wore.

"What is wrong with me?" she muttered as she flopped onto her back and stared up at the ceiling. "I'm not a silly teenager. I don't get crushes on guys. I haven't since I was nineteen."

She winced at the memory. She didn't like thinking of that period in her life, not even now when she knew God had forgiven her.

She reminded herself of one of her favorite promises from the Bible: *He will keep in perfect peace all those who trust in Him.* She could certainly use some perfect peace about now.

THEN TRUST IN ME.

"I do trust You, Lord," she whispered. "But what if this is just me and *my* desires getting in the way? How will I know what I'm supposed to do?"

TRUST, BELOVED.

Chapter Twenty-Four

Claire was breathless as she watched the curtain go down. Applause erupted all around her, but all she could do was sit still and savor the haunting strains of music that echoed in her mind. Finally she stood, clapping her hands, smiling as she looked toward Kevin.

"You enjoyed it," he said above the applause and cheers of the audience.

"It was magical."

He smiled and nodded. "I agree."

She couldn't help wondering what sort of strings he'd had to pull to get these tickets to *The Phantom of the Opera* on such short notice. She also wondered what it meant, that he'd gone to both the bother and the expense.

Looking back toward the stage, she watched as the cast took their bows, but her thoughts lingered on Kevin. She'd spent many hours with him since arriving in Seattle and had found she liked his company. He had a way of looking at her, of seeming to be truly interested, no matter what she was saying.

He could become a good friend.

She cast a surreptitious glance in his direction. Could it be that he wanted to be more than a friend?

She didn't think so. Beyond taking her arm, as any gentleman would, to help her in and out of a car or up a flight of stairs—and that moment at the miniature golf course when he'd shown her how to swing the golf club—he'd never touched her. There was nothing in any of their conversations that he couldn't have said to one of his male colleagues. And yet—

"Ready?" he asked.

She realized the crowd was beginning to disperse and felt a flash of embarrassment, almost as if she feared he might have read her thoughts. Kevin took hold of her arm as they slipped into the sea of theatergoers, keeping her close to him as they made their way toward the lobby.

It was rather nice, having a man protect her in such a way. Of course, it had been a long time since she'd given a man, other than her son, an opportunity to do so.

The night had turned cold while they were inside the theater. Claire shivered as they stepped outside. She turned up the collar of her wool coat and slipped on her gloves. When she was ready, Kevin cupped her elbow with the palm of his hand as they made their way to his automobile.

"I'm glad you could go with me tonight," he said, now that the buzz of the crowd had been left behind.

"Me too. It was an unexpected treat. I usually have to go to the musicals alone." The moment she said it, she was sorry. It sounded as if she were feeling sorry for herself. She tried to explain. "Dakota is busy with his friends or work, and musical theater just isn't Alana's cup of tea. But I don't mind going alone. I love it that much."

"I usually go by myself, too, ever since my wife died. Irene loved the theater. She had to drag me along at first. It took awhile for me to learn to appreciate it."

"Tell me about her. Irene."

"She was special." It was obvious from his tone that there was a wealth of feelings within those three simple words.

Claire almost wished she hadn't asked about her.

"She had a good and giving heart." He grinned. "And she was a notorious practical joker. You had to stay on your toes all the time with her around."

"How long were you married?"

"Twenty years." His voice softened. "We were blessed with twenty wonderful years together before she went home to the Father." He chuckled. "She's probably playing practical jokes all over heaven."

"You still think about her often, don't you?"

He briefly met her gaze. "I cherish the memories of what we had, sure. But I don't live in the past. Irene was in a lot of pain toward the end, and I knew that in heaven, she would be pain free. That made it easier to let her go on."

Claire was still pondering his comments when they arrived at his car. Kevin unlocked the doors with his remote as they drew near. He opened the passenger door and helped Claire in.

They talked about the play throughout the drive to her condo. It wouldn't be until later that she wondered if that change of subject had been by accident or by design.

Dakota hadn't expected to see Sara at the paint-a-thon that Saturday, but it sure made the day more special to have her there. The singles groups from five area churches had joined together to repair and spruce up the interiors of three homes in a poorer section of town. With just a little effort, Dakota managed to be paired with Sara, painting the kitchen of a tiny three-room house—perhaps *shanty* would have been a better description—while two others from Sunrise worked in the bedroom.

"Do you want the walls or the trim?" he asked her as they stared at their dingy surroundings.

"Trim, I guess."

"We'd better do some cleaning first or the paint will never stick."

"That's just what I was thinking."

Sara grabbed a plastic bucket, dumped in some pine-scented cleanser, and filled it with warm water. Dakota retrieved a couple of rags from the box of supplies they'd hauled into the house not long before. In a matter of minutes, he was scrubbing grease off the wall behind the stove, and Sara was down on her knees trying to remove grime from the baseboard.

"Can you feel the cold coming through the wall?" he asked her. "The old guy who lives here must have a hard time staying warm in the winter."

"Yes. Imagine having to live like this. It must make a person feel hopeless."

He paused and looked in her direction.

She met his gaze. "I thought I had it rough when I first went to Denver. Makes me ashamed of myself. By comparison, I was rich." She returned to her scrubbing.

She could have stayed home today, he thought as he watched her. Certainly she would have had a good excuse. For all practical purposes, she'd moved twice within the last couple of weeks, first home to Idaho, and then into her own place in Boise. Nobody would've faulted her for taking a Saturday to relax.

Pretty *and* caring. He found more to like about Sara Jennings every time he was with her.

"Dakota, can you toss me that wire brush?"

"Sure. Here."

She sat back on her heels and held out her hands. He lofted the brush, and she caught it easily, smiling as she did so. "Thanks."

"Tell me about Denver," he said. It was either that or ask her out on a date, and he was afraid she might turn him down if he asked too soon.

"Not much to tell."

"Must be something. You were there for twelve years."

"I guess you're right," she said with a laugh.

Over the next few hours, they talked about many different things, among them their college experiences, her passion for horses and acting, his interest in computer technologies, their shared love for the Lord. It seemed that in no time at all they were finished. The dingy little kitchen had been transformed, brightened with yellow paint and new curtains at the window.

As they packed up to leave, Dakota finally managed to ask the question that had been in the back of his mind all day. "Sara, would you be interested in taking a bike ride along the greenbelt? Maybe next Saturday, if it isn't too cold."

"Gee, I'm not sure. I haven't ridden a bike in a long time."

"They say you never forget how."

She smiled at him. "That's what they say."

He thought for sure that she was going to refuse.

"I'd like to join you, Dakota. I haven't had much real exercise lately. But I don't have a bicycle."

"I can borrow one." He sounded overeager, and he knew it.

"Okay. Give me a call later in the week. We'll see what the weather does."

He watched as she got into her car and drove away.

Please, God, I know the die-hard skiers wouldn't approve of this request. But I'd appreciate it if You'd make the sun shine and warm things up for next Saturday. Just for one day.

Chapter Twenty-Five

"So just what *do* you believe?" Kevin leaned back in his chair, looking relaxed and handsome in his navy slacks and burgundy cable-knit sweater. "I'd really like to understand."

Instead of answering him, Claire glanced out the restaurant window.

Dark, low-slung clouds made midday seem like evening, and a steady rain splattered against the windowpanes. Kevin had driven over to her apartment right after his church service let out and had brought her to Sequim—across Puget Sound and north from Seattle—to indulge, as he put it, in a seafood feast. It had been both an enjoyable drive and a delicious meal. The entire day had been perfect...until now.

"Do you even *know* what you believe, Claire?"

Her gaze snapped back to Kevin. "Of course, I do. But why should I tell you?"

"Don't be defensive. Please. Just hear me out."

He was right. She shouldn't be defensive. But she hadn't meant to send the conversation down this particular path. Not again. She'd always believed that discussing one's politics or one's religion was the quickest way to make someone angry or destroy a friendship. Yet she knew it was different with Kevin. In the time she'd been in Seattle, she'd learned that he talked easily about his God. He talked about God the same way he might talk about a dear friend or a close member of his own family. The same way Dakota did.

"All right," she said at last. "I'm listening."

"Thanks." His smile was warm. "Here's my reason for asking. The Bible tells me that as a Christian I'm to be ready to make a defense to everyone who asks for an account of what I believe and to give them a reason for my hope in Christ. Should anything less be expected of you and your beliefs? Shouldn't you be able to explain it to me so I can understand?"

He was right. She should be able to articulate her own personal beliefs. And to her great surprise, she realized she wanted to tell him. Perhaps it was because no matter what she said, she knew that he wouldn't belittle her.

She began slowly, feeling her way with care. "Well, I don't doubt the existence of God. I don't think something as incredible and intricate as this earth, let alone the entire universe, just happened by accident. So I suppose there must be a Creator, a Supreme Being. I can accept that much." She paused to draw a deep breath and gather her thoughts.

Kevin waited patiently.

"It's organized religion I can't accept. It seems to me it's just a...a control thing. Besides, who's to say that only one way is the right way to find God? Why can't there be many different paths?"

"Ah. I see."

His voice was soft, his words simple. Yet Claire thought she heard pity within them, and her temper flared again. She didn't want his pity. His or anyone else's.

"How can *you* be so sure of yourself and your religion?" she demanded. "Why can't there be more ways than just yours?"

"Do you really want an answer?"

Sharply, "Yes, I do."

"All right. I'll tell you." He leaned forward. "The Bible says that you do well to believe in God, that even the demons believe and they shudder. The difference for Christians is Jesus, His death on the cross, and His resurrection. The difference is *knowing* Jesus, having a personal relationship with Him. You see, Claire, He's alive. He isn't just some historical figure. He isn't just a good or wise man from the past. He isn't just a prophet. He's the Son of God and He is one with God. He's as much alive today as He was two thousand years ago, and we can know Him. And I mean *know* Him."

She'd heard Dakota say similar words over the years, but she'd always turned a deaf ear. Now, for some inexplicable reason, her heart was starting to pump double time as she listened to Kevin.

What would it be like to believe, as Kevin and Dakota did, in a living Jesus? What would it mean if He really was here beside her at this very moment? But that was crazy. That was impossible.

"Mankind is separated from God by sin, Claire. We're all sinners and fall short of the glory of God. He's holy and can't tolerate sin, any kind of sin, be it a tiny white lie or murder most foul."

Well then, if that were true, there was no hope for her. Claire was well acquainted with her own shortcomings.

"But God also loves mankind so much He made a way for us to be reconciled to Him. That way is Jesus on the cross, and Jesus Himself said that He is the *only* way." Kevin reached across the table and took hold of her hand. "Jesus died for you. He looked into the future and saw you and counted it joy to die on the cross for Claire Conway. He loves you *that* much."

Did she believe in a love like that? *Could* she believe in it?

She resisted the pull of his words. "If God loves me so much, why did He let my marriage fail? Why did my son have to grow up without a father? That doesn't sound like a loving thing to do."

"Are you blaming God for what your husband did? Or the things you chose to do?" He asked the questions without accusation. "God gave you the freedom to choose, Claire. That's part of His love. He gave us all free will. The choice is always ours."

Tears streaked her cheeks, and Kevin offered her his handkerchief.

"I don't know why I'm crying," she said as she dried her eyes.

"Don't you?"

BELOVED, COME TO ME.

Her tears fell even faster. "No," she half whispered, half croaked, not knowing if she was answering Kevin's question or rejecting those softly spoken words in her heart.

"Claire…" He tightened his grip on her hand.

She knew she was making a spectacle of herself in the middle of the restaurant, yet she seemed unable to stop. She felt broken, all her secrets exposed. The weight of a lifetime of hurts and disappointments, lies and betrayals, bitterness and anger, pressed down upon her shoulders.

If God cared so much for her, why hadn't He made her life turn out differently? Why was she all alone at her age? Why had He let all her dreams be destroyed? If God loved her, why hadn't He kept her from so much pain?

She'd heard the verse countless times, about God loving the world so much that He gave His own Son.

But what have You ever given to me, God? Tell me that. What have You ever given to me?

She had a right to feel bitter and angry. Her husband had left her in the cruelest way. For years she'd had to struggle just to survive. She'd slept alone in her bed with no one to turn to for comfort or encouragement. And the worst part had been seeing the pain her son went through, how he'd suffered because he didn't have a father.

What sort of love was that?

DAKOTA HAS A FATHER IN ME, BELOVED.

But I haven't had a husband!

FOR YOUR HUSBAND IS YOUR MAKER, WHOSE NAME IS THE LORD OF HOSTS.

She didn't know where those words came from or why, all of a sudden, she believed them. But she did. It was true. It was all true. She wasn't alone. The knowledge filled her, invading every pore.

I'm not alone.

A seemingly endless succession of memories drifted through her mind—days and weeks, months and years, countless incidents where she could clearly see that God had been calling to her, drawing her toward this precise moment. She had rejected Him over and over again, and yet, He had never given up on her. He had loved her then. He loved her now.

Why hadn't she seen it before? Why hadn't she heard?

But none of that mattered. She saw it now. She heard it now.

"Okay, God," she whispered. "I give up. I give it all up, Jesus. I won't run away from You any longer."

It was as if she could feel arms wrapping around her, holding her close. Something happened inside of her. Something beyond description.

WELCOME HOME, CLAIRE, MY BELOVED. WELCOME HOME.

Chapter Twenty-Six

Sara Jennings was undeniably the most beautiful woman in the world. Bar none. Even dressed in sweatpants and a faded denim jacket and her hair in its usual ponytail, she was without equal in the looks department. And Dakota would dare anyone to say otherwise.

Better yet, she was beautiful within. He was more aware of that every time he was with her.

As far as he was concerned, Sara was perfect. He still found it amazing that she'd agreed to go on a date with him.

Well, okay. She wasn't thinking of this as a date. To her this bike ride was just an outing with a friend. He was going to have to work on that aspect of their relationship. But at least she was spending an afternoon with just him and without all the others from their church singles group. It was a start.

God had truly answered his prayer. The January weather was mild, in the fifties. The sky was a clear and startling blue. The sun shone warm on their heads and backs as they rode along the greenbelt, a paved pathway that followed the Boise River for many miles, right through the heart of the city and clear up to Lucky Peak Reservoir, east of Boise. This time of year, the giant cottonwoods were brown and naked, but it wouldn't be long before spring adorned them in shades of green.

Not that Dakota was looking at the trees. His gaze was more often than not locked on Sara. Which was why he didn't see the young skateboarder until it was almost too late.

He swerved off the path to miss the kid. His front tire clipped a milepost marker, then hit a foot-high tree stump dead-on. The tail end of the bike rose off the ground, like the *Titanic* just before it sank, and Dakota went sailing through the air. He tried to protect his head with his arms as he crashed back to earth. He felt dirt and gravel scraping the flesh from his bare hands and burning the skin on his elbows and knees right through his clothes. Then the wind was knocked out of him as he flipped over and landed hard on his back.

For a split second, he didn't feel anything.

And then he felt too much.

"Dakota!"

He opened his eyes to find Sara bending over him.

"Are you all right?"

"Define all right." He tried to smile at his own joke.

"Do you want to try to sit up?"

"I'm not sure," he answered even as he started to do just that. A very unmacho groan rumbled in his throat.

Sara took hold of his upper arm, gently assisting him to an upright position.

The skateboarder stepped into Dakota's line of vision. "I'm sorry, mister. I didn't see you."

He waved the boy off. "It's okay."

After a moment's hesitation, the kid dropped his skateboard onto the asphalt and rolled away.

Sara sank to the ground beside Dakota. "I'd give it an overall score of nine-point-four. It wouldn't take much to make it a ten."

"Huh?"

"The hang time was pretty spectacular, but the landing could have been better. Poor use of hands, and the tuck-and-roll method wasn't used. Automatic point deduction. Sorry."

"You're rating my accident?" He groaned again. "Don't tell me. You're glued to the television for every Olympics, both winter and summer games."

She laughed, and the sound was husky and rich. Beautiful, like Sara herself. She met his gaze, and her laughter faded, along with the music of the rushing river and the distant voices of others enjoying the greenbelt.

He wasn't quite sure how it happened. He leaned toward her. She leaned toward him. Each looked at the other's mouth. And then they kissed.

It lasted no more than a few seconds. When they drew apart and he could gaze into her eyes once again, he knew that she was feeling the same thing he did, that there was something special happening between them.

A verse of Scripture sprang to mind: *Like a lily among the thorns, so is my darling among the maidens.* It seemed to describe Sara perfectly. A lily. A beautiful, white flower, a symbol of purity and goodness.

A blush rose in her cheeks, and she glanced quickly away. "Maybe we should start for home before you stiffen up."

"Not yet. Sara…" He didn't continue until she looked at him again. "Let's talk awhile."

"I'm seven years older than you. I don't think we should—"

"Why does it matter?"

"People will—"

"Does the age difference bother you? Personally, I mean. Do you see me as a boy instead of a man?"

She hesitated a moment before she answered. "No."

"It doesn't bother me either. So I guess it isn't important what others think." ·

She nodded but didn't look convinced.

"Sara, do you believe God brings people together for a reason?"

"I suppose."

"Then let's find out why He brought *us* together. I'd like to know." If that were just a line, he knew it would've sounded corny. But it wasn't a line. He meant it. He wanted to know God's purpose and plan. He thought it just might be because he and Sara were meant to share the future together. He hoped so.

Sara turned once more toward the river. She flipped her thick ponytail over her shoulder, hugged her legs to her chest again, and rested her chin on her knees. "I'd like to know, too, Dakota."

I think she's got me, Lord. Hook, line, and sinker.

With her hands stuffed into the pockets of her jacket, Claire walked beside Kevin through the park. "Are you sick and tired of all my questions yet?"

He grinned. "Not yet."

"Sometimes this all seems too good to be true."

"I understand. It was like that for me when I was born again."

Overhead, a flock of Canada geese flew in V formation. Claire paused to watch their silent passage, shading her eyes with her hand against the glare of a sun hidden behind a wispy veil of clouds. Once the birds disappeared from view, she lowered her hand and said, "Dakota tried to tell me the truth. All those years, he tried. I just didn't listen. I wasted so much time."

"Christianity and the Bible don't make much sense to unbelievers." Kevin touched her shoulder. "That takes revelation knowledge."

"I'm not sure I understand."

"Let's see if I can quote from the Living Bible. 'But the man who isn't a Christian can't understand and can't accept these thoughts from God, which the Holy Spirit teaches us. They sound foolish to him because only those who have the Holy Spirit within them can understand what the Holy Spirit means. Others just can't take it in.'"

"Where does it say that, Kevin? What chapter and verse?"

He chuckled.

She frowned at him.

"Sorry. I couldn't help it. Do you know how many times you've asked me that same exact question in the past week?"

"A thousand?"

"Could be." He took hold of her arm and they started walking again. "And to answer you, the verse is 1 Corinthians 2:14."

She wished she had her Bible with her so she could look it up. She was like that all the time. She couldn't seem to learn enough. She wanted to know it all, experience it all, and understand it all.

Kevin laughed softly, and Claire was certain he'd read her mind. It had been this way between them often this past week. She'd turned to him countless times in countless ways. He'd taken her to the Christian bookstore and helped her pick out her new Bible and a host of study tools. He'd recommended devotional books and study books. And on Wednesday night, he'd taken her to a midweek praise-and-prayer service at his church. Claire had tried to hide it, but she'd been positively giddy with joy the whole time. It was such a good feeling, this lightness of being, this sense of unfettered liberty.

"Have you told Dakota yet?" Kevin asked, breaking into her musings.

She shook her head. "No. I've called him a couple of times, but he hasn't been in." She smiled. "This isn't the sort of thing I want to leave on an answering machine. It's too special for that."

"*You're* special, Claire. Remember that. You're a new creation."

The way he said it made her feel soft and warm inside. She hadn't thought a man could ever make her feel that way again, but Kevin Quade did. She wasn't sure what it meant. Was it merely friendship or could it become something more?

Again, he must have read her mind. His expression sobered, and he gave his head a slight shake. "The most important thing for you right now is to deepen your walk with Christ. Don't let anything get in the way of that. Not even me."

It seemed a strange thing for him to say. "I won't." Hadn't Kevin led her to Christ? How could he get in God's way?

"Right now, everything looks rosy to you. But believe me, being a

Christian doesn't mean life will be easy from here on out. It doesn't mean all your problems go away, as if by magic."

"I know that."

Silence stretched between them as he stared down at her. She felt his tender concern and again wondered if Kevin could become more than a friend.

"Tell me about Dakota's father."

"No!" Her vehemence surprised them both. She would have turned and walked away, only his hand on her arm stayed her flight.

"Wait," he said gently.

"I never talk about my ex-husband. Never. I've worked hard to forget him, and that's how it will stay."

"But you can't have forgotten him if you're still this angry. Whatever he did to hurt you, you need to forgive more than forget."

The memory of Dakota telling her he'd forgiven his dad flashed in her mind. Along with it, she remembered her bitterness, her sense of betrayal.

"Claire, Jesus died for him too. He deserves your forgiveness."

"It isn't that simple." She turned her back toward him. "You don't know what he did."

"Will your unforgiveness make a difference to him? Will he be punished by it?"

Claire closed her eyes. "Dave's dead. He passed away nearly four years ago."

"I see."

What did Kevin see? she wondered. He hadn't known Dave. He hadn't known the way Dave had hurt his family, betrayed them, rejected them. He couldn't possibly know what it had done to her. From what Kevin had told her, he'd been happily married right up to the moment his wife died. As awful as that must have been for him, at least he'd known his wife still loved him, even at the end.

⁂

Dripping wet from the shower, a towel wrapped around his waist, Dakota grabbed the phone on the fifth ring, just as the answering machine picked up. "Hello."

"Dakota?"

"Yeah, it's me, Mom. Hold on a sec. Okay?"

"Okay."

He dashed back to the bathroom, dropped the towel, and pulled on a pair of cutoff sweatpants. He was back to the phone in just over a minute. "Thanks. I just got out of the shower and had to dry off." He sat down on the sofa. "So how're things going? You getting that office in shape?"

"A little at a time."

"What do you think of Seattle?"

"The skies are a bit gray and weepy, but I like it. You wouldn't believe all the things I've been doing—miniature golf, a Broadway musical, the art gallery, walks in the park. Kevin took me over to the ocean last Sunday."

Dakota grinned. "Kevin?"

"Mr. Quade. Jack's business partner in this venture. I told you about him."

Yes, she had, but he hadn't been *Kevin* then.

"How are things in Boise?"

"Your house is still standing. The thermostat is set at sixty. There's no mail in the mailbox. All the doors and windows are locked."

"All right, you." Wry humor laced her retort.

"Just wanted you to know I didn't forget your instructions."

"I meant, how are you?"

He thought of Sara. "I'm great. Really great." He wondered if he should tell his mom about her, then quickly decided against it. It was still too early, and she was sure to make too much of it.

"Honey? There's a special reason I called."

He had to strain to hear her.

"I wish I didn't have to do this over the phone."

Dakota leaned forward, feeling alarmed. "What is it, Mom?"

"No. It's good news."

"So tell me what it is." He wouldn't relax until she did.

"You see, I've finally understood...Well, Kevin has helped me to see that..." She sighed deeply. Then the words came out in a rush. "Dakota, I've found Jesus."

For a moment, he thought he'd misunderstood her. It would have been easier to believe she'd won a million dollars in the Washington State Lottery. It was only three weeks since he'd seen her off at the airport. He could still remember her expression when he'd said he was trusting God to bring him a wife. How could something this momentous happen in such a short period of time?

"Dakota? Are you still there?"

"I'm here, Mom. I'm just...surprised." *Understatement of the year.*

"Of course you are." Her soft laughter rolled across the phone lines and into the earpiece of the receiver. "So was I. I still am. A little."

For the next fifteen minutes, he listened as she told him what had happened to her. He heard many things in her words and voice. Her awe. Her joy. Her eagerness to learn and grow. But there was something else. Something she was holding back. He wondered if he should press her to tell him, but a small voice warned him that, whatever it was, she had to work it out for herself.

"Dakota…I want to thank you."

"For what?"

"For all the years you've been praying for me. It must have been hard, the way I rejected everything you believed in. It must have hurt. I wish I'd been a better mother to you."

His throat tightened, and he felt uncomfortably close to tears. Somehow he managed to say, "You've always been the best. Always."

His doorbell rang before Claire could respond.

"Hang on again, Mom." He set down the receiver, then strode to the door and yanked it open to reveal John. "Wait till I tell you what's happened." He hurried back to the telephone. "I'm back."

"You have company?"

"It's just John."

His friend made a face.

"Give him my love."

Dakota held the phone away from his ear. "Mom sends her love."

"Back atcha, Ms. Conway," John shouted.

She laughed. "You boys must have an evening out planned," she said. "I can't imagine you showering for John."

It was Dakota's turn to laugh. "You're right there, but I won't tell him what you said." He ignored John's suspicious glare. "A group from church is getting together to play Balderdash. I've got the game board, so I'm required to be there."

"Then I'd better let you go. I'll call again soon."

"Hey, Mom." He lowered his voice and turned away from John. "I'm rejoicing right along with the angels in heaven over what's happened."

"Thanks, honey. You have a good time tonight."

"We will."

"Good-bye."

"'Bye, Mom. I love you."

"I love you too."

After she placed the receiver in its cradle, Claire sat on the sofa, staring at the phone. "How did you do it, Dakota? How did you forgive him?"

Those were the questions she'd wanted to pose to her son, but she hadn't been able to do it. She just couldn't mention his father to him. She couldn't.

Will my unforgiveness make a difference to Dave?

No, it wouldn't make a bit of difference. Dave was dead and gone. Why couldn't she just forget it?

Forgive Dave, Kevin had said. But he didn't understand. He didn't know the facts. He'd never been betrayed the way she had. He'd never been deserted. No one could understand what that had felt like, what she'd had to live through. If Kevin did understand, then he wouldn't ask her to forgive.

"No one could possibly understand what I feel," she said with certainty. "No one."

I UNDERSTAND.

The breath caught in her throat, and her heart started to hammer.

I WAS DESERTED BY ONE WHOM I LOVED. PETER DENIED ME THREE TIMES. ONE WHOM I TRUSTED BETRAYED ME. JUDAS SOLD ME FOR THIRTY PIECES OF SILVER. I KNOW AND UNDERSTAND, BELOVED.

"But I can't do it, Jesus," she whispered. "Don't ask it of me." She covered her face with her hands. "I love You, but I just can't do it. I'm not strong enough. I'll never be strong enough."

Chapter Twenty-Seven

A thick blanket of snow covered the ground and lay heavy upon the limbs of majestic pines. Smoke rose from the chimney of the lodge, the woodsy fragrance reviving happy memories of evenings spent around campfires. Parents and kids, bundled in parkas and snow boots, hurried to and from parked cars.

Here in the mountains north of Boise, there was no hint of the unseasonable warm spell the valley had enjoyed for more than a week. It looked and felt like what it was—the last day of January.

But Sara didn't mind the snow or the cold. Not while she was clinging to an air mattress and floating in the natural hot springs swimming pool, with steam rising from the surface of the water to form a misty cloud around her head. She closed her eyes and let herself enjoy it all.

She couldn't remember a period in her life when she'd been this contented. Perhaps it was just being home again after so long. Perhaps it was having several weeks off before starting a new job. Or perhaps she had simply reached a new level of maturity. But she thought it probably had more to do with Dakota Conway.

They'd seen each other every evening since their bike ride along the greenbelt, taking long walks, going to a movie or out to dinner, talking for hours. She'd discovered in all that time with Dakota that there was much to like about him. His interests were many and eclectic. He expressed his thoughts intelligently and was an equally good listener.

And he made her laugh. She liked that about him, perhaps most of all.

"How does a dinner of steak and prawns sound to you?" Dakota asked, intruding on her thoughts.

"Mmm." The throaty response was the best she could do. She felt too lazy to speak.

"Or the Lone Star's got great barbecue." He sounded as relaxed as Sara felt.

"Mmm."

The water stirred around her. She opened her eyes to find Dakota, his torso draped over the top of another air mattress, floating directly in front of her. Close enough for him to reach out and take hold of her hand.

"You're not going to fall asleep and drown, are you?" he asked. "Because if you do, I'll have to use mouth-to-mouth resuscitation to revive you."

What a wonderfully enticing thought that was. It might be worth swallowing some water in order to be saved by him.

His grin was positively wicked. She should have known it meant trouble. If she hadn't been lulled by the warm water, her brain distracted by images of romantic rescue, she might have realized he was formulating a plot against her.

Suddenly Dakota disappeared beneath the surface of the water. A second later his hands closed around her ankles. She squealed in protest, but it was already too late.

Down she went.

When they bobbed up, in tandem, Sara brushed the water from her eyes and declared, "You got my hair wet, Dakota Conway, and that means war."

Using cupped hands, she took the offensive in an all-out water fight. When it became obvious he was beating her at her own game, she grabbed a plastic bucket from the side of the pool and used it to toss water in his face.

"Uncle!" he cried at last.

Laughing and panting, they made their way to the shallow end of the pool where they collapsed, side by side, onto the step.

"Sorry," he said, sounding totally unrepentant. "I couldn't help myself."

"You *should* be sorry. Do you know how long it takes to dry this hair of mine?" She scowled at him but knew the look was unconvincing.

"No. Tell me how long it takes."

A shiver of awareness shot through her. "Hours. Hours and hours. If I had any sense, I'd chop it all off, the way I used to wear it in high school."

"I like it long." He reached out and took hold of her soggy pony-tail. "I think it's beautiful."

Her mouth went dry, and she felt lightheaded.

"But you'd be beautiful no matter how you wore it." He slid closer to her. When he continued, his voice was low and husky. "I think it's time I kissed you again, Sara."

She swallowed. *Yes.*

He drew near, his eyes staring deeply into hers. He moved with extreme care, as if she were a skittish colt tangled in barbed wire. When he kissed her, she felt treasured, special, and utterly desirable.

His hands came up to cradle the side of her head, and the kiss deepened.

She would have had a hard time explaining why, but she knew in that moment—with water lapping around her shoulders, her sodden ponytail tugging at her scalp, and Dakota's fingertips stroking her temples—that it was no mere passing fancy she felt for this man.

And it wasn't simply physical desire. It was something much more. Something much better.

The moment was perfect...right up until the beachball smacked their heads, knocking them apart. Impish laughter regaled them.

"Tommy Johnson!" The woman's voice was stern. "You apologize this minute."

"But they were smoochin', Mama. They shouldn't've been doin' that in the pool."

Their assailant stared at them from about fifteen feet away. Maybe seven years old with carrot-red hair, freckles, and a face that said Trouble! with a capital T.

"You apologize to those nice people this minute, or you'll get the tanning of your life when we get home. When I tell your father..."

Dakota stood and turned toward the mortified mother. "No harm done, ma'am. It was just a beachball."

"All the same, he needs to apologize. Tommy, you do what I say right this minute."

Tommy scrunched his lips together and narrowed his eyes.

"Thomas Roy Johnson."

That did the trick. Reluctantly, Tommy moved through the water toward Dakota and Sara. Sara could read the rebellion in his eyes. This kid was anything *but* sorry. If she were his mother, she'd have scolded him too. But she wasn't his mother, and all she wanted to do was laugh. He was just too cute to be angry at. She had to fight to hide her smile.

"Sorry," Tommy mumbled. "I shouldn't've done it."

Dakota sank down in the water again. "Apology accepted. Only from now on, you do what your mom says the first time she says it. Okay?"

"Okay."

"Come on, Tommy," his mother called. "It's time to go."

"But I said I was sorry!"

Dakota leaned toward him, saying in a deep, solemn voice, "The *first* time, Thomas Roy Johnson."

Sara was amazed by how quickly Tommy decided he'd better mind. He scrambled past her on the step and hurried toward his mother, who wrapped him in a large beach towel and ushered him into the warmth of the dressing rooms.

Dakota chuckled. "His mom's in for it in another ten years."

"His mom's already in for it." She laughed with him, then said, "You're good with kids."

He shrugged and smiled at her.

"Do you want children of your own?" She hadn't known she was going to ask the question until it was out.

"Yes. Several. I'd like a family like the one you grew up in. I want to take my kids camping and do all the sports things with them like baseball and soccer." His voice lowered. "I want to be a dad who's there for his kids whenever they need him."

His comment seemed more intimate than a kiss. Perhaps because it revealed more about him than he knew.

She took hold of his hand beneath the surface of the water. "You know all about my family, but we haven't talked much about yours. Tell me about when you were growing up."

⚭

What Dakota wanted to do was kiss her.

"Please," she whispered, her gaze locked with his.

How could a guy resist the gentle caring he saw in her eyes and heard in her voice? He couldn't.

"Not much to tell really. Mom raised me by herself from the time I was twelve. My dad's dead. There wasn't ever any extra money, so we lived pretty simply. I know she worried all the time about paying the bills and about raising me right, and I sure didn't make it any easier on her. I was what they politely call a troubled teen, right up until I became a Christian."

"Losing your dad so young must have been hard on you. I'm sorry."

He realized she thought his father had died when he was a boy. He hadn't meant to mislead her.

"What's wrong?" she asked, apparently seeing the consternation on his face.

"Listen, Sara. I made a promise to my mom many years ago not to talk about my dad. Not to anyone. Not even when she isn't around. You see, things didn't end well between them. So until she tells me different, let's just avoid that topic. Okay?"

"Sure." She looked a little hurt.

He gave her an apologetic grin. "I'll tell you anything else you want to know. I broke my arm when I was fourteen. Had my wisdom teeth yanked when I was sixteen. Or were those my molars? Oh, I've got a mole behind my right ear here." He showed her. "And I'm a sucker for dark red hair and beautiful green eyes."

As she returned his smile, he couldn't help wondering if their kids would have hair and eyes like their mother.

Claire supposed it was just as well that Kevin had been called out of town on business this past week. Being totally on her own—during the day while handling the myriad duties associated with setting up the new office and at home in the evenings—had forced her to do a lot of reading and studying, thinking and praying.

It wasn't that she didn't know what she was supposed to do. The Bible was clear on the subject. She knew. She'd read the words every single day and could repeat them from memory.

For if you forgive men for their transgressions, your heavenly Father will also forgive you. But if you do not forgive men, then your Father will not forgive your transgressions.

Yes, she knew what she was supposed to do, but she didn't know *how* to do it. How did she forgive Dave for cheating on her, for going to bed with other women, for rejecting not just her but the son she had given him? He had left them with no money and a ton of debt and just skipped out. How was she supposed to forgive him all that? She was the innocent party here. Dave was the one who'd sinned. He should have been punished. She remembered hoping he'd gone to hell when he died. He'd hurt her. He'd wronged her. Why should she have to forgive him?

She'd nursed this hatred for so many years it seemed impossible to let it go.

"Obedience is better than sacrifice," the pastor had said last Sunday.

It took Claire the better part of the week to figure out what that meant. And this morning, she'd read something in her devotional that helped even more. Faith wasn't about feelings, it said. If we only obeyed God when we felt like it, then few would do it.

Not about feelings.

Obedience.

Forgive or you can't be forgiven.

Obedience, not feelings.

And so on this cloudy and rainy winter afternoon, Claire knelt beside her sofa, bowed her head, and prayed. "Lord, I don't feel forgiveness, but if that's what You want from me, I'll do it. As an act of obedience, I forgive Dave. Now if You want me to feel it, You're going to have to change my attitude because I can't do it on my own. Amen."

She rose and walked to the window.

That wasn't so bad, she thought. Now she could put Dave completely out of her mind, once and for all, just as she'd tried to do before. This time it would work. Besides, there were so many good things to think about, so many wonderful things happening in her life now. Who wanted to rehash things of the past?

❦

The Lone Star was packed to the brim when Dakota and Sara arrived. Rather than wait forty-five minutes to get a table, they decided to buy steaks and salad fixings at the grocery store and return to Sara's apartment.

Sara was surprised—pleasantly so—when she discovered it was Dakota's intention to prepare the meal while she relaxed.

"Hey, this isn't the fifties. Guys cook." He flashed one of his charmingly crooked grins.

"I have a dad and three brothers," she stated with authority. "Trust me. *None* of them cook. When their wives aren't around, the best any of them can do is operate an electric can opener. Pork and beans is the usual fare in such situations."

"Well, maybe I'll just have to invite them over to my place for a few lessons." He flourished his right hand in the air. "Maybe I should have my own television show. 'Men in the Kitchen with Chef Dakota.' What do you think?"

She tried to imagine her dad and brothers learning how to chop an onion or marinate meat or bake something from scratch. It was so ludicrous that she laughed out loud.

"And what's funny about that?" He looked offended, but she knew he was teasing her. "Do you think I *couldn't* teach them a thing or two?"

"It isn't you. It's them. They're all hopeless." She shook her head, trying to stifle her amusement.

"Do I hear a"—he made quotation marks in the air with his fingertips—"*typical male* hidden in those words? If so, I take exception."

There's nothing typical about you, Dakota.

Her heart fluttered, and she found herself wanting to step into his arms. Forget dinner. She wanted him to kiss her. Over and over and over again. She wanted to melt into his embrace. She wanted things she most certainly should *not* be wanting.

Hoping he hadn't read her thoughts, she asked, "Did your mom teach you to cook?"

It was his turn to laugh. "No. Although she could have back when I was a kid. She used to have these great dinner parties. Everybody loved to come to our house for one of Mom's parties because she always served the best food." As he talked, he rinsed and shredded the lettuce, then started chopping carrots and celery. "She wasn't into parties by the time I was a teen. Just not enough money for that sort of thing. After I moved out when I was in college, she quit cooking altogether. I think she's lived on takeout for years. If she has to feed herself from her own refrigerator and pantry, she opens a can of pineapple and mixes it with cottage cheese."

"I know what that's like." Sara reached into the cupboard and got down two glasses. Her hands were shaking, simply because she was standing close to him. "Diet Coke or Sprite?" She hoped he didn't notice the quiver in her voice.

"Sprite, please."

"Ah, a boy after Dad's own heart." That, at least, sounded normal. "The rest of us are caffeine junkies. Everybody except Dad."

She got the drinks out of the fridge, popped the tabs, and filled the glasses, all the while remembering the kiss they'd shared at the hot springs and hoping for another.

Unexpectedly, Dakota's hands closed upon her waist and turned her about. And there she was, right where she'd wanted to be all along. In his arms.

His kiss was infinitely sweet and heart-stoppingly amorous. When he drew back, he closed his hands around her upper arms; Sara found her legs useless, completely without strength. If not for his grip, she would have fallen.

"Sara."

She looked up at him, still breathless, still weak in the knees.

"I'm falling in love with you."

I'm falling in love with you too. In fact, I think I already have.

With his right hand, he caressed her cheek. "You're so wonderful."

So are you.

"I've been looking for you for a long time, Sara."

Her throat felt tight. "I haven't always made good choices in men. I've made awful mistakes. For so long—"

"It doesn't matter what mistakes you made in the past. I'm not like any of those other guys."

No, he wasn't. Dakota was someone special. To be told he was falling in love with her was almost incomprehensible. Too good to be true.

And maybe it wouldn't last.

With that thought in mind, she whispered, "We've known each other such a short time. How can you be so sure what you—"

"We're not going to rush into anything," he interrupted. He drew her close again, his lips brushing her forehead as he spoke. "We're going to seek God's will and His timing in all of this. Let's trust Him to work out the rest."

Sara released a deep breath as she closed her eyes and allowed herself to surrender to his embrace. She would trust God, and she would trust Dakota.

As long as she did, nothing could possibly go wrong.

Chapter Twenty-Eight

"Happy Groundhog Day!" Alana shouted cheerfully the moment that Claire answered the telephone. "I don't know about Punxsutawney, PA, but I'm thinking winter's on its last leg in Boise. How about in Seattle? How's the weather?"

Claire grinned as she settled onto the sofa, listening to her friend's chatter. "A little of this. A little of that. Rain, sunshine, chilly, pleasant. You know."

"Jack's been talking about flying over to meet with Kevin and go through the new office. I thought I might come with him. What do you think?"

"That would be wonderful. I'd love to see you. When do you think you'll come?"

Alana laughed. "You know how Jack is. He'll have to think on it for ages before he makes up his mind." She let out a dramatic sigh. "I'm told that's why he's such a successful businessman. He always studies his options from every possible angle. But spontaneity might be nice on occasion." She hardly took a breath before switching subjects. "So, tell me how you and Kevin are getting along."

"Fine." Claire really didn't want to say more. She *thought* she and

Kevin were getting along fine, but she hadn't seen him since his return to Seattle this morning. They hadn't even spoken by telephone.

"I've always thought he was a super-nice guy. And handsome too. Don't you think so?"

"Yes. Yes, I do think so."

"Aha!"

Claire groaned. "Oh, Alana, please don't get started on one of your matchmaking rampages."

"Why not, girlfriend? You've been on the shelf way too long. Not all men are scuzzbags like your ex. Kevin Quade is a peach of a guy. Maybe a little too square with all his religion talk, but a peach of a guy nonetheless."

Claire wondered what her friend would think once she knew Claire believed all that "religion talk." And when should she tell her?

"He lost his wife years ago," Alana continued, "and he's got to be tired of going it alone. I just know the two of you would be perfect for each other."

"Maybe."

"I knew it! You *are* interested! Oh, Claire, that's terrific. I want to know everything that's happened."

"Nothing's happened. At least, not what you think."

Alana laughed. "I'll just bet it hasn't. Something's up. I can tell. Now I know I'm coming over with Jack. I've got to see this for myself. Claire Conway, after all these years, interested in a man."

It was pretty amazing, at that, Claire thought as Alana's conversation veered off in another direction, this time about her kids.

Fifteen minutes later, they said good-bye and Claire hung up the telephone. But her hand lingered on the handset as Alana's voice echoed in her memory: *You* are *interested!*

Guilty as charged. She *was* interested in Kevin—and as more than her spiritual mentor. She thought she could learn to care for him as a man, not just a brother in Christ.

But she wasn't so sure he felt the same way about her. Was it because he was technically her boss? Or was he simply not interested in her in a romantic way? Perhaps he still mourned the loss of his wife, despite his statement to the contrary. Or perhaps he was content with things as they were.

She could understand that. There was much to be said for living alone. She never had to cook a meal. She ate when she was hungry and didn't when she wasn't. If she wanted to watch TV, she could do so without arguing over what channel. If she wanted to buy something, she didn't have to take anyone else's tastes into consideration. She could turn on the light and read in the middle of the night and not worry about disturbing someone on the other side of the bed.

The other side of the bed.

Was it possible she might want to share it with a man again?

Twelve years ago, she'd welcomed her husband's attentions. But after his betrayal, she'd repressed any desire. No longer a whole woman. Undesirable. Discarded like rubbish.

Was it possible that could change?

"Would it even be good for that to change, Lord?"

◈

By the end of her first day as the new personnel director at Master Resource Industries, Sara was exhausted. Her brain felt ready to explode. Despite what everyone else seemed to think, she had serious doubts about her qualifications for the position. She was scared to death that she—and they—would soon discover Sara Jennings was a complete and utter fraud. Maybe she hadn't even deserved her degree. Maybe that had been a mistake, a fluke, the result of a computer glitch.

She drove home, fighting the urge to cry the whole way. She hoped a soak in her whirlpool bath would ease away the tension, but she doubted it would help.

The instant the door to her apartment swung closed behind her, she began stripping off her clothes. First her blouse, then her skirt, then her slip. The bra and pantyhose didn't come off until she reached the bathroom.

"I made so many stupid mistakes," she muttered as she turned on the water. "The file clerks know more than I do."

She poured a capful of vanilla-scented bath salts into the tub, then grabbed a pair of hair claws from the basket on her bathroom counter. Bending over at the waist, her head even with her knees, she brushed her hair toward the floor, grasped the thick shank with her left hand, and after straightening, she gave the mass of hair a twist before capturing it on top of her head with the claws.

What if they fire me?

She tested the water in the tub with her toes. It was hot, but not too hot. She stepped in and sank down. Closing her eyes, she leaned her head on the spa pillow at the end opposite the faucet.

I'm the personnel director. I should fire myself and save them the trouble.

What would she do if she lost her job? She certainly wouldn't find another position in Boise as good as this one. If she wanted to stay in

Idaho, she would have to return to clerical work. And even if she did, she would never earn enough money to afford the rent on this apartment or the monthly payments on her new car. She'd probably have to move back in with her parents.

Failure...Idiot...

She remembered the countless times she'd had to buzz her secretary, Raquel Gonzalez, with one question after another. Things that she should have known—or at least should have guessed. She could just imagine Raquel going home to her family and saying, "This one won't last long."

What will I do if I lose my job?

Sara used her foot to shut off the water. She wished she could turn off her thoughts as easily.

DO YOU ADD A SINGLE HOUR TO YOUR LIFE BY WORRYING, MY DAUGHTER?

"I *have* to worry, Lord! I'm blowing the best opportunity of what is supposed to be my new career."

She punched the control button, and the whirlpool jets roared to life, quickly whipping the bath salts into a swelling blanket of white bubbles.

Relax...Don't worry so much...Be anxious for nothing...One day at a time...

She silently repeated the litany of positive phrases in her head. But it soon became painfully obvious that she wasn't going to heed the good advice.

Frustrated with herself and with the whole world, she got out of the tub and dried off, slipped into her terrycloth robe, and headed for the kitchen. When all else failed, a gallon of chocolate-chip-cookie-dough ice cream was usually what the doctor ordered.

She was seated on the barstool at the kitchen counter, the container of ice cream in front of her and tablespoon in hand, when her doorbell rang.

"Go away," she mumbled before taking another spoonful of ice cream.

A few moments later, the caller knocked.

She closed her eyes, trying to shut out the sound of the intruder, and licked the spoon clean.

The bell rang again, followed by another knock.

"All right. All right. I'm coming." She went to the door and yanked it open without first checking the peephole. "Whatever you're selling—" She stopped abruptly when she saw Dakota, a bouquet of mauve-colored rosebuds in his hand.

His eyes widened...and then he grinned. "Great first day, huh?"

She could feel tendrils of hair clinging damply to her neck. She knew that her natural curls, fresh from her hot soak in the tub, must resemble a bird's nest—or worse. She hadn't washed off her makeup, and there was no doubt in her mind that smudges of mascara streaked her face. And the clothes she'd discarded upon her arrival home still littered the floor, a trail from living room to bathroom.

Well, if this didn't cap an already perfectly horrid day, she didn't know what would.

Dakota stepped closer and brushed the corner of her mouth with his right thumb. "Ice cream, I think."

Lord, could You please open the floor and just let me drop through it?

He kissed her. "Mmm," he said as he drew back. "Unfamiliar flavor, but I like it. Have any left?"

"What?"

"Ice cream. Do you have any left or did you polish it all off?"

She didn't know whether to laugh hysterically or burst into tears.

"Would you rather I went away?" he asked, his smile vanishing.

"No." It couldn't get any worse than this. Right? "You can stay."

He entered, walking into the center of the living room before turning to face her. "Whatever went wrong, I'll bet it wasn't as bad as you think."

"Yes, it was." She closed the door. "Oh yes, it was."

"Sweetheart, almost nothing ever is."

His endearment succeeded in bringing those tears to her eyes. She tried to turn away, to escape before he noticed them. She was too late.

He caught her by the wrist and drew her toward him, at the same time tossing aside the bouquet of roses before enfolding her in his embrace. He was tall and strong, and it was easy to lean into him and cry her heart out.

So that's just what she did.

"Shh." He loosed her hair from the two claws, dropping them on the floor. Then he stroked her head with one hand while stroking her back with the other. "It's okay, Sara. I promise you, it is."

"You...don't know...what a fool I...made of myself...today."

He chuckled, and the sound in his chest rumbled against her ear. "You're no fool, honey. And no one would ever think you were."

"But I—"

"No." With a finger beneath her chin, he tipped her face upward. "You're no fool."

He kissed her again. His mouth was warm and firm, and he tasted wonderful.

Better than ice cream.

She forgot about crying. She forgot everything except the extraordinary feel of his body close to hers. She hadn't felt this strong need in what seemed a lifetime.

Yet even with her hormones raging, she knew that Dakota would always cherish her. She would always be safe with him. Loving him, wanting him, didn't seem wrong or frightening. She trusted him with herself, with her heart, with her all. She wanted him to hold and kiss and caress her.

It would be so easy…

Chapter Twenty-Nine

Desire flashed through Dakota like a fire.

All that separated them were a few clothes. With a quick flick of his wrist, he could untie Sara's belt. The bathrobe would fall open, and he could feast his eyes on the woman he adored.

Would it be so awful? We love each other.

But he knew the answer in his soul.

Not this way.

He took hold of her shoulders and carefully but determinedly set her back from him.

Sara opened her eyes, a question written in them, along with a fevered look of passion that mirrored his own.

"No, Sara." His voice broke. He cleared his throat, then repeated, "No."

"Oh, Dakota."

"It isn't right. Not now. Not in this way. And we both know it."

She sighed, and a quiver passed through her. "Yes, I suppose we do." She took a step backward, moving from beneath his hands. She clutched the front of her robe, the gesture exemplifying her sudden vulnerability. "Maybe I'd better get out of this robe and fix my hair."

"Good idea." The room was much too warm. He needed some fresh air, and he needed it *now*. "I'm going to step out onto the balcony while I wait."

"I won't be long." She fled as if pursued.

Once outside, he welcomed the sting of the winter's wind on his overheated skin. He needed the cold to clear his head. Only it didn't do the trick. His lustful thoughts remained on Sara and the way she'd felt in his arms.

"I'm just a man, Jesus," he prayed. "Help me."

It hadn't been this difficult before. Sure, he'd felt all the normal sexual urges, but this was different. This was Sara.

The good things we want to do when the Spirit has His way with us, Paul had written, *are just the opposite of our natural desires.* Never had he understood that truth as much as he did right now.

He closed his eyes. "I'm doing my best, God, but I'm not sure I can win this battle."

IT IS WRITTEN, "YOU SHALL BE HOLY, FOR I AM HOLY."

That's a mighty tough gig, Lord.

"Dakota?"

He turned quickly. She stood in the open doorway, clad in a navy blue sweater and faded jeans. Her feet were bare, her toenails painted with hot pink polish. She'd put her hair up, back in those claw things he'd removed just a short while ago. She looked every bit as beautiful, every bit as desirable as she had before.

"I'm sorry," she said.

"It wasn't your fault. I shouldn't have—"

"You've never made love to a woman, have you?"

Male pride warred with honesty. When he was a teenager, guys would have sex one night and then brag about it the next day in the locker room. Here he was, twenty-four and a virgin. The world said that was odd, abnormal, unmasculine. He didn't want Sara to think him anything less than a man.

"Have you?" Her expression was troubled.

What was he ashamed of? Obeying God? Striving to do what was right even when it wasn't easy, even when everything around him said he was out of step with the rest of the world?

He shook his head. "No, Sara, I haven't."

"Because?"

"Because I made a covenant with God when I was sixteen that I'd wait until marriage." He searched for the right words to explain. "I come from a broken home. I know how painful it is on everyone. I don't want to repeat that pattern as an adult. I want to give my marriage every advantage for success, and the only way I know to do that is to follow God's plan for sex and marriage."

This was tougher than he'd expected it to be. He'd never talked about sex with a woman before, not even in general terms.

"And what is God's plan?"

He shoved aside his discomfort and answered her as best he could. "Well, I think it's for sex to be special and unique between husband and wife, a joining of more than just bodies. The marriage bed should be undefiled. That's the ideal, and that's what I want."

She stepped to the balcony rail, gripped hold of it, and stared off toward the river. "Have you ever been tempted to break your vow?"

"I've been tempted plenty." *You may never know how much.* "I'm just like any other guy. It would be easy to give in. And I know there'd be pleasure involved. But it wouldn't last. Sort of like eating an entire chocolate cake by yourself. Tastes good at the time, but you regret it later."

"Dakota…" She hugged herself, whether against the night chill or against something within, he didn't know. "I'm not a virgin. I had an affair when I was nineteen."

He waited to feel upset by the revelation, then realized he wasn't surprised, that he'd suspected this was one of the "awful mistakes" she'd referred to in an earlier conversation.

"Maybe we shouldn't see each other anymore." She said it softly, still not looking at him. "You deserve someone better than me. Someone…pure."

His heart nearly broke when he heard her say those words. He moved to stand beside her, then placed his arm around her shoulders.

Give me the right words, Father. Give me wisdom.

He kissed the crown of her head. "My darling Sara, weren't your sins forgiven when you were born again?"

"What?" She turned toward him, at the same time shaking off his arm.

"I think you're letting guilt rob you of the joy He means for you to have in Him."

Sounding brittle, she responded, "Then what about your *undefiled* marriage bed? I certainly can't give it to you."

Lord? What do I say to that?

"Can I?" she challenged.

A peace descended over him, and he had his answer. "Yes, you can."

"How? Tell me *how.*"

"Because when you accepted Christ, His blood washed you white as snow. You've been born anew into someone totally different. He removed your sins as far from you as the east is from the west. They're gone, Sara. They aren't just covered over, like trash beneath the snow. They're *gone.*"

The defiance left her eyes. Her shoulders sagged. "Maybe that's true, Dakota. But *you'll* always know what they were. You'll always know what I've done. If we let this go any further, if we…if we let ourselves love each other, *you* would always know another man took me to his bed. Maybe you don't think so now, but there would come a time when you'd look at me and see me as…as soiled goods."

He placed his palms against the sides of her head, forcing her to look at him. He spoke carefully, letting everything he was feeling and thinking and hoping resonate in his words. "Sara, I see a woman who loves God, who is seeking His guidance and wants to serve Him. I see a woman who was forgiven of all her past mistakes, all her failures, all her sins, someone who was saved by grace through faith when she gave her heart to Jesus. Just like I was."

"But—"

"No buts. He didn't say, 'I'll remove everybody's sins *except* Sara's.'"

Even as darkness closed around them, he could see the glimmer of unshed tears in her eyes.

"You want to know what else I see?" He lowered his voice. "I'll tell you. I see the woman I love, the woman I know in my heart God has sent to me."

"But what if you're wrong? What if God has someone better in mind?"

Tenderly, "An excellent wife, who can find? For her worth is far above jewels. The heart of her husband trusts in her, and he will have no lack of gain. She does him good and not evil all the days of her life." He paused, then added, "You are the woman I want for my wife, the woman I want to live with all the rest of my days. You're the woman I want to make love to, the woman I hope will be the mother of my children and my companion in old age." He brushed his lips across hers. "Will you be all those things for me, Sara? Will you marry me?"

As if only now understanding what he'd been saying, she sucked in a quick breath. "Marry you?"

"Yes, marry me."

"You said we weren't going to rush into anything. You said we were going to go slow."

"*Are* we rushing?" He caressed her cheek with his fingertips. "I feel like I've known you forever. How can that be rushing?"

"But you *haven't* known me forever. There's a great deal you still don't know about me."

"Do you love me?"

She started to shake her head, then stopped.

"Do you?"

She nodded.

"And if we were married, would you be able to promise that you would stay with me, forsaking all others, till death do us part?"

"You don't understand. There are so many reasons I shouldn't marry you."

"Could you promise me those things if we *did* marry?"

She hesitated, then whispered, "Yes."

"Then I know everything I need to know, everything that's important."

Taking her by the hand, he led her back into the apartment and straight to the couch. With a gentle pressure on her shoulders, he urged her to sit. Then he dropped down on one knee in front of her and took hold of her right hand with both of his.

"Sara Jennings, I love you. I believe in my heart that God has ordained this moment. If you marry me, I promise I'll never be unfaithful, that I'll love you as Christ loves His church, enough to die for you. I promise I'll cherish you, and I'll try always to think in terms of two made one instead of just thinking of myself. I can't promise I'll be perfect. I'll make mistakes. I'll make you angry. But I'll never hurt you intentionally, and I'll strive to make things right when I fail you. Marry me, Sara. I love you. Make me the happiest guy alive."

For several tense heartbeats, while silence stretched between them, he feared she might refuse his proposal. Then, ever so slowly, a tentative smile curved the corners of her mouth.

"Yes, Dakota. Yes, I'll marry you."

Chapter Thirty

Claire leaned over the table and stared at the blueprints. "I'm not sure about the conference room layout," she told Adam Fogerty, the general contractor. "Maybe we should modify it slightly."

"Whatever you say, Ms. Conway. We'll just need to know no later than next Friday."

"I'll notify you right after I speak with Mr. Quade." She straightened. "He's supposed to be in the office today."

"I'm here now."

She spun around, and there Kevin stood, framed by the doorway, looking entirely too handsome for Claire's peace of mind.

Since it was Saturday, he'd once again foregone suit and tie. This time he wore stonewashed jeans and a sweatshirt that, judging by the faded slogan on the front of it, appeared to be a longtime favorite. He looked ten or fifteen years younger than his actual age, despite the gray that peppered his hair.

Her pulse skipped a beat even as Alana's words repeated in her head: *I knew it! You* are *interested.*

"Sorry it's taken me so long to get over here. This week's been a zoo." Kevin approached, his smile relaxed and friendly. "It looks like things are really moving along. You're doing a great job, Claire."

"Thanks." Hoping she wasn't blushing like a teenager, she turned toward the blueprints on the table. "You should look at these. I thought the conference room should be modified from our original plans. I'm not sure we're using this space to its potential. Mr. Fogerty said it wouldn't be a problem to change."

Kevin stepped up beside her. "Show me what you have in mind."

She could hardly answer him. He was standing too close. She would have sworn she could feel his body heat coming through his sweatshirt. And there was his cologne, a particularly appealing scent although she couldn't name the brand. She hadn't paid attention to a man's cologne in years.

Somehow, despite the distraction Kevin presented, she managed to express her ideas in a halfway intelligent manner instead of sounding like a blithering idiot.

"Hey, Fogerty!" a workman shouted from another area of the building. "We need you over here."

"Let me know when you've decided," the contractor said, striding out of the room.

As soon as he was gone, Kevin looked at Claire. "You've got a keen eye. Let's go with your ideas."

"Don't you want a little while to think about it?"

He shook his head. "Isn't necessary." He smiled again. "How are you? I've missed our talks while I was gone."

"I'm good." *I missed you too.* "I took your advice."

"My advice?" He cocked an eyebrow.

"About my ex."

Kevin didn't say anything; he waited for her to continue.

She drew in a quick breath. "I always thought forgiveness was something I had to feel first, and I knew I didn't feel it for him. But I understand now that my part is to be obedient. So I *chose* to forgive Dave, just as you told me."

"It wasn't me who said that's what we're to do."

She felt a twinge of irritation; she'd wanted his approval. She wanted him to tell her what a good person she was for having been obedient. To be honest, she wanted him to be impressed by her self-sacrifice. He didn't seem to be any of those things.

A bit perversely, she told him, "I still don't *feel* it, you know."

"That's one of the great things about our Father. He's able to use what we're willing to give to Him."

She knew he was right, but she didn't want to tell him so.

Kevin seemed oblivious to her rebellious feelings. "One thing I've learned after all these years—being a Christian isn't a destination; it's a lifelong journey. There's always something new to learn along the way, always something fresh to be revealed."

"So there's no hope of ever getting it right?" She sounded as churlish as she felt.

"Claire"—he touched her shoulder—"is something bothering you?"

You're bothering me. I want you to notice me. To see me as a woman, and you can't seem to do that. I was better off when I didn't want to be noticed. This is starting to hurt, and I don't want to hurt.

"Have I done or said something to upset you?"

"No." She stepped away from him, looked at her watch, and said, "I've got an appointment. I'm running late. I'd better go." It was a lie. She had no appointment.

"I'll see you in church tomorrow?"

"Yes. See you in church." She grabbed her purse and jacket off a folding chair before hurrying away.

⚜

"Nervous?" Dakota asked as his Jeep rumbled down the freeway at sixty-five miles per hour.

"A little." Sara glanced at her left hand. A small but beautiful marquise diamond in a gold setting glittered on her ring finger.

"You think your family will disapprove of our getting married?"

As she looked over at him, she thought of her matchmaking sisters-in-law and the way her brothers had already accepted Dakota as a part of the family, expecting her to bring him along when any of them got together. Her parents liked him too.

"No," she answered. "I think they'd be more apt to disapprove if I *refused* to marry you."

"That's good to know." He grinned. "Will they think I proposed too soon?"

"Do you?" She knew what his answer would be, but she never tired of hearing it.

"No way. I'd have asked you sooner if I weren't so shy."

"Oh, that's rich." She laughed. "You have many different facets to your personality, Dakota, but shyness is one I haven't seen."

His laughter joined hers.

After a few moments, Sara turned serious again. "What about your mother? Have you decided when you're going to tell her about me? About us?"

"I want to tell her in person." He quickly met her gaze, then looked back at the road. "Are you sure you can't get a couple of days off next month? You could go to Seattle with me and meet Mom."

"No, I can't. I'm too new at my job. Sometimes it seems that I'll never catch up." She let out a sigh. "But at least I don't still feel like they're going to fire me."

"I never thought they would. You're too smart. They knew what they were doing when they hired you."

She smiled at him, her heart overflowing with love. "But you're prejudiced, Mr. Conway."

"Yeah." He grinned as he looked at her, his gaze lingering a fraction longer than last time. "Yeah, I'm most definitely prejudiced, Miss Jennings. I'm also right."

Thank You, Father, for Dakota. I don't deserve him, but You brought us together anyway. I love him so much.

"As for telling my mom," he said, interrupting her silent prayer of thanksgiving. "Like I was saying, I'll wait until I go over for her birthday. I want to be with her when I break the news. It's only another three weeks. That's not all that long."

"Will her feelings be hurt if you wait?"

He pressed his lips together, giving her question some thought, and then he answered, "Not when I explain why. She'll be glad I did it in person."

He flipped on his right-turn signal to exit the freeway. Ten minutes later, they pulled into the Jenningses' driveway. Sara's feet had just touched the ground when the front door opened.

"Dakota," Kristina called, "you're just in time to settle something about the Olympic hockey team or coach or some such nonsense. The boys and their dad have been arguing for the past fifteen minutes."

"I'm no expert on hockey, Mrs. Jennings. Olympic or otherwise."

There was a wicked twinkle in her eyes. "It doesn't matter. Just speak with authority, and they'll think you know what you're talking about. None of *them* do, that's for certain."

Sara took hold of Dakota's right hand with her left as they went into the house, both of them pausing long enough for her to kiss her mom on the cheek. Inside, they found the kitchen in familiar turmoil. Myrna and Fiona were rolling out piecrusts in the center of the table while Darlene tried to keep her twins, J.J. and Lizzie, from dumping the cat food into the pet's water dish—but she was too late.

Seeing Sara and Dakota, Darlene pointed a finger at them. "Listen to one who knows, you two. Don't *ever* have kids!" Then she went chasing after the three-year-old troublemakers who were making a fast getaway up the stairs, giggles ringing in their wake.

Dakota leaned over and whispered in Sara's ear. "Does she know?"

"Just hopeful," she whispered in reply.

"We'd better tell them before someone sees your ring." He squeezed her hand.

With her heart beating double time, the best Sara could do was nod.

He gave her an encouraging grin and led her to the doorway between kitchen and living room. Sara's three brothers were still arguing with her father, their voices blending together in one loud crescendo.

"Hello," Dakota shouted above the ruckus.

"Dakota!" Eli cried. "I'm sure glad you're here. Come in and tell these blockheads a thing or two."

"Be glad to. But first I need to make an announcement."

Except for the sounds of little children at play upstairs and the low drone of the television, the house went instantly silent. Sara looked from the men in the living room to Darlene, who was standing midway up the staircase, to her mom, Fiona, and Myrna in the kitchen. No one smiled. No one moved.

She could have cut the air with a knife.

He placed his arm around her shoulders. "I've asked Sara to marry me, and she said yes."

Another moment or two of silence, and then the whoops and hollers began. Sara was pulled from Dakota's embrace and passed from one person to the next, hugged and kissed by everyone. Her ring was ogled and admired and oohed over. Her mother shed a few tears, and so did Sara. She was dizzy by the time she found herself once again beside her fiancé. And from the expression on his face and the traces of lipstick on his cheeks, he'd been subjected to the same jubilant congratulations.

"Have you decided on a date?" Fiona asked.

"Not exactly." He placed his arm around Sara again and looked down at her with an adoring gaze. "She's still getting settled in at work, and my mother'll be working in Seattle for another two or three months. But we'd both like to get married this summer."

She felt all soft inside, special, loved. A summer wedding. Golden sunshine. Emerald grass. Vibrant-colored flowers.

"Fourth of July's on a Saturday," Josh piped up. "That way you'd have the whole country celebrating your anniversary with you every year."

"Good idea. That way I'd never forget our anniversary, would I?"

"You'd better not forget it," she warned with a mock frown.

Her brothers groaned in unison.

"Forgetting your anniversary has got to be one of the seven deadly sins," Tim said. "Trust me on this. Been there. Done that. Darlene still hasn't forgiven me. Have you, Dar?"

"No way," his wife answered. "I'm milking it for all it's worth."

Dakota's arm tightened. Sara looked up.

"What do you think, sweetheart?" He grinned. "Is July fourth okay with you?"

Sweetheart. She forgot the question, drowning as she was in the loving look in his eyes and the tenderness in his voice. *I'm his sweetheart.*

"Is it, Sara?"

"Is what?"

"Is July fourth okay with you?"

"You could have an outdoor wedding," Myrna said. "It's almost always nice on the Fourth of July. They do weddings in the rose garden at Julia Davis Park. It might not be too late to reserve it."

Eli stepped up beside Dakota and said in a stage whisper, "Giving up your independence on Independence Day. Man, will you ever be in for some ribbing."

Sara hadn't taken her gaze from Dakota. He wore a secret smile, a smile that was for her and her alone. She felt it right down to her toes.

"For Pete's sake, Sara!" Tim exclaimed. "Give the guy an answer. Tell him the fourth is okay."

"The fourth is okay."

His grin reminded her of the proverbial cat who'd swallowed the canary.

And then, right in front of her entire family, he said, "I love you, Sara, and I'll love you till the day I die."

And he kissed her.

She hardly heard the renewed howls and whoops from her brothers. Only the feel of his mouth on hers and the rapid beating of her heart seemed real.

❧

Kevin stared out of his living room window at the lights of the city. Beethoven played on the stereo. Bob—an ugly mutt of a dog, complete with a missing ear and a bobbed tail, that had adopted him two years before—lay on the floor next to the recliner.

I like Claire, Lord.

In those first years after Irene died, Kevin hadn't conceived of ever marrying again. When his wife was in the hospital that last time, her kidney failing, she'd told him he should marry again one day. She didn't want him to be alone.

"It would be a great compliment to me," she'd said, "if you would."

He hadn't understood what she'd meant at the time. But later, he did. They'd been happy. Despite never having children, they'd had a full and joyous marriage. To marry again would be to say he'd been happy as her husband.

He got up from the recliner and walked to the plate glass window. Streamers of white lights flowed along freeways and streets, some drivers making their way home from the city, other drivers coming into the city for events of various kinds.

It had been a long time since he'd felt this emptiness in his home. He'd been satisfied living here with Bob for company. He enjoyed the work he did. He was active in his church. His life was full of interesting people and new challenges.

But I want more.

He'd thought about Claire often while he was out of town. More than he'd expected he would.

Delight yourself in the Lord, the psalmist had written, *and He will give you the desires of your heart.*

Kevin had believed those words all of his life. And he did delight in God, with his whole being. What he didn't know was whether or not Claire *was* a desire of his heart. He thought she might be. He thought he might want to be more than her friend; he thought she might feel the same. He wanted to find out for certain.

And yet something seemed to be holding him back.

"Why, Lord?" he whispered. "What is it You're trying to tell me?"

❧

Dakota leaned against the stall door and watched as Sara brushed the big reddish-brown horse.

"Rusty won me plenty of trophies and ribbons," she said without looking at Dakota. "Didn't you, boy?"

The two of them had slipped out to the barn to escape the continuing celebration going on inside the house. While an icy winter wind caused the door to rattle, here in the barn it was warm and cozy.

"Rusty's twenty years old now," Sara continued as she stroked the white blaze on the animal's face. "Hard to believe. He was still young when I was competing." She turned toward the gate. "We should go riding sometime."

"Riding? You mean, on a *horse?*"

She laughed. "Don't look so scared, Mr. Conway."

"I'm more of a cold-steel kinda guy. You know. Motorcycles. Cars. Airplanes, even."

"You'll need to learn how to ride before the kids get old enough. We'll want to take the whole family on trail rides up above Idaho City."

"Hey, I think we've got a little time. Don't rush me."

She gave the horse one final pat on the neck before walking over to the stall door. She stopped opposite Dakota. "Four kids. Two dogs. Maybe a cat. At least three horses."

"A Jeep and a minivan. A ski boat. A dirt bike."

"A house in the country, two stories with a wraparound porch."

"A family room with a big-screen TV."

"A queen-size bed and a heavy down quilt in the winter."

He leaned toward her, lowering his voice. "A king-size bed, but me to keep you warm."

"Deal," she whispered.

"Deal." He kissed her.

He really was the luckiest man on earth.

Chapter Thirty-One

Claire checked the kitchen clock. Six-thirty. She looked at her watch. Six-thirty-two.

Where is he?

She almost wished Dakota hadn't called her from Yakima.

"The Jeep's running great, Mom," he'd said, "and I'm making good time. Should be to your place around five-thirty, five-forty-five. My cell phone battery's dead or I'd call you when I hit town. Don't worry. I'll get there just fine."

Don't worry. Easy for him to say.

She walked into her bedroom where the window overlooked the parking lot. No sign of the blue Jeep. Turning, she glanced at the clock radio. It was three minutes faster than her wristwatch.

What if there'd been an accident? What if he'd run out of gas somewhere? What if—

He's a grown man, not a little boy. He'd call if he had trouble. Being anxious won't get him here one minute sooner.

Claire returned to the living room where she sat on the sofa and turned on the television, hoping she would find something to engage her mind until her son arrived. She didn't. She picked up a magazine and started flipping through it until she saw something that looked interesting. She read for a few minutes, then realized she hadn't a clue what she'd been reading. Tossing the magazine aside, she rose and went to the bedroom again. Still no sign of Dakota's Jeep.

She wished that Kevin were with her. He had a wonderful way of putting everything into perspective, of calming her fears, of reminding her to lean on the Lord. But he wasn't with her, nor had she expected him to be.

Something had changed between them during the past month. It seemed he'd erected some sort of invisible but impenetrable barrier. He'd continued to be there for her in many ways, and he seemed to genuinely care. He was always generous with his time, always willing to answer her questions.

And yet the barrier remained; the message was unmistakable. Kevin didn't want more from her than friendship.

She blinked away unwanted tears, angry with herself for shedding even a couple. She shouldn't be so disappointed. It wasn't as if she needed or wanted a man in her life. She'd done just fine as a single woman. She had a good job, dear and trusted friends, and a wonderful son. She didn't need anything—or anyone—more than that. Besides, in a couple more months, her work in Seattle would be done, and she would go home to Boise. Home where she belonged.

She heard the Jeep a split second before it came into view. Her heartbeat quickened with anticipation. *He's here!* She raced out of her condo and down to the parking lot.

"Dakota!" she shouted as her feet hit the sidewalk.

Standing at the rear of his Jeep, he turned when he heard her. "Mom!"

A moment later, he caught her in a bear hug, lifting her feet right off the ground. He kissed her soundly on the cheek before he set her down. Then he stepped back and studied her with his eyes.

"Wow! Seattle must agree with you. You look terrific."

"So do you. Did you find your way here without any trouble? I was getting worried."

"There was an accident on the freeway that slowed traffic to a crawl. Guess I should've found a phone, huh?" Looping his arm through hers, he drew her back to his Jeep where he removed his duffel bag from the back compartment. "Want me to take you out to dinner?"

"No, I've got a casserole ready. I'll just need to pop it into the microwave to warm it up."

"You made a casserole? You mean from…*scratch?*"

She poked him in the ribs. "Don't you tease me about it, Dakota. I haven't forgotten how to cook. I just don't do it often."

"Often?" He grinned that lopsided grin of his. "Define often."

"Remember who you're talking to, buster."

"The woman who made my dinner?"

"The mother who can still tan her son's hide if she's a mind to."

"Oh, right." In one smooth movement, he dropped his duffel and swept her feet off the ground. "Just try it."

They both laughed.

After a moment, he set her down, and she took him up to her condo. When they were inside, he paused in the center of the living room and looked around.

"Gee, Mom, this is nice." He tipped his head back and sniffed the air. "Smells good too. Let's see. Green peppers. Onions. Tomatoes. My favorite, right? You're the best."

"Thanks. Feelings reciprocated." She motioned for him to follow while still basking in the glow of his compliment. "Come on. I'll show you where to put your things. You can freshen up while I get the food ready." She took him to the small guest room, then pointed out the bathroom and the linen closet. "Take your time, honey. You've had a long drive. We can eat whenever you're ready."

"Thanks." He tossed his duffel onto the twin bed. "It won't take me long."

Claire left him there and returned to the kitchen. She put the casserole she'd baked earlier into the microwave, pulled a tossed salad and two kinds of dressing out of the refrigerator, and placed sliced sourdough bread into a cloth-lined basket. Next she poured ice water into the glasses on the table and lit the tapers in the cut-glass candleholders. In the living room, she put an instrumental CD into the compact disc player and pressed *Play*, setting the volume low. They had so much to talk about.

It was going to be wonderful to share with her son all that had happened. She'd anticipated this evening for many weeks. Ever since she'd come to the Lord.

"Anything I can help you with?" Dakota asked as he emerged from the hallway.

She smiled, feeling a rush of pleasure at the sight of him. What a blessing to have Dakota for a son. God was indeed good.

"No," she answered. "Just make yourself at home. I'll have everything on the table in a jiffy." She hurried back to the kitchen. "So what's new with you?" she asked in a raised voice. "I feel like I've been away from Boise for a couple of years instead of a couple of months."

"I sorta feel that way too. I've got plenty to tell you."

The microwave beeped. Claire took the casserole out and carried it to the table.

"Will you ask the blessing, Dakota?"

He grinned. "I'd love to." He pulled out a chair for her, and after she was seated, he sat opposite her. In unison, they bowed their heads in prayer.

There was nothing fancy about his prayer over the meal, only a genuine thankfulness for all that God had provided. The sentiment echoed the feelings in Claire's heart.

"In Jesus' name, amen," he finished.

"Amen," she added softly.

In a heartbeat, Dakota reached for the casserole and helped himself to a giant-size portion. "I didn't know how hungry I was till now," he said when he looked up and found her watching.

"Hmm." She lifted an eyebrow. "Seems to me you were always this hungry. Two hollow legs."

"I'm just a growing boy."

"Good grief! I certainly hope not. Six-four is plenty tall enough unless you plan to start playing pro basketball."

Their good-humored banter, interspersed with more serious topics, continued as they ate their dinner. They talked about the work Claire was doing in Seattle and all the new sights she had seen. They talked about Dakota's job and his chance for promotion. They talked about her church and Bible studies.

Nearly an hour later, Dakota pushed his dessert plate away from him. "Mom, I've got something else to tell you. Something important."

His tone of voice told her this was more than just "something."

"I've met somebody."

"Somebody?" she echoed, but she knew what he meant. She could see what he was feeling in his eyes. Dakota was in love.

"Her name's Sara." He smiled. "She's really special."

"You wouldn't care for someone who wasn't."

"I love her, Mom, and you're gonna love her just as much as I do."

"Of course I will." She returned his smile.

He leaned forward. "I've asked her to marry me."

She hadn't been prepared for that. She was glad he'd found someone special. She wasn't sorry he'd fallen in love. But marriage?

"How long have you known her?"

"Two months." He chuckled. "I told her if I weren't so shy I'd have asked her sooner. We met the day you left for Seattle. Remember how I told you at the airport that God would bring the right girl into my life at the right time? I didn't know how prophetic that was going to prove to be."

"Just how did the two of you meet?" She couldn't keep a note of suspicion out of her voice.

"I ran into her parents and brothers right after you got on the plane. They go to my church. They were at the airport to meet Sara. She'd just flown in from Denver." His grin broadened. "I had it bad from that moment on."

"Oh, Dakota, don't you think you should—"

"It wasn't easy, convincing her to go out on a date with me. Sara's a little older than I am. Seven years to be exact. She thought it should matter—to me and to others—but I convinced her it didn't." He paused a moment before adding, "She's made me the happiest guy in the world by accepting my proposal."

She was ashamed of herself for not responding better. It didn't take an Einstein to see how happy he was, how very much in love.

"She's a Christian, of course. We've been attending the singles' class together at church." He leaned back in his chair. "But not for long. We'll have to start going to the class for married couples after July fourth. That's the date we've picked for the wedding. We had to wait for you to get back from Seattle but didn't want to put it off too long after that."

Claire couldn't think of what to say. She was confused and disturbed, and it was more than because it had happened so fast. What was wrong?

I'm jealous of her!

The realization horrified Claire. But she knew it was true. She was jealous. Not because Dakota loved Sara. Not because he wanted to marry the girl. No, she was jealous because Sara was a believer, and now Claire would miss all those deep biblical discussions with Dakota that she'd been anticipating. He would be sharing all that with his bride instead.

Which was as it should be.

"Mom? I thought you'd be glad for me."

Father, forgive me.

She rose from her chair and went to give him a hug. "I *am* glad for you. Really I am. You just caught me by surprise. If you love this girl, I know I will, too, just like you said."

Sara was in bed when the phone rang. She knew it would be Dakota, and she answered it quickly.

"Hi, sweetheart," he said in a voice that sent chills right up her back. "Sorry I didn't call sooner."

"It's okay. I knew you'd call as soon as you were able." She nestled down into her pillow and closed her eyes, envisioning him in her mind. "How was the drive?"

"Uneventful."

"The best kind. How's your mother?"

"Great. I told her all about you. You know, that you're pretty and smart and sweet and perfect and—"

"And older?"

"Yep, told her you're almost ready for a walker, you're so old. She can't wait to meet you. She's thinking the two of you might take some sort of geriatric aerobic class together."

"Very funny, Conway." She chuckled, loving his teasing, loving the tenderness in his voice.

"I showed her that photo of us with the church youth group when we took them sledding, but you're half hidden behind the McGrath kid. Guess we need to get some good pictures taken of us."

"And what did she think about our rush to the altar?"

"She thinks it's great as long as we love each other."

Sara wondered if that was true. How would she feel if she were in his mother's place? She wasn't sure.

"Mom says she'll be back home by May, so July's no problem at all. Think you could order the wedding invitations tomorrow on your lunch hour?"

"The white and purple ones?"

"Those were my favorites, but you get whatever you like best."

"They're my favorites too. That's what I'll order."

"Hey, there's something I didn't tell you."

"What's that?"

His voice deepened. "I love you."

"Mmm." She shivered with pleasure. "I love you too."

"Wish you were here."

"Me too."

"Bet you could still catch a flight up. We could wait for the weekend to go over to Victoria. How about it?"

"I can't get away, Dakota. You know that."

Soft laughter came across the telephone wire. "Yeah, but you can't blame a guy for trying."

"It's nice to be wanted. I'm glad you keep trying." She sighed in contentment

"You sound tired. I'd better let you get some sleep."

She was reluctant to say good night, but he was right. She was tired, and it was late.

"Dream about me?" he suggested.

"Probably."

"I love you."

"And I love you."

"I'll call you tomorrow night from Victoria."

"I'll be here." *Waiting, just as I was tonight.*

"I miss you."

"Me too."

"'Night."

"'Night."

"Sleep tight."

"You too."

Silence, then, "We don't seem to be hanging up."

She laughed. "I noticed."

"I didn't know I'd miss you this much."

"I didn't know Seattle would seem so far away."

"Are you sure you can't—"

"Dakota, don't ask again."

He sighed. "Okay, I won't. I love you."

"And I, you."

"You know what, sweetheart?"

"We sound like bad movie dialogue?"

He laughed. "Yeah, I guess we do."

"Say good night, Dakota."

"Good night. I love you."

"I love you too. Good night." Reluctantly, she placed the receiver in its cradle, breaking the connection.

Still smiling, warmed by the memory of the sound of his voice, she rolled to her side.

Thank You, Lord. I know I don't deserve him, but I'm so grateful You brought us together.

Dakota and Claire celebrated her forty-second birthday in Victoria, British Columbia, with high tea at the Empress Hotel. On Friday they visited Butchart Gardens where the azaleas, tulips, and daffodils were a visual springtime delight. They spent hours and hours on Saturday poking around the Royal British Columbia Museum. And they talked and talked and talked. About all sorts of things, but mostly about Sara—or so it seemed to Claire.

On Sunday they returned to Seattle where they attended an evening church service; the experience of sitting beside her son and worshiping God in song and prayer was every bit as special as she'd known it would be. It was also a bittersweet experience, because she was aware of the many years she'd missed doing this very thing.

Monday morning arrived before she was ready for it.

As she watched Dakota toss his duffel bag into the back of the Jeep, she realized anew that she would never again be as important in her son's life. Soon he would be a husband. Eventually, he would be a father. These were all good things. All part of the natural order of life.

Knowing that didn't help much.

Dakota turned around. "I had a great time, Mom." He embraced her, hugging tightly.

"So did I." She tried to swallow the lump in her throat.

"Hey, don't cry." He kissed her forehead. "You'll be home in six weeks. Less if we're lucky."

"I know." She wiped her eyes with her fingertips. "Tell Sara that I can't wait to meet her."

"I will."

"Dakota…"

He raised an eyebrow. "Yeah?"

"I'm terribly proud of you."

"Ditto."

"I wish…" Again she let her voice trail into silence.

He seemed to understand. "Yeah." He kissed her again, this time on the cheek. "I know."

Oh, this was silly. She'd never had any patience with clingy mothers who didn't know when to release their children.

She patted his shoulder, returned his kiss, and then took a step backward. "You'd better get going. You have a long drive ahead of you. Call me when you get to Boise."

"I will."

"I love you.

"And I love you, Mom."

She stepped onto the sidewalk and watched as he started his Jeep, backed out of the parking space and, with a wave, drove away. Even after he'd disappeared from view, she remained standing there, feeling that wretched sense of loss.

Feeling old.

I'm not old, she silently argued as she headed for her condo. *Forty-two isn't old. Women are still having babies at my age, for crying out loud. I'm* not *old.*

But she wasn't young either. She wasn't in that first blush of youth when the world lay before her, filled with possibilities. She could hardly remember what it was like to be in love with someone the way Dakota was in love with his Sara.

She thought of Kevin. What would it be like to fall in love with him? To be loved by him?

God, why does everything have to be so confusing? My feelings are all mixed up. I don't know which way to turn.

Chapter Thirty-Two

"So how was your visit with Dakota?" Kevin asked when he saw Claire in the office the next morning. He almost added that he'd missed her while she was in Victoria but knew he mustn't, even though she'd been on his mind constantly. The time just wasn't right.

"Wonderful, but too brief." She clicked the *Save* icon with her computer mouse, then turned to look at him. "He's engaged to be married."

"Were you expecting this?"

"No, I wasn't. He met the young woman after I left Boise. He never said a word about her when we talked by phone. I suppose he was afraid I'd think he was rushing headlong into something." She shrugged. "I guess I do. At least a little." Softly, she continued, "He seems to be very much in love, and Dakota isn't the reckless, impetuous sort. Sometimes I've even thought he was too levelheaded for his own good."

Kevin stepped into her office. On this floor of the building it was the only finished room, and it was complete with carpet, window coverings, and framed prints. It was furnished with a bookcase and filing cabinets, desk and computer, and everything else Claire needed to do her job. Personal touches—a photo of Dakota and a chubby angel figurine—added warmth to the room.

Kevin sat down on a chair opposite her, as he'd done often in the past weeks. "What are you feeling right now?"

"Lonely," she answered with absolute frankness. "I feel lonely."

"That's understandable." He wished he could take her in his arms and offer comfort. But he knew he couldn't do that either.

"Is it?" she asked.

"I think so. I've seen my nieces and nephews grow up, move out, get married, and start families. And I've seen what it was like for their parents. They've invested so much of themselves for so many years, trying to raise decent kids who'll become decent, independent adults. And all of a sudden, that's what they are. Independent adults. I'm sure I'd feel lonely in your shoes too."

She looked away from him, toward the window. He could tell she was lost somewhere in the past, and he let her be.

Jesus, isn't it possible for us to be together now? She needs me.

IN ITS TIME, BELOVED.

⚜

Alone. Claire didn't want to feel alone.

But when she looked at Kevin again, she found herself asking something she hadn't meant to. "Have you ever wanted to get married again?"

He answered without hesitation. "Yes, I've thought I would. I've been waiting for the right woman and for the right time."

Waiting for the right woman…Obviously, he thought he hadn't met her yet.

She looked at her computer screen, smarting from his answer and not wanting his all-too-observant eyes to notice.

"Claire?"

She bit the inside of her lip, trying her best not to make a fool of herself.

"Look at me."

She didn't want to, but she did.

"God has made everything appropriate in its time."

"I don't know what you mean."

He looked at her with patience and tenderness. "I'm talking about you. And me. I'm talking about us."

Her chest tightened. *Us?* Her breathing grew shallow. "What about us?"

"I wouldn't be honest if I pretended I didn't care for you. I *do* care."

What do you mean, care?

"I'm not oblivious to what's been happening between us. I think there's a chance for more than friendship. Much more. And I think you feel it too."

She couldn't believe it. Was he really saying this?

"I've been praying about us, seeking God's will, and I think I finally understand what He's telling me." Kevin paused, his gaze thoughtful, his expression compassionate. Finally, in a soft voice, he continued, "This isn't the time for us. Not yet."

The wind went out of her sails.

"He wants us to wait."

"Wait for what, Kevin?"

"It isn't our season."

He was rejecting her, and he was blaming it on God. How like a man!

"There's something you have to do in Boise. I don't know what it is, but it's important. It's something you have to deal with before your heart will truly be ready to love again."

He was giving her the brush-off, telling her to go home, and he was using God as an excuse.

Angry, wounded, agitated, she rose from her chair and went to the window. "Who said anything about love? Unlike my son, I'm not the type to fall for someone in a matter of weeks. I've never wanted anything more from you than friendship."

"I've hurt you. I'm sorry."

"It takes more than something like this to hurt me. I can assure you of that."

"Claire?" He placed a hand on her shoulder.

Surprised that she hadn't heard his approach, she turned. The way he looked at her was nearly her undoing. She didn't want his pity.

"Hear me out. Please."

She didn't want to listen. She wanted him to leave her alone. "I can't imagine what more there is for you to say."

"Have you ever watched an artist painting a landscape in oils? While he's working, while you're standing up close to the canvas, it doesn't look like much at all. Just splashes of color that don't have much purpose or connection with reality. But when he's finished, when he adds those last brush strokes, and we step back to look, we can see what he had in mind all the time. And it's beautiful."

"What has that to do with our...friendship?"

"I'm telling you God has a plan for our lives, and when He's done with this particular landscape, it's going to be wonderful and perfect.

We'll be able to see His hand in all of it. He's creating something beautiful between us. I believe it with all my heart. Be willing to wait, Claire." He leaned forward and kissed her cheek. "Please wait," he whispered, his breath warm on her skin. Then he turned and walked out of the office.

She spun toward the window, fighting tears, trying to swallow the lump in her throat, wanting to escape the crushed feeling in her chest.

I've been waiting all my life. Why do I have to wait some more? Why do You want me to be alone, God? Why?

⤙⤚

The night after he returned to Boise, Dakota took Sara out to dinner. They ate at his favorite Italian restaurant, but he wouldn't remember later what he'd ordered or how the food tasted. He was too busy staring at her, drinking in every little detail of her—the dazzle of her smile, the sound of her laughter, the glitter of joy in her eyes, the perfection of her mouth, the gleam of candlelight reflected in her glorious hair. He hadn't expected to miss her so much. It was only a week since he'd seen her, but it felt more like a year.

"You're beautiful," he told her, for about the fifteenth time.

She laughed, then said, "So are you."

"No, I mean it. I've never known anyone as beautiful as you are."

"Except you. You're more beautiful." She laid a hand over her heart. "Especially in here."

"What I am is blessed." He leaned forward. "Did you order those wedding invitations yet?"

"Yes. Why? Did you change your mind about the color or verse?"

"Neither of those. I was thinking we should move the date up."

"To when?"

"Next week be too soon? We could drive down to Winnemucca and be married in a matter of hours."

Her laughter was as beautiful as she was.

He gave her a sheepish grin. "I take it that's a no."

Still smiling, Sara took hold of his hand. "Mr. Conway, since this is the only wedding either one of us is going to have, I want to do it right. No rushing, no matter how eager the bride and groom. The full church wedding with all the trimmings."

It's what he wanted too. Still...

"You wouldn't believe how many things there are to do before we'll be ready. Besides, my mom would kill me if I deprived her of fussing over each and every detail. Trust me, I know. She's in seventh heaven right now."

"I don't guess my mom would be too thrilled either if we just up and eloped." He shrugged. "But it would be sort of romantic, wouldn't it?"

She lowered her voice. "Yes, it would. Everything you do is romantic. You always make me feel special."

"It's only because you *are* special. I thank God every night for bringing you into my life." He squeezed her hand.

"It is rather like a miracle, isn't it?"

"Yeah, it is. A miracle."

They sat in silence for a long while, oblivious to the crowded restaurant sounds all around them, both of them recalling the moment they'd met.

Some would have called that day in the airport merely a coincidence. Just a chance meeting.

Dakota and Sara knew better.

⚜

Submit therefore to God.

Claire removed her reading glasses and dropped them on top of her Bible. She covered her face with her hands while resting her elbows on the table.

Submit therefore to God.

She felt as if He was trying to tell her something in this verse, but she didn't know what. Everything was confused and jumbled.

"I don't understand, Lord."

AND THOSE WHO KNOW MY NAME WILL PUT THEIR TRUST IN ME.

I do *trust You. But I want to understand what's going on.*

Was she being punished for something? Her son was about to get married, and she was all alone at forty-two.

The only man I've been interested in at all in years believes You don't want us together. And he's going to do what he thinks You're telling him, no matter what I say.

She raked the fingers of both hands through her hair, brooding because she was stuck in Seattle until her work was done. She was going to have to face Kevin's rejection every single day, over and over again.

He says it's all part of some perfect plan, but it doesn't seem very perfect to me. She looked toward the ceiling. "I'm trying to live right." She raised her voice. "What more do You want from me? When do I get a break?"

MAKE ME LORD OF YOUR HEART, BELOVED.

"I have."

OF *EVERY* CORNER OF YOUR HEART.

"I have!"

Exasperated, she got up and went to the couch in the living room. She sat down, grabbed the television control, and pushed the *On* button. The room was immediately filled with the noise of gunfire.

Good. A senselessly violent movie. Just what she was in the mood for. She wanted it to be loud enough to drown out the small Voice in her heart.

It didn't work.

I WILL NOT SHARE YOUR AFFECTION WITH ANY OTHER GOD!

"What other god?" She closed her eyes and covered her ears. *Leave me alone. I don't understand anything anymore.*

Part Five: *Gladness*

But let the righteous be glad;

let them exult before God;

Yes, let them rejoice with gladness.

— PSALM 68:3

Chapter Thirty-Three

MAY

The instant the *Fasten Seat Belt* sign was turned off, Claire jumped up from her seat and reached for her carry-on in the overhead bin. Her heart raced in anticipation of seeing Dakota again and meeting Sara for the first time. The last two months in Seattle had seemed years long.

Not that her work hadn't been both interesting and challenging. It had been. But ever since the day Kevin asked her to wait and see what God wanted for them, she'd felt herself in limbo. She'd prayed until she had no prayers left, asking for guidance, asking what God wanted. But if He was speaking to her, she wasn't hearing Him.

She saw passengers begin to leave the front of the aircraft and heard the attractive flight attendant spinning off her litany. "Thanks." "Have a nice day." "Thank you." "Good day." "Thanks."

When Claire reached the young woman, she returned a smile as she hurried by. The moment she turned the corner in the Jetway, she craned her neck in an attempt to see over the heads of other passengers, looking for her tall son. It wasn't until she was almost to the door that she saw him. He was grinning from ear to ear as he waved at her, and she felt a rush of joy.

"Dakota!"

A few seconds later, she was crushed in his tight embrace.

"Welcome home, Mom."

"Oh, it's good to be back." Misty eyed, she drew away from him and laid her palm flat against his cheek. "You look wonderful."

"You too. You've lost some weight, haven't you?" As he spoke, he took the carry-on bag from her.

"About ten pounds. Thanks for noticing." She looked around for Sara.

"She couldn't be here," he said, answering her unspoken question. "Her boss sent her to Pocatello yesterday afternoon." He put his free arm around Claire's back and steered her down the corridor. "But she'll be home late tonight, and we're coming over to your house tomorrow. She can't wait to meet you."

"Likewise."

He stopped walking. "You really are gonna love her, Mom."

"I know."

He grinned before giving her another hug.

Thank You, Father, for making my son so happy. He deserves it. Bless his marriage with joy all the days of his life.

Dakota took hold of her arm and started walking again. "Mrs. Jennings is planning a get-together next weekend with you as the honored guest. She thought you'd like a week to get settled in again before you're subjected to a big family dinner at their place. There's a bunch of them, remember. But you'll meet everyone at church on Sunday." His grip tightened on her arm. "You *are* planning to attend Sunrise Fellowship, aren't you?"

"Of course. I missed a lot of years when I could have been going with you. I don't want to miss any more."

"My thoughts exactly."

At the carousel, they waited with the crowd of other passengers for the luggage to appear, adding their voices to the cacophony rising all around them. Dakota asked her about Alana and Jack Moncur's visit to Seattle. By the time she'd finished answering, they'd collected her bags and were headed for his Jeep in the parking lot.

Half an hour later, she unlocked the front door of her house and stepped inside, pausing in the entryway as she looked around the living room. She felt a rush of pure pleasure. She was home again.

"Feels good, huh?" Dakota asked as he stepped in behind her.

"Mmm."

"And look. Not a single plant died in your absence."

She laughed.

"Want these in the bedroom?"

She glanced over her shoulder. He had a bag under each arm and another in each hand. "Oh, put them down anywhere, honey. I'll take care of them later." She walked through the living area and into the kitchen. Sunshine spilled through the windows of the eating nook, brightening the pale green and white room. A bouquet of daffodils and tulips sat in the center of the table, and a plate of frosted sugar cookies, covered with colored cellophane, waited on the counter near the stove.

"The flowers are from me," Dakota informed her as he entered the kitchen. "The cookies are from Sara."

She turned toward him. "Everything's so clean and sparkling. You must have worked hard to get it all spic-and-span."

"John helped since Sara had to be out of town. She wanted to do it for you. By the way, John sends his love. He said to tell you—" The ring of the doorbell interrupted him.

Claire raised an eyebrow. "Who knows I'm even home yet?" She went to answer it. Opening the door, she discovered a floral delivery-man holding a beautiful springtime bouquet.

"Ms. Conway?"

"Yes."

"These are for you."

"Thank you," she said as she accepted them.

As she closed the door with the toe of her shoe, she heard Dakota ask, "More flowers? Who're they from?"

"I don't know." She sniffed a sprig of sweet-smelling lilacs before setting the flowers on the coffee table. "Here's the card." She sat on the sofa as she opened it.

Thinking of you.

Kevin

Her heart fluttered at the sight of his name; she wished it didn't.

"An admirer, Mom? Are you holding out on me?"

She shook her head. "They're from Kevin, but don't go reading anything into it. He was just being thoughtful." How she wished it were more than that.

BE PATIENT, the small Voice in her heart whispered.

Be patient. Be patient. I hear You, Lord. But what am I being patient for?

Sara had a difficult time keeping the car at seventy-five miles per hour as she drove toward the setting sun. She wouldn't get home until after ten o'clock at this rate. Too late to see Dakota.

She wondered if his mother had arrived from Seattle okay. She'd wanted to be at the airport with Dakota and had been more than a little disappointed when she was required to be out of town, today of all days. She'd already waited several weeks for the first meeting with her future mother-in-law.

She and Claire had spoken a couple of times on the telephone at Dakota's urging. But what could they say to each other when they'd never actually met?

What if she doesn't like me?

Dakota adored his mother. It was evident in so many of the things he said and did. If Claire Conway didn't approve of Sara, if they couldn't get along, what would he do? Would he still want to marry her?

But that was silly. There wasn't any reason why she and Claire shouldn't get along. Mother-in-law horror stories didn't have to be the norm. Look how fond all of her brothers' wives were of Kristina Jennings. That alone was proof her worries were groundless.

She smiled to herself, remembering the last time she and her mother were together.

"Oh, Sara." Kristina's voice broke. "Oh, my baby girl. It's breathtaking."
She sniffed. "No, you're breathtaking."

Sara swept the beaded train of the wedding gown out of her way as she
turned around. "Don't cry, Mom, or you'll get me started too."

"I can't help it." Still sniffing, Kristina searched through her purse
until she found a tissue. She touched it to the corners of her eyes,
then blew her nose. "I wish your father was here to see you."

"I think he'd better wait until just before he walks me down the
aisle." She suspected her dad would be even more emotional than her
mother.

The salesclerk poked her head through the opening in the dressing
room curtains. "Oh, that's definitely the one, isn't it?"

Sara nodded as she looked toward the mirror again. She didn't
know if she'd ever seen anything more exquisite than this gown. And
she should know. She'd tried on at least forty of them in the past few
weeks. But this one was special. Yards and yards of satin, lace, and
tulle. Hundreds upon hundreds of shiny pearls and beads. An elegant
ten-foot train. This was most definitely the one.

"I have the perfect veil for it," the clerk said. "I'll be right back."

Dakota's bride, Sara thought, hardly aware that the salesclerk had
spoken. She pressed her palms against her stomach in an effort to still
the tingling sensations inside her. *Dakota's wife.* In less than two
months, she would stand before him in this gown and pledge to be
his, forever and always.

"Oh, Mama," she whispered, her vision blurred. "I'm so happy, I'm
almost scared. What if something goes wrong?"

Kristina released a halfhearted laugh as she dabbed at Sara's tears with another tissue. "What could go wrong? Dakota loves you so much. It's evident to everyone who sees you two together." She hugged Sara, careful not to crush the gown. "I've never known a couple more meant for each other than the two of you."

"Here we go." The clerk entered the dressing room. In her hands she held a white satin hat with a wide brim and a long, delicate veil. She waited for mother and daughter to release each other, then stood behind Sara, holding the hat over Sara's head. "It will be spectacular with your red hair. See? You'd wear it at a slight angle. Like this." She put the hat in place.

The woman was right. It went perfectly with the gown.

And her mother was right too.

What could possibly go wrong?

◈

The chirping of her cellular telephone brought Sara abruptly back to the present. She flipped the phone open and held it to her ear. "Hello?"

"Hi. It's me."

She smiled, the mere sound of Dakota's voice causing her heart to race. "Hi, me."

"Where are you?"

"Almost to Twin Falls. I didn't get away as soon as I'd wanted."

"Shoot. I was hoping you were closer than that. Guess that means I won't see you until tomorrow."

She heard the words he didn't say. "I've missed you too."

Twitter-pated. That's what the Wise Old Owl in *Bambi* had called this strange, wonderful feeling in her stomach. All jittery and fluttery, like she'd just gotten off a carnival ride.

"Did your mother get home all right?"

"Yeah. And she liked your cookies too."

"Did you tell her I was sorry not to meet her at the airport?"

"Of course."

"I wish I could've been there."

"She understands, Sara. Hey, guess what?"

"What?"

Softly, "I love you."

The warm, curling sensation in her stomach intensified. "I love you." She never tired of hearing it or saying it.

"I told Mom we'd be over about one o'clock tomorrow. How about if I pick you up and we go to lunch first?"

"I'd like that."

"Okay. I'll be at your place by eleven-thirty."

"I'll be ready."

There was a moment of silence on the other end of the line, then, "I sure wish we'd eloped so that you'd be driving home to me right now."

Me too.

"You call when you get in. I don't care what time it is. I'll be up."

She loved the caring tone of his voice. "I will. The instant I'm in the door, I'll call you."

"Drive safe."

"I will."

"Keep it under eighty, will you, please?"

She chuckled. He knew her tendency for exceeding the speed limit. "I will."

After a little more billing and cooing on both ends, Dakota said good-bye and hung up. Sara pressed the phone against her heart, as if doing so would bring her closer to him.

Twitter-pated, indeed.

She laughed aloud as she pressed her foot down on the accelerator.

Chapter Thirty-Four

Clothes littered Sara's bedroom. Dresses and slacks and blouses lay in puddles on the floor. They were also draped over the back and seat of a chair and were piled high on the unmade bed.

"It still isn't right," she muttered as she looked at her reflection in the mirror.

She unzipped the blue cotton dress, let it fall to the floor, and kicked it aside, letting it join the others she had also deemed inappropriate for meeting Dakota's mother.

"I should have gone shopping. I should have bought something new."

A glance at her bedside clock told her Dakota would be there at any moment. Out of time, she groaned as she reached for one of the few remaining items in her closet.

"Please let this one be okay."

She'd just hooked the clasp above the zipper of the lime green jersey dress when her doorbell announced his arrival. With another groan, she went to answer it.

He grinned the moment their eyes met. "Wow!"

"It's too short, isn't it?" She tugged on the soft, knit fabric. "Maybe it's too tight. Do I look like I'm trying to be younger than I am?"

"No, no, and no." He gave her a quick kiss. "You look perfect. The dress is just right. I love that color on you."

Unconvinced, she turned from him, heading down the hall. "I should've put my hair up. It's a mess. I look like I just got up." Another glance in the mirror made her want to crawl beneath the covers and clothes on her bed and hide there.

Dakota appeared in her bedroom doorway. "Would you relax? You're meeting my mom, not the Wicked Witch of the West." He chuckled softly.

"You don't understand!" She whirled toward him. "I could throw a bucket of water on the Wicked Witch and melt her. I want your mother to *like* me."

"Ah, sweetheart..." He went to her and gathered her into a warm and tender embrace. "We've been over this a dozen times already. Mom won't be able *not* to like you. She's going to love you." He kissed the top of her head. "And it won't matter if your hair is up or down. It won't matter what you're wearing. It's who you are that matters, and that's who she's going to see and love."

"You're just saying that to make me feel better."

Another chuckle rumbled deep in his chest. "Maybe. But it's also the truth."

"It's not fair."

"What isn't?"

"You knew my family before you met me. You didn't have to be nervous like this." She tipped her head back and looked up at him. "They already loved you before I did. I think my sisters-in-law had us married before we ever left the airport."

One corner of his mouth lifted in the lopsided grin she adored. "You never stood a chance, did you?"

The tension began to drain from her. "No." She tightened her arms around him. "Not for a moment."

Dakota lowered his mouth to hers. Sara rose on tiptoe to meet him. The kiss was slow and sweet, and it restored her confidence, at least momentarily.

Claire removed the freshly baked coffeecake from the oven. Her stomach growled as the warm scent filled her nostrils, but she knew she couldn't eat a bite. There wasn't room in her stomach for food with all those butterflies in there.

Setting the cake on a rack to cool, she opened the refrigerator and removed the container of decaffeinated coffee from the tray in the door. As she measured the dark grounds into the filter, she noticed her hand was shaking.

An old saying repeated in the back of her mind: *A son is a son till he takes a wife. A daughter's a daughter all of her life. A son is a son till he takes a wife… Till he takes a wife… Till he takes a wife…*

Was she going to lose Dakota to Sara? She was prepared for things to be different, just as when he'd moved into a place of his own, but she couldn't bear to lose him completely. She knew it sometimes happened. She'd seen it with her own eyes in other families. She didn't want it to happen to her.

Claire closed her eyes and drew in a deep breath. She let it out slowly. She hated herself for having these thoughts again. It showed a weakness in character that she despised.

"I'm behaving like an idiot," she scolded aloud. "I will not cling. I *refuse* to."

She took another deep breath and pressed the button on the coffee-maker to start it brewing. A glance around the kitchen told her everything was in readiness. On the island counter was the silver tray that had belonged to her grandmother. Claire had polished it last night when she couldn't sleep. Three china dessert plates, three forks, and three cloth napkins in silver rings, along with the china creamer and sugar bowl, were already in place on the tray. Three matching china cups waited near the coffeemaker. All that was left to do was put the coffeecake on the platter. She would wait and do that after her son and Sara arrived.

She was just headed for the living room to watch for their arrival when the phone rang. She hoped it wasn't Dakota calling to say they weren't coming.

"Hello?"

"Hi, Claire. It's Kevin."

It wasn't necessary for him to identify himself. She'd know his voice across a million miles of phone line, let alone five hundred. "Kevin. What a nice surprise." She gripped the receiver with both hands, cradling the mouthpiece with one palm.

"I'm not calling at a bad time, am I?"

"No. Not at all. I'm glad you called. I wanted to thank you for the flowers. They're lovely."

There was a moment's hesitation before he said, "Claire, is everything okay there? Are you okay?"

"Why do you ask?"

"I can't explain it, but I've felt all morning like I'm supposed to be praying for you. I just don't know why."

309

She'd fallen in love with him while in Seattle, despite his words of caution. She'd tried to deny it. She'd tried to pretend she merely thought she *could* learn to love him. But the truth was it had already happened. She loved Kevin.

And now she missed him fiercely. She wanted him to love her in return. But it was obvious that he didn't want the same. Not yet anyway.

"Claire? Are you still there?"

"Yes. Yes, I'm here."

"*Is* something wrong?"

"No." A desperate laugh slipped up from her throat, and she was glad she had an excuse to give him. "Except for a bad case of the jitters. I'm due to meet my future daughter-in-law any minute. I guess you're supposed to pray about that."

"Then I will."

Claire listened as he spoke to their Lord with a quiet confidence she both admired and envied.

He finished with "Amen," and after a moment of silence, he added, "If you need to talk, I hope you'll call me."

Do you really want me to? "Thanks, Kevin. I appreciate it." She wouldn't call him, of course. She'd already felt the sting of his rejection once. She couldn't bear it again. It hurt too much.

"You'll continue in my prayers."

And you in mine.

"I'd better let you go. I'm sure you and Sara will hit it off instantly."

"I'm sure we will too."

"'Bye. Talk to you again soon."

"'Bye, Kevin."

She replaced the handset in its cradle, shaking her head in futility. Unrequited love might make for great romance in a movie, but in real life it was the pits.

⁂

Dakota glanced sideways at Sara. She looked as if she were headed for her execution. He'd hoped they'd taken care of that back at her apartment, but apparently the cure wasn't permanent. He reached over and grabbed hold of her left hand.

Startled from her thoughts, she turned toward him with wide eyes.

He gave her a wink, then looked at the road again. "Hon, you've gotta calm down."

"I'm trying. It's just…" She let the words drift off unfinished.

"I told you, you two are going to love each other."

With another glance he caught her nodding as she forced a pitiful smile.

He released her hand so he could downshift. Then he turned into the subdivision. A few minutes later, he pulled up in front of his mother's house.

"We're here."

He got out, hurried around to her side, and took hold of her hand again. He gave her fingers a squeeze.

When her gaze met his, he said, "I love you. So will Mom. She's standing at the door now, waiting to welcome you into the Conway family. Relax and just be yourself." As he helped her out of the Jeep, he added, "Everything's going to be perfect."

Part Six: *Despair*

I am poured out like water,

and all my bones are out of joint;

My heart is like wax;

it is melted within me.

My strength is dried up like a potsherd;

and my tongue cleaves to my jaws;

And Thou dost lay me

in the dust of death

— PSALM 22:14–15

Chapter Thirty-Five

When Sara's gaze fell upon the small snapshot, a disquieting shiver ran through her. As if she should recognize something about it.

She leaned in for a closer look. The colored photo in the inexpensive gold-toned frame was grainy, but it was good enough to see the broad grin on the little boy's face as well as the happy expression on the woman's face. They were seated on the grass in front of a house. A bicycle, complete with training wheels, lay on the lawn behind them, and off to the right she could see a few purple blossoms on a lilac bush.

"Who is this?" she asked Dakota, that unsettled feeling growing in her chest.

"That's me and my mom when I was...oh, about five, I think."

That house. That front door. What was it that made her feel like she'd been there?

"Where was it taken?"

"That's our old house on Garden Street. It's where I grew up. Mom sold it after she got a divorce, right after I finished grade school."

Garden Street.

It wasn't possible. It was just a coincidence. Nothing more.

"Dakota...what was your father's name?"

After a moment's hesitation, he answered, "I've told you why I never talk about him. I promised Mom I wouldn't."

It can't be. It can't be.

She looked up into Dakota's eyes. "What was his name? I need to know. I *have* to know."

"Does it matter that much to you?"

Just tell me his name is anything but Dave, and this will all go away.

"Yes," she answered. "Yes, it does."

"Porter. His name was David Porter. Why?"

No!

Panicked, Sara turned toward the kitchen. Dakota's mother was standing in the doorway. "Claire...*Porter?*" It couldn't be. It couldn't be. In just a moment, this nightmare would end. *"Dave* was your husband? He's Dakota's father?"

Claire dropped the coffee tray.

"What's going on?" Dakota asked.

Sara spun toward him. Surely, if she asked the right question, this would all go away. "Did your dad call you Mikey?" *Tell me no.*

"Where did you hear that?" His answer was as good as a yes.

She stepped away from him, needing him to hold her and yet unable to bear the thought of it. Was he Dave's son? Had she had an affair with his father? "It can't be," she whispered. "It can't. God wouldn't do this to us. He wouldn't do this."

"Would someone *please* tell me what's going on?" Dakota demanded, his voice rising. "Mom?"

Sara looked toward Claire, too, silently pleading for words that would make this all turn out right. And in that instant, as she looked at the woman who was supposed to be her mother-in-law, she knew this wasn't a nightmare. She wasn't going to wake up. It was all horribly, unbelievably true. Every sordid detail of it.

And yet, still she pleaded, "Say it isn't true. Please say it isn't true."

But, of course, Claire couldn't oblige.

Sara wanted to die.

Claire had once been Dave's wife.

Dakota was Dave Porter's son.

Sara had slept with his father.

She was going to be sick.

"I have to go," she whispered as the bile rose in her throat. "I have to leave."

"Sara!" Dakota called after her, but she was already running for the door, tears blinding her.

O, God, please let me die. Strike me dead. Please!

Dakota stared after his fleeing fiancée, then turned toward his mother. She stood like a statue, frozen in place.

"What's happening?" he asked again. "Mom?"

Without answering, she knelt and began picking up the scattered items from the tray.

Dakota didn't know what to do. Should he stay with his mother or go after Sara? Something horrendous had happened right in front of his eyes, but he didn't know what it was. He only knew both Claire and Sara were in pain.

"You've got to tell me what's wrong."

"Look at this," Claire said softly. "The sugar bowl is chipped. A tiny piece is missing. It must have broken when I dropped the tray."

He knelt in front of her. "Mom?"

She didn't look up. "How will I find a sliver that small in the carpet?"

"Mom, you've got to tell me."

I'm supposed to honor my mother.

"Please."

I'm supposed to cleave to Sara.

How could he do both?

Claire looked up. Their gazes met.

He wished they hadn't.

"I've got to find Sara," he said hoarsely. "I've got to go after her. I'll be back."

He took off running, his heart hammering in fear. As much from what he'd just seen in his mother's eyes as from anything that had gone before.

❦

Claire stared at the open door.

The spring day was bright and sunny. The happy sounds of children at play drifted through the neighborhood. The smell of newly mown grass was evident on the breeze.

How could this be? How could everything else seem so normal?

"I'm in hell."

NO, BELOVED. YOU ARE IN MY EVERLASTING ARMS.

A sudden rage gripped her, and she shook her fist toward heaven. "How could You do this? How could You let it happen?" She stood and shouted, "She *slept* with my husband! She destroyed my life. And now she's doing it again."

LOVE COVERS A MULTITUDE OF SINS.

Not this. Nothing could cover this. Nothing could fix this. Not ever.

Dropping the sugar bowl a second time, she left the house, not knowing where she was going, only knowing she had to escape, just like Sara and Dakota before her.

Dakota found Sara a half-mile from his mother's house. She wasn't running any longer. Nor would he have said she was walking. It was more of a stagger, like a drunk after a long night with the bottle.

He pulled his Jeep alongside her and shouted, "Sara, get in."

She kept walking.

"Sara!"

Still she ignored him.

He braked to a halt, cut the engine, jumped out. "Sara!" He ran after her, grabbing her by the arm and spinning her to face him.

Her cheeks were streaked with tears. There was no color in her face; she was as pale as a ghost. Her eyes, like his mother's, were filled with incomprehensible pain.

"Sara, you've got to tell me what's going on."

"I can't," she answered in a voice devoid of life. "I can't tell you."

"Come on." He guided her toward the Jeep. "I'm taking you home. Then you can tell me what's wrong." He felt like a broken record, playing the same bars of music over and over again.

She didn't argue with him. Listlessly, she allowed him to put her into his vehicle.

God, what's happening here?

As he hurried around to the driver's side, he replayed the scene in his mind, from the moment Sara had asked him what his father's name was to the moment she'd run out of the house. But he still couldn't figure it out. His mom and Sara had never met…and yet somehow they knew each other. Somehow they were connected.

He pulled out into traffic, his thoughts churning.

"I can't marry you, Dakota."

The Jeep seemed to roll back to the shoulder of the road by itself.

He gripped the steering wheel as he looked at her. "What are you saying?"

"I can't marry you." She stared straight ahead. "I'm going back to Denver."

"This is crazy. Why? Why can't you marry me? Why would you go back to Denver?"

"I…I can't tell you."

He felt a spark of anger heating his chest. "Well, I don't accept it. You can't break an engagement without *some* reason. Explain it to me."

She didn't reply. Instead she started to weep, her head bowed, her hands clasped in her lap.

His anger vanished as quickly as it had come. He'd never seen anyone cry this way before. Absolute silence, absolute stillness, while a flood of tears poured down her cheeks. It was like watching her die before his eyes.

He made a quick decision. He wasn't taking her to her apartment.

Not until she told him the truth. Not until they had this out and he understood it all. He would take her to his place. He'd keep her there until she talked to him. He wasn't letting her go without a fight.

Help me, Jesus.

⤜⤛

Claire didn't know where she was going. She simply got into her car and drove, following a gray ribbon of road without seeing it.

She ruined my life. She ruined Dakota's childhood. He was only twelve years old when she was with his father. Only twelve. It's her fault he grew up without a dad. It's all her fault.

Hatred filled her, blinded her, consumed her.

What was happening between them at this moment? Was she poisoning his mind against his mother? Was she telling him more lies, making sure he would believe her rather than the truth?

Of course she was. A woman like Sara Jennings always told lies. That's what she was all about.

How could You let this happen? she railed against God. *How?*

Could Sara have done this on purpose? Was it no accident they'd met? Had she sought him out because he was Dave's son?

Anything was possible. That woman was wicked and dishonest and—

A flash of color appeared in Claire's peripheral vision. A dog. A collie with a bright red handkerchief tied about its neck. A child running behind it.

She jerked the steering wheel to the left to avoid hitting them. The car swerved, felt as if it would overturn. She corrected, jerking to the right. Overcorrected yet again.

After that, a series of images flashed in her head.

The blacktop country road…

Tall field grass on an embankment…

A creosoted telephone pole…

The car crashed to an abrupt halt. The seat belt cut into her chest and waist as she flew forward. Her head struck the steering wheel. Pain shot through her.

And then she mercifully blacked out.

⁂

Sara was too numb, too cold, too empty, to realize where Dakota was taking her until he pulled into his driveway. She stiffened as she gazed at his house. "What are we doing here? I thought you were taking me home."

"Not until we talk."

Without a word, she unfastened her seat belt, got out of the vehicle, and started running.

Dakota was too quick. He caught up with her before she reached the corner. Grasping her firmly by the arm, he spun her to face him. "We're going to talk."

"Let me go!" She tried to pull free.

"No."

She pulled harder.

With a look of grim determination on his face, he said, "If that's the way you want it, then that's how it'll be." He picked her up, slung her over his shoulder like a sack of potatoes, and carried her toward the house with long, purposeful strides.

The fight went out of her. She hadn't the strength to continue. It was hopeless anyway. Everything was hopeless.

Dakota stopped at the Jeep and pulled his keys from the ignition, then proceeded to the back door, unlocked it, and entered. He carried Sara into the living room and set her on her feet in front of the sofa. With a gentle but firm hand, he caused her to sit.

"Now," he said, "you *are* going to tell me what just happened at my mother's. I don't care if we have to stay here until the Second Coming; we're going to get to the bottom of this. I want the truth."

The truth? Nausea rose in her throat, and all she could do was shake her head while pressing her hand over her mouth.

He sat beside her and grasped her other hand. "I love you. There isn't anything we can't overcome with love. You know that."

"Not this," she managed to whisper.

"Even this." A pause. "Whatever this is."

"Not this. I'm being judged, Dakota. This is my punishment for the sins I committed."

Pain, like the blade of a knife, pierced her middle. She bent over, moaning, hugging her belly.

Why didn't You just take me, God? Why must Dakota suffer for what I did? It was my sin. Not his.

"Sara, sweetheart, please." He tried to draw her into his embrace, but she wouldn't let him.

I want to die. Be merciful, Jesus. Just let me die.

Chapter Thirty-Six

Claire awakened to bansheelike screaming. It took a few moments to realize that she was in an ambulance, its siren wailing directly overhead.

Cautiously, she opened her eyes. Her vision was blurred at first, then it began to clear.

A male attendant leaned over her. "Hello."

"What—"

"Don't try to talk, Mrs. Conway."

She wondered how he knew her name.

"You've been in an automobile accident. You're on the way to the hospital."

An accident?

"You smacked your head and have a nasty bump. You've also broken your left arm. But you're going to be all right. You don't need to worry."

She must have been driving somewhere. But where? She couldn't remember.

"Was I...Was I alone?"

"Yes. The sheriff's deputy found your ID in your wallet. He said your family would be notified."

Her family…Dakota…

Something twisted inside her at the thought of his name, but for the life of her, she didn't know why.

⁂

Dakota listened from the other side of the bathroom door while Sara emptied her stomach into the toilet bowl. He wanted to go in, wanted to hold her, wanted to comfort her, to help in some way. But he sensed it would be a mistake to try, no matter how well intentioned.

He placed his hands on the doorjambs and closed his eyes. *Father, I need answers.* He leaned his forehead against the door. *Help me help her.*

The toilet flushed, and water started running in the sink.

He breathed a sigh of relief. Maybe now she would be able to talk to him. He took a step back from the door, waiting for her to come out.

The disruptive jangle of the telephone broke the silence. He ignored it. Let the machine pick it up. He wasn't moving from this spot.

"This is Dakota…" The words of his recorded message droned from the kitchen. "So leave a message and I'll get back to you. Thanks."

Beep!

"Mr. Conway, this is Ms. Barth at St. Alphonsus Hospital. Your mother has been in an accident. She's in with the doctors right now and will probably be staying—"

Heart racing, he grabbed the phone. "Hello? This is Dakota Conway. What about my mother?"

The woman briefly told him what had happened.

"Tell her I'll be right there." He hung up.

What more could go wrong? When would this nightmarish day end?

He'd never felt so helpless in his life. He didn't know which way to turn. He knew he should pray, but he couldn't seem to gather his thoughts enough to do so.

He turned. Sara was standing in the hallway, watching him. She looked wan and shaken, like he felt.

"It's Mom," he told her. "She was in a car accident. I've got to go to the hospital."

She nodded, silent, expressionless.

"I need you to come with me, Sara."

She shook her head.

"Please. I *need* you." He took a step forward. "Please, Sara."

He thought she was going to refuse. But after a long pause, she said, "All right. I'll come with you."

Claire felt just a moment of solace when Dakota appeared around the curtain. And then she saw Sara.

He'd brought *her* with him.

Claire had remembered, of course, what had happened prior to her accident. She'd remembered why she was out driving aimlessly. She wished she hadn't. The temporary memory loss had been bliss compared with this gnawing pain and the return of an ancient bitterness, a bitterness made worse by its brief absence.

I hate you. She willed Sara to read her thoughts. *I hate you.*

"Mom, are you all right?"

She tore her gaze from Sara and looked at her son as he approached her hospital bed. "They tell me I'll be fine."

"What happened?" He took hold of her hand.

"I swerved to keep from hitting a child, and my car went off the road. I hit a pole." She lifted her left arm, showing the cast. She tried to keep her tone light. "Six weeks. That's not so long."

"But the nurse told me you've got a concussion and that you're going to have to stay in the hospital for a day or two."

"It's nothing. Just routine observation."

"I think I'd better talk to the doctor." He turned around. "Stay with her, Sara. Please. I'll be back as soon as I can find someone to tell me something more." He hurried out into the corridor.

The expression on Sara's face mirrored the feeling in Claire's heart. Neither wanted to be alone with the other.

Tramp. Adulteress.

Claire wanted to do Sara physical harm, to get even. If she could get out of this bed…

"You don't have to worry, Ms. Conway. I told Dakota that I can't marry him."

Claire took in a quick breath, surprised. "Then why are you here?"

"He made me come. He begged me to. He was worried about you. I couldn't…I couldn't refuse when he didn't know how badly you were hurt."

"How kind of you." Sarcasm dripped from each word. "It would have been convenient for you if I'd died, wouldn't it?"

Sara took a step backward, as if Claire had struck her.

She wished she had.

"I'm sorry," Sara whispered. "I didn't know. I'm so sorry for everything."

A likely story.

"I was young and stupid. I never meant—"

"Stop!" Despite the pain it caused, Claire sat up. "Do you think being young and stupid excuses you for what you did to my family?"

"No." Tears ran down Sara's cheeks. "No, it doesn't excuse anything."

"Leave Dakota alone before you destroy him." She lay down and turned onto her right side, showing Sara her back. "Leave us both alone. Just go away."

Claire held her breath, listening to the hospital sounds—the swish of rolling gurneys, footsteps muffled by paper shoe-covers, whispered conversations between staff members. She wasn't certain how, but she knew the moment Sara slipped out of the hospital room.

It should have made her feel better to know she was gone.

It didn't.

Maybe nothing ever would again.

Chapter Thirty-Seven

Claire leaned against Dakota as he unlocked the front door of her house. Exhausted by the drive home, she desperately needed to lie down. Before they'd left the hospital, she'd thought the doctor's lengthy list of do's and don'ts and other precautions were unnecessary. Not so. She was weaker than she'd realized.

The two of them were midway across the living room before her gaze fell on the scattered china cups and other items from the coffee tray.

Dakota must have seen the mess at the same time. "You sit down and I'll clean it up."

She scarcely heard him, her thoughts plummeting back to that moment two days before when she'd dropped the tray, spilling its contents.

"Mom." With his hand in the small of her back, he urged her toward the sofa. "Sit down."

She did as she was told, watching him as he carefully returned all the items to the tray, then carried it into the kitchen. A minute or two later, he returned with a damp rag and some spray cleaner and began working to remove the cream and coffee stains from the carpet.

"Look." He held something up between thumb and forefinger. "I found the chip out of the sugar bowl. A little glue and it'll be like new."

"I'm glad." Claire leaned back and closed her eyes. She didn't want to remember how the bowl had been broken. She wanted to forget it all. She wanted it to go away. She wanted to pretend it never happened.

Moments or minutes passed. She didn't know which.

"Are you asleep?"

"No." She opened her eyes to find her son seated on the chair next to the sofa. "But I'd like to be. I think I'll take one of those pills they sent home with me. They knock me out pretty good."

"Before you do, I need to ask you about Saturday." He raised a hand to forestall any protest she might offer. "I let it be while you were in the hospital, but I can't wait any longer. I haven't seen or talked to Sara since I left her with you in the emergency room. I've left countless messages on her answering machine. I've been by her apartment. Her car's there, but she doesn't answer the door. I called her office this morning, but they said she's out sick."

I hope she is sick. I hope she's deathly ill. Claire pressed her lips together to keep from speaking her thoughts aloud. *I hope she's suffering the tortures of hell itself…just as I am.*

"I need your help, Mom. What happened between you two?"

It was on the tip of her tongue to blurt it all out. But then the haze of her hatred lifted enough for her to see his agony, and she knew she couldn't be the one to tell him the truth. It was going to break his heart, perhaps irrevocably. It was better for him to be confused than destroyed.

"I can't tell you," she said, closing her eyes again. "And it's for the best that you don't know. Honest, it is. Just forget you ever knew her."

"I'm not going to let her go without a fight." His voice rose. "I love her, and I want the *truth!*"

She sighed deeply. "Then you'll have to get it from Sara." In a whisper, she added, "It doesn't always set you free, you know."

The silence that stretched between them caused her nerves to screech. Finally, unable to bear it any longer, she opened her eyes. He was heading for the door.

"Dakota, where are you going?"

"To do just what you suggested. Get Sara to tell me the truth."

"You said she wouldn't talk to you."

He stopped, turned, and pinioned her with his gaze. "She will, because I'm not leaving her in peace until she does." With that, he left, slamming the door behind him.

DO NOT LET THE SUN GO DOWN ON YOUR ANGER.

She ignored the Voice in her heart. God was asking too much of her. She'd tried to be obedient before, but this was asking too much. She *refused* to listen to that still, small Voice. Not this time.

AND DO NOT GIVE THE DEVIL AN OPPORTUNITY.

"It's too late. The devil's already had his opportunity, and he's done his worst."

BUT I AM GREATER, CLAIRE. HEAR ME.

"I have a *right* to be angry!" she shouted as she rose to her feet. "I have *every* right."

Dakota rang Sara's doorbell and knocked for ten minutes before he decided to get help. He went to the complex's rental office and told the manager, a Ms. Hopkins, that his fiancée was ill. He said Sara wasn't answering the phone or the door and that he was afraid she might need a doctor, maybe even an ambulance.

"Her car's in its parking spot, so I know she's inside. I'm worried about her."

His distress was real enough, and that probably helped to convince Ms. Hopkins that she might have a serious situation in one of her units. She grabbed the master key and hurried toward Building G.

When they arrived at the apartment, Dakota realized Sara might respond to Ms. Hopkins if she heard the manager calling to her through the door. She might tell Ms. Hopkins that she was fine and to go away. Then his plan would be ruined.

To keep that from happening, he pounded on the door before the manager could do the same. "Sara! It's Dakota. Answer me. Are you all right?"

Silence was all they heard. He'd known it would be.

Ms. Hopkins looked up at him with troubled eyes, then slipped the key into the lock. She'd barely turned the knob when Dakota placed his palm on the door and pushed it open. He rushed in.

"Sara!" She wasn't in the living room or kitchen. She wasn't on the balcony. "Sara!"

He found her in the bedroom. She looked as rumpled as the bed she lay on. Dark half-moons shadowed the underside of her eyes. Her hair was limp and tangled.

"Is she—?" Ms. Hopkins began.

"I'll take care of her." He glanced over his shoulder. "Thanks for everything." He looked at Sara again.

She rolled over, turning her back to him.

He waited until he heard the front door close behind the manager before he spoke. "I've come for some answers."

No response.

He walked to the opposite side of the bed and sat down. When she started to roll over again, he stayed her with a hand on her shoulder. Unable to escape him any other way, she closed her eyes.

Help me, God. I need Your wisdom. I need to understand so I can help Sara. And my mom too. But how can I help them if I don't know what happened? How can I get her to tell me?

A verse from the book of Job came to mind: *Now as for me, I said in my prosperity, "I will never be moved."*

He couldn't see the relevance and tried to clear his thoughts.

NEVER BE MOVED.

I don't doubt You, Lord. My faith's not shaken.

HEAR ME, DAKOTA. NEVER BE MOVED.

Understanding dawned. Of course. That was the answer.

Thanks, Lord.

He tightened his fingers on Sara's shoulder. "You might as well start talking, because I'm not leaving here until you do. Whether that's a day or an hour, a week or a month, I'm staying."

"You'll lose your job," she said without looking at him. Her voice was low and hoarse from disuse.

"Then I'll lose it. I don't care."

"Go away."

"No." He leaned toward her, kissed her cheek, and brushed the hair back from her face. "I love you. I'm not going until I know what terrible thing happened and what I can do about it." He kissed her forehead. "Don't you know this is driving me crazy?"

A moment later, bleak green eyes stared up at him, and the pain he saw therein was like a dagger through his heart.

Maybe she's right. Maybe I don't want to know.

When she rolled to her other side, he let her, still shaken by what he'd seen in her eyes, what he'd seen but didn't understand.

<hr />

An hour later, Dakota heated soup in the microwave and brought it to Sara. But she didn't eat anything. Even if she was hungry—which she wasn't—she couldn't have eaten. Just the thought of food made her queasy.

Two more hours passed. Dakota continued to sit in the easy chair in the corner of her bedroom. He hadn't attempted to force another conversation. He seemed determined to wait it out, no matter how long it took.

By evening she realized there was only one way she would be alone again, and that was if she told him what had happened with Dave. Only the unvarnished truth would drive Dakota away, out of her life.

And that, of course, was what she deserved: to lose him. Forever.

She remembered the conversation they'd had in this apartment three months before. On the night he'd proposed. She remembered telling him he needed to find someone else, someone better, someone without her tarnished past. He was a good and upright man. His heart was pure. He deserved a wife with a heart as pure as his own. He hadn't a clue what evil she had done, what wickedness she'd performed.

And only knowing it would send him away.

I don't want him to go. I love him.

But there wasn't any hope for them. The truth had to come out. It *would* come out, now or later. It might as well be now.

And then I'll never see him again.

With her heart breaking anew, she sat up on the bed. "You win." She pushed a heavy mass of tangled hair over her shoulder. "Let's go into the living room."

Claire grabbed the telephone before the second ring. "Dakota?"

"No, it's me. Kevin." A hesitation, then, "What's wrong?"

Softly, "Everything."

"Can you tell me?"

"No." She doubted he could hear her.

"Do you want me to pray for you?"

Louder, "No."

"Claire, I—"

"No! I don't want to pray. And I don't want to talk to you right now either. I'm sorry. Good-bye." She hung up before he could reply.

She stared at the telephone as if it were something that should be thrown out with the trash.

"I don't want to pray," she repeated. "I don't want to be told I need to forgive her, and I know that's what he'd tell me. I can't listen to any-body telling me I shouldn't be angry. I *want* to be angry."

An icy chill uncoiled in Dakota's chest as Sara revealed the details of her affair with his father. She didn't make any excuses. She didn't attempt to pretty it up. In fact, she seemed determined to make it sound as sordid as possible.

"I didn't know he was married, but that doesn't excuse me. I could have found out if I'd wanted to. All the signs were there. He was secretive, evasive. He didn't give me his phone number or his address. He took me to dark restaurants and out-of-the-way places." She laughed without humor. "But mostly just to bed. He never even said he loved me. I was that easy."

"Sara—"

"Get it through your head, *Mikey*." She nearly spit the name at him, her voice rising to a near shriek with each syllable. "You were twelve years old and I was *sleeping* with your father."

He understood now why she'd been vomiting on Saturday. He felt like being sick himself.

"Go away." Whatever strength, whatever anger, whatever else she'd felt, it was gone now. She spoke in a monotone, emotionless, listless. "Please just go away." She looked down at her left hand, removed the diamond engagement ring, and held it out to him. "I forgot to give you this the other day."

"Sara…" he tried again, although he wasn't sure what he wanted to say.

She rose from the chair where she'd been sitting, stepped over to him, placed the ring in his hand, and closed his fingers around it. "Lock the door on your way out."

He caught the glimmer of tears in her eyes before she turned and walked down the hall, disappearing into her bedroom. A part of him thought of following her. But if he did, what would he say? What *could* he say?

"Is this how it's meant to end, Lord?" he asked softly. "This certainly can't be how it's supposed to end."

He got up and left the apartment, the sharp edges of the diamond cutting into the palm of his hand.

Curled into a ball on the bed, hugging her pillow to her chest, Sara heard the door close. Dakota was gone. He was gone at last. She'd done what she'd set out to do. She'd made certain he didn't have any straggling illusions about her.

She remembered the night he'd proposed. She remembered his words of love and devotion. She remembered the hope she'd felt, the joy.

And now it was gone. Gone forever.

"Good-bye, Dakota," she whispered. "I love you."

Chapter Thirty-Eight

The Boise River gurgled and babbled over the smooth boulders and stones that lined the bottom of the swift-flowing waterway. An eighty-degree temperature had joggers and walkers out in force along the greenbelt.

Dakota had a favorite spot on this stretch of the river, a place hidden behind tall cottonwoods and dense underbrush, a place where he couldn't be seen and where he didn't have to see others. He thought of it as his private oasis. He'd come here many times in the past to pray and meditate.

And so he'd come today to seek answers. He'd wallowed in misery and self-pity for five days. He didn't want to remain in that place of sorrow any longer. He needed to hear his heavenly Father's voice again. He needed to know what to do, where to go, how to cope.

Taking a deep breath, he gazed at the beauty of God's creation that surrounded him and suddenly remembered the first time he'd seen it. He'd been with his dad, both of them carrying fishing poles. He couldn't have been more than six years old at the time. He remembered the two of them laughing as his dad put his favorite fishing hat on Dakota's head.

Strange that he'd forgotten that day until now.

"How come you had to have an affair?" he asked his long-absent earthly father.

Sunlight glinted off the surface of the water. A dog barked in the distance. A hawk soared against a crystal blue sky.

"And why did it have to be with Sara?"

A trout jumped. The breeze whispered.

"She was only nineteen. You used her, and you betrayed Mom. Why'd you have to do it?"

He reached into his pocket and withdrew the engagement ring. The marquise diamond captured the brilliance of midday and nearly blinded him with its reflection.

"I miss her so much."

A pause. A heartbeat.

"I *love* her so much."

Sara with his father.

He closed his hand around the ring, squeezing tightly.

"Why?"

He could hardly remember what his dad had looked like. The only photo he owned of Dave Porter had been tucked away for years, first in a bottom drawer, then in a box of old keepsakes out in the garage. He hadn't looked at it in ages, not since the last time he'd moved.

No, he couldn't remember what his dad had looked like. Could Sara remember?

"Why, Dad?"

Sara with his father. Sara kissing his father. Sara in bed with his father.

"Why'd you have to do it? Why'd you have to cheat on Mom? Now you're dead. It's just like you ran out on us all over again. You're gone, and look at all the pain you left the rest of us to deal with." He knocked the heel of his athletic shoe against the dark, hard-packed soil, pounding it in an expression of frustration, anger, pain. When he stopped, he added, "What were you thinking? Why didn't you care what you were doing to others? Why'd you have to be so selfish? Why'd you have to misuse Mom and Sara the way you did?"

He didn't know the answers, of course, because he'd never known his dad. Not really. He hadn't had the chance to.

"You're gone but the hurt remains. Hurt always lasts, doesn't it? It takes on a life of its own, and it lasts and lasts."

NO, DAKOTA. IT'S MY LOVE THAT LASTS. ALL ELSE WILL PASS AWAY, BUT NOT MY LOVE, BELOVED. NOT MY LOVE.

Hearing that familiar Voice in his heart, he released a sigh. For days now, God had felt far away, remote, inaccessible. Dakota had tried to pray, but ever since Sara revealed why she couldn't marry him, he'd felt all those prayers bouncing right back to him.

Abba, I don't know how to handle this.

I WILL BE YOUR COMFORT.

"Jesus," he whispered, the name a prayer all its own. "Take this from me, because I can't bear it." He pressed his fist—the ring still clutched within—against his forehead. "It hurts."

He sat in silence for a long time after that, listening to the soothing song of the river, to the gentle whisper of the cottonwood leaves, waiting for the pain to ease.

The sanctuary at Sunrise Fellowship was cool and dim, the only light filtered through stained-glass windows. The building was totally silent, seemingly deserted.

Except for Sara.

She paused midway up the center aisle and stared at the huge oak cross that hung on the wall above the pulpit. It was draped with a purple robe and crowned with a circlet of thorns. She dropped her gaze, feeling unworthy to look upon the symbol of Christ's sacrificial love.

With slow steps, she proceeded to the prayer altar. She knelt on the carpeted step and leaned her arms on the wooden banister, bowing her head and clasping her hands. There were no words, no expressions for what she was feeling. The most she could do was whisper, "Forgive me…I'm so sorry…Forgive me…"

God was silent, as He'd been all week, as she expected Him to remain. After all, she was only reaping the harvest of what she'd sown. This was her justly deserved punishment.

GRACE…

The single word seemed almost audible. She opened her eyes and looked behind her, halfway expecting to find the pastor standing there. But she was still alone in the sanctuary.

Turning her head, she stared upward at the cross.

"Forgive me."

There was only silence.

"I thought I'd find you here," John said.

Dakota looked over his shoulder and watched as his friend pushed aside the dense growth to make his way toward the riverbank. "Shouldn't you be at work?"

With a shrug, John answered, "Nobody else seems to be working today. You're not. Your mom's not." He sank down beside Dakota. "Something's going on, and I figured you might need an ear. I'm willing to listen."

"I needed to think and pray before I could talk about it with anybody."

John nodded, his expression neutral. He wasn't the sort to press.

"Sara broke our engagement last weekend."

That caused a slight widening of John's eyes. Nothing more.

"The reason has to do with both Mom and Sara. And me, too, in a way. I can't tell you the whole story. It would be betraying a confidence if I did."

"That's okay. God already knows the details."

"Yeah." He picked up a rock and tossed it as far as he could. It landed just short of the other bank, water splashing high, ripples circling the surface.

John placed a hand on Dakota's shoulder.

Dakota wasn't surprised by the comfort he gained from it. His friend had been at his side in more than one crisis in his lifetime. John didn't judge or try to find immediate answers. He was a quiet and steady presence. Just what Dakota needed at the moment.

"It looks really hopeless, John. No matter how hard I try, I can't find a solution."

His friend's grip tightened.

"But while I've been sitting here, I got the feeling it isn't over yet. The Lord's doing a work of some kind. I just don't know what it is."

"Maybe you don't need to know. At least not yet."

In God's time, Dakota thought, knowing that was one of the things he'd learned that afternoon beside the river. He was supposed to wait upon the Lord. He was supposed to take his hands off the situation and not try to fix it himself. He was being called to love Sara and his mother and to pray for God's will to be done in their lives as well as in his own. That might not mean what he wanted it to mean. It might mean Sara left his life forever.

But losing her wasn't what he wanted. He wanted everything to be the way it was before. He wanted things to miraculously be all right.

He wanted Sara never to have had that affair with his father.

The raw ache in his chest flared anew.

Could he have been wrong about her being the woman the Lord intended for him? Perhaps. How could he love her, knowing what he now knew?

God's voice in his heart was undeniably clear. THOUGH YOUR SINS ARE AS SCARLET, THEY WILL BE AS WHITE AS SNOW; THOUGH THEY ARE RED LIKE CRIMSON, THEY WILL BE LIKE WOOL.

He'd once told Sara the same thing. He'd told her that Jesus' blood had washed her clean from her past. Had he meant it? Did he believe it? Would he have said it if he'd known about her past?

"Dakota?"

"Hmm."

"Maybe what's happening here isn't what you think. Maybe God's taking something bad and turning it into something beautiful."

He looked up at the sky. *Turning this mess into something beautiful.* "That would take a miracle."

"But God's in the miracle business, Dakota."

Chapter Thirty-Nine

For Claire, the days passed with agonizing slowness.

Dakota was the dutiful son, checking on her daily, seeing to her needs, driving her to her doctor's appointment, and picking up her medication at the drugstore. Yet even when with her, he wasn't really with her, and she knew why. Not that he explained anything to her. He didn't so much as mention Sara's name. But Claire knew she must have confessed everything; the younger woman had made good on her promise that she wouldn't marry him.

Claire should have felt victorious. She should have felt vindicated. She didn't. Not when she looked at Dakota and saw his misery. Not when bitterness overtook and consumed her like a putrefying wound.

She recognized, reluctantly, that she was still shaking her fist at the Almighty, just as she'd done on the day her son had brought *that woman* into her home. On that afternoon, her fist shaking had been a physical act. Now she was doing it in her heart. And perhaps that was worse. Even though she hadn't been a Christian long, she knew this wasn't what God the Father had called her to feel and to be. Yet knowing it and doing something about it were totally different things.

The doorbell rang just as Claire hung up the telephone, a call from Alana, checking on Claire's physical well-being. She considered ignoring whoever was at the door. Dakota had been by this morning, so she knew it wasn't him, and she didn't want to deal with a salesman or some kid trying to raise money for a school or church project. She didn't want to deal with life. Period.

The second time the bell rang, she knew this person wasn't going away without being told to.

Moving a bit stiffly, her muscles aching, she walked to the front door and jerked it open with obvious irritation, an angry send-off perched on the tip of her tongue. She swallowed it the instant she saw him.

"Hello." Kevin's smile was warm, his gaze concerned. "I was in town on business. Jack told me about your accident. I thought you might need…" With a shrug, he let the explanation drift into silence.

Confusion raged in her chest. She was glad to see him. More glad than she'd thought possible. More glad than she wanted to be. At the same time, she wished he weren't here. Instinctively, she knew his mere presence would shine a light on the dark things in her heart. She didn't want them exposed.

He raised an eyebrow. "May I come in?"

Send him away.

"Please."

She stepped back, holding the door open wide. "Of course. I didn't mean to be rude." With her good arm, she motioned toward the sofa. "Would you like some coffee? I can make decaf. Or I've got a few diet sodas in the fridge."

"No. I'm fine. Thanks." He sat on the sofa, leaving room beside him. She took the chair instead.

"You've got a lovely home," he said as his gaze roamed over the room. When he met her eyes again, he added, "It's just the sort of place I'd imagined you in. Warm. Inviting."

She acknowledged his compliment with a tip of her head.

He leaned forward, resting his forearms on his thighs, his expression serious. "I told you a lie. I didn't come to Boise on business. That was only an excuse. I came to see you."

"Why?" There was a challenge in her question.

"Because you're in trouble."

She stiffened. "In trouble? Where did you get such a ridiculous idea?"

"You told me so yourself. On the telephone."

"Well, it was a poor choice of words then. I just had a little car accident, got a bump on the head, a few bruises, and this broken arm."

"Claire...be honest with me."

"Have you come all this way to call me a liar?"

His gaze was penetrating and unwavering.

She got up, feeling a need to put distance between them. He saw too much already.

"Don't run away," he said softly.

"You presume too much." Anger was her only defense. "I'm not running away from you."

"I didn't mean from me."

The words stung her heart...because they were true. She *was* running, and they both knew from whom.

A strangled sob was wrenched from her throat. A moment later, she felt Kevin's hands turning her toward him. Then she was gathered into his arms, her face pressed against his chest. She hadn't cried since this nightmare began. She'd been afraid to, afraid that if she got started she might not ever stop. It was easier to hate and rage than to crumble into helplessness.

"The Lord is near to the brokenhearted, and saves those who are crushed in spirit." Kevin stroked her hair. "Many are the afflictions of the righteous; but the Lord delivers him out of them all."

How can He deliver me from this? It's real. He can't change the past, and neither can I.

"The sacrifices of God are a broken spirit." His voice was soft, soothing. "A broken and a contrite heart, O God, Thou wilt not despise."

I'm broken. God, I'm so broken. Tears coursed down her cheeks, dampening Kevin's shirt.

"Cast your burden upon the Lord, and He will sustain you; He will never allow the righteous to be shaken."

But I'm not righteous. I'm angry and resentful and filled with hate. And I am *shaken. I've been shaken to pieces. I can't bear it. I can't bear it.*

His arms tightened, and he pressed his cheek against the side of her head. "He hasn't forsaken you. No matter what's happening, you aren't alone."

"If you knew what has happened…It's so hard. It's *too* hard."

"Life is often hard, dear one, but God is always good."

"I thought I was supposed to be happy for the rest of my life." She drew back slightly, enough to look into his eyes. "What about *that* promise?"

He shook his head, his gaze filled with infinite patience. "God didn't promise you happiness, Claire. He promised you joy and peace. They're something different altogether."

She frowned. "Well, I don't feel joy or peace either." She lowered her chin toward her chest and closed her eyes, fighting another flood of tears.

He cupped her chin with his hand and gently forced her to look at him again. "Whatever is going on, you're not going through it alone. God's here." He paused, then added, "And so am I."

Chapter Forty

With her family gathered around her—like a warrior's shield in battle—and her mother holding on to her arm, Sara entered the church narthex on Sunday morning.

She'd told her family nothing except that the wedding was off. She could do nothing to reassure her parents, brothers, and sisters-in-law. She had no intention of telling them the reasons why she'd given Dakota back his ring. All she could do was maintain a stoic silence.

She made certain not to look around her as they headed toward the sanctuary. Instead, she kept her gaze trained directly in front of her, fastened on her father's back.

But she didn't have to see Dakota to know he was there. She recognized his voice, despite the din of myriad conversations. A sixth sense told her the precise moment he noticed her. Kristina's grip tightened an instant before Sara heard Dakota speak her name from only a short distance away.

Unable to stop herself, she glanced up. He was standing next to Tim, ignoring the glowering look her eldest brother was giving him. She recognized the pain in his eyes, for it was like looking into her own heart. And yet there was something else in them as well. Something she couldn't describe. Something…peaceful.

He took a step closer. "Sara, may I talk to you? Privately?"

Frantic, she turned toward her mother and gave a quick shake of her head.

"Not now, Dakota," Kristina answered for her. "Perhaps later."

"All right. But I want you to know something, Sara. I love you. That hasn't changed. Do you understand?"

Her throat was constricting. Her chest was about to collapse.

"No matter what you decide to do, I'll go on loving you."

She saw the questions swirling in her mother's eyes, questions she didn't want to answer. Because in answering them, she would have to confess to her parents what she'd done, and she couldn't bear to do that. How many people did she have to hurt before this was done? Weren't Dakota and Claire enough? Did she have to cause her parents pain as well?

I should have stayed home. I shouldn't have come.

BUT I CALLED YOU HERE, BELOVED.

A shiver ran through her.

Kristina must have felt it, for she put her other arm around Sara's back and gently propelled her through the double doors and toward the two rows the Jennings clan filled every Sunday. Sara sank to the seat, glad to have something solid beneath her.

O Lord, don't let me fall apart in front of everyone. Get me through this.

Frustration welled in Dakota's chest. If only she would talk to him. He wanted to share with her what he'd discovered by the river yesterday. He wanted to impart some hope into a hopeless situation. The Word said, *Fix your hope completely on the grace to be brought to you at the revelation of Jesus Christ.* If he could tell her that, maybe it would help.

John came to stand beside him. "She's hurting bad."

"Yeah."

"Wish I could do something. I always thought you two were perfect for…well, you know what I mean."

"We *are* perfect for each other. I still believe it. But there's a mighty high wall between us right now, and I'm not the one who's got to climb over it."

Just then his mother, escorted by Kevin Quade, came through the main church doors. Despite her arm in a cast and a fading bruise on her forehead, she looked much improved from the last time he'd seen her, which was only yesterday morning. He suspected Kevin had something to do with that.

He felt a flash of irritation, realizing that he and Sara could be separated forever while his mother might be falling in love with this man. Not that he begrudged her some happiness. She deserved it. She'd given up plenty over the years. But her unforgiving attitude would have to change before any of them—Claire, Sara, Dakota—could be truly set free from the web of heartache that entrapped them all.

Seeing Dakota, Claire drew Kevin across the narthex. When she stopped, she gave her son a kiss on the cheek. "Honey, you remember Kevin."

"Sure."

The two men shook hands.

351

Claire continued her introductions. "And this is Dakota's good friend, John Kreizenbeck. John, this is Mr. Quade from Seattle."

"Nice to meet you, Mr. Quade," John responded. Then he added, "You're looking good today, Ms. Conway."

Claire smiled. "Thanks. I'm feeling better too."

"Bet you'll be glad to get rid of that cast. My youngest sister broke her arm once, and she just about drove us all crazy 'cause of the itching. Complained all the time."

Dakota heard little of what his friend was saying as he glanced toward the sanctuary, wondering where Sara was sitting, wondering if she was all right. Would it upset her even more if she saw Claire? And what would his mom do if the two of them met face to face?

Don't lose hope, Sara. Remember that we've fixed our hope on the living God. Don't forget it. Not ever. Hang on to it.

⧬

Claire sat down between Dakota and Kevin. It wasn't until then that she saw Sara's distinctive red hair.

Anger instantly glowed hot in her chest. She'd hoped Sara wouldn't have the nerve to show her face in church. After all, she had to know Dakota would be there, and if Dakota was there, then Claire would be there too. Surely, she had known it.

But she'd come anyway.

As the service began, Claire was only vaguely aware of the pastor, of the choir, of those around her. The very core of her being was focused on hating the younger woman whom she held to blame for every wrong that had occurred in her life.

She didn't know for certain what drew her back from her secret rage. Perhaps it was the minister's voice: "Galatians 6:1 and 2 say, 'Brethren, even if a man is caught in any trespass, you who are spiritual, restore such a one in a spirit of gentleness; each one looking to yourself, lest you too be tempted. Bear one another's burdens, and thus fulfill the law of Christ.'"

Something stirred inside her, one word repeating in her mind: *Restore...Restore...*

"John 20:23 says this: 'If you forgive the sins of any, their sins have been forgiven them; if you retain the sins of any, they have been retained.'"

She knew what God was saying to her, and yet she resisted.

I'm the wronged person here. Me!

Chapter Forty-One

The negligee on the mannequin was made of white satin and trimmed in delicate lace. It would have been perfect for a bride on her wedding night.

Claire watched from behind a display as Sara, longing and loss written on her face, reached out and touched the nightgown. Then, as if stung, she quickly pulled back her hand. Her shoulders slumped, and she turned away, an aura of futility lingering in her wake as she left the lingerie department.

Claire drew in a deep breath, not realizing until then that she'd been holding it. She'd been afraid Sara would see her, and yet she'd been unable to move so much as an inch. She'd been like a deer caught in the headlights, mesmerized despite the danger. Something in the girl's expression had caused a crack in her hardened heart.

She knew she was supposed to forgive Sara, and it wasn't anything Dakota or Kevin or even the pastor had said that told her so. She knew she had to let go of the anger and bitterness a second time. She'd laid it all down once, when she first came to believe. But how quickly those old traits had replanted themselves when she'd met

Sara. Like the demons returning to the man because he didn't put anything else in their place after Christ cast them out.

I don't want to be like that man. I don't want to feel this way. I don't want to be worse off than I was before.

Wanting suddenly to escape this place, she hurried toward the escalator. And that's where she came face to face with Sara. Each of them stopped, looked in the other direction, as if they could pretend they hadn't seen each other, then met the other's gaze a second time.

Sara was the first to find her voice. "Claire."

"Sara."

"I…Please, go ahead."

She had an affair with my husband and then she wanted my son. The thoughts raced through Claire's mind in an instant. *She took him like an innocent lamb to the slaughter. Did she seduce Dakota? Is that how she got him to propose? She must have entrapped him, her and her wicked ways. He never would have fallen for her otherwise. She hasn't changed. It's obvious she isn't good enough for him. So what difference does it make if I forgive her or not? She's gone from his life. He'll get over her and meet some nice girl and get married. It'll be better that way. Better for everyone.*

Sara took a step backward. "I just remembered something. I've got to go. Excuse me. I'm sorry." She turned and hurried away.

But not before Claire saw the tears.

The tears shouldn't have affected her. She didn't *want* the tears to affect her.

But they did.

Another chink appeared in her armor of bitterness.

It was good to know Sara'd gone to work today, Dakota thought as he leaned against a support post on one of the apartment complex carports. But remembering the way she had looked yesterday at church kept him from feeling much relief. She'd lost weight, appeared too thin, her clothes hanging loosely on her frame. He suspected she wasn't sleeping much, judging by her eyes.

Of course, he wasn't sleeping much himself these days.

He saw her car turn the corner. He straightened and stepped deeper into the shadows of the carport as he watched her pull into her designated parking space. She didn't immediately get out after cutting the engine. Instead, she leaned her forehead against the backs of her hands, hands that clenched the top of the steering wheel.

Was she crying?

I've got to go to her.

But an invisible hand stayed him from doing what he wanted.

After a long while, she opened her car door. When she stepped out, he could see she was carrying a purse and what looked like a sack of carry-out food. He hoped she ate it. All of it.

Ah, Sara, it's hard to see you like this. I love you so much. I want to make it better. I want to take your hurt away.

With listless steps, she crossed the driveway and followed the sidewalk to her building's entrance. The way she grasped the handrail as she started up the stairs reminded him of an old woman, a grandmother with brittle bones and hunched shoulders.

If I can't show her my love, Lord, show her Yours.

He waited until she disappeared from view before heading in the direction of the nearby office complex where he'd parked his Jeep.

❦

The popular Mexican restaurant was busy and noisy. Three times in the past half-hour servers had yipped and shouted and serenaded someone with a birthday or an anniversary or some other special occasion.

But at the moment, it wasn't the decibel level that was giving Claire fits. It was trying to eat her chicken fajita with only one hand.

Seeing her dilemma, Kevin chuckled and said, "Here. Let me help."

"Are you going to spoon-feed me like a baby?"

He wasn't put off by her mood. He just grinned and teasingly said, "No, but that might be fun." Then he pulled her plate toward him and cut her chicken and vegetables into bite-size pieces. He even cut the soft tortilla. "Won't be quite the same as holding the rolled-up version, but you won't starve trying." He pushed her plate back in front of her.

"Thanks." She wasn't sure why there was a lump in her throat, but there was.

For a time they were silent, lost in their private thoughts as they ate. Claire was remembering Sara, the white negligee, and Sara's nearly palpable heartache.

From the next booth came a woman's voice, intruding on Claire's memories: "Do you think he'll leave Maggie and marry that girl he's having the affair with?"

"Wouldn't you?" another woman responded.

"They've been married almost twenty years. They've still got kids at home."

"Well, Maggie isn't exactly blameless, you know. She's nearly suffocated that poor man with those needy ways of hers. Have you ever listened to how she whines at him? Maggie may be a friend of mine, but if I were Jim, I'd have left her years ago."

Claire felt like standing up and shouting at the two women, telling them they had no right to gossip about their friend with such cavalier disregard. What did they know about what really went on in Maggie's marriage? What did they know about a wife's hurt over that kind of betrayal? How dare they side with the adulterous husband? What if the wife *was* needy and whiny? That was no excuse to—

"Claire?"

She looked at Kevin.

"You can't change yesterday, no matter how hard you try."

"I know that."

"Do you? It doesn't show in your actions."

"What gives you the right to—"

"Because I love you."

She sucked in a gasp.

"I love you, and I'm tired of watching you fight so hard to prevent God from doing a work in your heart."

"I'm doing no such—"

"Yes, you are." He leaned forward. "There's a scripture that goes something like, What's crooked can't be straightened. Quit striving against the wind, Claire. Let go of the past. Really let it go."

Why was he doing this to her? With one breath he told her he loved her, and with the next he criticized her. Handed her happiness with one hand and took it away with the other.

His voice softened, gentled. "You already know what God's telling you to do. Don't fight Him so hard."

"It's not that simple."

"Yes, it is. You don't have to be strong. His power's perfected in our weakness."

Clichés! Trite answers to an impossible situation. The only way he'd quit offering his unsolicited advice was if she made him understand.

She looked down at her plate. "Sara Jennings had an affair with Dakota's father. She was the cause of my divorce. Because of her, I could hardly manage to keep a roof over Dakota's head because Dave never paid child support. It was her fault my son didn't have his dad around to go with him to father-son games or to play ball with."

She kept on, venting her rancor, not caring what he thought of her for saying it. She was tired of Dakota and Kevin thinking *she* was the one in the wrong. *She* hadn't had an affair with a married man. Why was *she* the one who had to forgive and forget? What about the price *Sara* had to pay for the wrong she'd done?

What about justice?

❦

The dinner Sara had brought home from the deli remained in the paper sack. She had no appetite. She'd tried to watch some television, but she couldn't concentrate. Everything was all jumbled in her mind.

When the knock sounded at her door, she ignored it. She hadn't the energy to get up and answer it.

"Sara, it's Mom. Open up."

With a sigh, she obeyed.

Kristina stepped into the apartment and immediately wrapped Sara in a tight embrace. She didn't say anything for a long time, just held her daughter, rubbing her back as she'd done when Sara was a child.

Sara fought her tears. She was tired of crying, tired of thinking, tired of feeling. She was weary beyond belief.

After a long while, her mother took her by the hand and led her to the sofa. She didn't release Sara's hand as they both sat down. If anything, she held on more tightly. "I want you to tell me what's happened."

"I can't." She tore her gaze away, looking out the window toward the river.

"Sara...I know this is more than just a broken engagement."

She shook her head.

"There isn't anything you can tell me that will alter how much I love you."

But you don't know what it is.

"Sara. Please. Whatever it is, there's an answer."

"Not for this. There's no answer for this."

"Have you tried God?"

Her heart fluttered even as she answered, "You don't understand."

"Then tell me so I can."

"Years ago," she began, haltingly at first, "when I was at Boise State...I had an affair. With a married man."

Her mother said nothing, but Sara sensed her surprise.

"When I found out Dave was married, I ran away."

"To Denver." More softly, Kristina added, "Now I understand."

"I was heartbroken and ashamed."

"And now Dakota's learned of this affair? He hasn't been able to forgive you?"

She met her mother's eyes, then pulled her hand away and stood up. She walked toward the mantel, looking at the bear figurines that Dakota had helped her unpack nearly five months before. It seemed longer.

"That doesn't sound like him," Kristina said softly.

"No, he could forgive that. He knew that I'd had an affair." She faced her mother again. "But he didn't know the man I had an affair with was his own father."

Kristina gasped.

Sara shuddered, the renewed reality of her confession striking her like a sledgehammer. When she spoke again, agony thinned her voice until it was nearly inaudible. "I didn't know who Dakota was. I didn't know he was Dave's son. But it doesn't matter. It doesn't change it. I can't marry him. Claire...knows who I am."

A groan was torn from her throat as she fell to her knees.

"Oh, Mama. Oh, Mama." She bent forward at the waist, touching her forehead to the floor. "Why won't God let me die?"

❦

Kevin kept his expression neutral while he listened. But he was silently, frantically praying for guidance and wisdom the whole time. Never in his wildest dreams could he have imagined such a tangled web as the story Claire was spinning for him.

"Well?" She asked when she finally ran out of both words and rage. "Don't you have *anything* to say?"

TELL THE TRUTH IN LOVE, BELOVED.

Oh, Father, can she handle the truth?

TELL THE TRUTH IN LOVE.

Jesus, You'll have to give me the right words. I'm out of my depth here.

Looking at Claire, seeing the despair in her eyes, he knew what he was about to say could drive a wedge between them that could never be removed. But still he had to speak it.

"Tell me, did Dave play ball with his son before the divorce? Was he involved in father-son things before he walked out on the two of you?"

"What?" She seemed confused by his questions.

"Was Dave close to Dakota? Did they do things together?"

She was silent a long while, and he guessed she was searching through memories.

"No," she answered at long last. "Only rarely."

Next came an even tougher question. "And did you ever suspect him of having other affairs?"

"That isn't any of your business." She closed her eyes, shutting him out.

"*Did* you suspect him?"

"Yes. Yes, I *did* suspect him. But we were working things out. Things were better between us until *she* came along."

He knew she was lying, but to herself rather than to him. He also knew he couldn't let up. He had to force her to see the whole truth, whether she wanted to see it or not.

He covered her hand with his, causing her to meet his gaze again.

"Tell me. Did Sara make him *not* pay child support or never see his son? Was it her fault, the type of man he was?"

"Why are you defending her?" The raw ache in her voice revealed her wounded spirit.

"I'm not defending what she did, Claire. But are you looking at the splinter in her eye when there's a log in your own?"

She stiffened. "I was never unfaithful. I was a good wife. I'm the injured person here. Why can't you see that? Why can't anyone see that?"

❦

Sara's mother held her as she wept. She didn't condemn her. She didn't express horror or disgust or even disappointment. She simply held her in arms of love.

When Sara's tears subsided, Kristina said, "Darling, your heart is broken, and judging from Dakota at church yesterday, so is his." She drew back, cupped Sara's chin in her hand. "But I want you to think about this. If you look in the Bible, you will find great tragedy but never true despair. Instead, there's tremendous hope, no matter what the situation."

What can I hope for? I've lost Dakota.

"God is greater, Sara."

"Claire hates me."

"But God doesn't."

Part Seven: *Forgiving*

And so, as those who have been chosen of God,

holy and beloved, put on a heart

of compassion, kindness, humility, gentleness

and patience; bearing with one another,

and forgiving each other,

whoever has a complaint against anyone;

just as the Lord forgave you,

so also should you.

— COLOSSIANS 3:12–13

Chapter Forty-Two

Normally, June was Claire's favorite month. She loved the warmer weather, the long days of sunshine, and the blue skies. She loved taking walks in her neighborhood or along the greenbelt in the evening, as the temperature began to cool. She loved the glorious sunsets, watching as heaven's paintbrush turned clouds from pristine white to brilliant orange, blood red, soft lavender, and delicate pink. She loved the distinctive cry of the killdeer as they faked broken wings and ran across horse pastures. She loved the sweet green smell of new growth.

But this June was different. A dark cloud of gloom covered the days and took pleasure from her normal summer pursuits.

She missed Kevin. He'd returned to Seattle, and although he called her several times a week, it wasn't the same as his being there. And despite his declaration of love, she knew he was waiting for her to let go of her bitterness before their relationship could move forward.

She missed the comfortable bond she'd once shared with her son. Dakota frequently came to see her, but things weren't the same. She knew he loved her and would go on loving her, no matter what. And in her heart she recognized that she held the key to her son's happiness. Because she also knew that he still loved Sara.

More than anything else, she missed the feeling of God's nearness. She knew the fault was her own, yet she couldn't seem to change, for to change she would have to admit her own responsibility, and that she was not ready to do.

Sara sought answers in the Bible. She had loved God's Word from the beginning of her Christian walk, and she knew she needed spiritual food to sustain her now.

Perhaps she hoped to find a passage that would make her forget the look in Claire Conway's eyes as the two of them had stood near the escalator at the Bon. It didn't seem to matter how much time passed; that look of sheer hatred lingered in Sara's thoughts.

On this evening, three weeks after that fateful encounter, Sara took her Bible and a blanket and walked down to the river. For a long while, she simply stared at the rushing water, her thoughts similarly rushing over the events of the past, from the day she'd met Dave to the last time she'd seen Claire.

So much hate in her eyes.

Shame washed over her afresh.

She has good reason to hate me.

She bowed her head as she crushed her Bible against her chest.

O God, help me. I know You're here, but I don't feel Your presence. I feel so far from You. I feel so unworthy, so hopeless. Help me to hear You. Quiet my heart and my mind so I can hear Your voice.

With more desperation than faith, she opened the Word, reading a passage, flipping pages, reading more, flipping more pages, and reading again. And as daylight faded, a brighter light began to burn in her chest as the Lord answered her prayer.

I have loved you with an everlasting love...He will exult over you with joy, He will be quiet in His love, He will rejoice over you with shouts of joy...For God is love...

"For God is love," Sara repeated in a whisper. She looked off toward the sunset. "And You rejoice over me with shouts of joy."

Surely she had known this before, that He loved her, that He'd forgiven her, that her only hope was in Him.

Hope in Him.

That was the difference. That's what He'd wanted her to come to understand. Her hope was in Him and Him alone, because He loved her so completely.

"This is what I saw in Dakota's eyes, isn't it? This hope, despite the circumstances."

No wonder the world didn't understand. It went against all reason that, with her heart still broken, she could feel this blanket of peace wrapped around her, keeping her warm. It didn't change the circumstances, but it changed Sara.

Her mother was right. Hope was greater than despair. No matter how deep she sank, God's provision was there to raise her up again.

Grace. At last she understood what He'd been telling her these many weeks. His grace wasn't earned. It was freely offered, not just when she'd first believed, but throughout the remainder of her life.

"Awesome," she whispered. "Truly awesome."

As if summoned by her discovery came a most beloved voice. "Sara."

She wasn't even surprised. Without turning to look at him, she said, "Hello, Dakota."

"Mind if I join you?"

"No, I don't mind."

He sank onto the ground beside her. "Beautiful sunset."

"Yes."

"How are you?"

She turned toward him at last. Her heart did a little skip. "I'm better."

He smiled gently, and she knew he understood the deeper meaning in her words.

"You've been reading quite a while." He pointed to the Bible in her lap. Then, in explanation, he added, "I was watching. I hope you don't mind. I didn't want to intrude."

She considered his comment. "No, I don't mind." *I'm glad you're here.*

The sun sank beneath the horizon. The clouds faded from pastel to gray. Night settled over the earth like a gigantic black cloak. Crickets chirped their evening songs. Someone was barbecuing, and the delicious aroma was carried to the river's edge on the evening breeze.

Tenderly, "I love you, Sara."

"I love you too." *I always will.*

"I need to tell you something, and I think you need to hear it."

She waited.

"You're still washed white as snow in my eyes."

Tears welled. A lump formed in her throat. "Oh, Dakota."

"There's more. I don't know why I feel so sure. I can't predict the future. But I know this is going to turn out all right, no matter what happens between us or with my mom. It's going to be okay."

"I know." Still fighting tears, she rested her arms on her knees, her chin on her arms. "I feel it too." She straightened and placed her right palm over her heart. "I feel it in here."

Neither of them had to say aloud that they couldn't marry without Claire's blessing. They didn't have to. It was simply understood. Like it or not, they were bound by his mother's unforgiveness. Unhappiness and heartache accompanied the knowledge, but a greater comfort triumphed over all.

"You've decided not to move to Denver?"

"No, I'm not going to Denver." Shrouded by the newly fallen darkness, Sara smiled sadly. "I'm not running away again. I'll stay." She looked toward him even though she could no longer see his face. "I was brought back to Boise for a reason. I thought for a while that it was to meet you, but now I'm convinced it was to experience God's love in its fullness."

"I wish my mom could—"

"Don't."

"Yeah, you're right. It doesn't change anything, but I still wish—"

"No." She drew a deep breath, then let it out on a sigh. "Sometimes, Dakota, God says no."

❦

Are you looking at the splinter in her eye when there's a log in your own?
How unfair it was of Kevin to have asked that, Claire thought as

she made herself a late-night decaf cappuccino. Even weeks later, his question continued to echo in her mind.

"I'm so tired of it all," she whispered.

She was tired of feeling guilty. She was tired of her own unhappiness. She was tired of the anger that rose so quickly whenever she thought of Dakota and Sara together.

Turning her back to the counter, she noticed her Bible lying on the kitchen table. She felt a pull toward it, but she resisted. She hadn't read the Word in weeks. She hadn't prayed either. She missed that special fellowship with the Lord, but she just couldn't seem to do it.

A log in her own eye. Maybe that was why. Maybe she couldn't see because of the log.

"I forgave Dave already. Isn't that enough?"

She knew the answer. She knew it wasn't enough.

She walked over to the table. Still standing, she placed her fingertips on the leather cover of her Bible.

LAZARUS. The Voice was clear and strong. LAZARUS.

Claire's concordance was in the den. She could find the story of Lazarus. She could find answers if she was willing to look for them.

She riffled the pages of the Bible, then stubbornly turned her back toward the table, muttering, "I can't. I just can't do it."

Chapter Forty-Three

"I can't change the way I feel," Claire told Kevin when he called her the next day at the office.

"Of course you can. It's your choice. You have the ability to forgive and be set free from your bitterness. If you'd just—"

"Everyone always has such pat answers. It isn't that simple. I've read that feelings aren't right or wrong, they just are. It's what you do in response to your feelings that counts."

His silence said more than any words would have.

"Let's not talk about this anymore, Kevin. Please. Let's talk about when you'll be in Boise next."

"I can't get away until the Fourth of July weekend."

The Fourth. The day Dakota was to have married Sara.

"I thought I'd fly in on Friday and stay until Tuesday afternoon. Does that work for you?"

She shook off the memory of what was supposed to have occurred on the fourth, then said, "Perfect. I'll plan a barbecue. We'll have Alana and Jack over and a few other friends. But no shoptalk. One word from you and Jack about the Seattle office or any other business, and I'll burn both your steaks. Agreed?"

"Agreed."

"Kevin?"

"Yes?"

"Keep praying for me." *Because I'm unable to pray for myself.*

"You know I will."

"I'd better get back to work. Do you want me to put you through to Jack?"

"No, I'll have to call him tomorrow. I've got an appointment in half an hour."

They said their good-byes and hung up. For a long while afterward she stared at the phone, thinking how little she deserved someone like him.

Would her stubbornness—her unwillingness to let go of the past, once and for all—ruin things between them? She knew he loved her. But would he continue to if she didn't change her attitude?

She turned her chair toward the plate-glass window and stared out at the golden summer day.

The Fourth of July. A perfect day for a wedding. Only not anymore.

But wasn't it better this way? Dakota *seemed* willing to forgive Sara, but surely that couldn't last. Marriage was a difficult proposition. The first time dissension or disagreement arose, he would remember that she'd once had an affair with his own father and the past would rise between them. They couldn't possibly be happy. It would eventually destroy them. No, it was better that it had ended.

O God…

But that was as far as she could go with a prayer, and it wasn't enough. It just wasn't enough.

LAZARUS.

Her pulse quickened. This was the third time she'd heard that word in her heart and known what she was to do. The story of Lazarus held the answer. She would find a message there, if only she would look.

But she was afraid of what she might have to do once she read it, and so she refused to obey. Sometimes, she thought, ignorance was bliss.

"Hey, Mom. You ready to get that cast off?"

She spun her chair around to find her son leaning his shoulder against the doorjamb. "I didn't expect you so—" She glanced at the clock on the wall. "Oh my goodness. I didn't know it was that late." Quickly, she grabbed her purse out of the bottom drawer of her desk.

"Bet it'll feel good to get rid of that thing," he said as she came toward him.

"You have no idea how good." She touched his shoulder. "But I *will* miss seeing you so often, not to mention all this private chauffeuring about town."

"I'm glad I could do it for you."

Looking into his eyes, Claire saw nothing but love.

LAZARUS, BELOVED.

⚬⚬⚬

The medical center's elevator doors opened before Sara—and there was Dakota with his mother. Panic threatened to smother her. There was no graceful way to escape. The best she could hope for was to avoid eye contact while she slipped past them.

Only she made the mistake of looking up instead of down. Her gaze met his, and she found herself unable to move.

"Hello, Sara." He stepped into the elevator, bringing his mom in with him, steering her with a hand on her back.

"Hello."

"What brings you here? You're not sick, are you?"

"No. Just an errand in the building."

"Thank God." He smiled sadly. "Mom gets her cast off today."

She couldn't avoid it any longer. She glanced toward Claire. "You must be relieved about that."

"Yes." The single word couldn't have seemed colder.

"Well…" She forced herself to smile, hoping it looked friendly rather than frightened. "I'm glad you're feeling better." Before the doors could close and trap her within, she stepped out of the elevator.

"Take care," Dakota called after her.

She turned just in time to catch a final glimpse of Claire. But instead of anger and hatred, Sara thought she saw confusion in the woman's eyes. Then the doors closed.

I know you've forgiven me, Lord. But is it possible she'll be able to do the same one day? Or do I want too much? Is this merely the cross I must bear?

Sara walked out of the lobby and into the bright sunshine. A mirage shimmered on the parking lot's surface as heat waves rose from the blacktop. A siren screamed as an ambulance exited the freeway and sped toward the emergency entrance of the hospital. She could smell the exhaust from the many cars waiting at the busy intersection on Fairview Avenue.

When she opened her car door, a blast of heat rushed out to meet her. A swim in her complex's pool sounded like a good idea, she thought as she got in and started the engine. But when she pulled out of the parking lot and into traffic, she steered her automobile toward the freeway on-ramp instead of heading for her apartment, realizing that what she needed most was a dose of her mother's unconditional love.

She found Kristina weeding the vegetable patch. Her mother wore a large, floppy-brimmed straw hat and a loose-fitting denim dress. Her feet and legs were bare.

After a quick greeting, Sara hurried inside and up the stairs to her old room. In the dresser she found a pair of worn cutoffs and a faded, sleeveless blouse. She removed her suit jacket, skirt, and pantyhose, then dressed in the shorts and summer top before hurrying, bare-footed, back outside.

"Where can I help, Mom?"

Kristina removed her hat and brushed red curls away from her forehead with the back of her wrist. Squinting up at her daughter, she said, "The carrots could use thinning." She pointed with her spade.

Sara nodded, then went to the far corner of the garden. Kneeling in the dirt, she asked, "Where's Dad?"

"He's over taking a look at Frank Eden's new tractor. He's probably salivating by this time."

Sara laughed, knowing it was true.

"I'm looking forward to the day he retires, and he's trying to figure out how we can buy the forty acres behind us. Men." The single word was spoken with great affection.

Men.

Sara thought of Dakota. She missed him so much. Seeing him this afternoon had only made the missing worse. She knew in her heart that God would cause all things to work together for good. Even in this situation. She'd found a deeper peace and joy in her new closeness with the Lord and in her fresh understanding of His great love for her.

But only time would ease the sense of loss that lingered whenever she remembered Dakota and the happiness they'd once shared, however briefly.

At his mom's invitation, Dakota stayed for dinner. It wasn't like he had any place urgent to go.

After asking if he could help prepare the food and being refused, he went outside to the backyard. He set the oscillating sprinkler and turned on the water. Then he settled in one of the lounge chairs on the covered patio.

And he thought of Sara.

No surprise there. He thought of her a lot. The memory was always bittersweet, poignant. He wondered if it would always be so. He closed his eyes, remembering the way she'd looked when those elevator doors opened and they'd seen each other. As pretty as ever, but too thin. He hoped she was eating better, now that she'd found that place of peace in the Lord.

He heard the patio door open and looked toward it as Claire stepped outside, carrying a large bowl of tossed salad in one hand and a bottle of salad dressing in the other. He quickly got up to take them from her.

"The rest will be right out," she said.

He placed the bowl in the center of the round patio table and followed his mother back inside.

It wasn't long before they were seated at the table, enjoying both the food and the occasional mist off the sprinkler. They laughed over Claire's clumsiness when using her left hand, weakened as it was from weeks in the cast. They talked about work and church. It was almost normal. Almost.

Suddenly, Claire's expression turned solemn. "You still love her, don't you? Even knowing what she did, you still love her."

"Yes, I do."

"And you still want to marry her?"

He could see her struggling to understand. "Yes, I do."

"I know your readiness to forgive." She looked off into the distance. "You've been like that for many years. But how could you forget? How could you forget that your father...*touched* her? That he was *intimate* with her?"

He searched for the right words with which to answer.

"Dakota, isn't it better just to let her go? There are other women for you to meet, women who—"

"Mom." He waited for her to look at him again. When she did, he continued, "I can't tell you why or how I can forget. I just know God's made it possible. There's a part of me that understands what you're saying. It's a normal, human reaction. I won't say I wasn't shocked, that I didn't feel anger and disappointment and confusion. But then, something happened inside me. Something..."

He let his words drift into silence, seeing in his mother's eyes that she couldn't accept what he was saying. Not yet. Besides, how did one illustrate the power of God to change a person's heart? It was a miracle, and miracles couldn't be explained.

Claire looked away a second time. "You won't marry her as long as I have any objections, will you?"

"No."

She released a sigh. He couldn't be sure if it was out of relief or sorrow.

Chapter Forty-Four

No condemnation.

There'd been no condemnation in Dakota's eyes or in his voice when he'd answered Claire. Not even when he'd admitted he still loved Sara and wanted to marry her. Not even when he'd said he wouldn't marry her as long as Claire objected.

Even with all that, he didn't condemn her, he didn't judge her. He simply loved her. He'd forgiven her without even being asked.

How was it possible? Claire didn't understand.

No, that wasn't true. She *did* understand. He didn't forgive out of his own strength. It was Christ in him, the hope of glory. It was what Kevin had tried to tell her, but she'd refused to listen.

At midnight, restless and sleepless, her thoughts churning, her emotions raw, Claire could bear it no longer. She retrieved her Bible and concordance and carried them to her favorite chair in the living room. Once there, she looked up *Lazarus*. With a glimmer of hope, she turned to the eleventh chapter of the Gospel of John and began to read.

She wasn't unfamiliar with the story of Lazarus and his sisters, Martha and Mary. She'd read the entire New Testament while in

Seattle. And because she knew the story, she hadn't understood what possible relevance it could have in her situation. It seemed completely unrelated.

Martha therefore said to Jesus, "Lord, if You had been here, my brother would not have died. Even now I know that whatever You ask of God, God will give You."

Claire believed that. She didn't doubt Christ *could* do miracles, even raise the dead. But He couldn't wipe out the past.

She continued reading.

Jesus therefore again being deeply moved within, came to the tomb. Now it was a cave, and a stone was lying against it. Jesus said, "Remove the stone." Martha, the sister of the deceased, said to Him, "Lord, by this time there will be a stench, for he has been dead four days."

Dead four days...A stench...The stench of death. The stench of decay.

Jesus said to her, "Did I not say to you, if you believe, you will see the glory of God?"

"I need to see your glory, Father," Claire whispered.

And so they removed the stone...

She stopped reading, then went back a few verses. Had she nearly missed the lesson she was supposed to learn? Was there a stench of death and decay around her?

She felt like there was.

And when He had said these things, He cried out with a loud voice, "Lazarus, come forth." He who had died came forth, bound hand and foot with wrappings; and his face was wrapped around with a cloth.

Raised from the dead. Symbolic of the new birth in Jesus. But there had to be more than that. She *needed* there to be more than just symbolism.

Jesus said to them, "Unbind him, and let him go."

Her heart began to race. She read it again.

"Unbind him, and let him go."

An inexplicable excitement burbled up inside her.

"Unbind him," she repeated aloud. "Unbind him, and let him go."

And suddenly she understood why God had brought her to this book, this chapter, this verse. Jesus raised Lazarus from the dead, but Lazarus was still bound by his graveclothes. Jesus had to tell those who were watching to unbind him, to free him from those rags.

"That's me, isn't it, Lord? You raised me from death into life, but I'm still dragging all that old stuff along with me. All those old graveclothes are still binding me." She closed her eyes. "But how do I get out of them? Who's going to unbind me and let me go?"

FORGIVE SARA.

The command didn't surprise her. She'd heard it before. "I don't know if I can, Lord."

FORGIVE HER, BELOVED.

Almost without realizing what she was doing, Claire slipped from the chair and to her knees, folded hands pressed tightly against her forehead.

"Father, I don't want to live in these rags. I don't want the stench of death hanging over me. I forgive her. Not by my power but by Yours."

NOW GO TO HER. TELL HER.

She caught her breath. A chill rolled over her.

No. No, she couldn't.

RESTORE HER.

"No." She shook her head as she began to weep. "I can't. I can't do it. Not that."

TELL HER, BELOVED.

Tears streaming down her cheeks, she raised her head and shouted, *"You're* God! *You* tell her! Don't ask this of me!"

Chapter Forty-Five

Sara was up early on that Saturday morning, early enough to be sipping a cup of coffee as the first fingers of dawn began to play across the earth. The sun rose slowly over the mountains in the east, spilling its rays upon ripples in the river's surface, causing them to dance with flashes of gold.

The air was chilly, but Sara didn't want to go inside for her bathrobe. She didn't want to miss even a moment of daybreak's breathtaking display. Instead, she drew her knees to her chest beneath her nightshirt and stayed where she was.

Perhaps she was hoping with the new day would come…something.

Last night had been one of the worst. Loneliness had been building within her for days, and last night it had overwhelmed her. She'd clung to every promise of God she could remember, repeating them over and over in her mind, but they hadn't been enough to stop her tears. She'd cried until her pillow was wet with them. She'd cried until there were no tears left.

Shades of gray faded and colors brightened as the sun triumphed over the last vestiges of night, escaping the mountain peaks and soaring in freedom over the valley, its brilliance reflected in windows of the homes and apartments along her street.

O God, let me soar free like the sun. Let me escape this wretched sorrow.

She swallowed the lump in her throat.

Grasping for comfort, Sara repeated aloud a verse she'd memorized many months before: "Give ear to my words, O Lord, consider my groaning. Heed the sound of my cry for help, my King and my God, for to Thee do I pray."

She choked over a sob. Quickly, she pressed her face against her knees.

"Did you see the sunrise, Dakota?"

How she longed to share these little pleasures with him. For a few short months, it had been within her grasp, to have the man she loved beside her. But no longer.

She lifted her head, looked toward the river.

"Oh, Dakota, how shall I ever bear losing you?"

How shall I bear it, Abba Father? I feel so utterly alone. I know You're with me. Let me feel Your comfort.

The fullness of morning was upon the earth now. Joggers appeared along the greenbelt. Already outside to play, children shouted in the distance. A car door slammed somewhere in the parking lot.

Life goes on.

"And so must I," she whispered. "So must I."

❧

Claire stood in front of Sara's door, unable to knock. It had taken her three days to get here. Three days of fighting the will of God. Three days of rationalizing and reasoning. All to no avail. She'd surrendered in the wee hours before dawn, and once she did, she knew she had to come immediately. She couldn't wait. Not even until a more reasonable hour.

Quivering, both inside and out, she lifted her arm and rapped her knuckles against the door.

Perhaps Sara would still be asleep and wouldn't hear her knock. Perhaps she wasn't even at home. Perhaps...

The door opened.

Surprise flashed instantly across Sara's face.

She's been crying.

Claire felt the young woman's heartbreak and pain as if they were her own. She drew in a deep breath, and asked, "May I come in?"

Sara nodded and took a step backward, holding the door open wide.

As Claire walked in, the enemy assaulted her with memories of the past, of her own heartbreak years ago, of the part Sara had played in her life's drama. But before self-righteous anger could overwhelm her, she felt an invisible hand on her shoulder, steadying her.

She turned around.

Sara stood in her nightshirt, her abundant red hair caught in an unruly ponytail. She was holding a coffee mug; Claire could see that her hands were shaking.

How do I begin, Lord?

Sara motioned toward the sofa. "Would you like to sit down?"

"Thank you."

"I...I think I'll get my robe. Excuse me."

God…how do I find the words?

PEACE I LEAVE WITH YOU; MY PEACE I GIVE TO YOU; NOT AS THE WORLD GIVES, DO I GIVE TO YOU. LET NOT YOUR HEART BE TROUBLED, NOR LET IT BE FEARFUL.

Sara returned, now clad in a terry-cloth bathrobe. She'd washed the tear stains from her cheeks, but her skin was abnormally pale, her hands still shaking nervously.

PEACE I LEAVE WITH YOU.

"Sara, I've come to ask your forgiveness."

"My forgiveness?"

Softly, "I've hated you in my heart." She stared at the floor. "Even before I knew your name, I hated you. All these years. So much bitterness. So much wasted emotion."

"You had every right to hate me."

Claire looked up, met Sara's gaze. "No. No, I didn't have every right. I thought I did." She offered a weak smile, tears beginning to blur her vision. "But I was wrong. I have no right to hate anyone."

"But it's me who needs to be forgiven."

"You already are." As she spoke those three simple words, something miraculous happened inside Claire. The graveclothes fell away. There was no longer the stench of death lingering in the air. Instead, she smelled the sweet fragrance of God's abiding love.

Joy warmed her heart. She was set free. Free forever. No longer chained to the hurts of the past.

She blinked back the tears, wanting to see Sara. The younger woman had covered her face with her hands; her shoulders shook as she wept. Claire rose from the sofa and went to her, kneeling on the floor in front of her chair. She reached out and drew Sara's hands from her face.

Help me to unbind her too, Father. Help me to unwrap her grave-clothes.

"Please don't cry," Claire whispered, choked by her own emotions.

"I…I never meant to hurt anyone. Not you or Dakota. I sinned against you both so grievously."

"What sin, Sara? God's forgotten it." Wonder and awe flooded Claire's heart as she spoke. "And now," she added softly, "so have I."

It was a sweet hour of the morning, that hour of forgiving.

And as the two women embraced, a song of praise rose from Claire's heart toward the very throne of God.

Epilogue

VALENTINE'S DAY—EIGHT MONTHS LATER

The sanctuary of Sunrise Fellowship Church was filled with white and red roses. White tapers flickered in candelabra. The sides of each pew were adorned with huge red and white bows. The pianist played softly while guests continued to fill the church, music and voices drifting down the hall to the dressing room.

"Oh, Claire," Sara whispered, anxiety clear in her voice. "I look absolutely dreadful. This was a mistake."

Claire turned around to see Sara staring woefully at her reflection in the full-length mirror. "But you look lovely," she argued.

"Lovely? What I look is fat. You should have asked one of your friends to do this."

"But I *wanted* you." Happiness filled her as she spoke the words, for with them came a rush of love for Sara. Of all the things that had happened over the past year, the love she felt for her daughter-in-law was the most miraculous of all.

Sara faced Claire, both of her hands resting on her gently rounded abdomen. "I'm not big enough to look pregnant and not small enough to disguise it. Just think what your wedding photographs are going to look like with me in them in this getup."

"What could be more beautiful than an expectant mother? I'll love every photo you're in."

Before Sara could respond, a soft rap sounded at the door, followed by Dakota's voice. "Mom, it's time. Are you ready?"

An unexpected flutter of nerves erupted.

"Mom?"

Casting a smile in Claire's direction, Sara opened the door. "She's ready." She stepped back. "Brides don't come any prettier than your mother."

His look of approval was a balm on her frazzled nerves. "Wow! Mom!" He grinned that special lopsided smile of his.

The butterflies settled. Joy welled up again, spilling over like David's cup in the Twenty-third Psalm.

"Your groom awaits." Her son moved to stand in front of her. He lowered his head toward hers as he stared deeply into her eyes. "You really do look beautiful. Kevin's a lucky guy. And he knows it too."

"I'm the lucky one. Who would have imagined all of this? You about to become a father. Me getting married again." She released a shaky breath. "It doesn't seem real. It's almost too good to be true."

"Every good thing bestowed and every perfect gift is from above," he quoted softly. He placed her right hand in the crook of his left arm. "Let's go, shall we?"

As they left the dressing room—Sara, her matron of honor, leading the way—Claire thought back over time. The power to sting, to hurt, to destroy, had been removed from the memories. The chains had been broken, once and for all.

Thank You, Father. Thank You for never giving up on me.

HOW BEAUTIFUL YOU ARE, MY DARLING, HOW BEAUTIFUL YOU ARE!

Thank You, Jesus, for giving me such a wonderful son and a daughter to love. And Kevin. Thank You for Kevin.

LIKE A LILY AMONG THE THORNS, SO IS MY DARLING AMONG THE MAIDENS.

Most of all, thanks for loving me with an everlasting love.

PUT ME LIKE A SEAL OVER YOUR HEART, LIKE A SEAL ON YOUR ARM. FOR LOVE IS AS STRONG AS DEATH.

Yes, the past had lost its grip on her heart and mind because love was stronger. Now what she saw when she looked back were the many ways God in His faithfulness had wooed her, had reached out to her in mercy, had called to her like the groom to his beloved bride, drawing her unto Himself.

Into a place of forgiveness.

Forever.

Dear Friends:

Every so often, an author is given a special story to tell, one that is particularly meaningful to her and, in some ways, more difficult to write. *The Forgiving Hour* is such a book for me. While not truly autobiographical, I do know firsthand the heartbreak of an unfaithful spouse, and I also know what it is like to be called upon by our heavenly Father to forgive all parties involved.

The lesson—of forgiving others, of forgiving ourselves, and of accepting forgiveness from God and those around us—is one of the hardest and one of the most important lessons we must learn during our walk on this earth. But with the learning of this lesson comes a beautiful and incomparable freedom.

If you have a private heartache, if you are hiding pain in a secret place inside yourself, there is peace to be found in turning it over to God. I pray that you will reach out to Him today.

Romans 5:8

Robin Lee Hatcher
PO Box 4722
Boise, ID 83711-4722